I0657957

Also by David Stansfield

One Last Great Wickedness
The Seventh Coming
Take Nothing For Granted
Blood
Got a Couple of Minutes?
Attack at Noon

David Stansfield

Praise for
The Man Who Murdered Time

"Have you met Eadweard Muybridge? I loved this extraordinary man, I identified with him at times, David Stansfield makes him so alive, so human, so present.

I savored the different levels of the text offered by the author. They complement themselves, nourish themselves, enrich themselves: the child aching for love; the grown-up lover, sincere and immature, murdered and murdering; the father of pure invention at the mercy of his brilliant, tyrannical sponsor; the genius embraced by both the artistic and the scientific community; a man both of and ahead of his time who meets the brilliant opportunist Edison, who is a friend of Nadar, of the obese and charming Prince Edward, of the Lumière brothers…

Stansfield takes us on a journey. This is a book about Talent, about the strange proximity of the artistic and the scientific world, about Love, about the World at the end of the 19th century and the ties that bind the cultural elites of America and Europe. This is a jewel."

Cécile Moulard
former Managing Director of Amazon.com France

"An astounding and amazing account of the life of a true genius. With a book written this well, I'm not even sure where to begin writing a review. It has been quite some time since I had the pleasure to enjoy a well written novel based on non-fiction factual evidence and "The Man Who Murdered Time" by David Stansfield ranks right up there with my all-time favorites. Stansfield does not present the life of Eadweard Muybridge (aka Edward Muggeridge) in some sort of boring academic history lesson. Rather, his view of the man comes directly from Muybridge's personal experiences and his interpretation of how Muybridge may have reacted to his circumstances with thought and emotion.

My overall summation of this text is one of delight and fulfillment that did not let me down throughout the entire course of reading. I had a difficult time putting this book down while reading it and I looked forward to picking it up with each sitting to learn more about Muybridge and his views on life and how he would attack his next goal. Muybridge had many successes, as well as failures, both in his career and in his personal life. "The Man Who Murdered Time" is a top read that offers much insight into the life of a true genius, while bringing his amazing journey to the readers of our modern age. Bravo Mr. Stansfield. Bravo!"

Larry Davis, photographer

"A fantastic evocation of the advent of the modern world, including speed of travel and communications happening before our eyes, so well integrated that the reader actually feels astounded and disturbed by it."

Charis Conn, Contributing Editor to
Harper's Magazine

"Stansfield conjures the soul of the man and in so doing, the reader must confront his own soul, stare into the abyss or the eye of a turtle and surrender. I just finished the book, it's so human, it's a For Whom The Bell Tolls… The writing is full of Life beginning and end. It touched me profoundly."

Jimmy Hall, Broadway actor and poet

David Stansfield

"David Stansfield's work on the life and times of Eadweard Muybridge is indeed a tour de force. Stansfield displays an incredible ability to combine artfully historical fact and the imagining of what Muybridge must have thought and felt. Only someone with Stansfield's background, born and raised in England and with many years living and working in Canada and the United States, could have written a book that has such a luxuriant textural feel for character and environment.

The Muybridge story provides a rich and panoramic view of the late 19th Century's age of invention. It is filled with both the often tragic romance of the American West and the sense of adventure and frustration of a man driven with ambition and brought low by betrayal – the betrayal of his own ambition and that of others whom he trusted.

This tale is pitch perfect and makes the reader care deeply about the protagonist and the world around him. This work is an incredible combination of a Dickensian eye for place and character with the broad social understanding of an American time and environment of an Edna Ferber or an E. L. Doctorow."

Charles Nanry
Professor of Sociology and former Dean of Rutgers University

"Muybridge is a triumph. It is everything a novel should be: a true portrait of both the man, Muybridge, that celebrated pioneer of motion picture making, and of the idea which thrust Muybridge into the limelight, the terrifying notion of looking under the skirts of Nature. Stansfield's descriptive prose bears the reader along as effortlessly as a horse photographing itself. There is Oscar material in this gripping love story, and somebody should send a copy of Muybridge to James Cameron as soon as practicable. Many congratulations to the author."

Anthony Barton
author of On the Structure of Didactic Tales

"Stansfield conjures the soul of the man and in so doing, the reader must confront his own soul, stare into the abyss or the eye of a turtle and surrender. I just finished the book, it's so human, it's a For Whom The Bell Tolls… The writing is full of Life beginning and end. It touched me profoundly."

Jimmy Hall, Broadway actor and poet

THE MAN WHO MURDERED TIME

A Novel
based on the Life of
Eadweard J. Muybridge

DAVID STANSFIELD

SULBY HALL
PUBLISHERS
Malibu & Toronto

v

David Stansfield

The Man Who Murdered Time/David Stansfield

ISBN-13: 978-0615845937
ISBN-10: 0615845932

Sulby Hall Publishers

USA: PO Box 6867
Malibu CA 90264

Canada: 28 Duncannon Drive,
Toronto ON M5P 2M1
www.sulbyhall.com

Cover design by Denise Boiteau & David Stansfield
Printed in the United States of America

For my wife Denise
and the children

David Stansfield

"Men who leave their mark on the world are very often those who, being gifted and full of nervous power, are at the same time haunted and driven by a dominant idea, and are therefore within a measurable distance of insanity."

Sir Francis Galton

David Stansfield

PART ONE

David Stansfield

CHAPTER ONE

There was something about the movement of the coach Edward didn't like. He'd ridden on stage-coaches before, even on a couple of steam trains back in England, but this was different. He couldn't put his finger on it. He braced himself between his bench and the coach door, his heart beating as rapidly as the horses' hooves. Fear or exhilaration? He glanced again at the poster above his head.

> YOU WILL BE TRAVELING THROUGH
> INDIAN COUNTRY AND THE SAFETY
> OF YOUR PERSON CANNOT BE
> VOUCHSAFED BY ANYONE BUT GOD

The driver and Mr. Stout, the road master riding shotgun, had sworn blind there was no danger: two years' traveling the Oxbow Route without a single incident, fresh horses changed every twelve to fifteen miles; if there were any Injuns, they could outrun 'em, easy. And it was true they hadn't seen a single Red Man so far, except for that one dead Comanche nailed to a tree, naked as a brown Jesus. The depth of our contempt for these people! But still Edward fingered the Bowie knife in his pocket that Mr. Stout had lent him.

What pictures were flashing by – astounding! The landscape was unearthly: a desiccated procession of bouncing rocks, flying cactus and scudding oaks. He had always been fascinated by movement: the shudder of a horse's haunch, the spring in a leaping dog's back, the tremble in the arms of the housemaid as she climbed the ladder to reach the plums behind their house in England. He would stand in front of the cheval glass beside the window of his little bed-room for hour after hour in his hand-me-down nightgown from John, watching the flocks of seagulls screaming encouragement at the horses on the riverbank as they pulled the coal barges downstream. He never tired of seeing them wheeling and dancing in the milky air, raising and lowering his arms as he switched his gaze between window and glass, gull and boy, fine-tuning his movements to the birds. Their wings hardly moved! How do you do it? If only I could stop you in mid-flight to find out.

The other passengers were all asleep now, rough workingmen mostly. Cattlemen or ranchers? Or miners perhaps, as exhausted of prospects as the gold fields? Sad men who'd rushed out to California for whatever precious substance haunted their nights and now rushed back empty-handed to God knows where, to God knows what.

They were crammed shoulder to shoulder on the wooden benches, three to a row, each squeezed into a space fifteen inches wide. The middle bench where Edward sat had only a leather strap to support his back, knees dove-tailing with those of his opposite number. He'd been suffering this indignity for almost two weeks now, ever since leaving San Francisco: dropping off mail in Los Angeles, Fort Yuma, Tucson and now traversing Texas. The reek of cheap whisky and stale tobacco, the endless glare of the Texan sun, the creaking and groaning of the springs, the thudding of the mailbags and trunks bouncing on the roof.

His eyes went to the young woman. She'd smiled at him when he'd swung her massive leather trunk up to Mr. Stout on the coach roof with such ease, but then wrinkled her nose at the smell of burning. It was his cigarette, one last one before he climbed aboard; no smoking allowed in the coach when there were ladies present. As usual when he was otherwise occupied, he'd placed it on the brim of his hat, which had started to smolder.

He looked at it now, wiggling his fingers through the holes. Perhaps she would find this amusing too. But she was as fast asleep as the other passengers, her little lapdog snoozing peacefully beneath the gentle rise and fall of her breast in her tight bodice, her bonnet loosened, auburn curls spilling onto the shoulder of her companion, a middle-aged man in an elegant sack coat, also dead to the world.

Her father? Edward had been asking himself this question

ever since he clapped eyes on him. Her husband? Surely not… Tell me he's her father. Then, as the man stirred, his hand went to the young woman's. Something about the movement said not a father's touch. How could she be with someone so old? But you saw it everywhere, didn't you? If the man was rich enough… That beautiful almost baby face, so innocent, so perfect, so easy to buy.

He wished she'd wake up so he could see her blue eyes once more.

Instead, the little dog opened his brown ones, staring right at him. He never tired of looking into animals' eyes. They either knew everything or they knew nothing. So much easier to talk to than people. He reached to touch the silken hair of the little dog, his hand inches from her breast. The flush of his face, the hammer of his heart.

The Chihuahua closed his eyes with a faint sigh, as if sharing Edward's small moment of bliss.

He withdrew his hand and stuck his head out of the narrow window. The bite of the wind and the sting of the sand was almost blinding. Blink a few times. That's better. Spit out the grit. Still no Injuns in sight – perhaps we've killed them all? – just a couple of diamondbacks coiled behind those rocks and a splatter of dead insects across "Butterfield Overland Stage" on the faded red panels of the Concord. The driver's whip cracking like a rifle over the six mustangs, the sweat pouring off the black satin, silk ribbons of mouth-foam streaming in the wind, eyes bulging, white as pearls.

He settled on his bench and leaned back against the strap; try to get some sleep.

However fast they traveled, he was going nowhere fast himself. Backwards, in fact, back to the East Coast and Boston for his last chance, and if that failed, then back across the Atlantic to that old crone, his grandmother. Although he was now thirty years old with a shaggy blond beard and the strength to wrestle an ox, whenever he thought of her he was still the poor asthmatic child lying sick in bed in his soiled sheets as they crowded round him, mocking his wheezing, the chorus of nightmare crones: grandmother, mother, aunt, in descending order of authority.

And all the while, big brother John, who could do everything — music, painting, writing, languages — chanting his favorite quip from behind the empty brass parrot cage they said they didn't have anywhere else to store, but which he always knew was meant for him: "Poor Edward, why does one always get the distinct impression when you enter the room that someone's just left?"

At such moments, he had vowed to himself never to inflict such misery on another: never, ever to hurt another human being

John. He was dead now of course. But he still loomed over Edward. Dead at twenty-one of "abdominal tumors and intumescence," caught from a rat on one of the barges that carried the Wellington and Scotch Splint down river from the family coal business of J. Muggeridge & Sons in the Royal Borough of Kingston-on-Thames.

Edward had been so full of hope that last day when he'd said goodbye to his grandmother, announcing that he was going to California to be an agent for a publishing company, arranged by his uncle George Lawrence. She'd laughed, her voice breaking up into fragments like pellets of small coal, her great cap of white silk ribbons and roses bobbing up and down. "*California!*" Never did a word have so many disreputable syllables. She put down her steel knitting needles. "You might as well be going to China. What are those dreadful miners going to do with *books*? Use them as doorstops?"

A purple velvet purse came from beneath the black satin and white pearls to be emptied on the table. He could still smell the lavender. She pushed the gold sovereigns towards him.

"No, thank you, Grandma, it's very kind of you, but I'm going to make a name for myself. If I fail, you will never hear of me again."

Another laugh. "You may live to regret that remark."

"I don't care."

She slipped the coins back into the purse, tightened the drawstring round its neck and swung it slowly back and forth. "Don't Care was made to care, Don't Care was hung."

It had been nine years since his promise to Grandma, most of them spent stuck in his stuffy little illustrated books store upstairs at 113 Montgomery-street (between Lecount's and Austin's), staring at shelf upon shelf of volumes of which he was almost the only reader. If it were possible to die of boredom, he would be long gone. Although he had enjoyed gazing at the Snowy Egrets, Whooping Cranes and Bald Eagles frozen so skillfully in time by Mr. Audubon in his magnificent volumes. What he would have given to see these noble creatures lift off the page. He'd thought it was his name itself that was holding him back, so he'd changed it from Muggeridge to *Muy*gridge, to reflect possible Spanish blood in his ancestry.

Would he keep his promise? Would Boston finally bring him success? He'd always enjoyed tinkering with machinery and had invented – on paper at least – many new gadgets, from a washing machine to an apparatus for tipping picture plates into books. It was the latter he had decided to return to. And Boston, the publishing capital of America, was the place to do it.

Watch out! This was even greater speed. In spite of his black mood, this was intoxicating. They couldn't be going any faster.

And yet they were. Cresting a hill they plunged down the other side at a breakneck pace.

He leaned out. The wind and sand had redoubled in force.

"*Woah! Woah! Steady!*" The driver was lurching back in his seat, yanking the reins to his chest.

But the horses were beyond control.

The driver and Stout were both standing, using their combined weight to pull on the brake lever. The screech of metal against metal only made the stage a sled, the spokes standing still, the coach careering faster than ever. One of the wheels was working loose now, splaying like a broken leg. They were veering off the road, skidding through a graveyard of jagged rocks, mailbags tumbling off the roof.

The young woman jerked awake, tipping her little dog onto the floor. She stared in horror, her eyes even more beautiful. He reached for her dog to help. She held it back, crying out.

A miner leaped up, knocking Edward off balance, forcing his way to the door. Edward hurled the man back where he'd come from and reached for the young woman, who shied away, the old man hiding his face, groaning.

The passengers avalanched from one side to the other of the madly tilting coach.

Edward pressed up against the door, stretching out his hand for the young woman again. She was hidden by a windmill of arms and legs. He wrestled with the door handle. Jammed shut, trapping them tight as a tomb.

Fighting for breath, gasping for air, lungs bursting.

Time slowing... slower... and slower... How could time change like this? Through the slit of the window, the granite boulders outside were blurring into a single pulsating entity like that revolving optical toy, the Daedalum, the Wheel of the Devil. A tumbling lump of granite changing its shape over and over again in slow motion, a thundering quivering amoeba.

All over. He didn't care. Let night fall.

Don't Care was made to care. His grandmother's voice.

Something flapping behind him.

He jumped onto the rear bench, pulled out Stout's knife, reached over his head and stabbed and stabbed at the back wall of the coach, slashing at the undulating black canvas, clawing at the gash he was carving, opening it wider and wider, forcing himself through...

Ahhh! The air! The blessed air! He could breathe again.

Amidst the screams of the passengers, the coach pitched forward, shooting him free. He glimpsed the splintered wheel striking a rock, the coach lurching sideways, the harnesses tearing loose from the horses, the coach catapulting into a giant oak, smashing itself to pieces.

He was flying. His arms spread out like the wings of birds wheeling and dancing in the air, he was flying on and on. Out of the blackness. Out of the night.

CHAPTER TWO

Two phosphorescent moons. But they weren't moons. They were two faces staring down. The double-mouth in the double-face starting to move, but no sounds emerging.

Twin blackboards appearing, twin hands chalking a silent message:

> *YOUR HEAD STRUCK A BOULDER. YOU HAVE BEEN IN A COMA FOR THREE DAYS. YOU ARE DEAF, EACH EYE HAS ITS OWN VISION, YOU HAVE NO SENSE OF SMELL OR TASTE.*

CHAPTER THREE

Edward gripped the arms of his chair. What would the verdict be? He stared at the bent head of Dr. William Withey Gull as he read his notes.

Would Gull give him a clean bill of health or condemn him to yet more bloodletting and purgatives and phrenological massages? He'd suffered six long years of this in hospitals and sanatoria from Arkansas to New York and back, fighting for his body as his adopted country fought for its soul.

The settlement of his lawsuit against the Butterfield Stage Company had enabled him to pay for everything. As for the other passengers, were there any survivors? He'd never found out. That lovely young woman and her little dog…

Now he'd come back to England, not to see Grandma – he was not here for her now, Heavens, no – but to see the Great Man himself at the Royal College of Physicians in Regent's Park for a final assessment of his condition. And now, twenty years after Edward had seen him bending over John, he was a Great Man was Gull, elevated to the post of Physician-in-Ordinary to Queen Victoria. What strings Edward had pulled to get this medical giant to see him, to plead for this final verdict, to suffer through the doctor's fond recollections of poor John. "Such a tragic loss," Gull had said. "We did our best of course, but… simply tragic. I don't think I've ever encountered such a gifted young man."

He was right of course. It was a tragic loss. Edward could see that now. The harrowing image of his elder brother stretched out in his etherized coma on the wooden table came back to him, a shriveled cartoon of himself, as the barber-shop Sawbones sharpened their knives, their frock coats freckled with blood and pus, and Dr. Gull, then a brilliant young lecturer in comparative anatomy from Guy's Hospital in the thick of it, ignoring the taboo on real doctors stooping to the surgeon's trade.

But where John might have gone! And John had known it too, hadn't he? He had always been convinced he was destined for great things. It was odd: they'd both gone to the same local grammar school and both come from the same pair of trades people, but to judge from the way John *sounded*, you'd have sworn he'd gone to that Eton College he talked about so bitterly as if it had been stolen from him, his rightful place among the toffs and swells. Indeed, you'd swear he hadn't come from Edward's family at all, but really was directly descended – as he never tired of claiming – from the seven Saxon kings on the coronation stone in Kingston Market Place.

Another odd thing: Edward had checked the names: Ethelred, Athelstan, Edmund, Edred, Edwy, and two Eadweards. Not a John in sight. And yet, wherever it had come from, at the time he would have given anything for his brother's cultured voice instead of his own flat-voweled Surrey whine, his "trine" for train, "nime" for name, and so much else. But now he realized he didn't care about any of this any more, he really didn't. How extraordinary.

Gull looked up from his notes, unfolded himself from behind his desk like a deckchair, a billiard cue of a man, although his grip was of iron; Edward had felt those hands on his body on the examination couch.

Edward stood to face him.

Gull cleared his throat and studied him for a moment over his spectacles. "I've verified all the data from my American colleagues, checked and double-checked all their tests – in addition to performing a number of my own devising – and I am pleased to say that the frontal lobe has returned to complete normality. Furthermore, I have been unable to detect any lingering physical side effects from the injuries. No more double-vision, ears, nose and tongue functioning as they should. Even the asthma seems to have quite disappeared."

A pause. A crooked smile.

Edward stopped breathing. Asthma: the other shadow in his life, although it was only during his first ten years that it had been truly severe. How he had struggled to draw breath through the great ball of seaweed in his lungs for so long his chest had become as pointed as the prow of a ship. Or a pigeon, as his schoolfellows had kept chanting when he was occasionally well enough to get out of bed: "pigeon-chest, pigeon-chest." But most of the time he hadn't been able to go to school at all, the ordinary things schoolchildren learned passing him by, leaving curious gaps in his mind about the simplest games and the simplest facts. What comes next in the alphabet? What's the capital of Egypt?

But that was all long past of course. His chest was now flat, he knew his ABC, he knew it was Cairo. And now Gull was saying all his ailments from the accident were cured. He was ready. Now he was really going to make something of himself.

At last it came: "I now pronounce you fit and well, Mr. Muygridge."

Edward let out a huge sigh of relief, his whole body relaxing as if he had slipped into a warm bath. He grinned to himself. Should he tell Gull he'd changed his name again, this time to Muy*bridge*, to celebrate the fact that, oddly enough after surviving that terrible accident, he felt he truly was a new man, building "my bridge" to a new world? No, perhaps not. He didn't think Gull was a man for puns. But what a wave of relief was still washing over him. Fit and well. *Fit...* and *well...* Surely the two most beautiful words in the English language.

Gull's hand rose to meet Edward's. Then he paused and frowned again. "Physically, that is. Psychologically, may be another question."

What? What was he trying to say?

"In patients with frontal orbital damage such as you have suffered, there can be profound personality changes, a different person altogether. One common symptom is the willingness to take risks. In some cases, this can be dangerous: failing to appreciate the consequences of one's actions. In your case, having observed you for some time now, I think that is unlikely... but not impossible."

Taking risks. Yes. He could take any risks now, couldn't he? He could carry oxen on his back, leap off tall buildings – well, perhaps not the latter, if there was one thing he had not got over, it was the vertigo.

Gull's hand again, shaking his in a rather odd way: pressing his thumb down on the back of Edward's knuckles, his little finger curled into his palm, then quickly letting go.

"Congratulations. All you need to complete your transformation is fresh air. It is quite the fashion in Germany now, 'natural therapy,' I like to call it. Try a more outdoor profession instead of one closeted with books. I suggest sun painting. Focus on landscapes perhaps, get out into the countryside." He handed Edward a carte-de-visite. "Look this chap up. He'll show you the ropes. One of the finest gentlemen-photographers in England, they tell me, friend of my colleague, Henry Southey, the alienist – you may have heard of him: Physician in Ordinary to George IV, then made a Physician in Lunacy by Lord Brougham. Although, lunacy is hardly the word," he added as if the thought had just struck him, "more a question of the multiplication of oneself. Yes, that's what it is to be mad of course, a form of multiplication…"

And on he went, the voice Edward had so longed to hear now fading from his ears. Sun painting… photography. He'd never paid much attention to it, and yet there was something strangely familiar about the whole idea.

"Paramnesia," said Gull.

"I beg your pardon?"

"A distorted or perverted memory, an illusory feeling of having previously experienced a present situation." Gull stared at him quizzically. "Perhaps of having experienced photography before?"

"How did you know that's what I was feeling, doctor?" He thought back to Matthew Brady's Daguerreotypes at the Great Exhibition in fifty-one, so wondrous, those silver pictures… Grandma had dismissed Brady as a vulgar tradesman selling the latest scientific novelty, play-pretties, shiny bits of tin for magpies, but still, such fascination…

Gull's crooked smile again. "If I am anything, I am a clinical physician, I saw your thoughts playing out on your face."

Make light of it. "So I may be destined for Dr. Southey's madhouse?"

"No, no, do not alarm yourself. It's a very common illusionary state. But then, on the other hand, so is madness, isn't it? Common,

I mean. Not one of us is far from madness, from the very edge of madness."

The glint in Gull's eyes; it gave him a shiver. Edward hadn't noticed this before, no doubt because all his attention had been focused on what Gull thought of *him*, not what he thought of Gull. He tapped the carte-de-visite. "Thank you very much, Doctor. I shall certainly look this man up."

Gull ushered him to the door. "Although I should warn you he can be somewhat difficult at times. Put your best foot forward. No time to waste: spring is the perfect season for photography, the sunlight, you know." Another oblique smile. "Although it's in rather short supply in this country."

Edward knew where he was going now. There was still money left in his Butterfield settlement; once he'd learned his way round the elements of photography, he was going to start his new life exactly where it left off, but set on a totally different course.

"I won't be staying in this country, Dr. Gull. I'll be going back to California."

Gull raised his eyebrows. "Really? Is that so? I hear there are some wonderful landscapes. Yosemite in particular is said to be quite spectacular. California: the land of grapes – which reminds me."

He dived into a drawer, fetched out a small brown paper bag and opened it to show its contents to Edward.

"Raisins, dehydrated grapes, I highly recommend them. Whenever I'm fatigued I refresh myself by eating some. They are always in my traveling bag and when in Scotland or the hills they form my luncheon with a biscuit and water. I eat no cane sugar but the sugar of the grape. Remember, Muybridge, the sugar of the grape, there's nothing like it."

The man who had England at his feet, went around carrying little bags of grapes?

Edward let himself out of the room, trying to resist skipping along the corridor like a child as he heard the old nursery rhyme echoing in his head: "I do not like thee, Dr. Fell/The reason why I cannot tell."

CHAPTER FOUR

Photography... thought Edward as he sat in the train up to Oxford. What did he know of it? He'd already starting reading about it, but he had trepidations. Was he going to pass muster with the great photographer who could "be somewhat difficult at times"?

He looked down again at the photograph on the carte-de-visite Gull had given him. What a pretty little girl, in her pale satin dress, reclining on a garden sofa. "When May was young;" that's what it said under the picture. It was dated ten years ago. May was no longer young, May was always young. Her fleeting shadow arrested, a single moment fixed in time no more capable of change, the corpse of an experience, embalmed like an Egyptian mummy in a photographer's chemicals. What did they use as a preservative instead of the Pharaohs' resin? Gold chloride, wasn't it? That's why the pictures turned sepia. May... the golden girl.

The photographic studio was a conversion of the former quarters of Richard Babcock's upholstery shop, just across the way from Christ Church College.

He knocked on the door. No answer. He knocked again. Still nothing. He was expected this morning, the letter from Southey had confirmed it. Could his host have forgotten? He was eccentric, according to Gull. He tried knocking one last time. Still no response. He started to leave. Then turned back and looked at the two windows on either side of the studio, but the blinds were drawn. He tried the door, it was unlocked. He gave a gentle push and stepped inside.

Into sunbeams.

They were shafting down from a skylight set into the ceiling and onto an armchair that was set against a painted backcloth of a riverbank and a gypsy encampment. A canvas awning was stretched above the chair and at an angle to it. On a tripod facing this arrangement, sat a large rosewood box that looked as if it had been sawn in half, its midsection replaced by a red leather accordion. A short brass tube was sticking out of the front of this contraption, and from its rear a black shroud bulged like a bustle.

Edward felt as if he were coming home after all, but this time to the real home that had been awaiting him all along. Was this an echo of his first experience of a *Camera obscura*, the "dark chamber," when he'd walked into that outsize one on Brighton Pier on one of the rare occasions he'd managed to get away from Muggeridge & Sons? At first he hadn't been able to see anything at all, it was so dark. Then somebody pulled a lever and a shaft of light shot down like the finger of God, splashing a dazzling moving picture onto the round table in front of him: a 360° degree view of the beach, the sea, the terraces; the fishermen in their red woolen caps stretching out their nets, the bathing machines hauled into the shallows by their teams of horses; the lady cavaliers on the cliff above, trotting with their beaux in their cylindrical beavers or plumed cocked hats, a stray gust of wind catching at the hem of a habit revealing a tiny brilliant boot snapped over a riding-trouser. How those steeds moved! How at home he'd felt in there, in that friendly darkness so different from that of the coach to come.

Edward turned the carte-de-visite over to read the name again: the Rev. Charles Dodgson. What will he be like, this mathematical lecturer turned gentleman-photographer?

A door at the back of the sunlit room opened to reveal a tall slender good-looking man. He closed it carefully, then strode up to Edward.

"Mr. Mmmuybridge, I presume."

He'd got his name right, that was a good start, even if he had difficulties with the "m." Edward held out his hand.

Dodgson stepped back, holding up his own hands, palms facing Edward, as if in surrender. They were almost pitch black. "Cccan't shake hands, sorry, the chemicals, you know," he waggled his hands, "in my dddarkroom," he gestured at the door behind him. "But how do you do. I'm Charles Dodgson – Reverend, although I mmmust say I don't feel so most of the time. Mmmy undergraduates call me dddodo because of my hesitation – my speech impediment – although I dddon't think I'm extinct."

The Reverend pushed up one of the black-stained cuffs of his shirtsleeves and pinched himself. Even his fingernails were stained black and looked as if he'd been biting them since birth.

"No, I'm dddefinitely still here, but you never know, do you? I told Southey I wanted you to come today of all days because I'm making ppportraits of two dddistinguished guests, Mrs. Latham and her daughter. I think you'll find one of the pictures I'm going to take of particular interest. Very particular interest."

Something odd had come into the man's voice, quite apart from his stutter.

"Oh, how I love photography! Would you like to see what I see?" exclaimed Dodgson, rubbing his blackened hands together.

"Yes, Reverend, I'd like to very much."

Dodgson motioned to him to duck under the shroud. It was certainly as dark as that other Camera Obscura. But there was a peephole in the rear revealing a small circle of light in the front section. It must have been the lens of the apparatus, but curiously it showed an inverted chair against an inverted riverbank.

Dodgson giggled: "It's quite literally ttturned my world upside down. I change the focal length by shortening or lengthening the bellows…"

The lens moved slowly towards Edward and the chair became sharper and sharper as the riverbank grew ever more misty. The lens moved away from him and both chair and the riverbank became sharp.

" …perceiving and not perceiving, solid objects dddissolving into the ether, large becomes small and small becomes large." Dodgson was chanting a spell that seemed strangely familiar. Where had Edward heard this before?

"In my dark-room," continued Dodgson, "I can conjure images out of thin air, make the invisible visible, the negative positive, the transient permanent, *mmmemento mori*. Nothing is quite what it seems. It's because of the train, you know."

Edward backed out of the shroud. "The train?"

"The window as it speeds: all you can see is the bbbackground, the landscape in general, objects that are far away. There's no foreground, no dddetails, just a blur."

The granite boulders blurring into a single pulsating entity. "What has this to do with photography?"

"It gives us back immediacy, close-ups, we can now delight in the tiniest detail that the train's pace takes away."

Yes, that's it, thought Edward: no time for sights or sounds or tastes or smells on a train, no panting and reeking animals yoked to the car, no individual flowers or trees going by, but only streaks of red and green and blue, surging by in an endless tartan ribbon celebrating the song of the rail – *diggady-ding, diggady-dong, diggady-ding, diggady-dong* – as the iron horse ate up the miles.

"All of these new inventions are related, I believe," continued Dodgson, "and I love them all – especially photography, it's a coming together of art and science – technology, optics, chemistry – preparing your own dddipping baths, mmmaking your own cccollodion – "

"The collodion doctors use to form a skin over a wound?"

"Yes, but in photography this 'skin' – once I've ppprepared the basic collodion from the chemist's for use in photography – serves as a transparent support for the light sensitive chemicals we need to apply. Let me show you."

His dark-room had a small window framed by thick half-open yellow calico curtains. One wall was covered in shelves of bottles and vials, tall glass jars and earthenware bowls piled high with what looked like salts.

"I start the preparation of my photographic collodion by dddissolving cotton fiber in a mixture of nitric acid and sulfuric acid."

"What the call 'gun cotton'?"

"Exactly. But don't worry, I only shoot ppportraits. But what I've dddiscovered you can do with gun cotton is dddissolve it in a mixture of bromide and iodide of potassium and alcohol to obtain the proper collodion mixture." He held up a bottle of a syrupy mixture. "Looks as if it comes out of a treacle-well, doesn't it?"

A "treacle-well"? Another strange familiarity.

Footsteps in the studio.

"That must be the Latham's now," said Dodgson. "That delightful child. Quite dddelightful."

Mrs. Latham could have been Grandma's sister. Dodgson took his time in posing her on the armchair in just the position he wanted, her little daughter at her feet. What a pretty girl: another May. Although this one was "Beatrice," as she'd announced proudly, "I'm seven."

Dodgson adjusted the overhead awning. "I'm deflecting the sunlight so as to throw the face into greater relief."

He was carving a picture out of light and shade... Extraordinary. "It's all a matter of light!"

"Yes, indeed. Light is everything." Dodgson cocked his head to one side, surveying his sculpture. "Good." He turned to Edward. "Now to sensitize the plate."

Back in the dark-room, the photographer slowly poured the gooey collodian onto one corner of a small glass plate. "The collodion has to be ppperfectly even. There is no room for error." Holding the plate by its diagonal corners, he tipped it at a slight angle so that the collodion flowed evenly across its surface, working from corner to corner in such a way that the liquid never flowed back on itself.

Dodgson closed the curtains, turning them yellow. "Next, I dip the plate in the compound that actually creates the picture: a solution of nitrate of silver – what we call 'Lunar Caustic.' And it is, believe me." He made a face at his blackened shirtsleeves, then pushed them even further up his arms as he set to work. "That's why they call photography the 'black art.' I don't know how many times my housekeeper has threatened to leave. Although I fear the real origin of the phrase is rather more sinister: some delicate souls believe that posing before the camera is the same as signing their death warrant."

Edward had never heard this before. Could there be some truth in it? Selling your soul to a black box?

Dodson checked the plate. "No streaks. Good." He laid the

plate face down in a wooden holder and closed its lid. "We only have a few moments before it dddries."

They rushed back into the studio.

"Are you ready Mrs. Latham? Miss Latham?"

"Yes, Reverend," said the ladies.

Dodgson hung a bowler hat over the camera lens and ducked under the black cloth with the plate. A few moments later, he was out again.

"Quite still, ladies, please." He looked up at the north light pouring into the studio. "I should be able to keep my exposure down to a mere thirty seconds." A proud grin to Edward. "I've thrown away all my head braces. No need to ccclamp the subject's head for minutes at a time."

Edward saw his point: Dodgson's two subjects were doing their own clamping, still as statues, literally holding their breath.

He checked his timepiece and removed the bowler hat from the lens. It seemed like an eternity of waiting.

He replaced the hat. "Thank you ladies. You may relax yourselves."

The ladies gasped for air.

Back in the dark-room, Dodgson picked up a second chemical bottle. "I've also prepared my developer in advance to save time: a solution of Pyro-gallic and Glacial acetic." He poured this concoction into a bath and immersed the plate.

"Why such a hurry to develop the plate?"

"The collodion dries so quickly. That's the ppproblem with wet plates."

"So there's such a thing as a *dry* plate?"

"There wasn't until quite recently until a Belgian chap came up with an emulsion that still retains its sensitivity when dry. Much more convenient, you can sensitize as many ppplates as you like ahead of time."

"So why don't you use dry plates?"

Dodgson looked hard at him. "My goodness, you dddo ask excellent questions, Muybridge, you have a good head on your shoulders. I rather tend to lose pppatience with unintelligent souls.

One of my numerous sins."

Edward breathed a sigh of relief. He'd passed the test.

Dodgson looked even more intensely at him. "You're a curious man, that's what you are, Muybridge? Want to know everything. Curiouser and curiouser – " He clapped his hand over his mouth. "Oh, dear."

Now Edward knew what had been nagging at him: *large becomes small, small becomes large; the treacle-well; curiouser and curiouser.*

"You're Lewis Carroll, aren't you?"

He sighed. "And I try so hard to kkkeep my lives separate."

"I loved your children's book. Alice was truly in a wonderland, in every sense of the word." Lewis Carroll... he could hardly believe it.

Dodgson sighed again. "Yes, that's what everyone says, apparently. Sometimes I wish I hadn't written it. It's been so hard to be taken ssseriously since. To answer your question, I don't use dry plates because they're frightfully slow – not very light sensitive, you see – you need exposures times of up to fffifteen minutes."

The image of Mrs. and Miss Latham was slowly appearing on the plate.

"It's like the Shroud of Turin," said Edward.

"Exactly. Only in the negative. Black becomes white and white becomes black, pure alchemy. Soon we really will be able to turn base metals into gold. Now I have to 'fix' the image so it won't be affected any further by light, get rid of all the iodide of silver from the blanks and shadows, and for that we need a particular salt of Soda: cyanide of potassium."

"First you shoot 'em, then you poison 'em?"

Dodgson laughed as he poured another chemical bottle over the plate. "Which do you think would interest you more, portrait or landscape?"

"Landscape, I think – particularly in California, it's such beautiful country."

"Is the sky as blue as they say?"

"Blue as a baby's eyes."

Dodgson shook his head. "Oh, dear."

"Why? I love blue skies – after all our English clouds."

"You may love them, but plates don't, they're oversensitive to blue. If you give the correct exposure to your foreground, the sky will be greatly overexposed – one of the reasons I limit myself to portraits. Now, that pppicture of particular interest I mentioned. The time has come."

Back in the studio, Dodgson addressed Mrs. Latham: "And now… *sans habillement*, as we agreed?"

"Yes, of course, Reverend." She nodded to her daughter.

The little girl unbuttoned her dress, slipping it off, now another item of clothing, now another and another. When was she going to stop? She wasn't going to stop. The last garment dropped to the floor.

The blood rushed to Edward's face. Why was this so shocking? It was merely a little girl without any clothes; she could have been about to step into the bath. He was being ridiculous, lots of photographers took pictures of nude children, they appeared on Christmas cards. But still…

Had Dodgson noticed his burning cheeks? No, he was adjusting his awning to get the shadows just so on her body. He might have been setting up to paint a plate of oranges. So why was he so disturbed by this? Was it simply the shock of two fully dressed men standing beside a girl with nothing on? The same shock people felt on first seeing Manet's *Déjeuner sur l'herbe?*

Dodgson leaned towards him: "I take many pictures of children, Muybridge. For me they represent the innocence of Eden, never more so than when unclothed. Children are mmmagical, a gggift from God that gives meaning and purpose to my life."

The perfect body of an innocent child… And she was so lovely. "Beatrice"… what a name… Dante's guide to Paradise.

Afterwards, when a new plate had been exposed to the young girl's beauty and mother and daughter had left the premises, Dodgson elaborated. "For me, the camera is a tool to help us understand to what extent the world really is what it appears to be."

"So there is *nothing* that cannot be the subject of a photograph?"

"Nothing – provided the work is done with art and pppurity of spirit. For example, when I was a young man I observed a mmmedical operation and was intrigued by the soporific effects of chloroform on the patient."

It hit Edward like a bolt of lightning. This was why he'd felt so drawn to photography, why he'd been so fascinated by the daguerrotypes in the Crystal Palace, the picture of little May that arrested her fleeting shadow, the seagulls over the Thames. This was what he would like to achieve with his own camera. What he'd been yearning to do all along. Now he would have a way to capture the things that had never been shown before, the movements and moments we could never normally perceive. To lift all the stones to see what was underneath; the secret things – the forbidden things. This was what he was meant to do. This was his calling. To stop the clocks to see what made them tick. To stop the seagulls to see what made them fly. He didn't know how he was ever going to be able to take a picture fast enough to capture movement, to capture time itself. But he knew as surely as he knew anything that he was going to do it.

Dodgson was continuing: "I wondered if there was a difference in the expression on the face between the state of anesthesia and that of normal sleep, so I took a series of photographs to try to dddetermine this."

Edward was trembling with excitement. "And did you succeed?"

"Not yet, alas, but I persist, I persist – and I am not alone, Dr. Charcot at the Salpetrière in Paris, has been photographing hysterical female inmates to provide visual proof of the specific form taken by their disease. He says he was inspired by the pictures the great French photographer Nadar took of the 'expressions of the passions' when the facial mmmuscles of the insane were electrically stimulated."

Dodgson shook his head. "But those poor women of

Charcot's: an unhappy uterus, nerves that are too thin, black bbbile from the liver? We still don't know the precise cause. But I'm planning to take some pictures myself of the insane. When do you plan to return to America, Muybridge?"

"A week on Tuesday."

"Plenty of time, then."

Edward smiled at him: "Dr. Southey, Physician in Lunacy?"

Dodgson smiled back: "I see we are of the same mind."

CHAPTER FIVE

This tripod was surprisingly heavy even for him – and felt even heavier in the circumstances – but Edward was Dodgson's "assistant" today and the great photographer was carrying the camera, which must have weighed even more. Behind them, a pair of Dodgson's students were bringing along an orange and red dark tent with the chemicals and equipment, and all of them were following the white-haired Dr. Henry Herbert Southey, who was setting a brisk pace along the institutional corridor.

Edward had been so carried away by Dodgson's enthusiasm he hadn't thought this through. He very much wanted to see Dodgson in action in such an unusual setting, but here of all places? He now felt it was the last place he wanted to be, the place where he might very well come face to face with himself.

Clanking. Growing louder and louder. Chains being dragged across a flagstone floor. Low moans. The stench of human excrement, urine and sweat, combined with what Edward could only describe as the smell of despair. It was almost unbearable.

The sickening odors and sounds were coming from heaps of dirty white sacks strewn across the floor of an iron cage, floundering and writhing like the ghosts of beached sea lions in San Francisco Bay. These bags of grief were emitting agonized screams as if trying to say that deep down they knew something about the soul of man the rest of us would never fathom.

One of the sacks was staggering towards him. She – for he thought it was a she, it was hard to tell – was shackled with iron manacles, hand and foot and neck. Between what remained of her teeth a string of saliva was hanging.

The rattle of a dinner trolley. The string grew longer.

The others were heaving themselves upright to shamble towards the bars of their cage.

Oh! The woman was sticking her leprous nose within an inch of his, all but asphyxiating him with her breath. She was so ugly, she was almost beautiful.

Dodgson adjusted his camera as his students set up the tent

and prepared to sensitize the plate. He was as calm as he had been with his Beatrice.

Meanwhile, Southey was studying the poor creature like something pinned under a microscope. The great alienist explained to Edward that this new Bethlem Asylum in Lambeth – or "Bedlam" as everyone called it – was a great improvement. Not so long ago the lunatics were kept stark naked and on display to visitors for a fee. Londoners could enjoy the zoo animals at the Tower of London then stroll up to Bedlam's former home in Moorfields to see the human animals, whose antics they were encouraged to stimulate by poking them with long sticks.

A man in a blue uniform was shoving tin plates covered in a slimy mush through the bars at the inmates.

The poor wretch in front of Edward was not moving, her cankered eyes looking everywhere but in his direction as if desperate to avoid the chasm between her world and his. Or was there a chasm? *Not one of us is far from madness.* Had Gull been referring to himself? Who knew what demons were troubling that man? Or this poor woman? Edward didn't know whether to cry for pity or to take notes as to the exact nature of the contortions deforming her features and body.

The camera was ready, the plate inserted. Dodgson removed the bowler hat from the lens. The creature wrenched down the front of her smock in synchrony with Dodgson's movement, exposing a nakedness as far from Beatrice as Hades from Heaven.

She became completely still, as if counting off the seconds with the Reverend, as if fully aware of the exposure time required.

Dodgson replaced his hat.

The madwoman crumpled to the floor, her mouth stretched wide in a *scream* that split Edward's ears.

CHAPTER SIX

"Don't forget to keep me up to dddate with how you get on with your photography," said Dodgson as he saw Edward off at the Oxford train station.

"You've been most kind, reverend, putting me up in your college rooms and letting me try my hand at making those portraits and landscape views of the Oxfordshire countryside." "Your sense of cccomposition and lighting is remarkable, as well as the speed at which you've become quite a chemist yourself, I have no doubt that this time you will have success in California. "

"It's very generous of you to say so."

"Not generous, it is simply true. A ddduck to water."

"I hope I don't drown."

"I only wish my students learned with your alacrity." He shook Edward's hand. "God speed, Muybridge. Oh, one more thing." He produced a slip of paper. "Just in case you get your chemicals confused." He grinned. "I stole it from Longfellow. Memorize this, Muybridge, and you have it."

Edward scanned the words:

First a piece of glass he coated
With Collodion, and plunged it
In a bath of Lunar Caustic
Carefully dissolved in water;
There he left it certain minutes.
Secondly my Hiawatha
Made with cunning hand a mixture
Of the acid Pyro-gallic,
And the Glacial Acetic,
And of alcohol and water:
This developed all the picture.
Finally he fixed each picture
With a saturate solution
Of a certain salt of Soda.

"Well, thank you, Reverend. I shall treasure this, just I shall treasure the time we have spent together."

"Oh, one more thing about cccchemicals: stay away from mmmercury, it drove poor Daguerre mad from the fumes, like the Mad Hatters who used it to cure their beaver fur."

The glint in his eyes as he said this. Like Gull, but at the same time quite different. If Gull's glint was a flash of steel in the dark, Dodgson's was a sparkle of fairy dust in a rainbow.

What a pair of strange birds to lend him their wings: the Dodo and the Gull.

The train gathered steam, and the Reverend Dodgson grew smaller and smaller on the platform as he raised his own beaver topper, all he was missing was the 10/6d sign in the band.

Lewis Carroll. Of all the men in England to have taught him photography, and to have given him his first glimpse of his true life's work, and now to be sending him off to his own adventures in wonderland!

CHAPTER SEVEN

Why couldn't he have climbed a short ladder, thought Edward — even the one the housemaid used to reach the plums — and then a medium-height ladder, and then a tall one, and so on, taking it in stages, like Hercules with his calf. But no, he had to go to the other extreme, from being earth-bound to climbing one of the highest points in the whole of California. He couldn't go much higher, short of a balloon ride. It was his last great fear and he had to conquer it. He had to. And this latest photographic trip had been the perfect opportunity.

Five years had elapsed since Dodgson has seen him off from that Oxford railway station, the starting point of his return journey to California. This second period in San Francisco had been as different from his first as sunbeams from shadows. After setting himself up as a photographer in the city, he had rapidly advanced from Silas Selleck's Gallery to the Photographic Studio run by those two athletic German brothers, the Nahls, with whom he had continued building up his body; and then most recently to none other than Bradley & Rulofson's, the premier studio in San Francisco, nay, in the entire state! And how industrious he had been throughout this time! Quite apart from Yosemite, he must have photographed half the Pacific Coast, not to mention all the portraits he had made.

Only a few more feet and he'd be able to see the lip of the ledge. Ah, there it is. Now reach up and grasp it. It's not even a hand-hold, just a finger-hold. Pull, pull, *pull!* There. Done it.

He stood up. And immediately wished he hadn't. He swayed; he thought he was going to faint. He shook himself. Was it the vertigo again? Now was the moment to find out. Conquer this moment and you will be able to do anything.

It was such a narrow ledge he was perched on, sticking out over the valley like the prow of a ship. Only this ship was flying three-quarters of a mile above the ground.

He looked down.

No vertigo. Thank God.

He was literally above the clouds: far below him, hugging the hollow of the valley, the giant Seqouias poking through the cumulus like toothpicks. He'd told his assistants nothing of his fear of heights, of course, simply saying he wanted to take this side trip so that they could procure a dramatic view of himself perching on the edge of an abyss. They'd obviously thought even this insane, but had kept their peace.

There they were now: Joseph and Arthur, both looking up at him, stick men a good hundred feet below. They were signaling: another couple of minutes. How attached he'd grown to these two over the last years, and what a contrast they made: lanky Arthur Townsend, just seventeen, always with his head in a book, a regular walking encyclopedia, towering over Edward's other man, Joseph Pocket, who must have been fifty if he was a day and to Edward's knowledge had never opened a book in his life. Arthur, though, was a prodigy, he not only read everything, but remembered everything, as if he'd photographed every page.

Joseph was muttering something to Arthur. Edward didn't need to read his lips. After so many trips together, he could read his mind. He would be saying something like, "I still swear some permanent damage was done in that coach accident, I don't care what the doctors say," or simply, "I can't wait to tell my wife of this, she'll never believe it."

Joseph's wife was as small as he was and he told her everything. They were almost a pair of dwarfs were Mr. and Mrs. Pocket, one on each side of the mantelpiece. How Edward envied them, but he had neither the time nor the inclination to "gather orange blossoms" as the coy euphemism for sexual congress had it. Inclination? He corrected himself: that wasn't the problem, the real problem was still buried.

Wu and Lee had now joined Joseph and Arthur, having got everything unloaded from the mules. His little audience of four. They said such cruel things about the Chinamen. But he'd trust these two with his life. Not least because they seemed to have more strength packed into their slim little bodies than most people twice their size.

There was a *cheeping* and a *tweeting*. He would have taken it as a sparrow or a chaffinch if he hadn't known better; it was the bald eagle he'd been observing for days now, soaring so high above their heads. An added bonus to scaling these heights: if he couldn't photograph its flight, he could at least climb to its level to observe it closely.

As if reading Edward's thoughts, the eagle was now hovering not twenty feet from him, staring at him from under its blinding white cowl with the accusing eye of a schoolmarm: "What are you doing up here? You should be in class."

One flap of his wings and the great bird was soaring, rising higher and higher, hardly stirring a pinion.

Edward struck a match and held it up. Not a breath of wind. How did the eagle do it? It had puzzled him with his Kingston seagulls and it puzzled him now.

One day, Mr. Eagle, I promise you, I will capture the ruffle of every feather in your wings and uncover the secret of your flight.

Contemplation Rock, that was what they called this little piece of granite sticking into nowhere. Good name. There was no shortage of things to contemplate. Not just the spectacular scenery, but life itself – and death. He was so close to death up here. One false step.

God, this was a beautiful place, so apparently untouched by human hand, you'd never guess that up until a mere twenty years ago it had been the most densely populated corner of California before the coming of the White Man (Arthur had read all about it). But of course the indigenous population had to go for they had committed two unpardonable sins: one, they were not White Men; and two, they occupied land in the foothills of the Sierra Nevada that contained deposits of gold. So the mere fact of having lived here for a thousand years was a poor excuse for being allowed to remain. Hence the "Mariposa Wars" in which a lynch mob of Forty-Niners saved the valley for civilization and dubbed it "Yosemite" in honor of the local tribe they were exterminating. So much more "suggestive, euphonious, and American," someone said, than the name the Yosemites themselves gave the valley, *Ahwahnee,* "Land of the Gaping Mouths," referring to its deep ravines surrounded by saw-toothed mountains, and also no doubt to the expression on the Yosemites' faces when the intrepid patriots put their villages to the torch, castrated their men, raped their women, and smashed their babies' heads like egg shells against the rocks. The redskins had long relished the edible roots of the local mariposa lily, but could never have imagined it could bear such fruit. How cruel people could be! Sometimes Edward felt like giving up on the human race.

Now the gold was gone, the miners were gone and the Indians were gone and the valley was a Garden of Eden once more, and quite empty – except for them.

"Ready, Mr. Muybridge?" came Joseph's shout from below.

He signaled that he was.

Joseph dived into the dark tent to fetch the plate.

He shifted closer to the edge, forcing himself to lean forward as if he were about to jump. Make the picture even more dramatic. One more inch and he would be flying. Contemplation Rock... Of course, they also called it the Devil's Diving Board, didn't they? The very tip of temptation. *...the willingness to take risks... this can be dangerous... the edge of madness.* Nonsense, surely? This wasn't the edge of madness, it was the edge of the final conquest of his fear. He was on the brink of it. Amazingly, at that moment, Edward realized, he was actually over the brink. He *was* no longer afraid. By tempting fate he had defeated it!

Joseph ducked under the camera shroud. So agile for his age; he moved like a little terrier. It always amused Edward the way the accordion rocked to and fro when Joseph was inside the camera as if it were having him for lunch.

Arthur removed the lens cap.

Edward stared down into the tiny speck of the lens so far below him, bracing himself for the two-minute exposure that would be necessary in this light.

Joseph swayed slightly as he looked up at his master, saying something to Arthur over his shoulder, as the latter counted off the seconds on Edward's timepiece. It would be Joseph's favorite Yosemite exclamation no doubt: "I hate this place." He always said that when he looked up at the mountains.

Edward wondered if like him Joseph could still hear the screams of the Indians in his head, as loud as the madwoman of Bedlam.

CHAPTER EIGHT

Edward cracked his whip over the head of his two black mustangs. He had to go faster, make up what time he could. He grinned. People were stopping and staring as his carriage rattled over the cobblestones. They always stared at his black box on wheels. He could hardly blame them. It could have been taken for a cubic hearse if it weren't for the gold-leaf words on its sides and rear: *Helios, The Flying Studio*. It was his portable dark-room and contained everything he needed: large landscape camera, small portrait camera, tripods, lenses, plates, chemicals, albumen paper, tools, camping gear, food and drink. It could go at quite a clip too, his horses were now weaving in and out of the early morning San Francisco traffic like trained seals.

Still, he was very late and would no doubt receive a proper drubbing from his employer. He hated letting him down. He also hated not being there to show his new re-touching assistant around; a Mrs. Stone, as he recalled. Sarah Louisa had told him the woman's tragic story: orphaned in infancy, then put out to a foster-father who molested her, then married to another monster, who treated her even worse. Both of them drunkards into the bargain. Poor soul, suffering through all of this by the age of twenty. No wonder she needed work.

And Sarah Louisa, left all alone to look after the newcomer. She already did so much for him. Like him, she was from England: Whitechapel in the East End. Same name as Grandma's side of his family, funnily enough: Smith. She was one of the best re-touchers in the business, having learned her trade in Chicago before moving out to California. Edward smiled to himself: Sarah Louisa had never forgotten "the Windy City" as she called it and never tired of talking of the steamship trips she'd taken on the Great Lakes, even kept an engraving of an imagined aerial view of them on the wall of her workroom. But in California, she'd been a tower of strength as Edward added more and more views to his portfolio, retouching every one of them herself. She certainly needed an assistant of her own. Although they had made an excellent team, the two of them. He'd even taken her to the theater and the Italian opera a couple of times as a reward for her good work; with her mother along of course; even in the "Wild West," one had to keep up appearances.

Here we are at last: 429 Montgomery-street. Three stories of Renaissance Revival splendor taking up the entire street corner and shouting out in six-foot white letters daubed across its red brick crest: *BRADLEY & RULOFSON'S FIRST PREMIUM GALLERY.* The studio prided itself in its advertisements as having "The only Elevator connected with Photography in the World", shuttling several dozen employees from floor to floor to tone and fume, trim and silver and re-touch and print and mount *his* photographs (well, to be honest, they weren't *exclusively* his, but a good portion were). That dreary little book store just a few hundred yards down the street was a thousand miles away. What a distance he had covered since he was last in this city.

He looked up. Was that a twitch of the curtains at the window beneath the *F* in *RULOFSON?* Probably Sarah Louisa. She always looked out for him and must be especially anxious today.

The soft padding of Wu and Lee as they dropped down from the rear of the carriage. Wu grabbed the reins of the horses and led the carriage away, while Lee held out his hands for the stack of plates on the seat beside Edward.

"*M'goi*," said Edward, 'no need'; he'd picked up a few words of Cantonese and as usual wanted to carry the plates himself. Lee gazed at him through those narrow eyes everyone made fun of. He gave one of his strange deep oriental bows and evaporated into the rear of the building.

Through the lobby and up the winding staircase, his usual three steps at a time. At forty-one, Edward could still outrun men half his age. All those new exercises on the parallel bars and pommel horses at the Olympic Club and the hours of sparring with Mr. Gerichton the boxing teacher had made him stronger and fitter than ever, not to mention all his turns round the track. They'd even had him do a spot of target practice, and he'd become quite a decent shot. Indeed, he'd made such progress, they'd presented him with a Smith & Wesson of his own. Had he remembered to lock it up in his desk? Think so. Soon see. Never know when he might have recourse to it; especially if he was ever called on to photograph one of the more unsavory areas of the city, leftovers from the rowdy Gold Rush days when people were shooting each other right and left.

There was a *clanking* and *hissing*. Growing louder and louder. The flash of the brass cage of the elevator, as it drew level with him. Come on now. *Four* stairs at a time.

It still wasn't enough. The elevator was already catching up with him again, Rulofson and Burckhardt with their little potbellies and close-cropped Prussian hair grinning at him through the bars like Tweedle Dum and Tweedle Dee.

"Vy don't you shtep into ze modern verld, Muybridge?" said Burckhardt, his tiny eyes almost disappearing into the pink pillows of his cheeks, his accent still as thick as the chopped steaks of his native Hamburg. Curious combination: the vulgarity of a fishwife coupled with the charm of a schoolboy.

The elevator pulled ahead of Edward as he heard Rulofson's usual grumble, only a trace of his origins left in his voice: "We go to all this expense for a hydraulic elevator and what does he do? He takes the stairs."

On the second floor landing, Edward passed the two men as they lit cigars and entered the reception room. He loved this room; it was so spacious, its great skylight so brilliant. Through the half open doors surrounding the gallery, he saw the young men and women hunched over their photographic prints look up and return his nod.

Oh, there they are, just inside the door of the ladies' dressing room. The dark hair and angles of Sarah Louisa, towering over what must be Mrs. Stone.

Sarah Louisa turned to greet him, coming close to whisper with that hint of cockney.

"Your cravat."

"What's the matter with it?"

"It's undone."

"It's the latest fashion, didn't you know?" It was usually so easy for Edward to make her smile. But not today, apparently.

"When did you last eat?"

"I don't remember – before the flood."

Her eyes narrowed. "Not maggots again, was it? That make the cheese taste better? Along with your blooming raisins."

She turned to Mrs. Stone. "That's all he eats half the time, raisins and cheese – with the maggots still in the holes. Can you imagine?"

The breath a hundred stairs couldn't knock out of him was gone. It wasn't just the lovely face, the tumbling mass of golden hair, the astonishing figure. How could breasts swell like that? A waist curve in to almost nothing like that? But there was something else, something that shook him to his toes, as if the earthquake they were always predicting had taken place within him. Edward had a distinct sense of falling – that must be why they talked of "falling in love." But it wasn't a literal falling, it was more a sinking, a sinking into another person with perfect confidence, knowing that at last, at last…

He had he have this woman. He had to possess her, he had to. God, what was he thinking? How could he even dare to think of such a thing? She was twenty to his forty-one. He'd become the rich old man in the stage-coach.

Sarah Louisa cleared her throat, gazing at him with her big brown eyes. She took him aside, stepped closer.

He tried to shake the image of Mrs. Stone from his head.

"I know you asked me to get someone in to help with the re-touching," said Sarah Louisa, "but… well… now I… I've been thinking it over, I don't really see the need after all, we managed quite well before, just the two of us, all this time, we used to – "

"Never mind what we used to do, Sarah Louisa!"

She looked down at her feet.

"We discussed all this before," said Edward, softly now, "there is so much to do. Rulofson is in full agreement."

She curtsied. "Yes, sir. I beg your pardon."

She turned back to the vision beside her. "May I introduce Mrs. Flora Stone? Flora, this is Mr. Muybridge."

"How do you do, sir."

He had so many questions. What were Flora Stone's eyes saying to him? Could she possibly feel the same way? No, that was absurd. After a split-second? But what was she thinking? How could anyone's voice be so enchanting? Was that lilt in her speech from Alabama or Kentucky? He had to know, he had to know everything.

Burckhardt shoved himself between them, Rulofson at his elbow. "You're late, Muybridge," he gestured at Edward's plates, "zese vere promised for tomorrow."

But Burckhardt's eyes were already elsewhere. He was staring at her! Rulofson too!

Pull yourself together. "Sorry I was delayed, Rulofson, but on the way back from Sacramento, I took the California Pacific from Vallejo to Calistoga and – "

" – you couldn't resist making views of the hot springs, I know." Rulofson finally dragged his eyes away from Flora and back to Edward, "But any pictures of Stanford's *Central* Pacific Railroad by any chance – the object of your trip? He's the one paying the bills, after all."

Would Rulofson ever stop talking about money? "I'll show them to you soon enough."

He escaped into an empty re-touching room, sensing the two women following him.

He spread his plates out on a table. Concentrate. Check the skies above the trains. Did they all come out blank? Go through them. Yes, good. Thank goodness he'd been able to devise that Sky Shade to get over the problem of the pesky California blue Dodgson had warned him about. So simple: merely a little board flap inside his camera to block the brighter light from the sky during a portion of an exposure. But now he was just sorting through the images, again and again, making busy work.

The eyes of the two women were boring into the back of his coat.

"There isn't any sky," mumbled Flora.

"That's because he holds it back," said Sarah Louisa.

"Like King Canute," said Flora.

"Who?"

"You know, holdin' back the waves, in the story."

Wa-eves. Edward closed his eyes, his back still to the women. That voice! What was it about the South?

"I don't know about that. He just wants to – "

"Make the clouds go away?" said Flora.

"Well, the whole sky," Sarah Louisa sounded impatient, "but if there are clouds, it'll be your job to help me put them back in."

"How do we know what sort of clouds Mr. Muybridge wants?" said Flora.

Sarah Louisa leaned past Edward's shoulder to pick up a positive paper print of a photograph and turned it over to reveal some notes.

"He gives them numbers."

Still behind him, Eadward could hear her finger tapping the print.

"Here, you see, 'California Pacific train crossing the Sacramento River: clouds 4 & 7.' Always write the name of the subject and the cloud number on the back."

"I've never heard of anyone numberin' the clouds before," said Flora. "How do you know which numbers to choose, Mr. Muybridge?"

Edward turned to face her. His mouth was locked and bolted. Force it out. "Please show her, Sarah Louisa."

Sarah Louisa glared at him, then turned and stomped to the rear of the workroom and started rummaging through piles of negative plates.

Flora came close to him. "Paintin' with light."

"What?" Her eyes were bluer than the sky. They would burn right through his Sky Shade.

"Sun paintin'," said Flora.

"You heard that from Sarah Louisa?"

"No... paintin' with light is what the word 'photography'

means, isn't it? And Helios, the sun god, on your carriage."

The heat was everywhere. In his neck, his forehead, his cheeks. Behind those curtains, perhaps it hadn't been Sarah Louisa, perhaps it had been her? Beneath the "F" – for Flora?

She looked up at the skylight, the light bathing her face. It took Leonardo months to paint Mona Liza. He could have done it in a few seconds. And that perfume she was wearing… Jasmine…

He called out, too loudly. "Sarah Louisa, where the blazes are those negatives?"

The evening traffic along Montgomery was as clogged as ever. It would be quicker to walk back to his lodgings, no point getting Helios out. He'd better tell Wu and Lee he didn't need it.

"It doesn't get any better, does it, the traffic?" Flora was at his elbow. Out of the blue.

He'd been avoiding her all day, leaving her to Sarah Louisa, and he didn't dare look at her now. He wasn't ready for this. He was torn.

He looked about him for an escape. Thank the Lord, there were his Chinamen now, with some of their friends from the billiard saloon clustered at the rear of the studio. Just in time.

"Huddle 'em, huddle 'em!"

A dozen or more schoolchildren were careering down the street. Only these children had never seen the inside of a school. Instead of school caps, they were wearing what looked like a fez with a Chinese pigtail, and instead of schoolbooks they were brandishing hickory sticks, knives and broken bottles. Racing along: elbowing, shouldering, kneeing any passer-by getting in their way, the girls as bad as the boys.

Edward had read about them in the newspaper: Irish ragamuffins they called the "Hoodlums," after their custom of shouting "huddle 'em" (to beat up Chinamen) and adding "lum" at the end of word. He searched his pockets. No pistol. Damn. The one time he needed it.

Everything sped up, the world flashing by as fast as the rocks outside the stage-coach: pedestrians ducking into doorways, flattening themselves against the sides of buildings; women giving yelps of fear; men pretending not to notice as the tornado tore through them.

"Fockin' chinklums! Fockin' chinklums! Huddle 'em, huddle 'em!"

Edward turned to see Wu and Lee and several of the other Chinamen shrinking back against the wall of the back of the studio building, pressing their bodies against the bricks as if they wanted to pass clean through them to Canton.

"Shall we pepperlum, pepperlum, Muldoon?" shouted one of the girls at one of the boys as she brandished a jam jar of red pepper in Wu's terrified face. "Owd yer like this in yer slant eyes, yer fockin' dog-eatin' piece of shite? Does yer mum's crack go sideways too? Oy'll slit that for 'er an' all."

"Oy gotta a better one, Little Dick!" cried Muldoon, flicking a cutthroat razor to and fro under Lee's nose, "let's slit their tonguelums and their earlums to match their fockin' eyes!"

Other Hoodlums stretched out an assortment of kitchen knives in search of pigtail trophies.

As if it were being moved by someone else, Edward watched his hand knocking Little Dick's jam jar out of her grasp and then doing the same to Muldoon's razor, sending it skittering along the ground.

The sheer shock of being challenged sent the Hoodlums into a huddle of their own. Then they turned to glare at Edward.

He glared back. "GET AWAY FROM HERE, I'M WARNING YOU!"

The words come from somewhere deep inside him, deeper than he knew existed. This wasn't him, yet it was, the new Edward, who had arrived just in time.

"It's a fockin' limey!" said Little Dick. "A fockin' old manlums."

Before Edward could stop him, Muldoon snatched up his razor from the ground. "Yer wanna be cut up yer daft old limey cunt?"

The world turned red. Never, ever hurt another human being,

his childhood vow to overcome all the hate, yes, but these weren't humans, these were demons exuding injustice and unfairness. The unfairness was always the worst thing, the cruelest thing, whether towards red Indians or yellow Chinamen or black Africans. Everything that was fast became slow; the stage-coach again, but he was in the driver's seat now. His world collapsed into a sluggish composition of crashing fists and flashing steel and splintering glass as he waged war on the devil's spawn, on the devil's unfairness.

But now that Edward's Chinamen had a leader, they added their deftness and agility and wiry strength to the brawl, and for once in their brief and brutish lives in America, the Hoodlums knew defeat, scattering in all directions. And for once in their long and nightmarish lives in America, these slender yellow men knew victory.

Battered and slashed but smiling, Wu and Lee looked down at Edward in the gutter, holding out their hands in thanks.

Something soft and cool with the scent of jasmine came between them, wiping the blood from his lips and cheek. A face stared down at him, a face with dimples and the sweetest smile he'd ever seen. Moving closer, blurring. A kiss planted on his forehead, like the seed of his future, right here, in broad daylight on Montgomery-street.

CHAPTER NINE

Edward's hands were trembling as he held the reins, his heart racing. This was ridiculous. He could overcome his fear of heights, he could overcome a street-full of hoodlums, and yet when faced with the prospect of being alone with a delicate creature half his size and half his age and one tenth of his strength, he was as nervous as a schoolboy. What would he say to her? Nothing in his life had prepared him for this.

It was his fault. He was the one who'd suggested they come to this remote beach, which he knew would be deserted on this weekday, precisely so that they could be alone together. But although he was so nervous, he was so happy at the same time. Was that possible? Can you be frightened and happy at the same time? He knew nothing of these matters, of these strange new feelings.

Clip-clop, clip-clop went his Helios steeds, clip-clopping so merrily. He reined them to a halt for a moment to collect his thoughts. What a view! From up here by the Cliff House Hotel at Point Lobos, you could see the whole of Ocean Beach. He'd photographed this view many times of course, but it had never looked like this. The choppy water was sapphire sprinkled with diamonds, the sand was gold dust. If only his camera could capture color. James Maxwell had achieved such a thing a few years back, using three cameras, each with a different filter: red, green and blue, but there'd been no advance since.

Edward snapped his whip in the air to get the horses started again and then down the slope from the hotel, down to the endless vista of sand and spume, not a soul in sight. The surf had little thunder in its voice this morning, just a long sigh in and out as the planet breathed. The sandpipers skittered to and fro on matchstick legs, ferreting for crabs between ebb and flow. A steamer sounded its horn in the Bay.

The canvas flap at the rear of the great black box was still down. His hands were shaking even more now.

The flap lifted aside, a curtain at the opening of a play.

"It's all right, you can come out," he said, "we have the place to ourselves."

Flora leaped into his arms.

She was lighter than a baby and just as soft. What was he doing? He released her. She looked up at him, a happy child ready for the next game. He wasn't afraid of anything now, so why was he afraid of her? This strange new person in his life.

"I know you can box – I saw that outside the gallery – but can you run?" Flora pointed at a jagged chunk of granite poking up through the sand a hundred yards down the beach.

She was wearing some sort of day dress of the palest blue. She hitched up her skirts and broke into a run. Edward couldn't stop staring at her. But he had to follow. She moved remarkably well for a woman, although he could easily have overtaken her of course, but instead he hung back. Was this a gallant gesture to let her win? Or because he couldn't resist the sight of her ankles?

She slipped on a straggle of wet seaweed, fell flat on her face and lay still.

Oh, Lord! She wasn't moving. He kneeled down beside her and gently touched her shoulder. Through the muslin it was soft and warm. But there was no response to his hand. *The jasmine, the curve of her spine.* He couldn't hear her breathing. He touched her neck. He couldn't detect a heartbeat, although his own was fit to burst. Gingerly, he eased her over onto her back. Her eyes were closed, a glisten of perspiration on her forehead. His hand automatically reached out to stroke her skin. So smooth... But still no response. Her chest against his cheek. A heartbeat. Was that a heartbeat? A faint thump? He couldn't be sure. There was nothing else for it. He shut his eyes and put his hand on her breast.

Suddenly, her arms were around him and she was kissing him on the lips.

"You tricked me!"

She looked up at him, into him. He was a pat of butter on a stove. "I'm sorry. I'm sorry – I just thought that – "

"This is not proper, it is not proper." Edward was almost shouting. "You shouldn't have. I was so alarmed."

"Please forgive me. I was carried away." She held out her arms for him to help her up.

CHAPTER TEN

Three weeks. It only took three weeks to change the world. They talked of the whirlwind of romance; Edward's head hadn't stopped whirling. A new vertigo. Another transformation of his life; this one surely the most profound?

Woodward's Gardens: they'd gone with Joseph and Arthur so Edward could take pictures of her in the stuffed animals exhibit: Flora popping up from behind a Bengal tiger, a gorilla, a polar bear, like a mischievous child, like one of Dodgson's little girls. Flora in the Garden of Eden, innocence among the beasts. He'd always loved Woodward's, but she'd made it their special place, returning with him again and again to sample its merry-go-rounds, theatrical displays, parlor-skating and wonderful zoo.

And those balloon ascensions! He'd once been afraid at the very thought of them, but no more. He'd begged Flora to let him take her up, but she was the one frightened now. They'd spent hours watching the huge globes swaying in the wind as they threw the ballast out and loosened the cords to allow the vast masses of silk to rise slowly into the blue, some of them ascending as high as half a mile, almost touching the heights of Heaven.

Imagine taking views from such a balloon one day! The spectacle must be sublime, turning the whole world into a Yosemite. Why not? After all, Nadar had done it, hadn't he? The famous Félix Nadar, whom he'd been reading about ever since Dodgson brought up his name. Nadar had not only photographed every well-known person in Europe, he had also photographed Paris itself from his hot-air balloon; one of the first pictures ever taken from the air, although how he'd managed to work with wet plates up there was a mystery.

Such delicious moments... leading inexorably to the most delicious moment of all when Edward sank to his knees before her.

May again. The bells were pealing at the Church of the Advent of Christ the King – the closest in liturgy to the Church of England he could find – the Reverend Mr. Sawtelle presiding.

"Perfect!" It was going to be a perfect picture. Quickly, out of the shroud. "Now, Joseph!"

Joseph stared up at him. What's got into the man, today of all days? "*Now*, I say. What are you waiting for?"

"*Edward!* You're meant to be *in* the picture!" came Flora's laughing voice.

"Oh, my Lord!"

He ran up the steps, laughing himself at the sight of her white wedding dress. She was so blindingly beautiful in the sun he doubted Rulofson and Burckhardt and the others from the gallery in their Sunday black would come out in the picture at all.

She clutched his arm so tightly it burned, her hand trembling.

A few feet away, Maid of Honor Sarah Louisa was muttering something to an elderly version of herself in a tangerine dress and a straw hat topped by an Everest of roses. That must be Mrs. Smith, her midwife mother. Now there was someone who could only have been born within the sound of Bow bells. All she was missing were the pearl buttons the constermongers sewed on their waistcoats. But poor Sarah Louisa, she must be thirty-one now and still single. He did so hope it wasn't too late for her to find a husband. She certainly deserved to be happy. Although he was a fine one to talk: it'd taken him until his forties to find the girl of his dreams. Married… Edward could hardly believe it. Who would have thought? Especially having vowed that he'd never do such a thing after what he'd seen of his parents' marriage. But this was going to be different, he knew it was. It was funny, by making that vow inside the church just now, he had broken another one.

Flora nodded to him.

He signalled Joseph that they were ready.

Joseph grasped the lens cap. "Everyone quite still please."

Edward knew it wasn't done in a photograph, but he was smiling so broadly his mouth hurt.

He was nervous as a virgin, his limbs frozen as up it came, the terrible memory he had been suppressing for so long. The awful falsetto voice thick with beer coming through the wall of his parents' bed-room. It was like a girl's, wheedling, begging, groveling, so different from Father's everyday voice, Mother might be sharing her bed with another man. "Susannah, please, please… let me… I want to… I have to do it, Susannah, please. Please let me." A loud slap on flesh. "No, I said *no*! Get away from me. Take your hands off me!" The sound of what used to be a man sobbing. Mother screaming: "Get away from me! You disgust me! You make me sick! You monster!" Now that stranger's voice was angry: "I saw that chit of a girl again, Susannah, wiggling her bottom along the tow-path. She hiked her skirt up to her ankles, Susannah, then to her knees, then to her thighs, then all the way up to her navel, showing to her cunt, and I raped her, Susannah, I raped her and raped her!"

Then later, after many more such nightmare voices, Edward's twelve-year old self squatting on his bed looking down at his father's razor, wanting to die, wanting to cut his penis off, his original sin. The thin red line of blood beginning to spurt at the base of the thing, just press a little harder. Although he hadn't of course. Thank the Lord. But he had been so close. God, how close. But he hadn't. All he had done was curl up like a fetus.

From that day to this, apart from the occasional guilt-ridden thrashing about with some hussy in a midnight street, he'd never known the love of a woman. Only the guilt of forbidden pleasures, such small pleasures, such small joy. Oh, St. Paul and St. Augustine, what have ye wrought? What did that poor, self-hating Paul who threw such discord into Christ's lovely song say? "The law of sin dwells in my members." Augustine had gone even further: "The diabolical excitement of the genitals is the clearest evidence of original sin." So much shame, so much guilt, and all because a woman urged a man to eat an apple.

"I'm nervous, too, Edward."

Was she? Was that possible? Oh, thank God… the darling.

"Stroke my brow, it's so calmin'."

This time it was calming him too.

"Tell me about your city, Edward."

"My city?"

"San Francisco. You love it so much. The city that's founded on gold."

Oh, that voice, that southern voice. The breath of air in the magnolias.

"You know what you have to do, to find the gold?" whispered Flora.

"What do I have to do?"

"You have to explore your city, go up and down all the highways and byways, climb all the hills, so soft and round, so many hills, delve down into the valleys, the soft warm valleys. Explore everythin'."

"Everything?"

"Every rooftop, every chimney, every avenue, every alleyway, every passage. You have to search everywhere to find the secret gate that guards the gold."

"And when I find it, how do I open it?"

"Oh, it's open, Edward, it's open."

It felt like – what did it feel like? There were no words for this. How can you describe something you have never experienced before in your life? No, that wasn't quite true: Edward had had an intimation of it before when he'd first caught sight of Flora. And now that falling in love feeling again, but multiplied a thousand-fold. And even more than that, a feeling of complete freedom, of letting go completely, of finally, finally giving himself. To her, of course, but not just to her, to the whole world, to the whole universe. Take me, I am part of you, you are part of me. He had no idea such pleasure, such joy, existed, that his whole body could be on fire like this, burning to the tips of his fingers like this, the tips of his toes, the end of every nerve. Inside, he laughed with the ecstasy of it, the pure joy, for they were all wrong, weren't they? St. Paul, St. Augustine, the school chaplain with his endless sermons about burning in Hell. They were all wrong, so utterly wrong. It wasn't in Hell where you burned. It was in Heaven.

He was flying with the seagulls, wheeling and dancing in the air.

"Oh, again, please Edward, oh, my love, my love!"

And again and again.

Finally, finally, that awful voice through his bedroom wall had been silenced, the ghosts of his past laid to rest – by what was surely the greatest love any man could know.

"It's my dream come true, my love," Flora was whispering, "not only this, but everything that has happened – and this house: in South Park of all places. I never dared dream of this."

Nor did Edward. It was Berkeley Square in San Francisco, a stone's throw from the Embarcadero as the man who leased it to them had said, its three-story residences curving round the gated oval park complete with gingko trees and sage palms, shady walkways and residents-only key. They even have a china closet imported direct from Thomas Twyford of England. Was he a gentleman at last?

"I'm going to make you proud of me, if it's the last thing I do."

Flora smiled at the ceiling. "You just did. Several times."

CHAPTER ELEVEN

A picnic on a Sunday summer afternoon: the Belmont Park pleasure-ground surrounding Edward with reflections and scents of her: tulip trees, pepper trees, catalpas, magnolias, geraniums, stephanotis, jasmine, passion flowers – his passion flower. It was hard to believe a year had gone by since their wedding.

He watched all the prominent San Francisco families parading past them in their sumptuous carriages, the men about town weaving in and out between the wheels, tipping their hats. There was one young blade in particular who seemed to know everyone, sporting the tallest white topper he'd ever seen. He looked vaguely familiar, but Edward couldn't quite place him. If only he could get an introduction to one of these eminent gentlemen, this could change everything, then he could really make his name, make Flora proud, accomplish his dream of capturing movement with his camera.

He looked down at his love now beneath her white parasol amidst their picnic spread. So young, so pure. Beatrice. Manet's naked woman on the grass. He could cope with that now, after Dodgson. She was the artist's own wife, they say. How he'd love to photograph Flora like that, but of course he'd never dare – especially with so many notable personages around.

"People will talk you know."

He flushed. Could she read his thoughts? "Will talk about what, my darling? We're only having a picnic."

"They'll think you're in love."

"Oh, I am and I always will be."

"With that." She pointed at his camera, which he'd set up a few feet from her next to Helios, its rear end opened up into a dark-room. "How many more pictures are you goin' to take of me? You even take pictures of me when you think I'm asleep."

His cheeks burned.

"You may well color, Edward Muybridge. Don't think I haven't noticed. Hiding behind the curtains, like a Peeping Tom."

It was like an electric shock. Is that what he was? With his obsession with seeing things that nobody had ever seen, that perhaps nobody was ever meant to see? Was there something salacious in him? Something libidinous? Something that had crept through the wall of his parents' bed-room into his soul? Was that part of why he'd shared Dodgson's fascination with the naked Beatrice? Why he'd thought of Manet?

"You know what happened to Tom when he looked at Lady Godiva," said Flora, "he was struck blind."

The sky was very bright today. Concentrate on that. "We might get away with a three in this light."

She sighed. "Oh, Edward, what *does* it matter? A five or a four or a three?"

A pair of swallows were swooping and soaring above them. "You see those birds?"

She glanced up quickly. "Yes... But *why*? Why do you want to see so much?"

"Look," he pulled a shred of crumpled newsprint out of his pocket, "from *Photographic News*, an article by another photographer from England, Stephen Thompson, it captures exactly what I'm trying to say." He scanned the words. "He writes about the fact that so far we can only capture nature in repose, landscapes, ruins, and so forth, but then he says, 'but life, motion, and all its poetry: nature – living, warm, pulsating nature, with her April face and her April eyes, her stormy passions and sudden calms, the power and mystery of nature, not only her outward form, but her beating heart – lies beyond our domain.'"

He gazed up at the birds again. "I want to go into that land... beyond...I want to look into that 'April face, and stop the birds.'"

Flora studied the swallows for a moment. "If you stop those birds, they'll die."

"It's not that," he muttered. He shook his head. "My photographs have to be faster and faster so I can get to – well, the essence of it..."

"All right, one more... for my 'essence.'"

He loaded the camera and watched her as she put down her

parasol and struck a pose.

"One… two… three…"

She looked at him. Was that a tiny hint of sadness in her eyes? "I know," she said, "five minutes to develop and fix and varnish: the tyranny of the wet plate." She reached for her book: *The Lady of the Camellias*, Alexandre Dumas, *fils*. It was one of Edward's favorites too. Now there was a writer, even better than his father. Flora even loved *La Traviata* because it was based on the novel.

Five minutes, when Edward emerged from Helios, Flora didn't even notice. She wasn't concentrating on her book, but on the dance pavilion nearby where couples were moving languidly to a Negro band under the banner "Wilson's All-Star Minstrels." They were playing "Silver Threads Among the Gold." Edward watched as Flora mouthed the words:

> *Darling, I am growing old,*
> *Silver threads among the gold,*
> *Shine upon my brow today,*
> *Life is fading fast away.*

Her hands touched her hair. She couldn't possibly imagine she was growing old surely? Is that why she'd looked sad just now? The silly darling. At twenty-one?

A little boy ran by with a hoop. Her eyes followed him. Was that what it was? His lips brushed her temple. "I know, Flora. We will have a son, some day soon, God willing."

"Shh, Edward, you're makin' *me* blush now."

The minstrels finished the song and the young conductor took a bow. That must be Mr. Wilson, thought Edward, since he was the only white man. What a fine figure he cut, such perfect bone structure, he could have been in the theater.

He saw Flora pick up her book. Talk of camellias… On the plate, where the lights and shades were reversed, she appeared even more beautiful.

Those black minstrels would be interesting to render, Edward thought, not only the dark complexions, but the brightness of the white round the eyes, the red round the lips, the glaring colors of their clothes, so many shades of gray to balance. What irony: they dress up as Golliwoggs to caricature the white minstrels who'd dressed up as Golliwoggs to caricature them.

"Don't tell me, you're wonderin' about the exposure for the dark skins."

She'd caught him again. "Sorry, there I go again – but I think I could do it, I've already photographed a colored boxer at the gymnasium, I just keep several different sensitizer mixtures ready for such occasions – oh, dear – " He clapped his hands over his mouth.

Flora shook her head fondly. "Oh, Edward, what am I going to do with you? You're such a dodo."

"Dodo? That's what everyone called Dodgson."

She shielded them with her parasol so she could embrace him. "Well, that's what you are too: my sweet dodo bird, the last of his kind. As strong as an ox and as delicate as a flower."

More drumming of horse's hooves. The splendid carriages were completing another loop of the park, circling them like Red Indians. One in particular was coming quite close: a four-in-hand Edward hadn't noticed before with a heavily-built middle-aged man and his family, who looked even more distinguished than the other grandees, if that were possible. Edward wondered who he was. And then he realized. Oh, it's *him*. He should have known. He looked almost as imposing in real life as in that Last Spike painting.

"Look, Flora."

"I know, I know, you want to capture the movement of the wheels."

"No, no – the man in the carriage."

She looked. "Who is it?"

"The Governor. You must have seen his painting."

"Leland Stanford? Why didn't you wave? You've taken enough photographs of his railroad."

"I've only seen him at a distance, we've never met in person." He refrained from mentioning that Stanford had refused to pay the creator of the Last Spike painting the $50,000 he owed him because he wasn't displayed prominently enough. "But if only I could get an introduction? A commission to take a family portrait? Who knows were that might lead?" *Even if he never got paid.*

He turned to Flora. "Amongst all your clients, all the people you're acquainted with, there must be someone who's close to the Governor?"

"No... I don't know anybody."

"Are you sure?"

"Why not the Major?" she said, "you could ask him, the two of them are as thick as thieves by all accounts." She pointed at the white topper, who had also reappeared and was now saluting them as he paused for a moment to chat with Stanford.

"What a splendid day, Mr. and Mrs. Muybridge!"

Edward saluted him back. So that's who it was? He hadn't recognized him under that extraordinary hat: Major Harry Larkyns...

"He owes you a favor, doesn't he?" said Flora. "Didn't you tell me he once dropped into the gallery to ask you and Sarah Louisa for some points in regard to photographic matters he was writing about in the *The Evening Post* along with his dramatic criticism?"

Edward nodded. The Major... Who could forget that much-quoted article about him in *The Examiner* a few years back: writer, poet, musician, soldier of fortune, boxing like Jem Mace, fencing like Agramonte, hitting bottle necks at twenty paces; a speaker of diverse foreign tongues with a princely command of his own; all this combined with his mastery of the chafing dish, Delmonico simply wasn't in it... He was almost too good to be true. So why not seek his help?

On the other hand, Edward went on to himself, everyone seemed to know a "story" about Larkyns, not all of them as flattering as *The Examiner*'s. One rumor was that he often farmed out his dramatic articles for *The Post* to a down-on-his-luck hack named Henry Coppinger, who ended up being paid so erratically for his work by Larkyns he'd exposed the Major to the newspaper, almost getting him fired. Apparently – at least so the gossip went –

Larkyns got his revenge by accosting the poor fellow in public, taking him by the nose and jaw, spreading open his mouth and spitting down his throat, forever after burdening him with the name "Cuspidor" Coppinger. Probably all nonsense, but all the same.

He turned back to Flora. "You're right, my darling. What have I got to lose?"

He stood up and waved his hat. "Major Larkyns! A minute of your time, if you please, sir."

CHAPTER TWELVE

This was his moment to show what he was made of, thought Edward, as he crouched over his camera, it was now or never.

"Quite still, please, ladies and gentlemen."

The former farm boy, attorney, grocer, governor, railroad magnate and now multi-millionaire froze in the haughty pose of the newly very, very, rich, his eyes fixed on Edward's camera lens as if were gazing into eternity. He who pisseth highest… to misquote *Samuel*. He was an impressive figure though, Edward had to give him that. There was nothing wrong with being rich of course, but the fiscal details of how Stanford came about his wealth would have warmed the heart of Mr. Micawber: bill to investors for constructing Central Pacific railroad, $120 million, actual expenditure on same, $58 million; result happiness.

Thanks to the Major, here Edward was, only a few short weeks later, in Sacramento, in one of the seventeen-foot high neo-Pompeian saloons of "Stanford's Palace," the Governor's forty-four-room monument to himself, which took up the entire corner of Eighth and N street. Sharing this overstuffed space with Stanford was his entire family including his golden-haired little four-year old son Leland in a brown velvet suit and lace collar, and his wife whose sprawling body was swathed from head to foot in purple velvet as thick as the Turkey and Brussels carpets, her hair, ears, neck and arms ablaze with precious stones. And coming from outside this museum of opulence, the sound of yet more wealth: the thunder of the hooves of one of Stanford's outrageously expensive thoroughbreds being put through his paces.

Edward removed the lens cap. Ten seconds. He couldn't get it below that today; the morning light wasn't good enough, too overcast. But he had arranged his canvas awning just as Dodgson had taught him to get the shadows of what light there was in the room thrown on his subjects exactly as he wanted. This was his main chance, his great opportunity handed to him by Larkyns to impress the most famous man in California by taking the best portrait of him and his family that had ever been made. "Thank you."

The Stanford shoulders relaxed for a moment in a flurry of operatic coughing and nose blowing.

"Thank *you*, Mr. Muybridge, for the pitcher," said Mrs. Stanford, smiling warmly as she opened her mouth for the first time. "It's a great honor to have a photographer of your caleyeber in our house. How you do it is beyond my apprehension, and us bobbing from side to side like a metromoan."

Edward warmed to her as quickly as he had to Dodgson: an American Mrs. Malaprop; next thing she'd be asking him about the perpendiculars of his profession.

"You are too kind, but there is one more picture to need to take." Always take one more for safety, Dogson had said.

Joseph and Arthur dashed into the room like a pair of vaudeville tumblers: the first to remove the exposed plate from the camera, the second to insert a fresh one.

"Quite still please," said Edward.

Yet another lofty pose; that was all Stanford seemed to want. But he must give him what he wants, mustn't he? thought Edward. If he was to have what *he* wanted: for the Governor to sponsor him to pursue a more rapid method of taking pictures to fulfill his dream.

As if on command, Stanford stepped out of the tableau vivant. "What if we did move? Could you find a way to photograph that?"

Edward started. This was astonishing. "But – Governor – how did you? – I've been thinking about that all my life!"

Stanford gestured to Edward to follow him through the French windows onto a balcony, which overlooked a small paddock where a raven-black racehorse was pulling a sulky of such light construction the driver appeared to float between its Penny Farthing wheels.

"What if I were to ask you to photograph Occident moving at full trot?" exclaimed the Governor.

"Occident? The fastest trotter in the world?"

"Could you capture him? He's been clocked at twenty-five

miles an hour."

Edward did a quick calculation: thirty-six feet per second! What minuscule fraction of a second's exposure would that require? And even if he continued to make further progress with his chemicals, how could he ever get the lens cap on and off in time? No, no, he hated to say it, it was really the last thing he wanted to say, but...

"It's impossible – "

"*Impossible n'est pas français,*" said young Leland, pushing his way through the cathedral of legs. "That's right, isn't it Papa?"

His father stroked his head, beaming down him. "That's quite right, my boy."

Now there's a son. Edward immediately wanted one just like him.

Stanford turned back to him: "The French always say the word impossible isn't part of their vocabulary, nor should it be part of ours."

"Yes, but what you're talking about, Governor, has never been heard of, photography hasn't yet arrived at such wonderful perfection."

"Obstacles are only things to be overcome, Muybridge. Even my son knows you can do it." He looked fondly at the boy again for a moment. "Do you have children, Muybridge?"

Edward reddened. "I'm just recently married and we have high hopes."

"When you have a son, you will do anything to make him proud. Anything." Stanford hugged the boy, then handed him over to his mother.

"I want you to capture the exact position of every hoof," the Governor continued, ushering Edward him back into the saloon. "I think if you will give your attention to the subject, you will be able to do it, and I want you to try."

What could he say? It *was* clearly impossible. On the other hand...

"Do you read French, Muybridge?" Stanford reached for a pile of proofs on a nearby table.

"Why, yes, a little…" said Edward.

"Look at this." Stanford pointed at an underlined passage.

"…*dans l'intervalle de deux battues successives, l'animal est un instant suspendu au-dessus du sol.*"

Edward struggled to remember his schoolboy French: "'…in the… eh… interval of − between two successive hoof beats, the animal is… for an instant suspended above the ground.'"

"That's a very controversial statement, you've just read, Muybridge. Most students of the horse maintain that all four hooves never leave the ground at once. But this book, '*La machine animale*,'" Stanford patted the proofs, "which the French physiologist, Professor Marey, is going to publish next year, proves otherwise in a most interesting experiment. He attached rubber tubes to the horse's legs by a leather bracelet. As each hoof struck the ground, the pressure of the bracelet forced air through the tube to a mechanism held by the rider, which recorded at what point and for how long the hoof had been in contact with the ground. Marey then created bar drawings of the actions of all four hooves." Stanford held up a sketch of a series of regular curving lines above two rows of horizontal black and white bars.

"It looks like a cardiographic tracing."

"That's precisely where Marey got the idea − in fact, do you know − he *invented* cardiographic recording. Only here," Stanford tapped the sketch again, "instead of measuring heartbeats he's measuring *hoof* beats."

"It also looks somewhat like musical notation."

"Exactly − done graphically. I want you to do the same thing *photo*graphically."

"Capture the music of movement… "

"We understand each other very well, I see."

The Governor really did want him to try to do this, thought Edward. Should he take the risk?

"I took up horse breeding on the advice of my doctors," continued Stanford.

This was truly astounding now. All these coincidences. "I took up photography for the same reason!"

The Governor rubbed his hands together. "Imagine what could happen if we mixed the two prescriptions together."

Was he really ready for this? *Was* it possible?

"Major Larkyns spoke very highly of you."

"That was very good of him." He certainly didn't want to let Larkyns down, that was certain. Oh, very well then. He shook Stanford's hand. "I will do my best, Governor."

The Governor smiled, accustomed to winning. "You won't regret this, Muybridge. He really did praise you to the skies, you know. A fine man, the Major, although there has been some talk, that business with young Arthur Neil."

Another story?

"Some question of fraud, $3,000 I heard, running up outrageous bar bills at the Occidental at the poor fellow's expense, probably all just rumor of course. He has a good bottom to him. Put it down to malicious gossip – I've been a victim myself. And life's not been kind to him, you know. In fact, it's a tragic story."

"No, I didn't know, I had no idea. What happened to him?"

"You're an Englishman, Muybridge, you remember the siege of Kabul in forty-two?"

"When the Afghanis promised the British safe passage from the city if they'd return to India, and then slaughtered every man jack of them?"

"Including both of Larkyns' parents – "

"Oh, my Lord." And Edward thought that he'd had a difficult childhood. Now Larkyns was putting him to shame on another level.

"They were out there overseeing the opium plantations for the East India Company, doing such a splendid trade with China too, and then... those savages..."

The opium trade with China... how many Chinese had it killed? Some twenty million? How *splendid?* But now was not the moment. "Oh, my Lord... The poor man."

"Boy," corrected Stanford, "that's all Larkyns was at the time." He nodded sadly, "Just a little boy, not much older than my son is now. Tragic, to be orphaned like that."

"My wife is also an orphan."

The Governor turned back to gaze through the French windows at Occident. "Nothing like this has ever been done before, you know, Muybridge. But they said that of my railroad, didn't they?" He looked round at Edward with a smile. "I think I can safely say that your wife's fortunes are about to change."

CHAPTER THIRTEEN

Come on, come on! How many trains and ferries had he taken today? Edward had lost track, but here he was in San Francisco harbor at last. Another twenty minutes and he'd be running up the studio stairs. He couldn't wait to tell her. Although Stanford had committed larceny of the grandest kind with the financing of his railroad, the man was a colossus nonetheless, spanning the continent with his trains like a Gulliver, with Morse's telegraph strung alongside the rails to announce his triumph simultaneously from coast to coast. At the very second Stanford's hammer struck that spike in Utah in sixty-nine – captured so vividly in the painting, even to the man with the Hebrew face standing just behind him – *bang!* an operator clicked three dots for 'done,' sending an instant electric message along the wires to activate the cannons and fire-bells in every major city. Fast as lightning and just as miraculous. And now this miracle worker wanted to help *him*, Edward Muybridge, do the same with photography: take a picture fast as light! It would mean spending about six weeks up in Sacramento since that was where all Stanford's horses and equipment were, but he was sure Flora would understand.

Flora almost knocked him over, leaping into his arms, covering him with kisses.

"Oh, I missed you so much, my darlin'!"

"I was only away a day."

She turned away, her shoulders starting to shake.

"What is it, my love?"

"Leavin' me…"

"But it was your idea for me to approach the Governor – and I'm not leaving you, my darling, I'll never leave you."

Edward's fingers traced her temple, her eyebrows. "Listen, Flora, you are my love, my life… you know that, you must know that."

She looked at him through her tears. "You won't go up there

again, will you, Dodo? You won't leave me again?"

He didn't know what had possessed her, but he did know that he couldn't possibly tell her about the six weeks now. What a terrible dilemma. What on earth was he going to do?

She snuggled against his chest, her slim neck still quivering with emotion like a frightened little bird.

"No, I will not go up to Sacramento again, Flora."

"You promise, Edward? You cross your heart?"

"I cross my heart."

She hugged him tighter and tighter, as if she wanted to bury herself in him.

There was a sound from the reception room, a woman's tread. Flora slipped out of his arms. It sounded like Sarah Louisa, always something hesitant in her walk. But even she was acting oddly today, Edward had never known her take so long for lunch. But it was true she'd been more and more moody lately, just when he thought she'd come to terms with losing her position to Flora.

Sarah Louisa almost fell into the room, her face flushed.

"Where have you been all afternoon, leavin' me to do all the work?" snapped Flora. This wasn't his Flora, this martinet. And these sudden shifts of mood, almost hysterical one moment, a bully the next?

Sarah Lousia flopped into a chair. "What do you mean? Who are you to talk to me – nine years your senior… "

"Have you been drinkin'? You know how I hate drinkin'."

"No – well, perhaps one or two, but – "

"Where did you go?" said Flora, calming down somewhat.

Sarah Louisa was suddenly excited. "The Occidental, it's all the go, we had such a lovely lunch, and that new cocktail, the 'Martinez!' Gin and vermouth. Everyone's drinking it. Anyway, we bumped into Major Larkyns and he told us the news he'd just heard from the Governor – "

Edward gave a start. Oh, God, what was she going to say? He had to put a stop to this.

" – so of course we had to celebrate – "

"We have a lot to do, Sarah Louisa!" Now Edward was doing the snapping. "You really must get back to work."

"To celebrate what?" Flora shifted her glare to him. "What news?"

"They'll tell you themselves when they get here," said Sarah Louisa. "They're so excited, I don't want to spoil it – but, wait, wait, I have my own news: the Major's invited me to the theater – my mother will come too, it will be quite proper, look…"

She felt around in her handbag and took out a poster with *Johann Hoff's Malt Extract* printed across the top in large letters above an engraving of a portly actor with thinning hair:

> *Mr. Harry Edwards writes from the California Theater: "The secret of my Thespian art is perfect digestion. I use the genuine Johann Hoff's Malt Extract that greatly aids me in the proper assimilation of food."*

"Harry Edwards is at the California in *Othello*," continued Sarah Louisa. "I've admired him for so long, and would you believe it? He's the Major's very best friend – oh, I know," she touched Flora's arm, "why don't you and Mr. Muybridge come as well?"

"We're much too busy for that sort of thing, Sarah Louisa," said Edward. Now he was barking. "Perhaps later, if things slow down. Please, you must get back to your – "

"Oh, why can't we go, Edward?" said Flora. "It's like the jam in that book by your friend Dodgson, isn't it? Never theater today, only theater yesterday and tomorrow, but never today, because tomorrow never comes, does it? We don't even go to the opera."

"I – I – " stammered Edward. This was getting much too complicated. What was he going to do?

The sound of raucous laughter.

Rulofson, Burckhardt and Major Harry Larkyns himself stood in the doorway, beaming and red in the face. Well, the two Germans were red in the face; Larkyns had his usual immaculate tan that never seemed to vary, winter or summer. He was so youthful looking with his light ginger hair and piercing gray eyes he could have been in his twenties and yet he was only four years younger than Edward.

Burckhardt offered Rulofson a Havana with that lascivious look of his. Where did he come from? The gutters of the Reeperbahn? Burckhardt stifled a burp, making eyes at the oversized cigar. "'afn't you got zumzing longer?" He dug the Major in the ribs. "As ze actress said to ze bishop – *shh!*" He'd spotted Edward and the two women. He turned back to his companions, holding his finger to his lips, then slapped Larkyns on the back. "*Ganz gute Speise, nicht, Harry? Klasse!* Zat Martinez!"

"*La spécialité de la maison, aber alles ist ausgezeichnet bei dem Occidental,*" Larkyns glided between languages like a Dutchman on skates. Then it was his turn to notice them, tripping an instant switch to top-drawer English.

"Ah, there he is, the man of the hour, Mr. Muybridge!"

He strode up to Edward and started pumping his hand up and down as Burckhardt thumped him on the shoulder: "Ze talk of ze town!"

"Congratulations, Muybridge." Now Rulofson was patting him on the back. "News of the wager with James Keene is spreading like wildfire."

"What wager? What are you talking about?"

Burckhardt did a Tweedle Dum toe rise. "It's a lot off money." He rubbed his fingers and thumb together. "*Viel geld.*"

"Twenty-five thousand dollars, in point of fact," said Larkyns, "that's what Stanford stands to win if you can prove his theory of 'unsupported transit.'"

"*What?*" Edward felt has if his insides were collapsing.

"The flying horse, you know, the hoofs," Burckhardt frowned, getting stuck in the language, "the hoofez?"

Rulofson stepped in. "The hoary old question of whether all four hooves of a horse are ever clear of the ground at the same time, you know, Muybridge. Stanford maintains they are, and Keene takes the opposite position."

So that was what it was all about? thought Edward. And he, poor fool, had thought that Stanford genuinely shared his passion, when all along it was just a rich man's wager.

Larkyns put his arm round him. They were almost the same height. The smell of expensive Cologne. "I've pulled all the strings I can, old boy. Happy to do it, of course. At last I've been able to repay you for all those tips about photography. But now it's your turn. The eyes of the whole state are upon you, Muybridge – or Edward, if I may make so bold. This could change your life, you know that, don't you?"

He bowed to Flora, who hadn't said a word. "And yours too, Mrs. Muybridge, if I may make so bold," He bent to kiss her hand. "Please accept my congratulations. I know your husband couldn't have achieved this without you. Behind every great man... "

Flora went red in the face and turned away.

"When do you start, old chap?" asked Rulofson.

All eyes were on Edward as Flora made for the exit.

"He starts tomorrow, don't you, Edward?" said Larkyns. "That's what you promised, isn't it?"

The door slammed.

Edward started to run after her. Sarah Louisa caught him by the sleeve. "I'll go. She's too upset."

He tried to break away, but her hand was still on his arm. "Your project with the Governor, I had an idea: to uncover and cover the lens very fast, that flap you use for your Sky Shade... " She started to explain something, but he wasn't listening. He couldn't listen. All he could see was the door.

The squeak of bedsprings through the mahogany.

"Flora... Flora..." cried Edward for the tenth time.

Still silence.

"Stanford put me in a frightful position, don't you see, Flora? If I'd said no, I'd have been the laughing stock of California. The time'll go by fast, you'll see, you'll have Sarah Louisa and her mother to look after you. The weather's lovely now, you can go for walks."

Was she asleep? More bedspring noises. He pressed his ear even harder against their bedroom door.

"Flora? You do understand don't you? I know I lied to you – but I didn't – I'll never lie to you again. But, don't you see, the Governor isn't a man who takes no for an answer. If he can drive a railroad through the Sierra Nevada, he can…"

What was the use? Was she listening to a word of this?

"Flora, I beg you, let me in, please. If it really upsets you so much, I'm sure we can find a way to resolve this together. Stanford said that after the project is completed, he'll invite us to the great ball he gives every year to celebrate Washington's Birthday. I'll come back to escort you up there, nothing comes before you, Flora, I promise, I swear to you on the Bible, I give you my word! Everybody will be there, the – the cream of society, it will be like your coming out – you – you can wear the blue silk dress I bought you, you know, the one with the pearls?"

Her voice filtered through the door: "It won't fit by that time."

Finally Edward understood. My God! No wonder she was so emotional!

"Oh, my love, my love!"

The pain shot through his shoulder as it hit the door, the hinges giving way immediately, the door crashing to the floor.

How warm her stomach was against Edward's ear. Was that a tiny heartbeat?

Flora laughed: "I think it's a little early to hear anythin', Edward. We only just found out."

"We?"

"Sarah and I, she came with me to Dr. Sullivan – I'm sorry about the scene I made in the studio, but I was – "

"Oh, my love, in your condition, how could I be angry with you? It was all my fault, how stupid I've been, your sudden changes of mood."

He moved up the bed to kiss her. " I don't deserve this."

He felt a wetness on his face. Were those tears hers or his?

He had a sudden thought. "I know what I'm going to do, Flora? My cousin George Lawrence still lives near our old house in Kingston – you remember, I told you about him, it was his father who got me the position with the publishing company that led me to America and to you, my darling. I'm going to ask George to send over the christening dress I wore as a baby, that's what I'm going to do. That's what our little boy shall wear for his first photograph!"

"You don't know that it'll be a boy."

Edward kissed her again. "Oh, yes, I do."

Flora kissed him back. "Oh, you silly darlin'... " She laughed again.

"What?"

"The door wasn't locked, you know."

The happiness flooded through him. "I'd swear I'd known you all my life."

"Me too. Such a tiny little short time, and yet – "

"Love creates its own time, doesn't it?" Edward grinned. "I've suddenly realized – it speeds everything up – Oh, my Lord."

"What?"

"I hope that doesn't mean our life together will be short."

"Dodo, dodo... our life together will be long and happy." She stroked the back of his neck. "Provided you don't try to photograph every last second of it."

Edward jumped off the bed, made for the writing desk, picked up a pen and paper and began to write.

The bedsprings creaked as Flora sat up. "What are you doing?"

"I'm sending a message to Stanford. This time I'm really going to turn him down. I'm not leaving you now – especially now."

"I've been thinkin', Edward." She was out of bed and standing behind him. "Everythin' has changed..."

"Yes, indeed it has."

Her hand snaked round him to take the pen. "No, I mean, the funny thing is that now you *can* go?"

He turned to face her. "I don't understand. You were so upset at the thought of my being away for so long." Would he ever understand women?

"Yes, but that was before..." She touched her stomach, "I'll have to go into confinement soon, I mustn't be seen, it's not proper, and I have Sarah and her mother to look after me. I couldn't be in better care." She caressed his chest. "And when you come back..." Her voice dropped to a whisper as she gave a little smile. "I can show you round the city again."

"You're serious about this, Flora? You're quite sure?"

"Of course I'm sure." She put the pen and paper away in a drawer and closed her arms around him.

Edward could have stayed like this forever.

CHAPTER FOURTEEN

"Oh, for God's sake!" shouted Stanford. "Do you know nothing else but failure?"

Edward took slow, deep breaths, his fingernails digging into his palms. He was as frustrated as the Governor, but there was no need to be so unpleasant about it.

"We are doing our best, Governor. We are doing our very best."

For the last seven weeks, he, Joseph, Arthur and another equally young if not equally bright assistant named Matthew had been slaving away in one of the Sacramento mansion's brick stables that had been converted into a combination workshop, dark-room and dormitory (they'd even been obliged to sleep on cots; no room at the inn apparently). The air was redolent with machine oil, chemicals and horse manure. And desperation. For this was their last working day before the ball, at which Stanford was determined to demonstrate that he had found the means to prove his flying horse hypothesis – although he never stopped trying to convince Edward that there was no wager, that it was just a stupid rumor started by that idiot Charles Crocker.

Edward had made great progress on the chemical front, creating a new bromide-rich collodion and extra-strong developer, which made a better foundation image. But this was of academic character unless he could find a way to cover and uncover the lens at an unheard of speed, which he'd calculated must be one five-hundredth of a second if they were to capture Occident's stride. So they'd spent the bulk of their time up here working on device after device to do precisely that – what he'd taken to calling his "shutter."

It was Sarah Louisa who'd first planted the idea, back at the studio before they left. Being so upset about Flora at the time, he'd thought he wasn't taking in what she was saying. But it had come back to him up here, something of the order of: "That flap you use for your Sky Shade, couldn't you adapt that to go up and down in front of the lens, like a sort of automatic lens cap?"

So that's what they'd done. It looked like a guillotine: a wooden frame to be placed in front of the camera lens, housing two metal sheets designed to slide up and down at lightning speed, exposing the plate for an infinitesimal fraction of a second. To control this apparatus and simultaneously measure its speed, he'd turned a telegraph key into an electromagnetic switch linked to a miniature hammer hitched to a tuning fork, which attached to a spring made of rubber bands for the guillotine shutter that in turn was connected to a stylus poised over a spinning cylinder of smoke-blackened paper. His own version of Marey's cardiograph.

They had just run the latest of Edward didn't know how many trials of the shutter and he still hadn't been able to get it faster than one-thirtieth of a second. It was so damnably frustrating. They were so close to their goal now, the concept was understood, the mechanism was sound, it was just the manufacture that lagged.

"Do it again," commanded Stanford.

Edward's assistants crouched at their stations, runners on their starting blocks.

"Now!"

Joseph pressed the switch, releasing the hammer to ping the tuning fork and trigger the clattering shutter to expose the space, simultaneously measuring the speed on the cylinder.

Matthew tallied the tiny heartbeats with plodding care. "Just over one-hundredth of a second."

"Fuck," said Stanford.

Joseph shrugged wearily. "It's the best so far, sir."

What to do? wondered Edward. It came in a flash. "Tighten the spring."

Joseph picked up a wrench, fitted it onto the end of the shutter spring and pushed down on it. It didn't budge. "It's already as tight as it'll go."

"Oh, give it to me!" Edward grabbed the wrench, pushed down on it with all his strength and managed to move it very slightly, tightening the spring a fraction of an inch.

"One more time."

They went through the whole routine once more.

The shutter slammed down at almost unearthly speed. They all swung round on Matthew. Surely this was it? It must be!

But Matthew was staring past them at the shutter.

A crackle of gunshots as the wooden frame collapsed in on itself like so much kindling.

"Oh, for Christ's sake!" yelled Stanford.

Edward ground his teeth. "We'll build another one, Governor, twice as strong."

"You have until the end of the day tomorrow."

"*Tomorrow*? I'm not working tomorrow. The ball – "

"Exactly."

"What about your invitation to Mrs. Muybridge and myself? I have to go down to San Francisco to pick her up."

"This is more important. You'll have to work through."

His Cinderella pacing up and down in her blue dress, waiting for the carriage that never comes, her hopes and dreams turning to rags. Stanford or Flora? Flora or Stanford? There was no question what the answer was.

"I will *not* work through!"

"You will!! This is too important!!"

"NOT AS IMPORTANT AS MY WIFE!" That voice again. His and not his.

Stanford's voice dropped to a whisper. "Really? You may want to think that over."

The next day their noses were pressed against the workshop window, street urchins as the Queen goes by, with Edward hating himself again.

But the colors! He had to admit: the bottle-greens, the mustard yellows, the royal blues, the imperial purples of the broughams and landaus and cabriolets clattering up the great driveway to the mansion. It really was a wondrous sight. Then the powdered footmen handing down their masters and mistresses, the river of privilege flowing up the marble steps of the Grand Entrance to greet the Governor and Mrs. Stanford as Handel's Water Music washed over them from the orchestra within.

Edward's assistants ooh-ed and ah-ed. But this was not right. It was just not fair. After all their weeks of non-stop backbreaking work, who was going to reap the glory? And who was going to have to explain all this to Flora?

Edward glimpsed Stanford whispering something in his wife's ear, then heading across the enormous lawn towards them.

Stanford entered the workshop. "Well? Am I going to be able to make my demonstration this evening or not?"

His demonstration? Edward wouldn't reply, he would not. Let Stanford look for himself.

Stanford spotted their larger, much sturdier-looking version of the guillotine. "You've re-built it already?"

"Only twenty-four hours work without a wink of sleep," muttered Arthur.

Edward gave the signal and his three men sprang into action again, the metal sheets sliding past each other too fast to see the blink at all. The device itself solid as a rock.

"And...?" said Stanford, glaring at Matthew.

The young man pointed at a fresh squiggle of dots. "One five-hundredth of a second."

The Governor's face lit up with a gracious smile. Finally. Edward had been wondering if he'd ever see him smile again. It was as if the sun had come out after months of rain. This made up for everything. "Well done, Mr. Muybridge."

Where's my key? Ah, here it is. Edward's hand was pale in the moonlight that was finally breaking through the rain clouds like a night-time echo of Stanford. At least she hadn't bolted the door; he wouldn't have blamed her if she had. She'd left the gaslights on too. The little luxuries they could afford now. But it was so quiet. What's the time? Goodness, ten o'clock already. The maid must have gone up to her attic. But he couldn't even hear anything from the second floor; his poor darling had probably cried herself to sleep. Don't let the stairs creak for Heaven's sake. With any luck he could slip into bed without waking her; he couldn't face a row tonight. Everything would look better in the morning, especially after his success.

The door to their room was unlocked. That was a good sign. Their brand-new door, how they'd laughed. The bed curtains were drawn, but she'd left his nightgown out, another good sign. She might just as easily have burnt it. Now to blow out the light. No, just turn it low, she always liked a little light. But he wouldn't have any trouble sleeping tonight, he was exhausted. Slowly, slowly pull back the curtains, that's it, he didn't want the rings to rattle.

The bed was still made up!

Where on earth could she be? Could she have gone to see Sarah Lousia? But why would she stay so late? Could she have had someone escort her up to Sacramento to see him? That was most unlikely. At all events, sleep was out of the question now. While he waited, he'd try to work on the idea for triggering his shutter he'd had on the journey down.

Concentrate on your work, the time will go faster. But it was already quarter past eleven. Where is she? Where is she? The rain had set in again. Oh, he hoped she was all right. Stop it. Just do your work. These sketches helped, he had to admit. It was all much clearer now. How the string would run breast-high from the shutter to the other side of the track so that Occident would snap it just at the very instant he passed in front of the camera. Taking his own picture. Or snapping it, you might say.

Half past twelve. This was really beginning to worry him. Where on earth could she be? He pulled back the curtains. Nobody down in the street, not a soul out, just the full moon winking at itself in a puddle, as if in on a private joke.

A clock chimed. And now another chime. Then silence. That was all. Two o'clock! He must have dropped off.

Carriage wheels. Oh, thank God.

Who is that getting out of the hansom cab? Oh, no. No, please. It's Major Harry Larkyns helping Flora down, giving her his arm to the front door. Shielding her head from the rain with his topper, a black one this time. They're both in evening dress. Oh, God, oh, God.

A few moments later, the Major got back into the carriage and it clattered off.

She was in the bedroom, flinging off her cape. Oh, the décolleté of that blue silk dress, the pearls cascading off her breasts. Every inch of him ached for her. She took a running jump at the bed, turning on her back, lying still, staring up at the canopy. Then slowly walking her hands over her body like a blind man remembering a face.

Something broke at the back of Edward's throat.

Her hands stopped, night animals caught in a carriage beam.

She sat up. She saw him. She gave a little scream.

"Oh! You gave me such a turn, Edward. When did you get home?"

"Obviously too soon." He bounded up and stood over her. "WHERE HAVE YOU BEEN?" Again that stranger's voice.

"Where have *you* been?" She was shaking on the bed, the whole bed shaking. "You promised on your honor, you crossed your heart, you swore to me – "

"You don't understand, Flora."

She pushed herself off the bed, stood to face him. "I do understand. That's the problem. I'm fed up to the eyelids with understandin', I – "

She saw his raised hand and shrank away. "Edward!?"

"What were you doing with Larkyns?"

"What do you mean?"

"I just saw you coming home with Major Larkyns at two o'clock in the morning!"

"What do you expect me to do? You leave me alone, I miss the ball – "

"But you wear the dress, the very blue dress that I bought you and – "

"Oh, Edward, what's happenin' to us? I'm not myself, I – "

She fell towards him. His arms were around her. Her bare shoulders. That new *Eau de cologne* from Paris he'd bought her.

He spoke into her hair. Even that smelled of Heaven. "Where did you go with Larkyns?"

"Just to the theater. You remember, he said he could get passes for Sarah and her mother and since I had – well, since I had nowhere else to go tonight – "

"I had no choice, or Stanford – "

"Stanford, Stanford, Stanford, why don't you marry *him*?"

"It ends at eleven."

"What does?"

"The theater. Not at two A.M. Where have you been since?"

"Just to a restaurant."

"What restaurant?"

"The Poodle Dog."

Edward froze. The Poodle Dog. God. Burckhardt was always going on about it. "A layer-cake of temptation," rolling the words around in his mouth, smacking his fat lips, "the higher you go, the tastier it becomes." The words came back to torment Edward. The main floor was respectable enough, but already by the second floor, there were certain secluded areas where men about town could entertain their paramours. The third floor was even more daring, featuring "animated French postcards," and on the fourth and fifth floors – "the icing on the cake" – private rooms were available, provided you slipped a sufficiently large tip to "Old Pierre," who controlled the elevator, they said he'd had made a fortune playing the pimp. *Wunderbar.*

"It was full of people, Edward, just innocent fun, the whole cast of the play were there and – "

"And Sarah Louisa's mother?"

"Well, no, she went home, but Harry Edwards was there – I think Sarah's quite taken by him – and – you'll never believe this – Lotta Crabtree was there too. From the vaudeville? I know all her songs: 'You Bet,' 'Port Wine'..." Harry said – "

"Harry Larkyns?" The anger rose in his throat again.

"No, Harry Edwards, he's a good friend of hers, he said she's a 'millionairess' now – from all the gold nuggets the miners have tossed her way – she's a miner's daughter herself, you know – "

"I *forbid* you ever to visit that place again, you have no idea what goes on there – "

"But – "

Edward's hands were on her shoulders, pushing her away from him, squeezing the soft flesh. "Listen to me, Flora, just listen, I'm twenty years older than you, I know about the world!"

She struggled to get loose. "Ouch, you're hurtin' me!"

She slipped through his hands and staggered back, tripping on a small Ottoman and crashing onto the parquet floor, pearls bouncing across the room like hailstones.

"Oh, my Lord, the baby!" She was a baby herself in his arms. "I'm so sorry, my darling, I'm so sorry."

She sobbed into his chest. "It was so innocent, Edward, just innocent fun, I'm young, Edward, I never go anywhere, I just..." Her body shuddered, tears flooding down. "I'm so sorry..."

Her body was rocking with his, her forehead under his fingers, stroking, stroking. "It's all right, my love, it's all right. There, there... do you feel any pain?"

"No, no, nothin', it was nothin'." Her eyes closed as she breathed deeply, slowly letting the tension out.

"It's more about your reputation than anything else. People will talk. I just ask you one thing."

She looked up at him through glistening eyes. "Anythin', Edward, I'll do anythin' for you."

"I have to go back to Sacramento next week to finish the experiment for Stanford, it'll just be for a few days."

"Oh! Of course, yes. I understand, my dear, of course you must go, I don't mind, really."

"But will you – "

She stopped his lips with her hand.

"Shh. I know what you're thinkin' Edward, and I promise, I swear, I give you my – I promise I will never see Major Larkyns again."

CHAPTER FIFTEEN

You'd swear snow had fallen on the Union Park Racecourse at Twentieth and G streets in Sacramento on this sunny summer morning. But the dazzling white wasn't from the sky, it was from the wheelbarrows piled high with the Governor's bed sheets that his chambermaids were currently trundling out to Joseph and Arthur to drape along the rear of the racetrack, as Matthew sprinkled white lime on the length of track in front of this blinding backcloth, across which a string had been stretched a few inches above the ground.

Nearby, Edward checked for the twentieth time his new shutter and his new lens – the thinnest, purest Dallmeyer B "Quick Acting Portrait" short lens money could buy, all the way from London, with an f3 aperture and a wide-angle view. Surely with such equipment, he would have success?

But so much could go wrong. Would Occident shy at the white tunnel at the last minute, split-seconds before his forelegs were due to unleash Madame Guillotine by breaking the string? And would this occur at a moment in his stride when all four of his hooves were off the ground?

If only they could have had some rehearsals. But no, although Edward saw this purely as a scientific experiment, Stanford saw it as a "show," akin to his striking of the last spike. No tryouts were allowed for this drama. They had to go straight to the "first night" in front of a sell-out audience, exposing themselves for all to see.

The stands were packed with over-fed racing enthusiasts in bulbous black frock coats and silk top hats watching Jasper Tennant in his sulky through their binoculars as he warmed up Occident some seventy-five yards down the track. Everyone was here: Frederick MacCrellish, publisher of the *Alta California*, Henry George, Publisher of *The Evening Post*, James Keene, president of the San Francisco stock exchange, Charles Crocker, former shopkeeper, former construction chief, and now full-fledged railroad magnate, and – the sole exception to the obesity rule – the skinny but fiery General Jefferson C. Davis, Union hero of the Civil War. At the other end of the food line, a gaggle of lean and hungry minions of MacCrellish and George and sundry other newspapers were also gathered in their scruffy suits and sweat-stained bowlers.

As he staggered past Edward under a pile of bed linen, Joseph muttered: "There's Cuspidor." He indicated a particularly scrawny reporter with a face like a weasel. So that was Mr. Coppinger. A typical in-between man, a class-bridger, for although he was dressed as shabbily as a lowly scribbler, there was something in his eyes...

But no Stanford yet, of course. He had delayed his appearance to the very last minute so that he could make the grandest possible entrance. Edward wondered if there would be trumpets.

He hadn't gone quite that far as it happened; the only fanfare being the rumble of carriage wheels as his landau came into view. A pair of footmen helped him and his wife down. They approached an elevated platform not far from Edward.

Mounting the steps, the Governor boomed out, "You are about to witness a dream come true, gentlemen."

"Still not interested in my wager, Leland?" brayed Keene in a cultivated English accent that reminded Edward of John.

"If you wish to find another gentleman to lose your money to, please proceed," said Stanford.

"You're the one who's afraid of losing his shirt," sang out Charles Crocker.

"This is science, not gambling," riposted Stanford.

Oh really? grunted Edward to himself.

"At any event, I have every confidence."

"If pigs could fly." Crocker grinned, looking rather like one himself.

"I don't know about pigs, Charley," said Stanford, "but can *horses* fly, that's the point. And we're about to find out, once and for all, *exactly* how a horse moves. It's a proud moment for me. We've worked long and hard for this, many sacrifices have been made, family life has had to suffer." He made a rueful face at his wife.

"The highspeed shutter I've devised is many times faster than anything ever seen before."

I've devised? A slip of the tongue? wondered Edward.

He heard a reporter mumble, "Here he goes again, the 'Great Whangdoodle,' always faster and bigger and richer than anybody else."

"You know how Ambrose Bierce spells Leland?" said his companion, scrawling *£eland* on his note pad.

Stanford glanced over at the track. "When Occident passes in front of the camera, my shutter will ensure that the precise motions of his hooves will be frozen in time."

My shutter. Edward scowled: no slip of the tongue. Damn him.

"So will $25,000 of your assets, old boy!" cried Keene.

The Governor sighed. "First of all, you know perfectly well I have nothing to do with this absurd wager, and secondly, it's not quite as simple as that, James. Let me explain how this is going to work."

Now he was invading Edward's territory. He almost tripped on the platform steps as he dashed up them, stumbling over the words as he faced the crowd. "This is a scientific expe-experiment, you see, not only creating the shutter, but the developing fluid – you, you have to be your own chemist, you have to prepare your own dipping baths, all your own chemicals. I'll conduct the experiment a dozen or more times if need be – "

"So the horse will have to go past the camera at least a dozen times?" called out a reporter.

"If necessary, yes. And after each exposure, I shall have to go into my dark-room – "

"When will the picture be ready?"

" – to develop the plate and fix it and – "

"How long?"

"A day or two or three at the most," replied Edward. "We can't do more than a handful of exposures per day, it's impossible to predict exactly – "

"Occident is waiting!" interrupted Stanford, stepping in front of Edward.

Edward called over to the sulky. "Mr. Tennant?"

The driver waved.

Edward made one final adjustment to his camera.

"Excuse me, Mr. Muybridge."

More delays? "In Heaven's name!?"

A Western Union boy in his toy soldier uniform was holding out a telegraphic dispatch.

Edward stuffed it in his pocket. No time for this now. Arthur was now poised half in and half out of Helios, waiting for his signal so he could tell Joseph to start sensitizing the plate. Edward waved his hand and Arthur disappeared into the carriage.

A couple of minutes later, Joseph emerged from the carriage and passed the sensitized plate to Arthur, who passed it on to Edward.

He ducked under the camera shroud to make sure the view was just so. Then out again to stand facing Tennant.

The punters leaned forward, the reporters licked their pencils, the Stanfords tensed.

Edward raised his arm as all eyes turned to him. He looked up into the sky as if waiting for the perfect atmospheric conditions. God be with me now. He lowered his arm. "Go!"

Tennant cracked his whip and Occident started to trot towards the sheets, rapidly attaining his twenty-five miles per hour, his thirty-six feet or twelve yards per second.

Edward had paced out the distance from the spot where Occident should have reached full speed to the spot where he should snap the string: forty-eight yards. He counted down the seconds, "Four...three... two... don't shy, don't shy..."

Occident didn't.

"One..."

Occident broke the string and *shshleech-clunk* went the guillotine shutter.

"Good boy!"

Stanford almost toppled off his platform. "He's done it!"

Talk of jumping the gun. "Well, not quite," cried Edward, "the development, the stride – we still have to – "

"My wonder horse!" Stanford ran to embrace Occident. "Well done, well done!"

The crowd engulfed the Governor, shaking his hand and clapping him on the back as Edward watched.

But his apparatus worked! he told himself. It really did. Even if Stanford had stolen his thunder.

As the crowd moved into the drinks pavilion, Edward remembered the telegraph. Where had he put it? He found the right pocket and pulled it out. Oh, God save him. It was edged in black.

BABY STILLBORN RULOFSON STOP

CHAPTER SIXTEEN

Three days later, Edward felt like dying himself – for two reasons: not only had he lost a child and had still not been able to return home to console poor Flora, but every single test of their picture-taking experiment had been an unqualified disaster. Each day as planned, Occident had taken his own picture half-a-dozen times, each one followed by the usual developing session, with varying combinations of sulfates and nitrates and acids and alcohols. But for the first dozen or so attempts, no image whatever had appeared on the plate.

Finally, late yesterday evening, one particularly potent mixture based on the evil-smelling naphtha had yielded a pale wisp of fog against the negative black, better than nothing at all, but as informative as an inkblot.

It was now ten minutes to six, the time-limit set by Mr. Keene for this wretched wager. If Stanford wasn't interested in gambling, the number of punters and reporters gathered outside Edward's dark-room proved everyone else was.

The plate stared up at him. His last negative. They'd just run Occident for the seventh time today. If they didn't get an image from this exposure, he didn't even want to think what Stanford would do. The plate sank slowly under the fluid in the developing bath.

Beyond the dark-room walls, Edward could hear the rising buzz of conversation.

The cascade of coins falling onto a table. The familiar voices cutting through the chatter.

Keene: "You are quite sure, aren't you, Leland?"

Stanford: "The outcome is not in doubt."

If only he knew! The jingle of a handful of coins.

Keene: "We have an absolute heap of doubt here, Governor." He cleared his throat. "A number of you gentlemen have stated you share Stanford's belief that all four of Occident's hooves leave the ground at once when he's trotting, is that not so?"

A few scattered murmurs of assent.

Keene: "Well, now for *el momento de la verdad*. Who is prepared to back up his belief with some good old American double eagles?"

More jingling of coins. Then a long silence.

Gently now, Edward told himself. Just keep slowly sluicing and sluicing the developer over the plate. And pray for a miracle. The sweat was running down his forehead, getting into his eyes. Oh... another dizzy spell, he'd been getting more and more of them lately. It was so hot in here. And the chemical fumes, the mercury. Day after day. He'd even passed out a couple of times. But he couldn't stop now.

Now it was Keene again: "Mr. MacCrellish, as the judge of this event, you are the timekeeper. What is it now?"

MacCrellish: "Three minutes to."

Keene: "This is your last chance, gentlemen."

More silence.

Heavy footsteps. Gasps of surprise.

Keene: "I thought you were an unbeliever? An apostate?"

Crocker's voice: "I'll not be outdone by a limey." A second cascade of coins. "This says horses *do* fly."

Look at the plate. Force yourself to look at the plate. Agh! Nothing. Come on, come on! He could break something in his frustration! He slammed his hand down. A dagger of pain shot up his arm. Blood oozed from the side of his thumb. He must have struck the sharp edge of the bench. Iodine – where's the iodine? Here it is. Splash it on the wound. Spilling everywhere. Never mind. No time to waste.

A knock on the door.

"Time's up," said Keene.

What's that on the plate? Edward couldn't believe his eyes. Oh, Heaven be praised! There it is! A shadowy white-on-black silhouette of Occident, little more than a vague outline, but enough to show conclusively that, yes indeed, all four hooves *are* off the ground.

Blackness fell over his eyes. A curtain falling.

* * *

A hand was shaking Edward's up and down.

Stanford smiled down at him. "I told you your fortunes would change. Well, done Muybridge." He patted Edward on the shoulder. "I trust you've recovered?"

"Oh, it's nothing, governor, nothing. Just a trifle hot in there."

Keene came up to take Stanford's hand, smiling bravely. "Congratulations, old chap. You're a devilish stubborn man."

"The sun's written confirmation of my theory," murmured the Governor, "the world's first successful photograph of the horse in motion."

How had it happened, wondered Edward. By what miracle had it happened. And then it came to him. The iodine. Of course. About the only chemical he hadn't tried. He must have spilled some of it into the developing bath. For once his prayers had been answered. Even though he had been overcome by the fumes again. But a small price to pay...

Another jingle of coins as Crocker shoveled two pyramids of gold coins into his attaché case.

"I have something to discuss with you, Mr. Muybridge," said Jefferson Davis.

Stanford held up his hand. "This is not the time, Jefferson."

"I beg to differ, Leland, this is precisely the time." He held up an official-looking envelope. "This is a dispatch from the War Department."

CHAPTER SEVENTEEN

The sound of men singing:

Libiam ne' lieti calici
Che la bellezza infiora,
E la fuggevol ora
S'inebri a voluttà.

What was that? *La Traviata*? Was he at the opera with Flora?

Edward sat up with a jolt, rubbing his eyes. He must have fallen asleep. What was this rocking chair and these giant wheels churning the water? Of course – he was on a boat. And not just any boat: the Chrysopolis, the most luxurious side-wheeler ever built. She could carry a thousand and one passengers, a thousand and one dreams, strung out like Arabian nights in their canvas and walnut rocking chairs. So good of Stanford to arrange this for him; for once he could get home in comfort – not to say much more quickly – than if he'd taken the usual convoluted route: train to Davisville, second train to Vallejo, ferry across the Bay. Stanford was such a complicated man, unbearable and selfish one minute, and generous and kind the next. But between them they'd done it, they'd torn a rift in the veil of perception, exposed a reality beyond the realm of ordinary human vision.

What *were* those deep Italian voices he was hearing? The thick fog that now enveloped the boat was being broken by occasional flashes of bright green as the feluccas bobbed in the water and further snatches of *La Traviata* floated up to him. Oh yes, it was the local Genoese fishermen, wasn't it? That was how they communicated with each other through the murk. This could mean only one thing: they were about to dock.

Edward felt the precious package between his knees and the ache between his ribs even as his heart throbbed with victory. How could you have a dream and a nightmare at the same time? He rocked to and fro in the chair, the tears running down his cheeks for the triumph of his work and the tragedy of his child. A sudden terrible thought that hadn't occurred before. Had it been his doing, the stillbirth? When he'd knocked down Flora down? Some injury to the foetus in the womb? Oh God, pray it wasn't that.

A few minutes later, they docked. He put his misery aside and hurried down the gangplank.

"Read all about it! The Flyin' 'orse!" A newspaper boy stepped in front of him and held out the *Alta California*.

How life can turn on its head!

He flashed a silver dollar.

"Can't change that, sir!"

"You don't have to." He flipped the boy the coin and took his entire stock.

There he was at last, on the front page. He checked each of the copies. Sure enough, he was on the front page of all of them. How silly he was. He scanned the words he'd waited so long to read.

Mr. Muybridge, having studied the matter thoroughly... secured a negative that shows 'Occident' in full motion — a perfect likeness of the celebrated horse. The space of time was so small that the spokes of the sulky were caught as if they were not in motion. This was considered a great triumph as a curiosity in photography — a horse's picture taken while going thirty-eight feet in a second.

Thirty-six actually, but never mind. Edward pressed his nose to the newsprint. If only he could absorb the ink directly into his bloodstream like the Mohammedans who copied verses from the Koran on slips of paper and then soaked them in water like tea leaves so they could drink the Holy words.

The clatter of iron wheels on the cobblestones. A cab with blinds drawn stopped beside him. The hackman jumped down. "Mr. Muybridge?"

So soon, the word had got about? How his life was changing! Clutching his newspapers and his package, Edward backed through the little door the man was holding open, falling against the cushions.

The hackney pulled away, its already dark interior turning night-black as hands closed around his eyes and lips brushed his cheek with a fragrance even more intoxicating than printer's ink.

Flora kissed him. "I wanted so much to give you this baby. I'm so sorry. I don't even know if it was a boy or a girl, they took it away so fast."

The misery rushed back. "I was the one who pushed you down. I was the one who kill – "

She put her hand over his mouth. "I tripped, Edward, it wasn't you, it was all my fault, upsettin' you like that."

She removed the newspapers from under his arm, pulling him to her. "Now tell me everything, darlin'. Was it a success? A wonderful success? Tell me it was, my dear, to make up for my failure."

"'A great triumph,' they said. I'll show you the negative when we get home. It was everything I've dreamed of."

Flora kissed him again. "Well, you shall have everythin' you've dreamed of with me as well."

"Well, can you still – I mean, after – "

"Oh yes, I'm fine. Doctor Sullivan says we can try again in a few weeks."

"You're sure?"

"Remember, I am not yet twenty-three."

"But I am – "

" – as fit as a fiddle and as hard as those rocks you climb all the time, look at all the hours you spend at the Olympic Club, your wooden horses and your rollin' pins. "

Edward laughed. "You're so funny. They're called Indian clubs, my love."

"Whatever they're called. Just feel these arms."

Flora squeezed his biceps, then felt another hardness. She removed the wooden plate holder from between his legs, replacing it with her hand.

Oh, the pleasure. It had been so long.

He pulled away from her. "But should you be up and about so soon?"

"They say it does no harm. I went to Wood – "

"You went to Woodwards?"

"Oh, oh… it-it…" she stuttered, "it was just to stroll around with Sarah."

She seemed very nervous all of a sudden, the things that giving birth did to a woman.

"We visited the stuffed animals' exhibit – you remember? Where you took all those photographs of me." She touched him again.

How could he have forgotten? So why was he worried all of a sudden? What possible harm was there in her going to revisit the Gardens with her friend? The darling must have been as nostalgic for the place as he was. Oh, Flora… what are you doing? Gently, he stopped her hand.

"Perhaps you're right, Edward, we can't – not yet…" She slowly withdrew her hand. "But we will have a boy next time. I know it. I just know we will."

"So do I."

They sat together in silence. They didn't need to talk, they were so close. Then a thought struck Edward: the government dispatch he'd read on the boat. What an intriguing project… and so flattering – and tempting. Of course he was going to turn it down. He could hardly leave again so soon, could he? But perhaps he should at least talk about it with her, get her opinion…

Suddenly, he was a schoolboy again, trying to explain himself to his master. "You remember Jefferson Davis?"

She frowned.

"He was a hero of the civil war – "

"Not to me he wasn't, he was with Sherman. Don't forget where I'm from."

Oh, dear. He was off to a fine start. "Oh, yes, of course, I'm sorry, Flora, but that was nearly ten years ago, we have to – "

"What about General Davis anyway?"

"Well, he presented me with the most extraordinary proposal –

90

he's a friend of Stanford's, you know, he was there when I took the picture of Occident – you've heard of the Modoc War?"

"That's almost in Oregon, isn't it? He wants you to go all the way up there to take photographs of redskins?"

"Yes, but don't worry I'm going to turn him down – "

"I'm not worryin'," she moved closer to him again. "Tell me some more."

"Well, it's for the U.S. Army, actually – Davis is the commanding general of the force moving the Indians back to their reservation, I don't approve of all this hounding of the poor natives, but the conflict is almost over now and they want an official record."

"How long will this venture last?"

"Well, *if* I took it – which I'm not going to, of course – "

"How long, my love?"

"It would depend…"

"Well, what? A week, two weeks, a month?"

"Um… a month… I would think, perhaps a little longer."

"Well, you should – "

"I'm going to say no."

"No, I mean you should say *yes*."

"No, don't worry, my darling, I am not taking the project."

"It is the United States government askin' you to do this, Edward."

"I know, but – " He looked away. It was so tempting.

She took his hands in hers. "Edward, you're not listenin' to me. I'll be fine, really I will. You must take this opportunity, it's another huge step for us, don't you see?"

"Really?"

Did she truly mean this? he wondered. What a different Flora this was, more mature, more confident, less dependent. Perhaps it was living through that terrible experience with the baby?

He searched her face.

She nodded. "Absolutely positive, my love. And when you come back…" Her hands were on his chest.

What a woman!

Edward felt a burst of energy. "This is history in the making, Flora, right in front of our eyes, the last tribe to face up to us, in front of *my* camera! And they do the Ghost Dance, where they believe their dead ancestors will come back to save them and defeat the White Man, they dance in a circle, all night long for days on end, it's extraordinary. And – and – there's more, I forgot, the General has connections with *Harper's Weekly* and they'll make magazine engravings from my pictures, and publish as many as fifty, they say. *Harper's*, Flora, can you imagine! This will change everything."

CHAPTER EIGHTEEN

Edward opened his eyes. Ouch. He shut them again. A thunderclap. But thunderclaps went away, didn't they? Not this one. It was a permanent *bang* preserved in his brain like a fossil. Might as well open his eyes, it couldn't make it any worse, could it? Ow! Yes, it could. All that drink. Another vow broken. Hope to God Flora doesn't find out. After her experience with those two drunkards she'd had to live with, one of the things she most admired about him was that he was a teetotaler.

He looked around him. There was something strange about Stanford's dining room. It was decked out in the usual silk curtains, velvet cushions and plush upholstery. But why was the table so small, with only room for four? Oh dear, his head. But there wasn't just one little dining table, there were lots of them, rows of identical little dining tables. Everything was topsy-turvy. It was worse than being thrown out of a stage-coach.

But it wasn't a stage-coach, was it? It was a train. Of course. A train that was going nowhere; no pictures flashing past outside, the outside was dead, all the life was inside. Oh, now he remembered. Stanford had lent them his "Director's Car," his own special version of the CP Silver Palace dining car that he kept parked in the Sacramento Railroad Station. The most famous, most expensive dining car in the whole world. Of course. What else?

Stanford had been here, though, hadn't he, with his friends and with all the rest of them? And then he and his friends had gone, and it had just been Burckhardt and Rulofson and Edward and all the ladies. What ladies? Oh God, those ladies! Burckhardt's friend Fong See had brought them in, the man who made undergarments for the brothel trade, Heaven help him. Some of them were little more than children. So strange that Rulofson of all people should have been part of it. He was so strait-laced he even said the waltz was immoral, a "loathsome ulcer festering in our midst." How many times Edward had heard him say that! And yet at the same time, it was rumored that he'd had to escape from

Canada to California after seducing a fourteen-year old. It was all very confusing.

Not least because so much of it had been in German. *Eins, zwei, drei*, they'd shouted with Burckhardt, all the way up to *sieben* as Salome's veils fell to the clink of their champagne glasses. First the garniture on the skirt *prosit*! second the skirt itself *prosit*! third the outer petticoat *prosit*! fourth the inner petticoat *prosit*! fifth the corset *prosit*! sixth the chemise *prosit*! Until they'd gotten to the last of Fong See's veils, *oompah*! Mr. Lee's best selling garment: the drawers that were forever open, for they had no crotch.

Nor had he, he realized. God in Heaven. He buttoned himself up. What had happened last night? What had they done? What hadn't they done? And who with? Most of the time it had been too dark to see – or they'd been too drunk to care. Oh, he prayed the other two wouldn't breathe a word of this. It could ruin his career, his work with Stanford, desecrating his dining car like this. What had happened to them anyway?

What was that noise? A rising and falling sound like a pile of coal bricks tumbling backwards through time, then a windy train whistle of relief. Were they moving, after all? He peered out of the window. No, the platform hadn't budged. The sound was coming from under the table.

Rulofson and Burckhardt were snoring their heads off, spread-eagled across a wreckage of cigars and caviar and champagne and God knows what else. Oh, Lord, they'd even spilled some of Stanford's best Roederer Crystal on *Harper's Weekly*, right on its pompous sub-title: *"A Journal of Civilization."* At least he hoped that's what they'd spilled. Oh, Lord! It was the June 21st issue. Why was that important? His pictures! He picked up the magazine: *Photographs by Muybridge, furnished by the courtesy of Bradley & Rulofson, San Francisco. Modoc Brave Lying in Wait for A Shot… Warm Spring Indians and Scouting… On the Look-out for an Attack on a Picket Station…* And his tableaux of *Modoc Squaws.*

How bravely the Indians had stood up to the U.S. army although they'd been outnumbered twenty to one. The pictures were awfully good, he had to say, even reproduced as woodcuts.

Still, it was a poor excuse to drink himself into a stupor. To behave like a Hoodlum himself. Oh, his head. What had come over him? Thank the Lord Flora hadn't been there to see him last night!

Flora! The note! Now he remembered. Burckhardt had found it slipped under the door at the studio yesterday. Where was it? He searched in his pockets and smoothed out the crumpled paper and re-read the real reason he'd drunk so much. The nightmare was beginning all over again:

> *Your wife has been seen going about town with Major Larkyns, at Woodward's Gardens and elsewhere. Come to the offices of the* Evening Post *and I will tell you all. Henry Coppinger*

CHAPTER NINETEEN

The following afternoon, the minute he got off the ferry at the Broadway Wharf, Edward headed straight for the newspaper offices, Flora's words sounding in his ears: *"I went to Woodwards... to stroll around with Sarah..."* How could she? How could she? And as for Larkyns – well, he'd already worked out exactly what he was going to do with him.

He raced up the stairs to the main floor. What was this? It could have been the reading room of a public library, the atmosphere was so muted and serious. Long rows of tables, occupied by stern faced editors in morning suits – he presumed that's what they were – their top hats upended beside them like shiny black buckets floating in a flotsam of steel nibs, porcelain inkpots, massive green and gold reference tomes and sheets of pink blotting-paper with galley proofs propped up before them. So this is where Larkyns used to work before he lost his place? It seemed rather sober for such a dashing man of the world. In a far corner there was a series of small open cubicles occupied by much scruffier men: the reporters, no doubt. One of them, with a weasel face, stood up. It was Coppinger. Without pronouncing a word, the man gestured for Edward to follow him into a stairwell.

"I want to know everything, Mr. Coppinger," blurted Edward, "tell me everything. First of all, how do you know Larkyns went with my wife to Woodward's?"

"Well, Mr. Muybridge, after Larkyns did what he did to me – I'm sure you heard about it, who hasn't? – the greatest humiliation of my life, and after all I'd done for him, well, I swore to pay him back. And my chance came when I heard rumors about his seeing your wife."

"Oh, God."

"I'm sorry, but... " Coppinger paused.

"Go on, go on."

"Well, I started following him about town. One evening about a month ago, I trailed him to Woodward's Gardens where I saw him enter the stuffed animals' exhibit."

A sharp pain in his stomach. *Flora popping up behind the animals.* He didn't want to hear any more. But he had to. "Go on."

"After about an hour, having concealed myself inside a nearby shooting gallery, I saw your wife run out of the exhibit, adjusting her clothes and red in the face. She then dashed off through the crowds. A few moments later, Larkyns emerged, equally disheveled. He looked right and left for her, but eventually appeared to give up because of the mass of people surging about."

Oh, my Lord. "And then? What did you see then?"

"I saw Harry Edwards – you know, the actor – also come out of the exhibit with Flora's friend, Sarah Smith, on his arm."

"I mean what did you see of Larkyns and my wife."

"Oh, nothing further that day. Larkyns and Edwards and Miss Smith got into a cab and – "

"*That day?* What do you mean?"

"Well, about a week later, I followed Larkyns again – it was quite late at night – and I saw him enter the Gallery – "

"Rulofson's?"

"Yes. I didn't follow him inside, I didn't want to risk it, but there was a light on on the top floor, somebody working late – "

"My wife?"

"I don't know, it might have been. I've heard she does work late sometimes when you're away."

"Have you? Who from?"

"Well, let's just say I keep my eyes open. I am a reporter, after all…" Coppinger paused again.

"Go on, go on, man! Then what happened?"

"Well, again about an hour or so later, I saw Larkyns exit the building – "

"Alone? Was he alone?"

"Yes. Then I waited a few minutes longer, but no one else came out, so I went home."

"Take me to him."

"The Major?"

"Yes. If you know where he is."

Coppinger consulted his watch. "I think I have an idea where he might be at this time of day."

Edward followed Coppinger from the respectability of the newspaper offices to the narrow streets of the infamous Barbary Coast that Burckhardt never stopped talking about.

Oh, the double lives we lead. The place was a monument to the hypocrisy of the times, the desire and lust that lay just beneath the lace and the stiff collars and the top hats joining hands with raw capitalism as the Barbary pirates separated you from your money. If the pickpockets didn't clean it out of you in a tobacco shop, the cardsharps would trick it out of you in a gambling house where the crimps would paralyze you with Afghan Whisky before opening a trap under your bar stool to "shanghai" you to a tall ship. If all else failed, the buccaneers would simply entice the loose change out of your pocket with French novels and French postcards of Artists' Models coupling with men, women, children, dwarves, cripples, animals, bananas, broom handles and other handy objects. For live versions of the above, you'd be directed to rows of tiny windows, each framing a yellow face that could have been as young as ten if that was your cup of tea, pronouncing with a Mikado smile the only English words she knew: "Two bittee lookee, flo bittee feelee, six bittee dooee!" Or you might be tempted to take a step up the flight of fancy to the Nymphia, one of the many "cow yards" in these parts, according to Burckhardt. Multistory buildings housing a hundred tiny cribs with a window shade that popped up for a dime to give you a peep at a hundred Godivas bending over for their beaux. For more refined tastes, there were elegant French parlor houses such as Madame Gabrielle's Lively Flea where you could watch a woman with a Shetland pony. Or Madame Marcelle's where you could spy on a highly placed city official, who paid a silver dollar each day to dust the bed-rooms while wearing a dress.

Why was everything French associated with the naughty, the saucy, the oo-la-la: French novels, French postcards, French letters, French parlors, French pox? Edward wondered. Why did the very word "French" send a *frisson* up the Anglo-Saxon spine? But he'd no more time to think about this now. He had to get through these leering streets as fast as he could to face down the man who'd been leering at him the hardest.

They passed dead fall after dead fall with a quick glance through a grimy window: Cowboy's Rest, the Whale, The Roaring Gimlet, The Bull's Run, The Cock of the Walk, the Star of the Union, Every Man is Welcome.

Edward made a mental note to return here to take some views. As Dodgson had said, there was nothing that couldn't be the subject of a photograph.

"Ah, we've struck gold at last," said Coppinger. "There's our quarry inside Black Tom's."

"Thank you, Mr. Coppinger."

The man smiled. "Believe me, it's a pleasure, Mr. Muybridge." He turned to go.

"Oh, one more thing, do you have a pencil and paper?"

"Certainly," said Coppinger, sorting through his pockets and coming up a pencil and a grubby notebook. He tore off a page and handed it to Edward, who scribbled something on it and handed it back.

"Please have that delivered for me as soon as possible."

He gave Coppinger a handful of sovereigns.

"Much obliged, sir, very much obliged."

With that, Mr. In-Between spun on his heel and faded into the night.

Edward took a seat in a shadowy side booth with a direct view of the bar where Larkyns was sharing a stool with a young woman in a low-cut purple satin dress, who was wrapped around him like a boa constrictor. Edward could have rung his neck there and then.

He took a breath, calming himself as he looked around the place. Above their heads, the dingy walls undulated with coy nudes of Venuses and Psyches and alabaster Odalisques in oriental bath scenes by Gérôme and company – those French – that no "palace of masculine recreation" could seem to be without.

A deep voice: "Another one, Major?"

Edward went rigid.

Larkyns held out his empty beer glass to a towering Negro built like a Clydesdale.

"And one for Miss Mary Douglas?" said Black Tom.

Larkyns stroked the girl's bottom. "Uhuh."

"Tell us agin about the wine trick, Harry," said the girl. "What you did in the Poodle Dog to impress the ladies."

Edward's fist almost crushed his own beer glass.

"Actually, it's *La Poule d'Or* – the Golden Chicken," said Larkyns into Mary's neck, "and it certainly laid some golden eggs for me and my friend Harry Edwards last night – you know, the famous actor?"

"Ooh, is he as naughty as you?" Mary stroked his thigh. "Who was you two with then?"

"That'd be telling."

She arched her back. "Was they as pretty as me?"

Larkyns ogled her. "Who could be? But they made a nice pair." He kissed each of her breasts in turn. "One was tall and dark – her face wouldn't have launched many ships, but she disrobes well, Harry tells me, and you don't look at the mantelpiece. But the other one – well, good enough to eat." He bit one of her nipples through the thin material.

She cooed. "Show us yer wine trick agin."

Larkyns raised his beer to his nostrils as if were a *Château Lafitte.* He closed his eyes for a moment, then delivered the verdict: *"Pas de défaut majeur."*

Mary giggled.

Larkyns slowly tipped the glass until it was horizontal, lining it up against the girl's half-naked bosom, drawing out the words as if wanting even Edward to understand. *"Limpide, mais pas transparent... l'intensité est sombre... la vivacité lumineuse... et la couleur vire au pourpre."*

"Ooh, I love it when you talks like that, it sounds so dirty," breathed Mary.

Larkyns rotated his wrist like a ballet dancer, swirling the beer round the glass. He sniffed it delicately, then smiled at the girl, all

French pout and shoulder shrug. *"Arôme… tilleul… ou peut-être cassis. Et le bouquet… floral à dominante violette."*

"Mmmm… Harry…"

Larkyns took a sip, rolling the liquid across his tongue. *"Souple… nerveux… saveur de base: salée… le parfum en bouche…"*

Mary licked his ear. "Ooh, you shouldn't do that to a girl. How did that go down in the restront?"

"Well, let's just say the wine was drier than the ladies."

Crack. Edward's glass broke in his hand.

Larkyns whirled round, his bar stool tipping over, almost sending both him and the young woman to the floor. A wooden *crack* as one of the spindles broke.

A wave of snickers slopped through the bar like dirty washing.

Edward strode up to Larkyns, reaching inside his coat.

The snickers dried up. Mary gasped.

Larkyns backed away, almost knocking her over. "Muybridge. Don't! I beg you!"

"Why not? I owe you so much." Edward flipped two bits at the barman, his lacerated hand spattering blood. "The least I can do is buy you and your lady friend a drink."

Edward turned to Mary. All that was left of her were the swinging doors.

Black Tom hastily poured more beer for Larkyns then hurried to the farthest end of the bar to polish some tankards.

Larkyns' head swiveled to and fro like a nervous sparrow. "Look, can't we talk somewhere else?"

Edward picked up Larkyns's stool and *BANGED* it down. Another spindle *cracked*, sending up a storm of sawdust and pistachio shells. "Sit!"

Larkyns sank back onto what was left of his stool, shrunk as small as John in his hospital bed.

"You will not only never go out with my wife again, you will never speak to her, or even recognize your acquaintance with her wherever you see her."

"I – I don't know what you're talking about."

"I am her husband. I shall defend my rights, be assured of

that. I don't care what the consequences are. Are we clear?"

"I still don't know – "

"ARE WE CLEAR?"

Larkyns was trembling. "It was all very innocent, a pass to the theater – I even suggested it to Flora – Mrs. Muybridge – in front of you at the gallery…" He paused. Lost for words for once in his life.

"Go on," growled Edward. "What happened after the theater?"

"Well… nothing… a quiet drink afterwards – Sarah was there, it was all very – "

"I'm talking about a great deal more, you know perfectly well."

He stepped closer to Larkyns, who staggered back against the bar rail.

"I assure you, I still don't – "

"You were seen together at Woodward's."

The Major steadied himself. "Oh, that, well, we did bump into each other, quite by accident, it was all perfectly – "

"And again, you were seen entering the studio at night."

"Just to keep an eye – "

"Can you draw?"

"No, no, I'm…" Larkyns started to pat himself all over like a Customs man. "…I'm not armed!"

"Have… You… Studied… Drawing?" Edward spaced out the words as if were talking to a backward child. How he despised this man. "Don't let me down now, Major. The man who can do everything."

"Well, I did study at the Royal Academy for a number of years, yes."

"I'm talking about surveying."

"Yes, I've studied that too, in point of fact, at *l'Ecole des Beaux Arts* in Paris as part of my apprenticeship in architecture."

Edward let out an exaggerated sigh and pretended to wipe his brow. "That's a relief. For one awful minute I thought I'd discovered something you hadn't mastered." Now to brass tacks.

"You're going to Calistoga. One of my acquaintances, William Stewart, needs a draftsman – I've already had a note about you dispatched to him. He's the manager at the Yellow Jacket Silver Mine."

"Well, I was thinking of changing my profession, in point of fact, so, yes. I – I have to put my affairs in order, of course. I can't just up and go. The newspaper – "

" – fired you some time ago. I know. I'm not a complete idiot." Edward was all but snarling, so much hate rising up in him. "Don't worry, Major. I'll look after all your expenses. You will leave tomorrow."

He started towards the exit.

He stopped, waging a war with himself. *Never hurt another human being.*

He turned back. "Listen, Major, I know that in spite of all appearances, your life hasn't been easy. And I also know what happened to your parents. I'm sorry."

Larkyns also appeared torn. For a moment, they were strangely alike. "Do you promise on your honor as a gentleman that you will never see my wife again?"

Larkyns looked him straight in the face. "I promise. On my honor."

"So be it then. You were kind to me, very kind, in making that introduction to Governor Stanford that's led to so much. I don't know what your motives were, but the action stands, and I thank you."

He shook Larkyns' hand. "I wish you well at Calistoga. This can be a new start for all of us."

Larkyns looked down at the blood on Edward's fingers. "You should put some iodine on that."

Edward smiled. "Oh, I will, it always brings me luck."

CHAPTER TWENTY

Edward opened the door to the little sitting room that adjoined their bed-room, Flora sprang to her feet. They stared at each other, neither of them moving, as if daring the other to speak first.

Edward held out a small black box.

She continued to gaze into his face. "Have we met? Yes, you do look somewhat familiar, don't tell me, the name is on the tip of my tongue."

"Flora, I don't know what to say." She had every right to be angry that one month had stretched into three. On the other hand, what had she been doing while he'd been recording the Modocs for posterity?

He put the box down on a table.

Still she gazed at him. "I trust you had a pleasant time in Sacramento."

Was that it? Could she possibly know what had taken place that evening? He was not even sure himself. He marched to the window, staring out at the gingko trees and sage palms of the little park to hide his red face. "I know about Woodward's, Flora."

A sharp intake of breath.

"And about his visiting you at the gallery."

There was a long pause. Still Edward kept his back to her.

Her voice was so quiet, he could hardly make out the words. "Nothing happened with the Major. On my life, Edward. You must believe me."

He took a deep breath, still without turning. "I've sent him away, Flora. It's over."

"Edward... now *I* don't know what to say."

"I threw you into his arms, I neglected you shamefully."

"No, Edward, it was my fault, I should never have – "

"Shh, my love. Let's not talk about it any more. Let's start again."

He continued staring out of the window. Could they start again, after all this? Could they?

Flora came up behind him, put her arms round his waist, and buried her face in the back of his coat. "It was another great triumph, wasn't it, up in Oregon? I saw the magazine, the engravin's, your photographs are always like paintin's, but these... were extraordinary... even for you."

She released him and stepped back.

Edward remained motionless. Of course they could start again. They could, couldn't they? They had to. He loved her so much, he couldn't live without her.

He went over to the table to pick up the box. He handed it to her.

Flora stared at it. "I don't know what to do."

He kissed her forehead. "You could open it."

She noticed the plaster on his hand. "What's that? Did you get into a fight?"

"No, nothing like that. Just a little accident. It's nothing." He gestured at the box. "Are you going to open it?"

"Yes."

It was an eighteen-carat diamond bracelet set in gold and platinum. He'd been saving up for it for months.

Now it was her turn to stare out of the window. A catch in her voice, "Oh, my God. This must be worth a fort – "

"In itself, it's worth nothing, a few shiny bits of rock, that's all, completely useless in themselves The only thing that matters is what they *measure*: how much I love you."

"I don't deserve this."

Now he was putting his arms round her waist. "You deserve everything. And from now on, you shall have it."

Flora turned back to him and looked down at the bracelet, still in its box in her hand. "It's so... I don't know how to... I don't know what to say..."

Edward slipped the bracelet onto her wrist.

She gave a little cry, then whispered, "Close your eyes and hold out your hand."

He closed his eyes.

He heard a drawer opening. Something round and heavy

dropped into his hand.

"Open it"

It was the most beautiful gold pocket watch Edward had ever seen.

"Rulofson sent to Germany for it. He says it's one of the best in the world – what am I sayin'? It *is* the best in the world – just like you, my darlin' – *Lange und Söhne*." She clicked a tiny stud to release the cover and reveal the watch face. "Look at all those little dials. It'll even count off the seconds for your exposures, even the tenths of each second."

Now Edward was speechless. Never in his entire life had he received such a gift.

"Don't move," she said as she looked down at her bracelet and then at her day dress. "This dress isn't quite right – I know just what to wear to show this off. Don't come in until I tell you."

She disappeared into the bed-room.

Edward caressed his new watch slowly with the tip of his thumb. Oh, how he loved her! He took his old watch out of its fob, removed it from its chain, and attached the new one.

"I'm ready," called Flora.

The bed-room door opened.

Now she was only wearing the bracelet.

CHAPTER TWENTY-ONE

Edward was bored. Although he shouldn't have been. Larkyns was now out of the picture and life was back to normal with Flora, all forgiven and forgotten. He believed her when she said that nothing serious had taken place between her and the Major. A mere flirtation, nothing more. And best of all, she was expecting again and they were rapidly approaching the happy day. This was going to be his best year ever, he just knew it.

So why was he bored? The one word answer was Stanford. The man had insisted on yet more stereoscopic views of his damn railroad for some business reason or other, when all Edward wanted to do was get home to Flora to be there for the baby and to persuade the Governor to let him resume his instantaneous photography of Occident where he'd left off two years ago. All this assuming he could get out of Rulofson's commitment to the Pacific Mail Steamship Company that he go down to Guatamala to make views of their coffee plantations. So many interruptions.

For now, here he was in the ticket cum telegraph office of the Summit Station. Joseph and Arthur were unpacking his photographic equipment for what Edward sincerely hoped was their last day of railway pictures up here. He was dividing his attention between the snow falling outside the window and the telegraph boy who could have been the twin of the lad who had delivered the message about the miscarriage. He hoped to God this was not an omen.

The boy was a charming lad, he'd give him that; he only hoped his own baby would grow up to be such a fine young man. And that extraordinary brass contraption he was using: an electromagnet and armature linked to a tobacco tin of all things. But it made quite a good amplifier, spewing its stream of incoming Morse code. It sounded like a woodpecker, but there was something other-worldly about it too, like a message from an impatient creature from Mars who's finally made contact with Earth and hasn't a moment to lose.

The boy obviously spoke the Martian's language for he was taking down the message at an equally furious pace, passing his shorthand scribbles to the young woman sitting beside him, who copied them onto a blank telegram form in a neat copperplate. She made another charming sight: from the back she might have been be Flora – although of course nowhere near as plump as his darling had now become.

She turned. Good Heavens. She could have been Flora's younger sister. Oh, but she wasn't looking at him, she was looking past him at Arthur. Damn. Come on, you can't be jealous surely? But he did miss Flora so.

The woodpecker was starting up again. Arthur giggled in counterpoint, the young woman joining in.

"Exactly what's so amusing, Arthur?"

"Sworn to secrecy, sir, but people do send the oddest messages sometimes."

"Oh, I forgot," Edward gestured in the direction of Morse code receiver, "you used to do this, didn't you?"

Arthur nodded absently, still looking at the young woman.

"Here she comes now," said Joseph as he looked out the window.

The familiar deep breathy noise that always reminded Edward of drawers being shoved in and out of a giant dressing table. He joined Joseph to look down the railroad line.

Dense plumes of white smoke were billowing up from the mouth of the nearby Summit Tunnel, merging with the snowflakes. A red signal arm flipped up. The squeal of iron on iron. That's strange...

Edward called over his shoulder, "I thought you said this station didn't have a signalman, Arthur."

"It doesn't, sir."

"Then how does the signal know to turn to red?"

"It's an automatic block. They run a current up and down a section of the rail. When the wheels pass over this section they complete the circuit, which triggers the stop signal. Easy as pie."

"Really? I've never heard of this before."

"Not surprising. It was only invented last year – by a Dr. Robinson, if I remember rightly."

Was there any technical magazine the boy hadn't read? Edward stared at the raised signal and then at the rail itself. There was something about it all this... The beginning of an idea was hovering at the edge of his mind. Then it was gone. Clever invention though.

"Tarnation! Sorry, Elsie."

The woodpecker had started up again and the telegraph boy was scowling at something he'd just taken down. "That Henry in 'Frisco! I'd recognize his fist anywhere. Can't spell for beans." The boy showed the sheet to Elsie. "Look at the way he spells Edward! E-d-w-e-i-r-d."

Weird? Was the lad mocking him? Although, oddly he had been considering changing his name to "Eadweard" after one of the old Saxon kings from Kingston. But "What hath God wrought?" as Morse said. They even knew where he was.

"It's probably the Governor wanting you to do something else for him." grumbled Joseph.

More noises from Mars.

"What's the message say?"

"Dot-dot, dash, dot-dot, dot-dot-dot, dot-dash, dash-dot-dot-dot, dot-space-dot, dot-dot-space-dot-dot."

"Very funny, but what does it mean?"

Arthur grinned. "It's a boy."

"Three blind mice, see how they run! They all ran after the farmer's wife who cut off their tails with a carving knife..." sang his small mountain of packages as he tottered with it up the stairs.

At the top of the landing, he turned his back on their bedroom door, and tapped on it with his heel. No answer. She must have dozed off. But the door was starting to swing open as if she'd known in advance that he would have his hands full, the darling.

He was fast asleep in the crib beside her bed. The crumpled features and the tiny body. Edward felt his own face beginning to crumple too as if by osmosis, the tears seeping out of his eyes and running down his cheeks. "Oh, my Lord... my Lord." He could see his own future in the tiny being, his immortality. This was how a man lived on, wasn't it, through his boy? He bent down to kiss the tiny forehead, inhaling the perfect angelic baby smell.

He sat down on the bed beside Flora, whose head was hidden by a pink net sleeping cap. He kissed her neck. "You've made me the happiest man in the world."

There was a loud scream. Mrs. Smith popped up like a spring doll, hitting her head on the canopy frame.

Edward fell off the bed and scrambled to his feet. "Oh, Mrs. Smith, I do apologize. My Goodness. What on earth are you – "

Mrs. Smith struggled out of the bed in her nightdress, backing away, staring wildly at him, her hands groping for her dressing gown. Her Cockney so broad, it was almost unintelligible. "'ang abart – oy – oy – Fl – Mrs. Muybridge 'ad to go art for a little while and I woz wotchin' the baby, innit, and oy – oy must 'ave – oy mus' 'ave dropped orf."

"That's quite all right, Mrs. Smith – but my wife shouldn't be up surely?"

"It woz a veddy heasy birf, sir," she said, buttoning her dressing gown, "hastonishing reelly, o'course she's still young, innit, it's hallways heasier when yer young. "

"Well, Mrs. Smith, I want to thank you for – " he glanced at the darling boy, "everything."

"Yuss, well, oy'd better be – "

There was an odd smell that Edward hadn't noticed before. He looked round the room. A Havana? "Has someone been smoking in here?"

"Oh, nah sir, well, jus' the man – "

"The man?"

Mrs. Smith was also searching round the room. "The man – eh – wot woz 'ere fer the new bell." She pointed at a shiny brass bell pull on the wall beside the bed. "Oy tole 'im wot woz 'e finkin' vat's vy oy opened the winders – "

She went to close them.

Edward held up his hand. "No, that's all right, it's a warm

night, and they say in Germany you can't have too much fresh air – what new bell?"

"Well, Flora – Mrs. Muybridge – wannid to connect 'er room direkly wiv yours, innit, sir, wot oy'm usin' for nar, sir, if vat's all right, so oy can be near the baby and come prompt-like soon as she ring."

"Yes, that's a good plan when I'm away."

"Yuss, sir, fank you, sir, and Lily made up the spare room for yer – "

"Lily?"

"The noo maid."

The new maid?

"Wot you fink of yer noo baby, sir? Ain't 'e bootiful?"

Edward looked down at his sleeping child. He felt as young as springtime. "I've never seen anything so beautiful in my entire life, Mrs. Smith."

"You see the placement of the figures and the wings and the flies in rows one behind the other?" said Edward as he pointed at the tiny cardboard actors striking dramatic poses between layers of cardboard scenery that seemed to recede into the distance behind the Regency proscenium arch. "That's what gives us not only width and height but depth as well, so we imagine that we're seeing these flat cutouts in the round. When I was a boy, you could buy sheets of characters from the toyshop, 'penny plain and tuppence colored.' Oh, the colors of that water paint, the very names: crimson lake, gamboge green, Prussian blue – like your eyes, my darling."

He was squatting on the floor in front of the toy theater, gazing down at the baby boy in his arms, who shared both his and Flora's and Edward's father's eyes. Blue runs in the family.

He kissed the soft top of the baby's head, turning him to face the theater again. "You see the backcloth, Florado? You see how it's drawn in single-point linear perspective? That's to add even more depth."

"Florado?"

Edward looked up to see Flora standing at the door in her day clothes and a new bonnet that made her look even more beautiful.

"My love!"

He started to stand with the baby, almost letting him slip out of his arms in his eagerness to embrace her.

Flora hastily took the baby from him, turning away to settle him in his crib.

Was she frowning? Perhaps she still hadn't completely recovered? He should never have gone off so late in her pregnancy. He should have been here.

"I'm so sorry I missed his birth, Flora – the snow in the mountains was so – "

"Don't worry, Edward. I told you before you left, I'm in good hands. But 'Florado?' Where did that come from?"

"Your name and – well, the Flo part, and – you remember you used to call me dodo? I put them together." He curled his arm round her waist, kissing the side of her neck as they both looked down at the baby.

The tightness slowly drained from her face. "Of course, you'll always be my dodo."

"It also rhymes with *El Dorado*: the golden one."

The baby yawned, closing his eyes.

"His full name will be Florado Helios Muybridge."

Flora shook her head, but with a smile now. "Only you…"

"Why don't they tell you how incredible this is?" He touched the baby's cheek. "It struck me just now: it's – it's as if I'm touching infinity, as if this somehow makes me – makes us – infinite. We can see our own shadows in our child, Flora, long shadows stretching into the future. What we are, you and I, will be what he is, only he'll be much, much better. We'll make sure of that, won't we? Much better." He stroked the baby again, who gripped Edward's finger in his sleep, such a strong grip for such a tiny hand. He had his father's strength. "Our sun in the sky – our son from the sky. Just look at his color, how radiant he is!"

"He's pink from the bath, Edward."

Flora surveyed the bed-room floor, which was strewn with every mechanical plaything and toy Edward had been able to lay his hands on: a tinplate train set from Chicago complete with one of the new clockwork CPR Locomotives, a wind-up Whirligig and a Jack-in-the-Box from England; a spinning turnip top and a rolling hoop from California just like the little boy's in the park; sets of Mignot and Hyde lead soldiers from France and Germany…

"Are you sure you bought him enough presents? You have an entire toyshop in here."

He grinned. "Yes, I know."

He gazed at the sleeping baby again. "I'm going to photograph him at every stage, you'll see, Flora: crawling, walking, standing, running. I'm going to be here for all of it."

Flora frowned once more. "Well, he won't crawl for quite a while yet. Don't you have more photographic work of the railroad to do?"

"Well, yes, I'm afraid. Stanford's so demanding, it's endless, and of course I'm also hoping to do further rapid-motion projects with him and – "

"Well, you have time to do all that first, my love." She came close to him, touching him on the shoulder. "Nothin's goin' on here, just restin' and nursin'."

Her wrist was bare.

"What happened to your bracelet?"

She pulled her sleeve down. "Oh, the clasp broke, it's at the jewelers. But as I was sayin', you should go off and do your work – wasn't there talk of Guatemala too?"

"Well, I don't – "

"Don't worry, you have time to fit all that in, and then come back in a few months when he does start crawlin'."

She had a point. He could get a great deal done during this period. "Well, you know best of course, my love. But I want to take just one picture of him first. You know my old christening dress – the one that I had sent over from England?"

Flora stepped back a couple of paces. "Eh, yes…?" What do you want with that?"

"Don't you remember? I wanted it for when I take our first baby picture after we have him christened."

"Oh, yes, of course, it's somewhere in the house. But it will take a while to find it. But anyway, I'd rather have the christenin' when he's a bit older, he'll be so much more handsome."

"Oh, as you wish, my love, mother knows best."

"Meanwhile, don't worry, as I said, I have Mrs. Smith."

"I suppose Sarah Louisa could come in as well?"

"Yes, yes, of course."

There was a soft knock on the door.

Flora opened it on a very young chambermaid on the darkened landing.

"Beg your pardon, Madam, but Samuel has come for the shirts and he dunno which is which." A flash of white teeth behind her.

Edward looked at the shadow in the doorway. "Samuel?"

The shadow became a huge servant. He could have been Black Tom's brother. "Yes, massah."

"How do you do?" Edward shook his hand.

Samuel looked confused and stepped back behind the chambermaid.

Edward addressed her: "And you must be Lily?"

Lily blushed as she curtsied. "Yes, sir."

He smiled at her. "Well, welcome to my house, I'm sure you'll be of great help to Mrs. Muybridge…"

Lily seemed to relax herself somewhat. "Thank you, sir, I – "

"What shirts has Samuel come for, Lily?"

"Them for the Ma – "

"There's so much washin' with the baby," interrupted Flora, "we – we have to send some of it out. I wanted your shirts to be specially nice and starched for you – don't want your laundry to get mixed up."

She turned to Lily and Samuel, "I'll come down with you. I'll be back in a moment, Edward," she added, without looking at him.

The door closed behind them.

Edward stared at the door. *Mixed up with what?* What was going on? This was most odd.

A gurgle from the crib erased every worry and suspicion from his mind. Florado beamed up at him. And what a beam! To have called it a smile would have been absurdly inadequate. The sheer power of perfect purity and innocence almost knocked him over. It was a tear in the curtain, a glimpse of "elsewhere" and "otherwise" of God's true universe.

He gathered the baby up and walked to the window, holding the tiny face next to his, both of them gazing out at the rows of street lamps obeying the laws of linear perspective deep into the night.

"You see all those lights, Florado, receding in every direction? That will be your kingdom one day, my darling boy. You will have everything I never had. You will have your Silver Palace."

CHAPTER TWENTY-TWO

On this early morning run, the car might almost have been Edward's own private property. Apart from the "gripman" who started and stopped the thing by using a lever to grip and ungrip the wire-rope, there was only one other passenger: a smartly dressed fellow sitting at the rear of the car in business suit and topper, cradling a brief-bag on his knees. Odd fellow, though: each time Edward looked around to admire the view and their eyes crossed, the man's face twitched. Probably a *tic douleureux*, poor chap.

Having sent Flora and Florado up to her uncle's in Oregon to get a good long rest, the new father was feeling on top of the world. And that was precisely where they were going this very minute: to the top of the steepest hill in San Francisco so that Edward could petition Stanford to continue their fast-motion experiments. And the means of conveyance? A vehicle that hadn't existed a mere twelve-month ago dragging itself up a hill nearly four hundred feet high by its own bootstraps. But that was exactly what was being accomplished by Edward's "cable car," all perky maroon paintwork and cream and blue trim with *Clay Street Hill R.R. Co* in gilt lettering on the side.

How such a wonder of transportation came about was due to a certain clever Scotsman by the name of Andrew Smith Hallidie. He'd been standing at the bottom of this same hill watching a team of horses about to pull their bus on the same journey that Edward was now undertaking in such comfort. Like Sisyphus, the poor benighted creatures lived for only one thing: to pull the bus up the hill, only to have it fall back down again of its own weight, so that they had to pull it up again, and again, and again, for all eternity. The epitome of hopelessness, like the lives of its passengers. Until recently such buses had been burdened with the poor and the exhausted returning after a twelve-hour workday to their miserable tarpaper shacks at the summit of the treacherous sand castle known as the "Hill of Golden Promise," the last resort of the truly desperate. And in an age when even horses were divided into classes, those that hauled these conveyances were the mudsills of equine society, as far removed from Occident as a beggar from Croesus.

On the day Hallidie had been watching, one of the beggars had been able to stand it no more and had fallen on its knees, pulling down the other four. Their agonized whinnyings had fought with the terrified screams of the passengers as the bus slowly toppled over and skidded faster and faster down the wet cobblestones to the very bottom of the hill, dragging the horses behind as they were flailed alive.

That's when Mr. Hallidie had his idea. A few years before, he had been faced with the problem of hauling giant buckets of rock and ore across deep chasms and up precipitous mountains for the gold and silver mining companies. He'd invented an endless traveling cable made out of plaited strands of steel, which ran both above and below the ground. On the day of the accident, in a sudden flash of inspiration, Hallidie realized that the same system could work for the self-propulsion of street-cars up and down the hills of San Francisco.

It turned the railroad inside out. Instead of the steam engine moving along the rails, the rails moved along the steam engine, which itself never moved at all. It just sat there in a five-storied powerhouse at the bottom of the slope, endlessly winding and unwinding Hallidie's wire-rope like Penelope's tapestry.

The cable car was now approaching the crest of the hill, rising above the thick mist with perfect smoothness and in almost complete silence broken only by the faint *clickity-clank* of the perpetually moving wire-rope beneath them, which sounded to Edward like some subterranean monk telling his beads.

As they arrived at the top, Edward saw that the sand castle had become an ant hill, pullulating with what must have been thousands of workmen swinging scythes, hefting pick axes, climbing ladders, sawing, planeing, hammering. He screwed up his eyes, stripping them naked, and blinked several times in rapid succession, capturing every instant of their movements, every flex and ripple of their muscles. He looked away. Then back. They were decent again.

And what all these man were doing was the talk of the town, mused Edward. Hundreds of wretched hovels were being razed to the ground to make way for a cluster of palatial mansions. Thanks to the new cable car service, the human rubbish was being transformed into the jewel in the crown of the state of California where what the British Raj called the *nabobs* could rehabilitate these few God-forsaken acres into what was already being referred to as "Nob Hill."

Just as little boys rejoiced in running up on top of anything they could find that was more than six inches off the ground and crying "I'm the king of the castle!" so were the newly anointed silver kings and railroad barons almost falling over themselves in their rush to the top of the very latest place to be.

The jumped-up shopkeepers, Charles Crocker (dry goods), Mark Hopkins and Collis P. Huntington (hardware), and Leland Stanford (grocer), were building some of the most elaborate architectural fantasies the world had ever seen, as they shouted out their untold wealth.

Stanford, standing outside a construction shed of what was to be the largest and most expensive private residence in the United States of America, was shouting the loudest as he commanded his workers to "get a bloody move on."

"Good morning, Muybridge," he cried as he spotted Edward, "I hear you're not afraid of heights." He pointed up at an observation tower built out of scaffolding.

"No fear whatever, Governor," Edward was delighted to be able to report.

Stanford started heaving his bulk up the ladder. Edward followed.

They reached a small platform at the top of the tower. It was the highest Edward had climbed since Yosemite, he realized. Not a trace of vertigo.

After a few moments to recover his breath – Stanford had obviously never seen the inside of a gymnasium – the Governor said, "You have the whole world at your feet up here, Muybridge:

cars from the city of Mexico and trains laden with gold and silver bullion from Senora and Chihuahua and grain from Washington Territory and Oregon. I can look out through the Golden Gate and see fleets of ocean steamers bearing the trade of India, the commerce of Asia, the traffic of the islands of the ocean."

Stanford pointed down at his building site, almost blowing Edward off the tower with a blizzard of facts and figures about the hundred-foot entrance hall, the seventy-foot supper room, the fifty-foot art-room, the neo-Pompeian ceilings...

When there was finally a pause in the gush of amber this, ebony that, marble whatdoyoucallits, and gold thingamyjigs, Edward opened his mouth to broach the subject of his visit. But too late, the Tycoon was already gesturing at some neighboring construction plots. "Next door is where Mark is building, and further down will be Collis's place, and," he chuckled, "there's where Charley Crocker is having his little difficulty." He indicated a nearby building site beside which workmen were erecting a giant wooden box around a small house. "When Crocker bought a pair of plots in that block for his house and stables, he discovered that a Chink named Nicholas Yung – he has something to do with a funeral home, I believe – had already built that dreadful little house next door. Crocker naturally couldn't put up with that, but – would you believe it? – the fellow refused to sell. So Crocker is building a forty-foot high fence round the place." He chuckled. "A 'spite wall,' he likes to call it. And quite right too, we don't want the wrong sort up here. For once, I agree with Charley. We can't spite these slant-eyes enough."

Should he object to this endless denigration of the Chinese? wondered Edward. No, what was the point? It was so ingrained. He turned his head to the Governor, started to speak, then stopped. He didn't know how to begin.

"What brings you up here to see me today, Muybridge?" said Stanford, solving Edward's problem for him. "I take it it wasn't just to admire the view?"

"Well, quite frankly, Governor, I'd very much like to continue our motion photography, our first attempt with Occident was – "

"A great success, you don't need to tell me." Stanford smiled. "And you also don't need to tell me that our first photograph of my horse was shadowy and indistinct. It was the proof I needed, but no more. For the last months, I've been too taken up with railroad business to pursue such experiments, but now things have settled down, I would like to resume our work. I want to capture a really clear picture of Occident's stride – a series of such pictures of every phase of his stride, in fact, on which I can base a scientific theory of animal training. And once again, you're the only man I know who can do it."

Once more, Edward was dumbfounded by the Governor, who again seemed to have his thoughts in perfect synchrony with his own. And now he was talking about science!

"I want you to give me all the details as soon as you can," continued Stanford, "the costs, the equipment, the people. My funds are at your disposal, my horses – whatever you need." He reached out to shake Edward's hand. "We're going to do great things together, Muybridge, you and I, great things!"

Stanford started to climb down the ladder. Then he paused to look up at Edward. "Just one more matter…"

"Yes, Governor."

"I know a great many people in California, many of them extremely affluent. Some of them have been rather offended by your behavior when they've asked you to make views of their estates or ranches and you have refused simply because it didn't suit your artistic tastes, however much they offered you."

"I'll never make a view for money if I don't see beauty in it."

"The artist and the scientist all bound up in one man. I admire that and I respect it. But you are also a very stubborn man, Muybridge. You know what you want and nothing will stop you from getting it." Stanford grinned. "It's almost like looking in the mirror. That is why I know we will succeed in our venture."

As he watched the Governor descend to the ground, Edward's mind was rotating as fast as a carriage wheel. Here he was, at the very top of the former Governor of California's tower at the very top of Nob Hill. Below him, the sun had burned off the morning mist, exposing the entire bay and the great city. He held out his arms and began to turn like a dervish, spinning a panorama of Montgomery, Pine, Mason, Powell, Market, Belmont Park, Golden Gate Park, Montgomery, Pine, Mason, Powell, Market…

A hand tapped him on the shoulder. It was the smartly dressed man from the cable car.

"What? What the – how did you get up here?"

"I thought we should be alone, Mr. Muybridge." The man looked around him at the view; there was no nervous tic now. "What better place for you to read this." He held out a scroll of parchment fastened with black silk ribbon and a red seal. "Mrs. Susan Smith has obtained a judgment against you in the Justices Court. I am her attorney. My name is Sawyer." He flourished a business card.

"A judgment against me, from Mrs. Smith? What in Heaven's name for?"

"For non-payment of services rendered at the time of the birth of the baby."

"This is nonsense. I gave my wife ample money for that."

"I'm afraid we have evidence that you did not, sir." Sawyer took a letter out of his brief-bag. "In this letter to Mrs. Smith, your wife acknowledges that she wasn't able to pay her because she had no money."

Edward's head was reeling as rapidly as the streets. He took the letter and skimmed through it. He could hardly make out the words, the letters were dancing so fast.

"Is that your wife's handwriting, Mr. Muybridge?"

"Yes, yes… What is this… ? What… ? 'I'm expecting some money that I lent to a friend.'"

Flora's bare wrist… the clasp broke… the shirts got mixed up…

Edward staggered back against the ledge of the scaffolding, almost breaking through the flimsy wooden planks.

He stared at the attorney, seeing nothing. "It seems I owe Mrs. Smith an apology, Mr. Sawyer, please forgive me… I – I must have been mistaken. How much?"

"One hundred and seven dollars, sir."

CHAPTER TWENTY-THREE

Edward tugged on the doorbell of the little house at 1032 Mission again and again, so hard he almost shook some of the crumbling roof tiles onto the pavement. He must be rousing the whole street, the whole city, the whole world. But not apparently Mrs. Smith – or Sarah Louisa, for that matter. Could she be at the gallery already? He looked at his watch. Of course she could: it was almost eleven o'clock.

He stepped over a flowerbed and peered through a tear in the faded lace curtains. Mrs. Smith was sitting at a little table in the front parlor, dozing over a tiny cardigan.

He banged on the windowpane.

Mrs. Smith looked up and started as if seeing a ghost. She jumped to her feet and bustled out of view.

The sound of the bolt being drawn back. Edward shoved the door open and marched into the cramped little room. Mrs. Smith recoiled from him. He reached for her hand. She jerked it away. He grabbed her wrist and forced her hand open.

"I believe this is yours, Mrs. Smith. I've rounded it up to one hundred and ten dollars for your trouble."

Mrs. Smith stared at the sheaf of bills.

"I would have brought coins, but I couldn't find my purse."

"Oh, fank you, sir."

"Who did my wife give the money to?"

She backed away from him again. "Oy – Oy don' unnerrstand."

"Who did she give the money to that was meant for you?"

"Oy dunno, sir. She didn't say nuffink in any of her letters – "

"There are *more* letters?"

"Beg yer parding, sir?"

Edward took as deep a breath as he could. "Are there any more letters?"

"Oy dunno…" She was trembling.

"I'm warning you, Mrs. Smith!"

Her eyes flickered. She was looking at something behind him: a chest-of-drawers in the corner of the room.

Edward rushed over to it, pulled open the top drawer and started rummaging through bills and tram tickets and postcards of naked cherubs. There were two letters. He unfolded one of them and started to read.

> *Dear Mrs. Smith, You'll be surprised to hear from me so soon after I left the city, but I have been so worried about that poor girl that I cannot rest, and it is a relief to talk or write about her.*

He skimmed down the page:

> *I have written to the morning and evening papers in Portland today and advertised in the personals so: "Flora and Georgie. If you have a heart you will write to me. Have you forgotten that April night when we were both so pale?"*

The letter was signed "Harry Larkyns." That "April night?" Oh, God. He hardly dared open the second letter, which was from Flora to Sarah Louisa:

> *Dear Sarah... I made a trip to the Columbia River with my Aunt on my Uncles Boat the scenery is perfectly lovely, I wish I had a nice little house with you know who, and your mother and all of you near me I would be so happy to get away from California from all my pretended friends... I am not ashamed to say I love him better than anyone else on earth, and no one can change my mind...Destroy my letters after reading them, for you might lose one, and it might get picked up.*

How could Sarah Louisa have connived with Flora in this

way? How could she have done this to him? He glared at Mrs. Smith. "What in God's name is going on?"

"Oy dunno, sir, oy swears on me muvver's grave."

Edward waved the first letter in her face. "This is addressed to you, Mrs. Smith, and signed by Harry Larkyns. And this," he brandished the second letter, "is from my wife to your daughter. You must have known what was going on!"

Mrs. Smith collapsed into a chair, holding a handkerchief to her face. "Oy didn't, sir, oy don't, oy – "

"How could you not know?"

"Oy dunno..." She was gasping for breath.

"If you say that once more, I'll – " he bunched his fists. "HOW COULD YOU NOT KNOW?"

"Oy can't – oy can't read, sir. Sarah reads 'em all and passes on all the messages."

So that was it. He still couldn't believe this of Sarah Louisa. She of all people.

"So you and your daughter were – were – playing the pimp for my wife and Larkyns? Is that it?"

Mrs. Smith blew her nose loudly.

Edward turned back to the chest-of-drawers and pulled out the entire drawer, letting it crash to the floor. He dropped to his knees, scrabbling through the jumble of paper. H e f o u n d a n o t h e r scrawled note from Harry Larkyns:

> *Why doesn't the old man get out of town and leave us alone? At the place on Montgomery Street they think you are my wife.*

He leaped up and advanced on Mrs. Smith. "More! I want more! You must have more!"

She got up from her chair and shrank away from him, knocking over a side table and sending her knitting to the floor along with a small square of cardboard, which she hastily kicked out of sight.

Edward lunged for it. It was a photograph of a baby boy

propped up in bed in an old-fashioned christening dress. His tiny hand was reaching out for a small velvet purse a man's hand was dangling in front of him. Edward felt as if he'd been kicked in the stomach by a mule. His baby, his christening dress, his purse — taken with one of his cameras, no doubt! God in Heaven! How brazen could she be? Taking everything from him and giving it to that man. Larkyns must have sneaked back from Yellow Jacket while he was away.

He spun round on Mrs. Smith. "Where did you get this picture?"

"Yer vife sent it to me from Oregon."

Edward turned the picture over to read two words in Flora's handwriting: *Little Harry.* Always write the name of the subject on the back. That's what he'd taught her, wasn't it?

CHAPTER TWENTY-FOUR

Edward was in the brass cage in his child's bed-room, pulling and pulling at the bars trying to reach Flora standing naked before him, his bracelet glittering on her wrist like a serpent. *That was what it was about, wasn't it? Standing there like that, naked like that, to make sure he would make love to her to allay any suspicion she was carrying the seed of the other? It had all just been a ruse, hadn't it? As she'd stood there wearing nothing but his bracelet. The bracelet she'd given to her lover.*

The bars gave way and he stumbled out into a pair of arms that gripped him like a vise.

"What's got into you, Muybridge?" said Rulofson.

Edward broke free of him with one shrug of his shoulders. What was Rulofson talking about? Where was he? What was he doing here?

Rulofson stared at him. "I've never seen you take the elevator before, not once, in all these years…"

"Not once in all these years…" Edward repeated like an automaton. They were in the ground floor lobby of the studio, he must have come down in the elevator. Why on earth had he taken the elevator? How had he even got to the studio in the first place – all the way from Mission-street?

He could feel Rulofson's hands guiding him towards the stairs, forcing him to take step after step.

They arrived at the second floor, then through the parlor into the ladies' dressing room. *That moment when he'd first seen her face.* He'd never seen the inside of the dressing room though: it was lined with lockers and hangars for feminine garments. He collapsed onto a lounge, his chest heaving as if his asthma had returned.

"For God's sake, Muybridge," exclaimed Rulofson, "what's the matter, man?"

Edward looked blank. He didn't know, he knew nothing; everything had gone black. Something about letters, a photograph… oh God, yes, the letters! He patted his coat. What was that large hard thing? He felt its shape. Oh, yes… But what was he doing with that? He didn't even want to name it. But the letters. He found them in his breast pocket.

"The weasel – the weasel told me, Larkyns spat in his face, Woodward's, the gallery, back here at night together, Mrs. Smith, the photograph, the letters!" He held them out to Rulofson.

Rulofson looked at them in bewilderment. "What's this? What is going on?"

"You'll find out soon enough. You've been a good friend to me, Rulofson. I want you to promise me that in the event of my death you will give my wife all that belongs to me."

"Death!? I don't understand."

Edward pointed at the letters. "Here is absolute proof that my wife has dishonored me."

He jumped to his feet and headed for the dressing room door.

Rulofson's arms were around him again. With a sudden burst of strength, he prized them off his body, then lifted the stocky German clean off his feet and threw him across the room as if he were a child.

He dashed out of the dressing room and across the parlor and made for the stairs.

Somehow Rulofson caught up with him in the lobby. "Listen to me! Listen to me, Muybridge! Many good women are wrongly slandered."

"One of us will be shot!"

"Who? Who are you talking about?"

"Is your watch set to city time?"

"Why yes, but – "

"What does it say?"

"Four minutes to four."

"I'm going to hunt him down, Rulofson."

He ran out into the street.

Rulofson grabbed him again. "Who?"

"Let me go! I have to catch the last ferry, the four o'clock!"

"That's impossible. It's twelve blocks from here."

Edward pushed Rulofson away and sprinted down the street.

* * *

Running down Market. A foghorn. "Last call for Vallejo!" Onto the Broadway Wharf. "Connecting with trains for Calistoga, Knight's Landing and Sacramento!" The smokestacks of the *Yosemite* belching white steam, the deck hands dragging the gangplank on board, casting off the mooring chains.

Edward charged through the spectators.

The stern of the boat was already a good six feet from the dock.

Run, run! You can do it, you can do it!

He jumped, hung in the air… and grasped the boat rail.

Pull, pull, *pull*! It was Yosemite again.

He toppled over the rail onto the deck.

A trio of young women gaped down at him. He scrambled to his feet. One of them looked familiar. Where had he seen her before? Black Tom's. It was Mary Douglas, the girl in the plummeting dress.

Three and a half hours later, Edward was sitting alone in the darkened smoking coach of the Calistoga train as it approached the end of its journey north from Vallejo Junction through Napa County.

There was a single gong clap as the conductor alerted the terminal station to their arrival.

He swung open the coach door, jumped onto the still moving platform and sprinted past the first-class carriage as the window slid down, framing Mary's face.

He vaulted the barrier at the end of the platform, ignoring the cries of the ticket collector.

Was does the sign say? It's getting so dark it's hard to see. But yes, this is the place: *FOSS & CONNOLLY'S LIVERY STABLE.*

Edward burst through the swing doors into a jumble of wagons, horse stalls and bales of hay – and his old friend William

Stewart whom he'd met up here before, long ago. Stewart was chatting with a man who must have been Connolly himself. But there was no time for niceties. "I need a rig!"

The two men stared at him.

"A wagon and team! I have business with Major Larkyns up at Yellow Jacket that cannot wait!"

"What are you doing here, Muybridge?" said Stewart. "What do you want with Larkyns?"

Edward ignored him and barked at Connolly. "Take me there."

The sound of giggling. Mary and her companions were at the stable door.

"I thought you'd missed the train," snapped Stewart to the young women. "Now hurry up, for God's sake, we don't want to keep 'em waiting. Into the stage with you."

The young women hurried across the stable and out of the rear door where a Concord was waiting.

Edward started to follow them. Stewart put a hand on his arm. "I'm afraid there isn't room for anyone else." He ran to catch up with the girls.

"Then I shall make my own way," shouted Edward after him.

"We don't have any other drivers, sir," said Connolly.

"Hurry, man, hurry!" came Stewart's voice from outside:

The crack of a whip, the crunch of wheels on gravel.

"The wagon, quick!" cried Edward. "I'll pay you handsomely to drive it yourself."

"The next stage leaves in the morning, sir."

"I have to see Major Larkyns tonight, I tell you!"

Connolly hesitated for a moment, then cried out, "George!" There was no response. "George!!"

In a corner of the stable, a bale of hay shuddered, then shuffled to one side, revealing a boy of about fifteen, rubbing his eyes and yawning.

Connolly started over to him. Edward pushed past him, hissing at the boy: "Is there a shortcut to Yellow Jacket?"

"Eh, well, why yes, sir, but it's a good seven mile and very bumpy and muddy…"

Edward showed him a handful of silver dollars. "This is for you if you can get me to the ranch before Mr. Stewart."

Screams of laughter. A blaze of light. Edward pressed his face against the ranch house window.

Larkyns was stripped to the waist, his chest gleaming as he strutted up and down a long trestle table, brandishing a sabre above the heads of a dozen or so miners with half-naked women in their arms as the Major slashed and slashed at a line of champagne bottles, decapitating one after the other, their foaming contents spurting into open mouths.

"Kill another one, Harry!" yelled someone. Was that James McArthur? The local prospector Edward had met up here not so long ago while taking views? Where were his polite formalities now, his starched shirt, his touching of his forelock?

"Which enemy shall we assail now, *mes amis*?" cried Larkyns. "Shall we go to Italy where I fought beside Garibaldi?"

"Yes, yes, yes!"

"*Avanti, avanti, porco cane, va, all'inferno!*" *Slash-schlick.* "Or shall we go to Germany to attack the Prussians as I did when under arms with *le Général* Bourbaki?"

"Yes, yes, yes!"

"*Verdammte Schweinhund, gehen sie zum Teufel!*" *Slash-schlick.*

The rage welled up inside Edward. Larkyns, the man to whom everything came so easily, his languages, his grace, his charm. The man who'd given him his greatest chance, only to take it back again along with everything else he had, his baby, his wife, his work, his reputation. Well, now we'll see who'll do the taking away, for one of us must die. There was nothing else now, nothing but death. His whole universe was shrinking down to this, falling in on itself to this, this single point…

Crash. His fist on the door. *Crash* and *Crash* again.

The door opened and the Major stepped out, screwing up his eyes against the darkness. "Who is it? Who are you? I can't see your face, it's so dark."

Edward reached into his pocket and raised his pistol. "My name is Muybridge, and this is a message from my wife."

Time stopped. I will never ever hurt another human being. It's Larkyns, it's John, it's Larkyns, it's John, it's Larkyns, it's John. I don't know who it is.

He fired.

He opened his eyes. He was scrunched up in the darkness, in the back of a two-seater, a buggy robe over his shoulders. In front of him, beside a driver, a miner was holding a lamp. His ankles were burning. He looked down: they were bound with cord. Black spots on his light-colored jacket – he touched them, put his finger to his mouth: hot and sticky. Blood.

A series of images jerked across his mind as they headed down to Calistoga. The black rosette growing on Larkyns' bare chest, his hands clutching his chest, the little spurt of blood between the fingers, his face as the life drained out of it, all seared onto Edward's retina in that one split-second as surely as by the Lunar Caustic. Larkyns staggering back, turning, stumbling through the house in front of Edward, who was following him, pistol upraised. Larkyns' dying voice, "Let me out, let me out!" as he almost fell through the parlor past the shattered champagne bottles and the smoldering opium pipes and out the other door of the ranch house, finally collapsing into the dirt beneath an oak tree, drowning in his own blood. Then McArthur holding a revolver in front of Edward's face: "You have shot a man, give me your pistol." Handing it over, sitting down, then looking up at the white faces of the girls struggling into their clothes, then his own voice: "Please forgive me, ladies, for this little trouble, but you must consider my wrong, the ruin of my happiness..." Then Prickett and two other men he'd also met up here before, McCrory and Murray, running up to him as he fell onto a lounge. Then a strange calm settling over him like a blanket of ether as he asked for a glass of water and the newspaper and offered his rig to McArthur to fetch a physician. Then Stewart bursting into the room followed by Mary Douglas and the other girls from the boat.

The ruin of his happiness. On the 17th of October, eighteen

seventy-four. The day he would never forget for as long as he lived. Which he prayed would not be long.

CHAPTER TWENTY-FIVE

Edward's moment of truth finally arrived after three and a half months incarceration in the Napa City Jail and a three-day trial.

The foreman, Sam Newcomer, a tall gaunt rancher with a white mustache and goatee, stepped into the jury box of the Napa City Court-House, followed by eleven grizzled farmers and carpenters and cattlemen as rough-hewn as the bare wooden walls; no time to apply plaster, the city had been growing so fast.

Mostly men were crowded here for Edward's day of judgment, with a sprinkling of women, some with babies in their arms — *babies, imagine, the power of the baby* — as well as a small army of attorneys, bailiffs, clerks and sheriffs. Every major newspaper in the region had reporters on the alert, while telegraph operators stood by to send the verdict across the land. The sensational shooting and lurid love affair had all the elements of melodrama: the cuckolded gray bearded husband; the beautiful young wife; the dashing lover; the child born out wedlock. The entire country was holding its breath to learn the outcome of what had already become known as "the trial of the century."

Out of the court-room window, workmen were testing the scaffold, dropping a man-sized sandbag through the trap door for about ten feet before snapping the rope tight to break the neck: the new "measured drop" to determine how much slack would be needed to ensure Edward would not be decapitated. He wouldn't suffer for more than half a second. How thoughtful! If he could have rigged a line from his high-speed camera to the rope, his falling body could have taken its own picture.

He was surrounded by hate, that was the only word for it. It was palpable. The courtroom air was thick with it. This was his guilt, the guilt he had been born with, the guilt as primeval as Adam's. Was this how it was to end? *Don't Care was made to care, Don't Care was hung.* He'd sworn to Grandma that he would make a name for himself. Well, he'd finally done it, hadn't he? He had kept his promise. And what a name he had made.

Murderer! He had shot and killed Major Harry George Larkyns, "willfully, unlawfully and of his malice aforethought," as the counsel for the prosecution, Thomas P. Stoney, had never tired repeating throughout the trial with his smirk of superiority as if to say, why are we wasting our time when the outcome is so obvious?

Why indeed. There had been no shortage of witnesses to what Edward had done, from the Yellow Jacket miners and prostitutes to William Stewart and Mary Douglas, trooping up to take the stand, one after the other. Then Edward's pistol being passed round the court and George Crummel, the Constable who had arrested him in Calistoga, confirming that this was indeed the weapon he had used. Then Stoney going into mind-numbing detail about whether the revolver was a Smith and Wesson Number Two or a Number Two and a Half, a thirty-two rim fire or not, a six shot or a five shot, and the exact dimensions of its barrel. Oh, what does it matter? *What does it matter, Edward, a five or a four or a three?* What did any of it matter now?

But it had gone on. Next, they had been treated to the gory medical details by the local physician, Dr. S.J. Reid, as to exactly how his bullet had killed Larkyns. "The orifice was one and a quarter inches to the right and below the left nipple, about an inch from the sternum, between the fifth and sixth ribs. It ranged inward and upward, penetrating the heart and causing hemorrhage, which in turn caused the death of the victim." His voice going round and round in Edward's head. And the spots of blood they'd found on the light-gray suit he was still wearing in court, long ago washed out of course, invisible to everyone but as clear to him as to Lady Macbeth. Dr. Ried had probed the wound, which was still fresh, proclaiming that a man with such a wound "would not live more than thirty or forty seconds" and that "the ball had passed clear through the body."

That had all been plain enough and – surprisingly – not too harrowing to bear. It was almost as if Edward had wanted all this, deep down somewhere inside himself, in his heart of hearts, he had wanted it, he had always wanted it. The martyr willing his own death. He wasn't afraid of the death of his body, having died once in that stage-coach and very nearly again at the hands of the Hoodlums; no, that wasn't his fear, not that form of death, but the death of his pride, death by public humiliation. That terrible moment when it had been the turn of his very own counsels to build the case for the defense on the grounds of "justifiable homicide"; that's when his real agony had begun.

Edward glanced at the two of them now: the florid, middle-aged Cameron King so proper in his black suit, such a jarring contrast with the bright bourbon and blue waistcoat of his pale-faced young partner, William Wirt Pendegast, a man Edward had become friendly with after he'd taken portraits of his family and – apart from his assistants – the only person to visit him during all his time in jail. (Not a word from Stanford of course throughout this affair; Pontius Pilate couldn't have washed his hands cleaner.) Oh, but there was one other visitor: Flora's attorney to inform him that she was filing for divorce and suing for alimony on the grounds of extreme cruelty. However, since the only instance she could cite was that "he peeped in at her when she was sleeping" – she could hardly name the real nature of his cruelty: that he had shot dead her lover – the judge had so far rejected her suit.

Mr. King's first witness had been Mrs. Susan Smith, who had begun with the events surrounding the birth of the baby while Edward had still been stuck up in the Sierras. How Larkyns "in an 'igh white 'at" had arrived at her house on Mission-street in a carriage containing Flora in labor. How he'd whisked them back to the Muybridge residence. How Flora had been so worried that the baby might have her lover's sandy hair. And then how Larkyns had held her in his arms and kissed her and caressed her and fondled her as if she were a spoilt child. How, after the baby boy was born, Flora had asked Larkyns who he thought it was like and he'd replied, "You ought to know, Flo." *Torquemada probing beneath Edward's fingernails.* And then how Flora had looked down at the baby and told Larkyns that they would remember the thirteenth of July, wouldn't they? Now they had something to show for it. *So that was the day?* thought Edward, wincing in pain. Where was he on the thirteenth of July, eighteen seventy-three? Taking pretty pictures of Modoc Indians.

But Mrs. Smith had had more to tell, much more. *Torquemada tightening the thumbscrew.* How Flora had passed on to Larkyns nearly all the money Edward had given her – even passing on her diamond bracelet when the Major ran into financial difficulties. *That bracelet... the clasp broke, it's at the jewelers...* How she'd employed a Negro to carry letters between them as often as three times a day, and how she'd used the same Negro to fetch her lover's washing to have it done with Edward's. *Oh, Samuel... so that's what you were about?*

The very proper Mr. King had then probed for even juicier details, prompting Mrs. Smith to recall how frequently Larkyns had visited Flora in our bed-room, staying there for hours, kissing and caressing her. *The man about the new bell... the smell of a Havana...* "Where did he caress her?" the relentless King had asked over Stoney's vehement objections. Mrs. Smith had duly testified that she'd often seen Larkyns sitting at Flora's bedside when she lay exposed with her bedclothes pulled down as he kissed her naked breasts.

But soon, in spite of this depraved behavior and Edward's attorneys' frequent quotations from the Bible condemning adultery, it had become clear that things were not going well for the defense. So King and Pendegast had decided to add to their plea of justifiable homicide, the plea of insanity.

When back in his cell, Edward had protested violently; his attorneys had insisted it was his only hope.

Besides, Pendegast had added in his lilting Kentucky accent that so reminded Edward of Flora that it almost tore him apart, there was a sound basis for it: a medical man in France was talkin' of the possibility of different personalities inhabitin' the same being. Stevenson, a writer friend of his, was workin' on an idee-ah for a story along the same lines: inside every civilized man there lurked a monster.

"That is *fiction*," Edward had shouted again and again as they argued back and forth and the dirty white sacks floundered and writhed on the floor, the madwoman crumpling at his feet, her mouth stretched wide`. He was not insane, he was not! Even when Pendegast had shouted so loud he broke into a fit of coughing (had that been blood on his handkerchief?), no amount of lawyer logic could overcome his memory of a scream.

But at last, they had prevailed. It was this or the gallows.

Witness after witness had been called to attest to Edward's madness. Dr. Willard Parker, who had treated him in New York shortly after his stage-coach accident, had discussed the traumatic effects of his injuries. With the aid of medical charts and phrenological diagrams, he had shown that such injuries often resulted in aberrant behavior and personality abnormalities, especially if there was damage to the frontal lobe. This had later been confirmed of course by Mr. Madness himself, Dr. Gull.

King had then re-called Mrs. Smith to relate in a torrent of Cockney how his client's discovery of the "guilty letters" had "struck 'im dumb wiv grief, staggerin' and gaspin' and foamin' at the marf and then juss as suddly becomin' as cool as hice." (None of which Edward could deny.)

Next, Sarah Louisa had stepped up to corroborate much of what her mother had said about Edward's disturbed state of mind, his "eccentric habits" in business matters, his personal peculiarities, the disarray of his attire, his nervous excitability. *His Sarah Louisa siding with Flora against him yet again*! But of course, as Pendegast had kept assuring him, both mother and daughter were only doing their best to save him from the gallows. And it was true that Sarah Louisa had kept looking over at him with those big brown eyes as if begging forgiveness.

Then Rulofson: Edward cared nothing for worldly goods. Even though he could afford the finest food, he would insist on cooking his own simple meals, he could survive for days on a diet of raisins and cheese, with the live maggots still in the holes (as if Sarah Louisa hadn't scolded him enough about this). This habit, his counsels had insisted, could have done little for his mental well-being, and what about the neurotic effects of all those chemical vapors in the dark-room? Daguerre had been driven mad by mercury fumes, had he not, like the hatters who used it to cure beaver fur? Dodgson's Mad Hatter again. How ironic that Edward's last image of the Reverend had been of him raising his beaver topper. What price that sign in the hat band now?

As if raisins and maggots and poisonous vapors were not enough to unbalance a man, Rulofson had then produced a photograph of Edward teetering on the very tip of Contemplation Rock in the Yosemite, three thousand four hundred feet above the valley floor. "No sane man would venture there, much less have his picture taken," his attorneys had cried, as the photograph of Edward's microscopic self dangling his feet over the Land of the Gaping Mouths was passed round the jury.

A number of other witnesses had presented accounts of "aberrant behavior," including Mary Douglas who recalled Edward smashing Larkyns' stool to pieces at Black Tom's bar, raging as if he wanted to kill him on the spot. And as for the ferry, the way he'd run onto the dock, knocking people over like ninepins, then leaping onto the boat when it was already "ten yards" out, why, she'd thought he was going to kill *hissself*.

Finally, as the *pièce de résistance*, Rulofson had been brought back to relate how Edward had always refused to set foot in the studio elevator and yet had taken that very same elevator on the day of the homicide and had then run the length of twelve city blocks in under four minutes to catch the ferry. In fact, Rulofson concluded, it would take two years to tell all the reasons he had for believing in Edward's insanity. How he'd make a bargain one day and break or forget it the next and had done so thirty or forty times in the years they'd been working together. Or how when Charles Crocker questioned a bill for $700, Edward had dropped the matter rather than argue. Rulofson, of all people. The traitor.

Then had come Stoney's rebuttal, beginning with George Wolfe, who'd testified that while he was driving Edward up to Yellow Jacket, he had wanted to be sure his pistol wasn't fouled and had proceeded to fire it off with perfect calm. *Had he really done such a thing? He remembered none of this.* Next, William Stewart had said much the same regarding how cool Edward had been after killing Larkyns, handing over his gun like a lamb and bowing to the ladies, saying how sorry he was.

King had jumped on the "coolness" argument to maintain that this wild swinging between frenzied behavior and utter calm was the very definition of insanity.

But then came Stoney's star witness, Dr. Shurtleff from the Stockton Insane Asylum. He promptly demolished the insanity argument: truly insane people were never cool under any circumstances. Such demeanor was in fact the strongest possible evidence of *sanity*. Insane people didn't carefully plan and prepare for an act of violence as Edward had done and they didn't admit the act afterwards. Furthermore, there was no evidence whatever that sudden shifts in temper from icy calm to passionate frenzy were an indication of insanity.

And so it had gone, batting Edward's life about the court like a tennis ball, the spectators' eyes swinging back and forth between Stoney and King.

But it had soon begun to look increasingly like game, set and match for the prosecution. All the defense's hopes had rested on the closing statement of Wirt Pendegast, looking paler than ever, but also even more determined.

It had been as if the young man had climbed inside Edward's head, knowing exactly what he was thinking and feeling and then asking the jury to step in there with him, to become the man who had loved his wife with a deep passion and then all at once with a clap of thunder, "from a clear sky, came the revelation that his whole life was blasted."

The counsel for the prosecution, declared Pendegast had insisted said that in such a case "the wronged man must seek redress, if at all, accordin' to law, but you – " he strode close to the jury box – "you, the gentlemen of the jury, who are all married men, you who have daughters whom you cherish, mothers whom you reverence, wives whom you love, you gentlemen, would not say so."

He had then pointed at Edward and proclaimed that there was

"no law" for the avengin' of the wrongs he had suffered. Oh, there was a law in the Bible, "the man that committeth adultery with another man's wife, even he that committeth adultery shall surely be put to death." But that wasn't the law of California. They must put aside the Bible, it had never been written. Jesus Christ had never died on the cross. Christianity had never existed. There was no law because there was no need of it, no need of... and there his voice had dropped into his boots... *human* law.

Pendegast had then spun on his heel and marched towards a woman in the public gallery who was breast-feeding her baby. He'd looked down at her with a tremble in his voice as if he were on the verge of tears. "Neither was there a law to compel a mother to give her nourishment to her child though it perished for the want of it." All great lawyers must be great actors, thought Edward; Harry Edwards couldn't have done better.

Having prepared the ground, Pendegast had launched into his grand finale, "an astonishing display of sustained oratory" as the newspapers said, extolling the virtues of his client and damning the sins of Larkyns. This culminated by his saying that he couldn't ask the jury to send "the wronged man" back to a happy home; it had been utterly destroyed, but he could ask them to let him go forth – Edward remembered the exact words again – "among the wild and grand beauties of nature in his present and beloved profession, where he may perhaps pick up again a few of the broken threads of his life." At that point, Pendegast had left his longest pause of all. "Or send him to the gallows. Ye are the judges!"

"Mr. Klam."

"Present."

The Clerk of the Court was calling the jury roll.

"Mr. Hervy."

"Present."

Tapping. It was Edward's own foot, which apparently had a mind of its own.

The Clerk ignored it. "Mr. Anderson."

"Present."

Louder tapping.

Pendegast leaned close to him. "You've acted the man all through this, Muybridge. Don't fail me now."

Edward struggled to still his foot and whispered back: "I'm prepared for anything except what I most desire." But what did he desire? Once again, he was torn in two. He wanted to live and he wanted to die.

The Clerk looked over at the jury. "Gentlemen of the jury, have you agreed upon a verdict?"

Sam Newcomer stepped out of the jury box. "Yes, sir." He handed the Clerk a sheet of paper.

The Clerk read it, then brought it to the judge, who studied it for a moment, then asked, "Gentlemen of the jury, is this your verdict?"

"It is," said Newcomer.

"Record the verdict, Mr. Clerk."

The pen scarcely seemed to move, so slowly and deliberately did the Clerk bring the nib across the page, the faint scratch of steel on paper tearing at every nerve in Edward's body.

Finally, the pen stopped moving. The Clerk rose to his feet.

"Gentlemen of the jury, listen to your verdict as it stands recorded." He cleared his throat. "The People versus Edward James Muybridge. We, the jury in the above case, find the defendant... not guilty."

David Stansfield

142

PART TWO

David Stansfield

CHAPTER TWENTY-SIX

The next twenty-four hours were a blank: Edward knew nothing of how he got down from Napa after the trial, whether he went home or not, or where he spent the night. Dr. Gull had talked of his paramnesia, his illusionary state; this must have been a case of plain amnesia, dropping him out of the world as if he'd fallen down a rabbit hole. All he knew was that he was now sitting at a secluded table in a small restaurant in some remote part of San Franciso, face to face with the man who had saved his life.

"Have you seen your wife since the shootin'?" asked Pendegast.

"Have I seen my wife?" The question slowly sank in. Had Edward seen his wife? "No... and I don't expect or desire to see her. I know she's in the city, but we're now completely estranged."

"You know she's still filin' for divorce?"

Edward shrugged. What was this to him now?

"She intends to seize your cameras in order to secure alimony..."

Pendegast broke into a fit of coughing, covering his mouth with his handkerchief, splashing it with specks of blood. It hadn't been Edward's imagination in court. Pendegast was chalk white. It must be consumption.

"I'm so sorry, I had no idea you were – "

Pendegast waved Edward's concern for him aside. "As your attorney, I advise you to take all your photographic equipment with you on the voyage."

"What voyage?"

"To Guatamala. That's what I brought you here to talk about: your undertaking to photograph the coffee plantations of the Pacific Mail Steamship Company. You gave your word. It is imperative that you protect your good name."

"My good name? I can't even look people in the eye."

Pendegast smiled sadly. "I've noticed – you haven't looked directly at me since we sat down. Your eyes are forever wandering somewhere else."

"I have nothing left now. I have destroyed everything. I have nothing to live for – "

The other held up his hand. "I'm rather well qualified to talk about death, you know."

"But surely you could – "

The hand again. "There is no cure – "

" – the sanatoria, in Germany, they get wonderful results, they say, the fresh air… "

"It's too far advanced for that, I'm afraid." Pendegast looked into Edward's eyes. "Listen, Muybridge, I know you, I know that in spite of everything, you are a man of honor and a gentleman who has much of worth to give to the world. I also know the hardest blow for you has been to lose a baby boy you thought was yours. I too have a baby, a little girl… Janet… born just three weeks' past, and I will never…" He couldn't go on.

So Pendegast's emotion in the courtroom for the breast-feeding mother was genuine? Edward reached out to touch his sleeve. "I don't know what to say."

"Say nothin', just hear me out. Your task now is to learn to love life again, you have so much ahead of you, so much more you have to do, your motion study experiments – Stanford will surely be willin' to continue after things have quietened down a bit." He put his hand on Edward's arm. "That's why it's so important that you get away as far as you can from the scene of the horrors of the last few months and once again immerse yourself in your photography – now there's a therapy that *will* succeed."

CHAPTER TWENTY-SEVEN

How could they have found out? wondered Edward as he sat behind Wu and Lee in their skiff, which was moored in a secluded corner of the wharf at the foot of First and Brannan. He was training his telescope on the two men in business suits and toppers on board, the Pacific Mail Steamship Company's *SS Montana*, who were scrutinizing the male passengers as they mounted the gang plank. The two gentlemen in question were Flora's divorce-court bailiffs come to seize all Edward's photographic apparatus before he left the city. How surprised they would have been to know that that very apparatus was stowed just a few feet below where they were standing. With the connivance of the skipper, a old friend of Pendegast's, Joseph and Matthew had delivered a wagonload of crates the previous night and concealed every last item of Edward's equipment deep within the hold of *SS Montana* before concealing their own persons below decks to await their employer's arrival. Edward was disappointed that Arthur hadn't been able to accompany them because of his recent betrothal to Elsie – those ardent looks across the waiting room at the Summit Station having sparked a wedding. He prayed that Arthur's marriage would be more successful than his own.

Edward continued to watch as the last passenger finally came on board. The two bailiffs shrugged their shoulders in frustration and hurried down the gang plank as the ship's foghorn sounded.

He nodded to Wu and Lee, who untied the mooring rope and bent to their oars, the little boat sliding silently across the bay, hardly creating a ripple in the surface of the water, which was still as a mill pond tonight. Just to be on the safe side, Edward pulled his hat low and his coat collar high to go over his face. He felt like a secret agent, but you never knew who might be watching from the shore. He kept turning round. Thank goodness: no sign of another rowing boat. This fog was helping them too.

As previously arranged with the skipper, they rendezvous'd with the ship just as she was approaching the Golden Gate. The vessel slowed to a crawl and Wu and Lee hoisted Edward into the arms of Joseph and Matthew, who hauled him on board.

The next few weeks were as foggy for Edward as the Bay. Vague impressions of Cabo St Lucas and Acapulco, then heading down the coast for a reception kindly arranged for him by Pendegast in Panama City. The days became steadily hotter and the landscapes more tropical.

Edward returned to his motion experiments, using the lush scenes they were passing as his subject. But just as in the case of Occident, in spite of all the best efforts of Joseph and Matthew dashing to and fro between his camera and the make-shift dark-room in his cabin, he achieved little more than blurry outlines, not knowing whether this was from the unsteadiness of the ship or the tears running down his face.

By the middle of March, everything depressed Edward, even the view from the steamboat as they docked in Panama City: a vista of decaying churches and crumbling public buildings overgrown by vines and creepers as the jungle strangled the place. Stanford's doing! A few years back, the Trans-Panama Railroad had been the only overland route between the Atlantic and the Pacific, making the country rich. Then Stanford had struck his golden spike. Now the only movement along Panama's pot-holed streets was the lethargic ebb and flow of unemployed Negroes, Indians, mulattoes and Chinese. It was always those at the bottom who paid the price.

But the morning after their arrival presented a very different picture. Edward found himself facing what looked like half the Panamanian army – in smart uniforms and bare feet – manning a long row of cannons lined up in front of the cathedral in La Plaza de Armas behind a constellation of generals smothered in gold braid. It was a reception committee in Edward's honor, welcoming him to the city with a volley of fire so regular and rapid it was hard to believe. It was as if the cannons were tied together like a bundle of dynamite rods. Afterwards, the generals kissed "Sr. Don

Eduardo Santiago Muybridge" on both cheeks.

Edward dutifully filled his days pleasing his hosts with *vistas fotographicas de nuestra Republica:* Panama's crumbling bridges, pre-Columbian ruins, rusting railway lines and the two-hundred-year-old remains of Captain Morgan's castle. All conventional views he could have taken in his sleep. Even the exploding colors of the countless species of tropical trees and plants and animals were as gray to him as his photographs.

A letter arrived from Sarah Louisa, forwarded by the steamship company. At first, Edward didn't want to open it. The infernal cheek of the woman. But she'd been his devoted assistant for all these years. He should at least give her the benefit of the doubt. He tore open the envelope. The first sentence wiped everything else from his mind. Pendegast had died two days after Edward left San Francisco.

This shocked him out of his self-pity. He scarcely noticed Sarah Louisa's profuse apologies that followed. His poor friend. Never again would Pendegast see the beauty of a landscape, smell the perfume of flowers, hear the song of the birds, touch the skin of a woman. But *Edward* was not dead. Pendegast was dead. And Pendegast, God rest his soul, had been right, Edward did have a choice. *Learn to love life again, Edward, that is your task now, you have so much ahead of you, so much more to do.*

He mulled over this for most of the night. In the morning, when he opened the threadbare curtains of his hotel room, the view was astonishing: it was if Maxwell's color filters had been pasted over the glass. The drab desolation had been replaced by eye-ravishing colors and textures, luxuriant forms and shapes, a baroque extravaganza. How fast the man he had grown so fond of had been able to turn Edward's mood around, just as he had with the jury. Even from the grave, Pendegast had worked another miracle.

Now Edward couldn't wait to capture the beauty of this land in the way it deserved. He smashed his earlier uninspired plates, gathered his crew together, transferred his equipment to the backs of a team of mules and set out over the next few months to do exactly that.

After he had completed a panoply of views of Panama, they sailed back up the coast to Guatemala. Here, Edward not only photographed the entire process of coffee production at Las Nubes as requested by his sponsors, but myriad other scenes, ranging from a vanishing point perspective of an avenue of antique mausoleums to bare-breasted campesinas doing their laundry in a forest stream. He also sun-painted sweeping views of the capital from the heights of El Cerro del Carmen. One of these consisted of a small panorama of five stereo cards designed to be viewed through a stereoscope to create the illusion of being surrounded on all sides by Guatemala City. But the picture which pleased Edward most was of the ruined church of San Miguel soaring up into the sky, escaping from the riot of spiny leaves and the confusion of foliage tearing at its walls, while a little naked black girl stood guard like an ebony Beatrice.

Thinking ahead, Edward spent every spare moment of the next few months working to make his high-speed shutter function even faster. Eventually, with the help of Joseph and Matthew, he was approaching almost $1/1,000^{th}$ of a second.

CHAPTER TWENTY-EIGHT

In late August, there came a second letter from Sarah Louisa, along with a clipping from the *Chronicle*. Flora had died on July 18 at San Francisco's St. Mary's Hospital of "natural causes" variously described as "influenza, paralytic stroke, and a complication of spinal complaint and inflammatory rheumatism, which baffled the skill of physicians." The newspaper went on to report that "the poor woman was out of her mind a great portion of the time and was unconscious at the time of death." During Flora's illness, Sarah Louisa had taken Florado and left him in the care of a French family in the Mission district. At the end of the letter, Edward read through his tears that Flora's funeral had been handled by Crocker's nemesis, Nicholas Yung, who had also overseen her burial in the pauper's section of the Odd Fellows Cemetery. She was twenty-four. Her last words were "I am sorry."

Back in Panama City for *el Dia de los Muertos*, the day the dead came back to visit the living, The entire city was draped in black, a funereal backcloth for the gaping eyes, the grinning teeth, the rattling bones of the clockwork skeleton dancing on the bar, *las Calacas, las Calacas, las Calacas* as Larkyns strutted back and forth, slashing and slashing, the ball ranging inward and upward, worming its way clear through his body, the Aztec worm at the bottom of the bottles of mescal lined up before Edward now as he sank lower and lower. He hadn't touched alcohol since Stanford's dining car and was hardly touching it now, pouring it straight down his throat.

"I am sorry." Was she really sorry? Had she really still harbored feelings for him? What if she'd come to him to beg forgiveness before she'd died? At least she would have died in peace. Perhaps he could have nursed her back to health? Perhaps she wouldn't have died at all?

The walls of the filthy little cantina were spinning round Edward like a whirlpool of yellow bilge-water pulling him further and further down into death. First Larkyns dead, then Pendegast dead, now Flora dead, all dead now on *el Dia de los Muertos*, the day the dead came back to visit the living.

Flora and Larkyns were sitting on the bed in the corner of the bar. Of course they were sitting there, for they will never really die, will they? Edward's life's work, his photography, preserved them forever. Like formaldehyde, like the bands of linen wrapped round the Egyptian mummies, embalming them all in sun and silver nitrate, the camera had defeated death, defeated time, made them all immortal. If he'd had his camera when he'd shot Larkyns, at the very moment he'd died, he wouldn't have died at all, would he? Edward would have undone murder. Larkyns was dead, *click*, long live Larkyns.

He staggered to his feet. He, Sr. Don Eduardo Santiago Muybridge, the man of a thousand names, not one of them worth a damn, let us salute him, fire all the cannons, fire every single one, *bang, bang, bang, bang*, for this is *el Dia de los Muertos* and Larkyns is dead, God Save the King. Now they were moving, Flora and Larkyns. He could capture that too, couldn't he? A microscope can see what is small, a telescope what is far, and his camera what is fast. It didn't matter how fast they moved, he could capture it all, capture everything, stop it stone dead. All the world was a bird, to stop stone dead.

But what were they doing now? Why was Flora naked, her burial shroud drawn down to her waist? Edward had never photographed her naked, she would never have let him, however much he'd begged, although he would never have begged, of course. He wasn't his father.

So what were they doing? What was Larkyns doing? Why was he cupping her white breasts in his hands?

Edward charged across the filthy spinning room, diving at Larkyns, smashing his fists again and again into the grinning face. Then hands were grabbing his waist, pulling him away. His own hands stretching out for her, her flesh coming away in his fingers, dissolving into a whisp of white smoke, whisping back into the bed... into the grave... into the empty bar.

Then the hands were lifting him, carrying him out of the dark. The drawn faces, the voices: "Worst I've ever seen him... high fever... local doctors can do nothing... ... call the steamship... I don't know if he'll live..."

Who were they, these men? He knew them yet he didn't know them.

Then there was nothing.

Then, much, much later, an eternity later, another voice joined in. "Since he received the letter?... two months... every night... the worst...?"

Burning, burning... not the burning of Heaven that Flora had induced in his limbs, this was the true burning of Hell the Church had always threatened him with. They had been right along, hadn't they? Everyone had been right all along. When would it stop?

Then at last – after hours? days? months? years? eons? – the yellow brimstone gradually, gradually became sweet white jasmine as Edward felt her hand, her sweet white hand.

He took a gulp of pure fresh air. Joseph removed his hand from his forehead, Matthew took his pulse. They were smiling.

Joseph's eyes brimmed. "The fever's gone, Mr. Muybridge. Oh, thank God."

"Fifty-two beats per minute, sir, perfect for your age," said Matthew.

His body was dry. His flesh was cool. His head was clear. His voice was calm. "How long was I – ?"

"Six days and nights," said Matthew, ever the one for counting.

CHAPTER TWENTY-NINE

A few days later, after nearly nine months' absence, Edward was finally embarked on his return voyage to San Francisco aboard another of the steamship company's vessels, the *SS Constitution*. Now all he was burning with was the desire to continue his work with Stanford as soon as possible and to focus his full attention on motion photography – assuming the Governor wasn't still too offended by the scandal of the trial, that is.

Over the next two weeks of the voyage, thanks to his even faster shutter and an even better combination of chemicals (after much experimenting, he had found that adding a small amount of iron was most beneficial), Edward was soon taking clearer and clearer views of the passing palm trees.

They dropped anchor in late November. Chinese porters, hotel runners and crowds of friends and family waited for their loved ones. But no one waited for Edward. He might as well have never lived here, the hole created by his absence had closed up like a perfectly healed wound. Joseph had replied to Sarah Louisa's last letter on his behalf when he was still in a fever telling her the date of his return, but it seemed she hadn't come, nor shared this information with anyone else in the city.

As he walked down the gang plank, a dark-haired young woman ran out of the crowd. She had come! Sarah Louisa grabbed his arms as if she were drowning, opening her mouth to speak, no words coming out. They stared at each other. He was riveted by those sad brown eyes, all the shouting and cursing and banging of packing cases around him falling away. He'd forgotten just how tall she was, so much taller than Flora, they were on almost exactly the same level. But she had aged, the frown on her face drawing wrinkles all across her forehead. How old was she now? She must have been nearly thirty-five.

He broke the silence. "The past is past, Sarah Louisa. We're making a fresh start now. And I need your help more than ever.

154

Did you order a cab?"

The wrinkles melted into a smile. "I did better than that."

A black box on wheels clattered towards them, a grinning Arthur at the reins and the golden words: *Helios, The Flying Studio.*

As they made their way through the streets, Edward told her of his plans. "So much to discuss, Sarah Louisa, I hardly know where to start."

"Why don't we begin by stopping by the studio to say hello to Rulofson and the others?"

"I'm not going back to Rulofson's – "

"What?"

"It's a long story"

"But what will you do if you leave the gallery? Where will you go?"

"I'm going to start a gallery of my own – "

"Oh, really?" Her voice sank. "That's splendid, but – "

"And I want you to join me, if you're willing – "

"Oh, yes, of course," her voice rose several octaves, "wherever you go, I – "

"Well, I'm not sure yet exactly where I'll set up, but I expect I could rent a space, perhaps on Clay Street, I've always liked that area. Once that's done, my first task – *our* first task – will be to make prints of all the plates I took in Central America and mount them. It's a great deal of work, there are nearly five hundred. I want to bind the best ones into albums and send them to Pendegast's widow, my other two attorneys, the steamship company, and Mrs. Stanford – perhaps she can help me with the Governor."

"Oh Edward, I can hardly wait to get started!"

"And I want to do something new. I want to transfer some of my images of Panama and Guatemala to glass slides and give a lantern exhibition at the next meeting of the Photographic Art Society – there should be one coming up in January. It's almost like a theatrical event."

Edward felt her lean closer to him. Her perfume. What was it?

"I'll never forget our theater evenings."

Jasmine… it was jasmine. He shuddered.

She pulled back. "I'm sorry, I'm sorry, Flora gave me some of her perfume. I'm sorry, I didn't think."

"Please don't wear it again."

"I promise."

Edward shut out the memories by concentrating on maneuvering the carriage through the thick stream of traffic.

"But if ever you don't have enough for me to do," murmured Sarah Louisa, "while you were away, I learned another occupation: telegraph operator. They're hiring more and more women now, you know. Arthur and Elsie taught me the Morse code when I went over to help with the baby."

"My goodness, Arthur a father?"

"Yes, an adorable little boy – which reminds me," she added quickly, "I need to talk to you about Florado."

Florado… He really didn't want to hear that name, any more than he wanted to smell the boy's mother's perfume. He calmed himself. "I wanted to thank you for placing him with that French family."

"I was pleased to help, but since I wrote to you, these kind people were finding it somewhat of a financial burden and – "

"Oh, of course, yes. I'll reimburse them naturally." Edward sighed: one more item on his long list of things to do.

"It was especially a burden because of all the doctor's bills."

"Has he been ill?"

"Well, not physically."

"What do you mean?"

"They suspected he may not be quite right in the head, a little slow – they even consulted an alienist at one point – "

In spite of himself, Edward burst into laughter.

"What's so amusing?"

"Larkyns – the man of all talents, the true renaissance man – fathering an idiot! I'm sorry. It's too rich."

"They didn't go that far, it was just that he's not been developing as rapidly as a normal infant of his age – he's twenty months now – and, well, they ended up moving him to a Catholic orphanage."

"And so? What is your point?"

"Well, I thought you'd have preferred he be brought up in the Protestant faith, like yourself."

Edward felt a sudden spasm of anger. "He is not my son!" He corrected himself. "No, that's cruel; the poor little chap, born with a handicap, it's no fault of his. But the fact remains, he was fathered by… "

He couldn't finish. But he didn't need to; they were at South Park.

CHAPTER THIRTY

Something soft and cool with the scent of jasmine was wiping his forehead. *Flora!* He opened his eyes. Sarah Louisa was leaning over him. He was lying on the lounge in his parlor covered by a blanket.

He sat up.

"You fell asleep, almost as soon as you sat down. You must be so exhausted after that long voyage."

He lay down again. She was right, he really was exhausted.

Sarah Louisa settled into an armchair.

There was a long silence.

At last, she broke it. "I know you said the past was past, but I'm so ashamed for my part in all this. I'm so sorry. Will you ever forgive me? But she was my closest friend. I was torn." She banged her fist up and down on the arm of the chair. "Stupid Sarah, stupid Sarah."

"But the past really is past, Sarah Louisa."

"Even though it wasn't quite what you thought it was."

"What do you mean?"

"Oh, nothing, nothing."

Now he was wide-awake. "Tell me."

"Well, even Larkyns – "

"Even Larkyns what? It's all right. Time heals."

"No, I know, but it's nothing, really."

"Tell me. *Even Larkyns what?*"

"Well, those 'guilty' letters – you only read in them what you wanted to read – or what you dreaded to read, the parts about Flora's infidelity, but you passed over the rest. You know why Larkyns wrote those letters to my mother and me about her?"

"Because he was having an affair with her and wanted to see her. I can remember Larkyn's exact words: 'I have been so worried about that poor girl that I cannot rest.'"

"You should have read on. He was worried about her because he was afraid of losing her. He went on to say he'd found out that the minstrels would soon return from Portland on the next steamer, but he could not and would not believe anything so bad as that 'rumor.'"

"The minstrels…" *Wilson's All-Star Minstrels... in Belmont Park… Wilson the bandleader… his fine figure, his perfect bone structure…* Even when she was with Larkyns, she had an eye for other men.

"It appears she was as unfaithful to Larkyns as she was to you."

His head felt it had been put through a mangle. "It's as if everything I love has been stolen from me twice."

"Not quite everything." Her voice was very soft. "There's still Florado. We can take him back – "

"*We?*"

The splash of color on her neck turned purple. "Don't you understand?"And then finally he did. He who lived by his eyes, how could he have been so blind to so many things, and perhaps above all to this?

He reached out to touch her. "I'm so sorry, Sarah Louisa."

"All these years, didn't you know that I… Why do you think I never married? Didn't you ever think about that? Didn't you think that was strange? I had my chances, you know, I had my chances." She slumped into an armchair and began to cry.

He fought to control his own tears. "There is – was – only one woman in my life, Sarah Louisa, only one great love – at least I thought it was a great love… I'm so sorry."

Her heaving chest, the quiver of her shoulders. He started to reach out for her again, but hesitated now, remembering. "But Harry Edwards, weren't you going to – I mean, I thought – "

"So did I. I thought he was the man – I mean, after Flora and you… I believed everything he said…" she looked back into the past, "from the moment we first met after the theater that night and then afterwards at the Poodle Dog…" She closed her eyes. "I drank so much. But he was so charming, so witty, he kept reciting the most wonderful passages from Shakespeare. You'd swear he really *was* Othello, Macbeth, Hamlet, Heaven knows who else. I – I was bowled over – well, almost – and…" She looked at Edward, appealing to him. "He was my only hope, my last chance. "ouse to get, furniture to buy, man to get in the mind o'ot,' as Mother always says." She slipped back so easily into the Cockney. "She was always saying that to me, going on and on at me to find a man… Anyway, after that night, Harry wanted to spend every free moment with me, we went everywhere together. He called me his queen… Then suddenly he had to go off with his stock company to the East Coast and he was away for months and months. But he kept writing to me and saying he was going to make me his wife. When he did eventually come back, we started up again, and I was only waiting for him to name the day. But the day kept being put off and put off for one trip after another. He was almost never there."

Just like Flora and himself, thought Edward. Was he just another Harry Edwards?

"He kept stringing me along with his letters, pouring out his heart to me… and then… suddenly, the letters stopped, not a word. I kept writing and writing and he never answered."

"So that was the end of it?"

"Not quite. After the Major was – well, I heard Harry had rushed back here from New York to read the eulogy at the funeral. So I had no choice but to try to confront him. Everyone was there, all the actresses and… Lotta Crabtree," she forced the name through her teeth, "sitting there all decked out in her man's suit, making cow's eyes at Harry as he gave the oration. Always wearing a man's suit. What's the matter with her?" She grunted. "And always after money. I remember Harry saying once – " she tried to imitate a booming histrionic voice: "'It is perfectly clear that Lotta can never extract enough from those around her – not for nothing is she a miner's daughter: the perfect gold-digger.' Haha. He always thought he was so droll.

"Well, she was digging what she could out of him, and no mistake. After we came out of the church, I looked everywhere for him, but he'd completely disappeared. I ran out into the street – and there he was handing Lotta into her carriage and climbing in beside her. 'Don't they make a lovely couple?' one of the actresses said, as the Stage-door Johnnies harnessed themselves to the shafts to pull her through the streets – they always did that with Lotta – before the footman could hitch up the horses. I could hear his voice right to the end of the street, quoting from his damned Shakespeare as she laughed and laughed... I could have killed her – I could have killed them both – oh, sorry, Mr. Muybridge."

Edward had never heard her make such a long speech. He took her hand. "Poor Sarah Louisa... How terrible... So then it really was over?"

"I never saw him or heard from him again. I've been alone ever since."

There was another long silence.

He tried to cheer her up. "Do you know what the Greek word for actor is?"

"No."

"Hypocrite."

"Well, he was that all right. But there was one bright point at the funeral, there was the great... 'hypocrite' – pompous old ass, I don't know how I ever fell for him, well, I do – but there he was, standing up at the pulpit blathering on and on about Larkyns being a gentleman in the truest sense of the word, distinguished upon the battle-field, superior to everyone else in manliness and honor, you've never heard such nonsense... and suddenly a scrawny little man stands up and everyone starts whispering and pointing, 'There's Cuspidor, there's Cuspidor.'"

"Coppinger!" He kept popping up in Edward's life like a bad penny. "What was Coppinger doing there? He hated Larkyns after what he did to him."

"Vengeance is sweet."

"What do you mean?"

"Cuspidor – Mr. Coppinger – strides the entire length of the church, bold as brass, amongst all these people – there must have been five hundred at least, it was packed – and he goes right up to the open casket – you've never seen such a handsome affair, all rosewood and silver, heaped with flowers – and he stares down at the dead man and he says – I'll never forget his words: 'There's a special Providence in the killing of this man! I'd walk twenty miles on the stormiest night that ever was seen to gaze on this sight!' And do you know what he does then?"

Edward almost felt like smiling. "I think I know what's coming."

"He spits all over Larkyns' face."

There was another long silence.

Sarah Louisa started to sob quietly again, talking through her tears, her hair falling across her face. "I don't ask anything, you know. Just to be with you – just to – " She pulled her hair aside, her big brown eyes crying out to him. "We work well together well, don't we?"

"We do indeed. Very well."

"So I can continue to be – "

"Yes, of course, you're the best assistant anyone could want, Sarah Louisa... and... and you're very dear to me, you're like the sister I never had."

She sat up straight, drying her eyes with a handkerchief, slipping back into her accustomed role. "So now... Florado... What are we going to do?"

Suddenly, Edward could hardly keep his eyes open. "Oh, I don't know, I don't know... I'm so tired..."

Gently, she pushed him back down on the lounge. "Of course you are, that long voyage... and the letter... Sleep now. You must sleep. A good night's rest is what you need. Up to bed with you."

Another smell now, the smell of England: the hot cup of tea that Sarah Louisa was setting down beside Edward's bed.

"Tea? I haven't had a good cup of tea for so long. Thank you."

"Mother used to do for a gentleman back in the old country and she taught me just how they like it. Bring the pot to the kettle, milk in first. One lump or two?"

She even had sugar cubes. "One please."

He took a sip. She was quite right. It was perfect.

The crackle of burning coal made him sit up in bed. She'd already got a fire going in the little grate in the bedroom – a welcome sight on a chilly November – what? morning? Yes, there was the morning sun smiling at him now as she opened the curtains. "But you shouldn't be waiting on me. I have the girl – by the way, where is Lily?"

Sarah Louisa laughed. "You've been away for a long time, Mr. Muybridge. Lily left some months ago and Mother and I took the liberty of coming in every few days to look after the house while you were gone. I hope you don't mind?"

"Another liberty?"

Her face dropped.

Edward smiled reassuringly. "No, of course, I don't mind. I'm teasing you, forgive me. It's a great comfort, what you're doing, it truly is, but of course I won't be keeping the house…"

She nodded slowly. "I understand. But where will you go?"

"I don't know, I can always take a couple of the rooms at my new studio – wherever it ends up being."

"But Florado – "

"I know. I kept waking during the night. I couldn't stop thinking about him." *Never, ever hurt another human being* "But… this is so terrible to say, but I can't take him in. I can't bring him up as my son – "

"But Mother could continue to come in to help and – "

"No, he was fathered by another man, we can't change that. Raising the son of the man who stole my wife, the man I shot in cold blood, the poor boy would be the laughing stock of California. I can't do that to him. An innocent little boy. And all my fault."

Sarah Louisa tried to break in. He held up his hand. "No, no, the whole tragedy began when I found that awful photograph that was brought about by my neglecting Flora, by my always putting my work before her. I know that now. Ultimately, the whole terrible affair was my fault. I don't intend to repeat that same mistake with my son, Sarah Louisa. He could be destroyed by it. No, the kindest thing I can do for Florado is precisely not to bring him up myself. All I can do is make sure he is well looked after and is never in want."

"But my mother and I could bring him up – "

"No, no, no, if you want to continue working closely with me –

and I sincerely hope you do – you'll be associated much too closely with me to have Florado on your hands, it would be too great a burden."

"But – "

"No more buts – I've thought it through, believe me. I'll go to the Catholic orphanage tomorrow and settle the financial side of things and then, when the boy's a little older, as you suggested, I'll transfer him to a Protestant orphanage, and subsequently find some new foster parents for him."

"But his name? What name will he go by?"

"He shall continue to be known as Florado Muybridge. At least I can give him that."

CHAPTER THIRTY-ONE

Imagine a small ant wishing to get a comprehensive view of a painted Japanese dinner-plate. He'd succeed if he could get a thimble upright in the middle of the plate, then climb to the top of the thimble and look by turn in every direction. The ant was Edward, the saucer was San Francisco and the thimble on which he was perched was the turret of Mark Hopkins' Nob Hill mansion, which towered over the corner of California and Mason. The rim of the saucer was decorated with various ridges and spurs: Point Bonita, the Golden Gate, Tamaulipas, Sonoma, Napa, San Ramon, Mt. Diablo, Telegraph Hill, Rincon Hill, and so on, in a perfect circle of views. Within the confines of this saucer, the homes of more than a quarter of a million people were distinctly visible.

What was not visible in the eleven 8 X 10 inch plates Edward was in the process of exposing in his 360° sweep of the city were the people themselves; the streets appeared as empty as if it were two in the morning. In order to capture every detail of every cornice stone, attic window and chimney, he'd slowed his exposure to such an extent that no movement could be captured, wiping out all trace of humanity. Far from instantaneous, these views were glacial, just like his own high-speed photographic career, for he'd come full circle, going from one extreme to the other, from nearly $1/1,000^{th}$ of a second to several minutes for each picture, traveling back in time to where he'd started. If he could not go fast, he must go slow.

Was this yet another unconscious echo of Flora? *To explore your city, go up and down all the highways and byways, climb all the hills, every rooftop, every chimney, every avenue, every alleyway, every passage.* Is this why he put so much effort into this monumental project? He did his best to bury the thought.

Or was he fulfilling his young man's dream of creating his own version of a revolving Camera Obscura, taking Guatemala City to the next level?

Or − yet another possibility − was he simply driven to make such busy work by his frustration that after thirteen months back in the city there was still no word from Stanford? Although during all this time he'd been so often at Hopkins' house, only a stone's throw from the Governor's finally completed home, each of his requests for an interview had been blocked by Stanford's private secretary − who'd turned out to be none other than Edward's old crony from the Olympic Club, young Frank Shay.

How Frank and he used to chatter like schoolboys about their biceps, wondering if they'd ever equal those of the club strong man, Louis Brandt. But in spite of their friendship, Frank had been obliged to offer so many excuses for his master that Edward was beginning to wonder whether the Governor was avoiding him deliberately: the Stanfords were out of town visiting friends, they were touring the country in search of yet more thoroughbred horses, they were off on yet another buying spree in New York for yet more marble statues for their new mansion. There seemed to be no limit to the thousands of miles that man would travel and the millions of dollars he would spend to prove over and over again that he was the richest, the most powerful, the most successful, etcetera, etcetera. If he thought a vase would impress visitors in the vestibule, it had to be the largest most expensive vase in the world − $100,000 they said he'd spent on the last one − but it wasn't any old giant $100,000 vase, it had to be a Sèvres vase, and not any old Sèvres vase, it had to be the very Sèvres vase that Marie-Antoinette gave to the Marquis de Villette. There was obviously no bottom to the depths of feelings of inferiority Stanford was struggling to overcome. For that's what it was, of course. Edward could see right through the man. Of course he could. Because Stanford was just like him − or at least the way Edward was before his stage-coach accident and immediately after the Larkyns affair.

However, the Governor was still not willing to see him. He still had to keep on waiting. His only consolation was that in all other respects his career had been steadily gathering momentum − thank the Lord there hadn't been a single mention of the murder trial in any of the newspapers. Sarah Louisa had settled down and seemed content to be simply a good friend and loyal assistant, often coming home with him in the evenings (Helios concealed a multitude of social sins) to sit by the fire in his parlor for a couple of hours to discuss how their day had gone. Although he still intended to move out of the South Park house, of course, as soon as he had time. And the old team of Joseph and Arthur and Matthew were also still with him, as were Wu and Lee when he needed them for the really heavy work.

So much accomplished since he'd returned from South America, beginning with his lantern exhibition at the Photographic Art Society last January, which, thanks to Arthur's able assistance, had been a great success. He'd seen various magic lantern projections back in England, from painted slides on Biblical subjects to educational drawings at the Royal Polytechnic, but the effect of throwing his own photographic images of real-life scenes in Panama and Guatemala clear across a darkened room to land in a dazzling circle of light on a large white screen struck him as another level of experience altogether. Even the magic lantern itself was a thing of wonder: a brass box on stilts with a hole in the front for the lens and a little chimney on top like a toy steam engine. He'd had no hesitation in following up with more such exhibitions, especially as Arthur had taken so well to the whole affair. He not only played limelight man with the hissing oxy-hydrogen torch, and deftly changed the slides when Edward pressed his steel clicker, but he'd also revealed a diplomatic side. When the bright red hydrogen cylinder had suddenly given a little pop during one performance, Arthur had calmed the nerves of some of the elderly female spectators by assuring them that although the press liked to make a sensation out of the very few times a lantern illuminant exploded, there was absolutely nothing to fear on this occasion.

Meanwhile, Edward had outfitted his new studio on Clay Street with the latest equipment and secured a number of new commissions – nothing from the finest families yet, but still very gratifying. With Sarah Louisa, he'd also processed all of his South American plates and completed all the special albums, eliciting showers of praise from their recipients. The note from Mrs.

Stanford had been particularly kind, "no more beautiful examples of your work exist." And not a single grammatical error or malapropism. Shay must have helped her.

Then there was this mighty panorama of course, not even finished yet, but already being hailed by the Hopkins family — who'd been peeking at the negatives all day — as the greatest achievement of its kind.

It was ironic that Hopkins' mansion had ended up several feet taller than Stanford's after all that Great Man's boasts, and right next door too. So near and yet so far.

CHAPTER THIRTY-TWO

Some four months later, Edward was driving up Laguna Street to the Protestant Orphan Asylum, having asked the Catholic one to deliver Florado there just before his arrival so that he could formally transfer the boy. And there it was, looming over the horizon at Haight and Buchanan like a gothic castle. He'd photographed this eyesore some years before precisely because it was so ugly – odd that ugliness pushed far enough, so often turned back into beauty, like the mad woman of Bedlam. Since his first visit the gardeners had done their best with the flowers and the shrubbery to make the grounds "a homelike abiding place" as it said in the prospectus, but its prison-like air was only reinforced by the twelve-foot high stone fence designed to keep in its two hundred juvenile "inmates," poor waifs who'd either lost their mothers or been deliberately lost *by* their mothers.

But the most depressing sight of all was what greeted Edward as he entered the lobby.

Florado was beaming up at him. For a moment, he was back beside his baby crib. He leaned down to touch the little boy's cheek just as he had done the last time he saw him, two and a half years ago. His miniature arms fastened onto Edward's leg, tight as an octopus. "Dadah, badah, dadah, badah, dadah, badah," he chanted over and over again. What was he trying to say? "Dadah, badah?" Was he a bad dada? Dadah, badah," on and on, like a clockwork toy. Why didn't he stop? This boy who had been his, and then not his, and now he realized, not anybody's. For the little boy who was beaming up at him was not seeing him at all; he wasn't seeing anyone; only the walls of his own lonely world that would confine him for the rest of his life more surely than any stone fence. Something in the birthing, something passed down, as the English scientist Francis Galton had suggested in his optimistic writings about how we would one day by careful selection be able to breed for intelligence and to breed out such unfortunate "accidents" as Florado. Whatever the case might be "one day," all Edward could think now was: so this is the boy I'd so looked forward to fathering? The boy whose baby photograph had driven me to murder? He knelt down to clasp Florado in his arms.

"He's a good boy, the people at the Catholic Orphanage tell me," the Head of the Protestant Asylum, Mrs. Ella NcNeal, said, as she gently prized Florado's arms loose from Edward, "always smiling, always willing to do any little thing to help."

Edward stood up and turned away, trying to disguise the heaviness in his chest and the sting in his eyes, knowing that in spite of all his best intentions, he would never again be able to bear the sight of this poor lost child. He would never again be able to bear to visit him.

CHAPTER THIRTY-THREE

Two more months passed before Edward finally found himself riding the little cable car to see the Governor for the first time in three years. Could this visit to his Nob Hill mansion possibly end as disastrously as his first one? He glanced round the car. There was no smartly dressed man with a brief-bag on his knees and a tic douleureux in his cheek; only an elderly couple sharing a newspaper. Come on! He had to pull himself together. He was nearing his goal at last, the goal that would surpass everything else he had accomplished. Not that everything else hadn't continued to go well. His panorama had been published by Morse's Gallery and had amazed everyone who saw it. When he'd set it up in a circle in his studio and had turned around inside it, although there was no movement in the individual panels, the entire city had seemed to revolve around me, as though he were inside more than a Camera Obscura, more like a *Daedalum*, or *Zoetrope*, as they now called it, a Wheel of Life, sounding so much better than the old Devil name as a demonstration of the persistence of vision. Persistence had also turned out to be the key to achieving his dream. Just when he'd almost given up hope of an interview with Stanford, a few days ago Shay had informed him that the Governor had acceded to his latest – and what he'd decided would be his last – request.

Ah, here we are. At the top of Nob Hill. Again. Now for it!

Edward leaped off the cable car. It was all he could do not to run up the marble entrance stairs to ring the massive doorbell. The double doors swung open and the butler led him through the vestibule, across a twenty-foot mosaic dog named "Fidelity" beneath a white, blue and gold ceiling representing the world's continents and a gargantuan oil painting of a cornucopia labeled "Abundance," "Pax Vebi," and "Welcome to Visitors." At last, they reached the largest private library he'd ever seen, its soaring rows of rare books sealed up tight as Pharaohs.

Governor Stanford held out his hand. "Good morning, Mr. Muybridge." He gestured to a deep leather armchair. "I trust you are well?"

"Oh, yes, very well, thank you, Governor."

"After your ordeal."

"I am quite recovered, thank you."

"I am not."

Oh God, here it comes.

"Quite frankly, Muybridge, I was deeply concerned over the whole affair… " He paused to light a cigar. "But at the same time, I feel somehow responsible."

What? Responsible? Of all the scenarios Edward had imagined, he had never imagined this.

"I was so caught up in our experiments that I did not follow your home life, Muybridge. Had I done so, I would have stepped in to warn you of what was happening, how the zeal and deep study you were giving to our work was blinding you to – well, too much has already been said about the whole affair. I knew Larkyns was a strange mixture of a man, but I had no idea he would behave so disgracefully."

Excitement swept over Edward. Stanford was on his side!

"But now to business. What brings you up here, Muybridge?"

Or was he? "Didn't Mr. Shay tell you?"

"No – or if he did, I have no recollection of it. I am a very busy man."

"Well, Governor, when we last spoke – you remember before the – well, you said that since our first photograph of Occident was so blurred – "

"It achieved everything I wanted to do at the time."

"Yes, it did, yes, that's perfectly true, but you said that the next step must be to take a really clear picture of Occident's stride as support for a scientific theory of horse training, perhaps eventually even a series of pictures of every phase of his stride.

Stanford looked puzzled. "Did I? Well, I suppose I may have said something of the sort, but get to the matter."

"You also said that I was the only man you knew who could do it. I did some very rapid work on my way back from the southern country and – "

The Governor laughed. "Ah, yes, but things have changed, have they not? The scandal – it is over now of course, I have made sure that no newspaper will ever mention the dreadful affair again." *So that explained the silence following the trial; he even controlled the newspapers!* "But my friends have all cautioned me to – well, quite frankly, they have cautioned me to stay well away from you."

"Yes, but Governor, I was hoping that the success of my panorama and my views of Central America – they are all over-subscribed, you know – would help me – "

Stanford gave him a knowing smile. "So that is why you sent the album to my wife?"

"No, not at all, it was a gesture of thanks to you and your family for your support." The man was a kitten playing with a mouse. Edward wasn't sure he could stand much more of this.

"Leland," came a female voice.

Mrs. Stanford entered the room, holding out Edward's album as she walked straight up to him. "Mr. Muybridge, some of them photographs was amongst the finest what I hever seen. I tickly liked your views of the Church of San Miguel with the little black girl. White people should never be seen naked, but among savages such impositions are natural and expected. Even when they're naked, they ain't, if you see what I mean. Like the animals. Anyways, congratulations, you're such a remorseful man. And thanks again for the gift." She turned to her husband. "I do hope you and Mr. Muybridge will have the opportunity to work together again real soon, Leland."

Her husband bowed to her. "Yes, well, that is just what we were discussing, my dear."

"Oh, he has a preposition for you? Splendid." She nodded to Edward as she turned to go. "Well, I'll leave you to it. Good day, Mr. Muybridge."

Stanford humphed into his beard. "Listen, Muybridge, upon reflection, perhaps my dear wife is right, I have not had much time to think about it recently, with forty or more enterprises going full blast, you will understand – " A condescending chuckle. "Or perhaps you will not. But it is true that I would be interested in obtaining a clearer picture of Occident's stride. Do you think you can do it?"

"Yes, Governor, I do," said Edward, resisting an urge to punch him.

"But I am taking a deliberate social risk, Muybridge, you do understand that, do you not?"

"Yes, Governor." Bite your lip.

"On the other hand, if you succeed, it will perhaps go some way to help bring you back into public life. I want you to report with your equipment and your assistants to the Sacramento race course next Monday morning."

And so Edward did. And so did almost the same collection of well-heeled turfmen and down-at-heel sports reporters who had witnessed his foggy picture of Occident five years before. Only Stanford was absent, having been called away on some "urgent business matter," a euphemism for buying more gewgaws, no doubt.

This time Edward's shutter was twice as fast and seemed to perform perfectly as Occident pulled his sulky in front of his camera at a cracking pace.

As before, all now hung on whether or not he could produce a clear negative in his dark-room. He prayed that his new mix of chemicals would prove to be as superior to his previous efforts as his shutter.

The newspapers' reaction to "Occident Photographed at Full Speed" told the whole story as Sarah Louisa prepared to read extracts to Edward over a cup of tea beside his parlor fire. She had been keeping a scrapbook of every one of his press clippings since eighteen sixty-eight and now she slipped the rubber band off the well-worn volume with its mottled board covers and dark green leather spine. She flipped past Yosemite and Alaska, the first pictures of Occident, Modoc Indians, railroads, measuring out Edward's life in newsprint before leapfrogging a murder to land in Panama and Guatemala, and finally onto Occident again.

"Mr. McCrellish writes in the *Alta California,*" said Sarah Louisa, "that the negative was exposed to the light for 'so brief a time that the horse did not move a quarter of an inch. The photographer had made many experiments to secure the highest sensitiveness and the briefest possible exposure and the result was a novelty in photographic art, and a delineation of speed, which the eye cannot catch. At 2:27, the spokes of the sulky are invisible to the eye, as they spin around so fast that, taken separately, they are not distinguishable... without blur... '"

Edward smiled to himself. Had he not stopped the very wheels of the stage-coach now?

Sarah Louisa ran her finger down the page to another clipping. "*The Resources of California* says, ' ...every essential part, even to the wheel, the particles of dust flying from the horse's hoof... is perfect in its outline and marvelous in the absolute fidelity, as made by the unerring action of light when controlled by... '" she paused for effect, "'genius.'"

She put the scrapbook down with a sigh of satisfaction. "'Genius,' did you hear that, Mr. Muybridge, that's what I've always thought you were. Isn't this wonderful? What we've always dreamed of! The Governor must be so pleased."

"I hope so." Edward had sent him a print, but the only reply had been a cryptic message to come to see him tomorrow morning.

As Edward was ushered once again into the library, he found the Governor sitting with his back to him studying an enlarged print of his photograph of Occident.

Stanford turned slowly towards him, then rose to his feet, extended his arms, and grasped both of Edward's hands in his. "You have done it, now you have really done it, my dear Muybridge. Remarkable, quite remarkable. You know what we are going to do now?"

Edward was speechless.

"We are going to undertake a *full-scale* study of the horse in motion. We are going to take a series of instantaneous pictures showing the step of Occident at all the stages, one after the other, matching the speed of the horse."

Stanford dropped Edward's hands and started to stride up and down the room. "If we can achieve this, Muybridge, we can represent for the first time the *precise* differences in the motions of different horses, a matter of great interest to us horsemen. For trotters vary greatly in their action, as you know, one having his fore-leg straight when it touches the ground, another crooked, and so on."

He stopped and took Edward's hands again. "So I want you to think about how such an undertaking can be accomplished. This is extremely important to me, Muybridge. You understand? I will fund whatever is required. Money is no object."

CHAPTER THIRTY-FOUR

Edward couldn't sleep. How on earth was he going to take a whole *series* of split-second pictures, "one after the other, matching the speed of the horse?" It was all very well for Stanford to talk, but how was he actually going to do it? There wasn't even time to replace the plate once every minute, let alone many times a second. How was he going to do it? Over and over again, the same question pounding in his head.

He found himself repeating it yet again to Sarah Louisa one evening as she sat on the floor beside his armchair, her head resting on his knee. How comfortable it was to be with her; she was like an old pair of slippers. He would find it hard to spend an evening at home without her now. Especially when she cooked for him. Such mutton, such roast beef, such Yorkshire pudding. How English she still was after all these years. "Better than maggots and raisins," she liked to say, their old joke. She could always make him laugh with that. They were "advancing now to some kind of confidence," as Flora's favorite author, Jane Austen, had put it. Could their friendship ever be anything but platonic? Could he ever feel for Sarah Louisa what he'd felt for Flora? Or was he simply not attracted to her in that way? Was she, as he'd told her when they were first reunited after his return from the South Land, simply the sister he had never had? Tell her everything, yet give her nothing? Was it really just a question of inches, like Cleopatra's nose? If Sarah Louisa's had been a fraction less long and her chest a fraction less flat? If the two women in his life hadn't been such a study in geometry, the one with all the angles, the other with all the curves, what might his life have been?

"How in Heaven's name can I manage to take multiple pictures with a single camera in the space of a half a second?" he asked Sarah Louisa yet again.

"I don't know, but if anybody can solve the puzzle, you can. Persistence, that's all you need now." She looked up at him with a teasing smile. "You already have the genius part."

Edward smiled back. "Oh, you…" He gently lifted her head from his knee, rose to his feet and began to stride up and down the parlor. He was getting more and more like Stanford every day. But there must be a way…

A few minutes later, Sarah Louisa sat up straight. "You take two pictures at the same time for your stereo views, do you not?"

"Yes…"

"Using two lenses on the same camera?"

"Yes…"

"Well, why don't you invent a camera that has a multitude of lenses?"

He couldn't help laughing. "Like the eye of a honeybee. Now there's a creature equipped for motion studies." But perhaps she did have something. He sat down again and stared into the fire as she snuggled back into position. A camera with a multitude of lenses... Why not? If you could have two lenses, you could have three, four – perhaps as many as you wanted? But how to trigger them, that was the question… The flames were getting low, they needed a bit of bucking up as they used to say in England. Like him.

As if reading his thoughts, Sarah Louisa reached for the fire-iron and gave the coal a good poke. A crackle of sparks, a volley of tiny explosions: *snap, snap, snap*. He wondered if this coal was Wellington or Scotch Splint and if it perhaps originally came from J. Muggeridge & Sons? Funny, he'd never thought of that before: how far that coal might have traveled.

Then his own head was exploding. *"Snap, snap, snap… bang, bang, bang."* Edward snapped his fingers again and again. *Bang, bang, bang.* That's it!!"

She stared up at him. "That's *what?*"

"When I arrived in Panama City, there was a whole row of cannons lined up in the plaza to fire a salute for me. They went off so fast, like a single organism, you should have seen them."

"I'm sure I should, but – "

"A battery of cannons, don't you see? A battery of *cameras*. I just have to line up a battery of cameras. I won't do it with one camera, I'll do it with many cameras, as many cameras as it takes."

His heart sank. "But those cannons in Panama City, they went off one after the other in such perfect unison, such regularity, like a drum roll, I could never possibly duplicate that." Then a thought struck him. "But you know it was strange, it was as if they were firing themselves somehow… Now if I could get a series of cameras to fire themselves! *Bang, bang, bang…* But how?"

"Remember what you told me about that Locomotive you saw up in the Sierras and how it stopped itself – "

"Dr. Robinson's automatic block to avoid collisions?" It was all coming back to him. "What did Arthur say? They run a current up and down the rail and when the metal wheels of the train cross the wire, they complete the circuit and trigger the stop signal… "

Now Sarah Louisa jumped to her feet. "Sulky wheels have metal rims, don't they?"

"So when the horse pulls the sulky over an electric wire – "

" – a *series* of electric wires – "

" – a series of electric wires, yes, of course… " In a flash, Edward saw it all. He set to pacing once more. "The wheels complete the circuit – the horse takes it own picture again, in a sense – only multiple pictures now, one after the other, in rapid succession as it moves past the cameras… so simple…" He started to laugh. "So wonderful… But to capture every stage in the horse's stride, I need to take at least twelve pictures in one half-second. That's a great many cameras – I'll need the very finest cameras, and the very finest lenses… and that's expensive… "

"You told me Stanford said money was no object."

"That's true, that's true. All right then, I'll order a dozen Scoville cameras from New York and every type of Dallmeyer lens from London that they have, a dozen of each, and I'll have the same number of guillotine shutters made… But… "

"But what?"

"How can I make sure they run fast enough? They'll have to be electric. Who knows how to do this?"

He stared out of the window, through the lace curtains, into the darkness. "Who knows? Who knows?"

Sarah Louisa cleared away the tea things and headed for the kitchen, talking over her shoulder.

"Who better than the man you're doing all this for?"

"Stanford, yes! When he hit that last spike, he sent an electric telegraph message that instantaneously set off all the cannons in the country and – of course – we want to do almost the same thing, don't we? Send an instant electric message along the wires to trigger the *cameras*! How perfect!" He hurried after her into the kitchen. "What we want to do *is* just like the last spike, it's the same thing: sending an instant electric message along the wires to trigger the *cameras*! How perfect! Now who's the genius?" He leaned over her to kiss her on the forehead as she stood at the sink.

She dropped the plate she was holding and it shattered on the stone floor.

"Oh, bother, these wet plates are so slippery."

She began to gather up the pieces. He bent down to help her. Then it struck him. "What did you just say?"

"These wet plates – "

"Damn, damn, damn!"

"I'm sorry, Edward, but I only broke one of them."

"Wet plates!" He slapped himself on the side of the head. "How could I have forgotten all this time? We've got to insert plates in each of the twelve cameras beforehand and there's no time to do that with wet plates, they're only good for a few moments."

"What about dry plates?"

"They're still too slow. They use gelatin now, but they still can't get any faster than about one-thirtieth of a second. No good for motion pictures. So we're stuck. Our idea is not going to work. Oh, damn."

"But you said there were many men working on developing faster dry plates in many different countries. Perhaps someone somewhere is getting close to the speed you need?"

"It's possible, I suppose. Who would know about this?"

They looked at each other, both getting the same idea.

CHAPTER THIRTY-FIVE

Finally, Edward's train was approaching Lyon railway station. Would he find what he was looking for in this city? The solution to his problem, the key to his future? In just an hour or so from now, he would know the answer. Thank you, Arthur, for that photographic memory Sarah Louisa and he had thought of at the same time.

When he'd told Stanford about his camera battery idea and who, according to Arthur, was the most likely person in the world to be able to supply the missing element, the Governor had insisted that Edward leave immediately, and in style.

Since Stanford was not only president of the Central Pacific Railroad Company with shares in just about every other railroad in the country, but also director of the Occidental and Oriental Steamship Company, this was easily arranged. For the railway leg of the journey, all the Governor had to do was scribble "Pass Edward" on a slip of paper over his signature for Edward to be given immediate access to his Director's Car and direct passage all the way to New York in five luxurious days. For the first time in his life, Edward experienced what it must be like to have more money than you know what to do with.

The electric telegraph poles flashed by, slicing the landscape into – as Stanford had once told him – sixty-yard chunks, roughly thirty to the mile. Profiting from the precision of his wondrous Teutonic timepiece, Edward had calculated the speed of the train by measuring the average time it took to pass from one pole to the next, 2.7 seconds, multiplied by 30 poles, equals 81 seconds to cover one mile – they were traveling at 44.4 miles per hour! What price a eight-mile-an-hour stagecoach now? The "iron horse" would soon be reaching the velocity of a cannonball.

For Edward's sea voyage, Stanford had actually had Occidental's liner the *Oceanic* re-assigned from its San Francisco-Hong Kong service to the New York-Le Havre route. Just for him. Such was the Governor's enthusiasm for their project! Averaging

14.5 knots, according to the captain, the passage had taken a mere nine days. Not surprisingly, given Stanford's tastes, the *Oceanic* was the most modern and most opulent steamer known to man. If the armchairs hadn't been bolted to the floor, its first-class dining room with its grand piano, coal fireplaces and marble mantels could have been mistaken for the interior of a luxurious country house. Even the stateroom reserved for Edward was equipped with running water, call bells, and bathing facilities.

The Governor had also put in a word with the owner of *La Compagnie de chemin de fer de Paris Lyon Méditerranée* to secure Edward the plumpest possible first-class seat on the last segment of his trip, the entire 6,500-mile span of which had totaled just over a fortnight, door to door.

The contrast with the seven grueling months of his original journey to the New World was staggering – the Liverpool-New York leg alone had confined him to the stinking hold of an emigrant sailing ship for fifty-three nauseous days. Canute couldn't hold back the waves, but man could now shrink the ocean to a village pond. How Edward's world had changed!

The hackney from Lyon railway station deposited him outside a small photographic studio on rue de la Barre in the heart of the city. Its street-front window displayed a number of studio portraits of *Célébrités lyonnaises immortalisées sur plaque sensible* and brimmed with cameras and lenses and tripods and other sun-painting equipment all jumbled together like an Old Curiosity Shop; a far cry from Rulofson's.

The shop-door bell jangled and a man advanced to greet him. He looked to be about ten years younger than Edward and had a bushy moustache under a long Gallic nose. His floppy Bohemian tie and velvet jacket would have done Monsieur Baudelaire proud.

"*Monsieur Muybridge, je vous ai reconnu de votre image dans* La Nature," said the man, kissing him on both cheeks. "*Antoine Lumière, enchanté, mes fils ont si hâte de faire votre connaissance. Suivez-moi, s'il vous plaît.*"

He led Edward to meet his sons, first through the shop and then down a steep flight of steps into a basement so dark Edward could scarcely see his hand in front of his face. The only light came from a gas lamp under a red shade beside a pair of small tables, one of which was set up for chess, the other for cards. Edward's eyes adjusted to the gloom: the basement stretched in every direction, an underground warren, part chemist's shop – he'd never seen so many bottles and jars of chemicals in one place – part laboratory, part operating room, and all of it, quite literally, a dark room. This must form part of the famous *traboules* of Lyon, he realized, the underground tunnels that wound beneath so much of the city. He also realized that the little street-level part of the Lumières' studio was merely the tip of a photographic iceberg, the submerged portion of which must have encompassed the cellars of half the buildings on the street.

"I know it's cramped," cried a shrill adolescent voice, "but we're planning to build a *gigantesque* factory in Montplaisir in a couple of years to manufacture my gelatin plates by the tens of thousand, *n'est-ce pas, Papa?*"

"*On verra, Louis, on verra.*" grunted Monsieur Lumière, as if he didn't agree at all, but smiling affectionately nonetheless at the small figure who was bounding up to Edward.

"This is a great honor, Monsieur Muybridge. Louis Lumière, at your service," said the young man.

"How do you do?" replied Edward as they shook hands. Arthur had told him that Louis Lumière was barely fourteen years old, and he looked it, and yet there was something curiously old about him at the same time; he already had the same long nose as his father. "Your English is excellent. Did you learn it at school?"

Louis shook his head. "I had to have a governess, but she was English, she taught me." He touched his temple as if it were tender. "My silly migraines – I had to leave school at ten – "

"And I couldn't go to school *until* I was ten because of my silly asthma."

Louis smiled. "Between us, we could have had quite an education. But now you'll understand why I like the dark. What else could I have taken up but photography? The '*lumière*' in the darkness."

At this point, they were joined by a slightly older boy, who was introduced as Louis's elder brother Auguste, two years older, although they looked so alike they could almost have been twins.

After their father had excused himself because of his lack of knowledge of English, Auguste addressed Edward nearly as fluently as his brother.

"We received your letter regarding the purchase of some of Louis's instantaneous dry plates. But you must realize they're still at the experimental stage – "

"Yes, that's what I wanted to ask," said Edward, turning to Louis. "What combination of chemicals did you came up with to make your dry plates sensitive enough?"

"Well, eh..." Louis looked at his brother and Auguste shrugged as if to say, go ahead, "...like many other researchers here and in England I'd tried everything for the emulsion from honey and beer to liquorice and ginger wine and raspberry jelly, until – "

"Oh, I'm aware of the process by which silver bromide is suspended in gelatine to produce the emulsion – "

"Yes, but I went further." Once more, Louis glanced at his brother with Auguste again signalling him to continue. "I developed a method of 'ripening' the emulsion by keeping it as warm as possible – like ripening fruit – keeping it at around thirty-two degrees Celsius for several days to make it not only as sensitive as wet collodion but fifty to a hundred times *more* sensitive."

"Good gracious! So what is the *base* of your emulsion?"

"Well, Father concocted an ammonia-based formula for coating both glass and paper that – "

" – is enough, Louis," interrupted Auguste. He turned to Edward. "I'm afraid we're now entering the realm of the professional secret, Monsieur." Then he laughed as if afraid he'd sounded too harsh. "You know how protective we photographers are – they must be like that in America too, I suppose?"

Edward had never really thought of it before, but now he told them, "I haven't yet perfected my own chemical formulae for developing my fast negatives, but when I do improve them as far as

I can, I've no intention of patenting them or keeping them secret."

"What I meant was," added Auguste hastily, "since Louis's plates are still experimental, well, they are not yet available commercially – "

"But I've come such a long way – "

"However, Louis and I found the article in *La Nature* last December about your high-speed photographs of Governor Stanford's horse so intriguing that we may make an exception in your case." He thought to himself for a moment. "I think we might be able to let you have half-a-dozen plates."

"That's most kind, but I was hoping to buy a great deal more than that." Edward then proceeded to explain how his plan to take a sequence of clear pictures in less than one second with twelve cameras couldn't possibly work using wet plates and how their dry plates were the only way to proceed. But since it would of course require a number of trials, he would need a great quantity of plates.

Auguste's eyes widened. "Twelve cameras taking twelve images, one after the other? In less than one second. *Vraiment?* You didn't mention that in your letter. This is most interesting." He glanced at his brother, muttering almost under his breath: "*Hallucinant, hein?*"

Loui, now sitting at one of the small red-lit tables, appeared to be off in a world of his own, as he lined up a series of playing cards, passing his hand to and fro over them like a boy magician, over and over again, the ruby images of kings and queens and hearts and diamonds flickering between his outstretched fingers as he murmured, "*Encore et encore et encore et encore… le mouvement…* "

"You will keep us informed of all the details of your work, won't you, Monsieur Muybridge?" said Auguste.

"Of course, with pleasure."

"How many plates did you say you needed?"

CHAPTER THIRTY-SIX

Everything was in place at Stanford's Menlo Park stock farm for the capturing of the world's first series of motion pictures. Now, will it work? thought Edward.

Each of his twelve "automatic electro-photographic" cameras were ready and waiting and loaded with a sensitized Lumière dry plate. After numerous experiments, he had established the exact measurements they needed: each of his twelve cameras spaced 21" apart and connected to twelve galvanized wires strung horizontally just above the lime-powdered track, on the far side of which a giant screen of white canvas was stretched over a scantling fence, thirty feet long by eight feet high, subdivided by heavy black lines into 21" vertical spaces like a giant ruler. How satisfying to cage a snorting, quivering, perspiring mass of horseflesh in a methodical grid of cold hard science, taking the steed's movement apart and then putting it back together again with the precision and beauty of a German watch. And all of it done – again, exactly as planned – with the assistance of electricians from the San Francisco Telegraph Supply Company, augmented by a team of railroad engineers and mechanics furnished by Governor Stanford.

Edward couldn't have asked for more cooperation from Stanford. As soon as he'd returned from France, the Governor had put the "Mile Race Track" at his new Stock Farm in Menlo Park at his disposal. So he'd gathered his group of assistants together and set out for "Palo Alto," as the Spanish called this area: High Tree. Edward's personal team had grown to five: Sarah Louisa, Joseph, Matthew, and Arthur as before, but now joined by Elsie – Mrs. Arthur Townsend. And thank goodness too, for her presence had made Sarah Louisa's respectable and allowed her to share Elsie's and Edward's lodgings at the boarding house where Stanford had put them up close to the Governor's new love: his Stock Farm. Having completed his Nob Hill mansion and crammed it to the rafters with every priceless knickknack known to man, he seemed to have promptly forgotten all about it like a spoiled child discarding an old toy for a new one, for now he thought only of Palo Alto, spending every spare moment here. When he wasn't in his immense ranch house, Mayfield Grange, Stanford was sitting in a custom-made rotating chair in the middle of his "kindergarten track," keeping one eye on the ranchhands training his colts until their hooves "struck the ground with the regularity and sequence of the stamps of a quartz mill," as he liked to put it, and the other eye on the experiment he hoped would make his horse-training even more efficient – and himself even more famous.

Meanwhile, nothing was too good for the denizens of this hippodrome. The Menlo Park stables were beyond lavish even by Stanford's standard; they would have been fit for princes let alone animals: marble halls, Brussel carpet, hot and cold water in every stall and large signs forbidding whipping, scolding, harsh language, swearing – even loud talking – in front of the precious beasts.

Through the window of the studio shed they'd set up beside the Governor's track, Edward saw that Abe Edgington, driven by Stanford's master trainer, Charles Marvin, was all set to go.

To some extent this gave *une sensation de déjà vu* as the French said, since the same colleagues and friends of the Governor were in attendance as at the Sacramento motion experiment. A similar gaggle of journalists had turned up, although these were a cut above the Coppingers of this world and included the Turf Editors of every major newspaper on the West Coast; highly respected writers expressly invited by Stanford to observe the entire process of the photographs' manufacture, from the horses' activation of the cameras to the on site development of the negatives.

The greatest difference of all, however, was that everything was multiplied by twelve: instead of a single blindingly white research laboratory designed to take one picture, there was one twelve times the size to take a dozen pictures; instead of one piece of string to break, there were twelve electric wires to trip; and instead of one shutter to trigger, there were a dozen – and a dozen opportunities for something to go wrong, fretted Edward. For again, Stanford the consummate showman had only permitted them to rehearse this experiment piecemeal, one or at most a couple of cameras at a time, reserving the full-scale twelve-camera spectacle for the largest possible audience for the greatest dramatic effect. Edward shook his head: do or die once more. It was like the charge of the damn Light Brigade.

Edward's "camera crew" from the telegraph company and the railroad had now readied their equipment. They gave him the nod.

He raised his arm and dropped it.

Mr. Marvin cracked his whip.

The wheels of the sulky gathered more and more momentum, accelerating and accelerating until they must have been going even faster than Occident: a 2:20 speed, at least.

Abe Edgington was approaching the first wire. Would he balk? Edward felt like closing his eyes, he almost couldn't bear to watch. Would the wheels break the circuit? Would this trigger the shutter? And even if all went well at this point, would it go well again, and again and again, twelve times over?

CHAPTER THIRTY-SEVEN

A few days later, Sarah Louisa was reading from her trusty scrapbook: "…the wheels of the sulky make a sound like the wings of a woodcock, as the wheels touch the wires, and in a trifle over half a second the twelve pictures are registered,"

"'The wings of a woodcock,'" echoed Edward, "goodness he writes well, your Mr. J. Cairns Simpson. And he certainly catches the spirit." He thought back to that astonishing moment at the stock farm when he had held his breath – when everyone had held his breath.

Click-click-click-click-click-click-click-click-click-click-click-click, the wheels had gone. Was that twelve? It had been too fast to tell. But when they checked the wires: yes, every one of them had been broken. And when they checked the cameras, yes again, every one of the shutters had been triggered, each one exposing a Lumière dry plate at precisely one-thousandth of a second. Exactly as planned!

"What else does Cairns Simpson write?"

Sarah Louisa handed him the scrapbook.

The Turf Editor of the *California Spirit of the Times* had gone on to describe the last stage of Edward's experiment in the studio shed dark-room:

> *There is a feeling of awe in the mind of the beholder, as he looks at the glass plate which is held before the yellow curtain, and he sees the miniature of the flying horse so perfect that it startles him. Reduced in size until it would do for the scarf-pin of a lady, and yet in the weird opal-tinted light it is as distinct as if cut on a gem. The eye runs rapidly over the series, and there are positions which could never be explained by any hypothesis, but which cannot be questioned by those who have witnessed the operation.*

* * *

After that, things had begun to move even faster than Stanford's horses. First, inspired by the Lumière brothers after all – not to mention nagged at by Sarah Louisa – Edward had applied for patents on his "Method and Apparatus for Photographing Objects in Motion."

Next, Edward had returned to the Photographic Art Association with Arthur for a repeat performance of their lantern exhibition, but this time presenting slides of a horse trotting past twelve cameras.

Something extraordinary had happened in the course of this exhibition. At first, Edward had projected the series of pictures of Abe Edgington very slowly so the audience could take a good look at each stage in the stride. Then someone had asked to see them in quick succession to reconstitute the motion Edward's individual photographs had stopped. So Edward had clicked through the slides as fast as he could, and really it was quite astounding – seeing movement itself; as Cairns Simpson had written: "The eye runs rapidly over the series." Was this what Edward had first glimpsed from the runaway stagecoach? Those tumbling rocks coalescing into a single pulsating object? Had he seen all this before? Who knows? But it was most entertaining, the members of the audience said, though of course that wasn't really the point, but such a synthesis could be absolute proof of how accurate his analysis was. If only he could find a way to project twelve images of a moving horse *automatically* at a steady speed, it would be even better.

The question had had to be temporarily set aside in the storm of publicity over Edward's publication of six albumen print cabinet-size cards entitled "The Horse in Motion." Each card showed a latticework of twelve pictures of various trotters spread out like Hogarth's *Rake's Progress* from left to right and top to bottom, with an analysis of the stride printed on the back. The cards had even received the supreme compliment of being parodied in San Francisco's *Illustrated Wasp* by a series of drawings of a horse's legs flying wildly in every direction. The cards themselves had made a similar impact all across Europe, "The Horse in Motion" becoming "Les Allures du Cheval" in *La Nature* and "Das Pferd in Bewegung" in Berlin's *Fremdenblatt*.

But it had been *Scientific American* that had given Edward the beginning of an answer to his question about automatic projection. Having devoted its cover to a series of engravings of his photographs, the magazine had suggested that Edward's pictures might be cut out and mounted on strips for use in a *Zoetrope*.

Zoetrope… That was the word that had really set him thinking, and what he was still thinking about now as he discussed it in his room at the boarding house with Sarah Louisa.

"But the *Zoetrope*'s a cylinder," she objected, "how do you project your motion pictures from inside a cylinder?"

"That's a good point… Maybe it should a *Phenakistiscope* – you know, the disk version of the *Zoetrope*. Instead of slots round the outside for viewing the images inside, it uses a slotted disk with drawings printed on it."

"Yes, I've seen one, and when you spin the drawings in front of a mirror and look at them through vertical slots, they give the illusion of smooth motion. Your persistence of vision again."

"If I can somehow find a way to spin the disk behind a series of vertical slots at the same time as I project the pictures through a magic lantern onto a screen…"

"A projecting *Phenakistiscope*. Doesn't exactly trip off the tongue, does it? What does it mean anyway?"

"'Deceptive view.'"

Hmm… that was rather good, actually. Very apt: he reconstituted his photographs of the true elements of motion to demonstrate that motion *itself* was deceptive. Seeing is believing, but what you are believing is not true. The perfect paradox: the very projection of motion pictures *proves* that they are false… But how to do it? That was still the question.

* * *

Edward spent the next few weeks thinking of little else, building apparatus after apparatus in his mind. But nothing came together. Even his daily discussions with Sarah Louisa, which usually bore fruit, were getting him nowhere. He was in despair. Perhaps he was really not meant to take his work any further? A fool's bolt is soon shot, as the saying goes.

And then one evening, Sarah Louisa knocked on his door for their nightly chat. The timid knock she had been increasingly prone to lately and the equally timid whispering, "It's only me," as if it were really no one at all.

"Come in," called Edward.

She slipped in like a ghost.

"What is it?"

"A letter from Thomas Eakins."

"Thomas Eakins? I admire his work above all else." Especially his detailed paintings of unclothed men and women, he refrained from adding: those controversial works that had raised so many eyebrows.

Edward took the letter and skimmed through it. "Ah, this is extraordinary; he's seen my motion pictures in *Scientific American* and he's been so inspired he not only uses them in his classes at the Pennsylvania Academy of the Fine Arts, but has begun work on a painting for his patron, Fairman Rogers, that will be based on my work. The painting is going to show Rogers driving his four-in-hand through the park, demonstrating for the first time in the history of art how horses really move. He says he only wishes *I* could be on the faculty of the Academy!"

This really gave Edward a lift. His enthusiasm for his projection project was rekindled: a vote of confidence from Thomas Eakins!

He turned to Sarah Louisa to share his excitement and noticed her woebegone expression. "What's the matter? You look so down."

"Oh, nothing."

"No, out with it, Sarah Louisa. I know you well enough by now. You can tell me."

"Well, I know you too, Mr. Muybridge, you and your sudden bursts of enthusiasm and…"

"And… what?"

"Well, you're not going to suddenly drop everything here and run off to Pennsylvania, are you?"

Edward laughed. "I doubt that very much, Sarah Louisa, with everything that's going on here. But if I do, I assure you will be the first to know. But in the mean time, I have work to do!"

It was amazing what a few words of encouragement could accomplish. Edward returned to his task with renewed vigor. Hardly had he begun when even more heartening words arrived in the post in the form of a clipping from *La Nature*: a letter to the editor from Professor Marey of all people. After he'd translated it, he read it through again and again.

> *"I am lost in admiration over the instantaneous photographs of Mr. Muybridge… what beautiful zootropes he could give us, and we could perfectly see the true movements of all imaginable animals. It would be animated zoology. So far as artists are concerned, it would create a revolution, since we could furnish them the true attributes of motion, the position of the body in equilibrium, which no model could pose for them… My enthusiasm is overflowing."*

Edward was also aided in his endeavors by a sad set of circumstances. Stanford had recently fallen ill and had been confined to his bed with fever and nausea, his sides, legs and back drawn up with extremely painful rheumatism. At first, no one had any idea of the cause of this malady; even his personal physician, Dr. Jacob Stillman (a Forty-Niner who'd become one of the

Governor's closest friends) was baffled. But then Stillman noticed the unpleasant odor in Stanford's quarters at Mayfield Grange: sewer gas was escaping from the privy vault in the cellar directly beneath him. That was the cause of his ailments. If it weren't so tragic, it would be funny, thought Edward: he who pisseth highest laid low by his own excrement. Happily, the leak in the vault had now been repaired, and Stanford was gradually on the mend. But in the meantime, Edward was left alone to forge ahead with his work exactly as he saw fit.

The first and greatest problem was the spinning disk itself. When he got it to revolve on a spindle in front of the beam of his magic lantern, the resulting projection was clear enough, but Abe Edgington looked as if he'd been squashed by a giant steam hammer. After weeks of experimenting, Edward finally discovered what was causing the distortion. Because the disc was spinning, the left side of each image was projected at a fractionally different rate from the right side. After yet more experimentation, he found the solution: to have a professional retoucher repaint and elongate each photographic image using an angled mirror to give a consistent correction. In this way, all the projected images were now correctly proportioned. Although these were admittedly paintings, not photographs, they were still taken directly from the life, still completely faithful to the actual movement of the horse, to the "true attributes of motion." They were also startlingly beautiful in their vibrant rainbow colors.

Edward's second problem was the flickering effect that was produced when these motion pictures were projected. They were not smooth, but jittery, as if looked at through constantly blinking eyes. How was he to get a smooth image?

Again, Sarah Louisa saved the day by suggesting that he go back to his original inspiration: the *Phenakistiscope*. How did that achieve smooth motion? By having the viewer look at the image through spinning vertical slots. So how could he introduce such slots into his machine? After even more experimentation, he came up with the solution: to use *two* disks, spinning in opposite directions, one made of glass bearing his twelve horse pictures round its perimeter; the other made of sheet metal with long narrow slots round its perimeter.

But it hadn't ended there. More trial and error revealed that to achieve the desired effect, he had to devise a gearing mechanism that not only spun the two disks simultaneously in two opposing directions, but in such a way that the disk with the slots traveled twice as fast as the disk with the pictures.

At last he had all the pieces of his puzzle, his motion pictures, his disks, his gearing mechanism, and his projection device: his magic lantern. Now to put them together into what he'd decided to call his "animal action viewing device" or *Zoöpraxiscope*.

When Edward showed the result to Sarah Louisa, she giggled. At first he was hurt, but then he saw the humor of it himself. The Zoöpraxiscope was a strange beast indeed. Its rear end consisted of half of the usual steam-engine-like magic lantern balanced on four long legs like a stork; its midsection was made up of what appeared to be a sewing machine with a circular handle and two spindles at its own front and back; and its front end was a simple wooden column supporting the other half of his projector: a giant lens. A one-eyed monster. But it worked. It worked!

CHAPTER THIRTY-EIGHT

They were moving furniture at Mayfield Grange. It had taken a total of seven months for this day to come, July 8TH, 1879, to be precise, or some forty years if Edward counted from his first inkling of it. The day he was finally ready to show the world something it had never been shown before. Even Stanford didn't know what Edward had in store for him. His exhibition this evening would be the first time the Governor had ventured from his sick bed for many weeks.

So they were moving furniture, Joseph, Arthur, Matthew, Elsie, Sarah Louisa and Edward; he had insisted they do this themselves, rather than the Governor's servants, so that everything would be just so. But he did have an additional helper this evening: Leland Stanford Jr., now aged eleven, and a fine, if not strapping boy, so charming and intelligent. Over the last few months during the Governor's indisposition as Edward had expanded his motion experiments from twelve cameras to twenty-four – all still firing within a single second – he and the boy had grown close and Edward almost felt like the father to him he could never have been to Florado.

They lined up the gleaming button leather sofas and armchairs like rows of sleek sea lions in front of the ten-foot square canvas that was angled out at exactly 30° from the far wall of the immense parlor as if awaiting a Rembrandt. Was everything ready? Any detail overlooked?

And how would the exhibition be received? As miraculous as Edward and his crew thought it was, would the world share their opinion?

A nurse wheeled in a wan-looking Stanford muffled in blankets, with all the other guests trooping in behind. In the lead was their hostess, Jane Stanford, with such a breast-load of diamonds it was a wonder she could walk; the newspapers claimed the jewels she'd recently taken to wearing were nearing the half-million mark. Frank Shay came in next, shooting Edward a quick wink of encouragement before sitting down not far from him, along with a couple of horse trainers whose names he had forgotten; Stanford had so many. Now a portly gentleman appeared, carrying a small black bag, his shock of white hair making him look like an Old Testament prophet – except for the long fluffy sideburns. Edward found something vaguely familiar about him. He glanced at Shay.

"Dr. Stillman," whispered his friend.

So this was the famous doctor. They'd never met, so Edward must have been mistaken about seeing him before. Now a small but wonderfully select group of grand personages and their lady wives were filing in. He knew that most of them were down from San Francisco (only eighty minutes now by private S.P.R.R. train to Menlo Park station). They included James Flood, the bonanza king of the Comstock Load, the only man in the state rumored to be richer than Stanford; David Jacks, the Treasurer of the CPR, who'd driven up from his 100,000 acre estate in Monterey; and Charles Crocker, who had been a frequent visitor since the Governor fell ill. Elsie had written out their names in her best copperplate, and they took their designated seats.

Edward nodded to Joseph and the rest of his team to start dousing the many kerosene lamps scattered about the room; no self-respecting millionaire stooped to gaslight nowadays.

A few moments later, they were in almost complete darkness, only relieved by the eerie flicker of the two small candles Arthur and Matthew were holding.

Edward stepped up onto a narrow platform rimming a six-foot high table.

The ladies inched closer to their husbands as if preparing to receive a communication from beyond the grave mediated by Madame Blavatsky. Mrs. Stanford, who'd recently taken up spiritualism, looked as if she were expecting a demonstration of immorality, as she would probably have called it. The room lapsed into a state of dead silence almost as complete as that of the court-house when they'd read the verdict. What would the verdict be tonight?

Edward's Zoöpraxiscope was perched on a table set thirty feet back from the canvas screen. Arthur slowly turned the control knobs of the oxygen and hydrogen cylinders to release the gasses into the mixing chamber. Edward crossed his fingers that nothing would pop tonight. Arthur lit a taper from his candle, igniting the mixture of gases in the chamber. A *hiss* and a *puff* and the nozzle of Joseph's torch shot out a flame. All was well; God was in his Heaven. Joseph then trained the torch on the small white cylinder of lime, gradually turning the calcium oxide redder and redder until it reached the required 500° Fahrenheit. A shaft of light streaked like a bolt of lightning across the heads of Stanford and onto the screen.

Joseph inserted the slotted disk and the image disk into the "sewing machine" section of the apparatus.

Edward grasped the handle and began turning. The two disks revolved in their opposite directions and at their different speeds.

A horse galloped across the room, and again, and again, exiting on one side of the screen and re-entering on the other. An endless procession of flying hooves. Although of course he had seen this many times in their rehearsals, it still astonished him. The action was so smooth, so real. Twenty-four pictures in one second: the precise number required to give the illusion of smooth movement, at least for humans. Arthur had said that some scientist had calculated that if you were to show such motion to an audience of honeybees, it would have to run at two hundred and fifty pictures per second, because honeybees lived faster than we did, cutting up their time into smaller increments. At the other end of the scale were snails who sliced their reality very thick indeed: their motion projections would have to be at two pictures per second, they lived in such a slow world, anything moving faster than that would be perceived as stationary.

How magical this was, this juxtaposition of images, thought Edward. When two or more images were placed together they created a third image, like a mosaic or a stained-glass window. But it was the spaces *between* the chips and the shards that really mattered, wasn't it? What was going on in the spaces between his images of the moving horse? For that matter, what was going on in the crevices of his own reality? What monsters lurked in the cracks between the paving stones he would never step on as a child? Why was he thinking of this? Was it because of the unearthly silence that still enveloped the room, only broken by the crank of his handle?

There was a slither of blankets as Stanford sat upright in his wheelchair.

Edward stopped cranking, freezing the horse in mid-stride.

His eyes adjusted to the dark. The spectators were as motionless as the horse. In fact, nothing was moving other than the gentlemen's cigar tips making devil's eyes through the gloom.

Why did nobody speak? Edward felt as if all the life in him was draining from his limbs.

After the longest and most agonizing pause, as if God Himself had put his hand on the spinning globe, a shaky voice said, "There, Governor, there you have a representation of Hawthorn galloping at a 1:42 gait."

Was that him?

Slowly, Stanford's head started to nod up and down as if he were retracing his memory of the horse's rhythm. "I think you must be mistaken in the name of the animal, Mr. Muybridge. That was certainly not the gait of Hawthorn, but of Anderson."

Edward grabbed Arthur's candle to leaf through his notes. No, no, according to his records, it was indeed Hawthorn.

"But, Governor – "

"Charles." Stanford beckoned to one of the horse trainers, who stood up sheepishly.

"I'm sorry, Governor, I forgot to tell Mr. Muybridge, but I substituted Anderson at the last minute."

The heat of Edward's life surged back into him as fast as it had left. He glanced over at Sarah Louisa, who smiled back in triumph. He was glowing: he'd just been paid the highest compliment Stanford could have given him. The very fact that Stanford had immediately recognized the difference between the gait of the two horses proved beyond doubt the excellence of what he had done.

Quickly, Joseph began feeding picture disk after picture disk into the magic machine as Edward turned the handle for all he was worth. The elegant parlor became a barnyard: a dog bounding, a goat bucking, a deer leaping, a cow ambling, a bull charging, in front of the gaping faces. He was Goethe's Sorcerer's Apprentice, *"die Geiste die ich rief."* The spirits were finally on his side.

They were at the grand finale: a boy on a pony being chased across the screen by yet another horse trainer holding onto his hat.

Joseph and company began re-lighting the lamps.

"When did you take those pictures?" said Stanford

"Mr. Muybridge took them of me last month, Father, I was riding Gypsy," piped up Leland Jr. "You know, papa, that Mr. Muybridge is helping to get me started in photography myself." He grinned at Edward. "I'm working on an album. I thought this might do for the cover." He showed his father a drawing of his slim form hunched under the dark cloth of a camera, a miniature of Edward.

Stanford struggled half up out of his chair, leaning over to shake Edward's hand. "Thank you, Mr. Muybridge, thank you for one of the most remarkable evenings of my life. And thank you for looking after my son." He winked as he assumed a French accent, *"Impossible, hein? Impossible..."*

There was another long silence as the audience gradually absorbed what they had seen. This was a séance, after all.

Later, hand still aching and shoulders still sore from all the cranking and congratulating – at one point he'd thought Crocker was going to kiss him – Edward watched the nurse wheeling a beaming Stanford out of the room, the guests following, still shaking their heads in wonderment.

He turned to help pack up the equipment. Dr. Stillman's great frosty head was bent over the Zoöpraxiscope as if examining a patient, Arthur muttering at his elbow, no doubt giving him the life history of every nut and bolt. Edward looked twice at the man. Now he remembered where he'd seen him before: the Hebrew face beside Stanford in the Last Spike painting. But they did say the Jews made excellent doctors, in spite of their strange beliefs. At least Stanford had no prejudice in that department.

Sarah Louisa grabbed Edward's sleeve, whispering in his ear: "Remember the Lumières: don't give away all your secrets."

"This is quite different," he whispered back, "he's one of Stanford's oldest friends. If I can't trust him, who can I trust?"

"Ah, Mr. Muybridge," Stillman was at his side, "It's such an honor to meet you at last. You have given us an astonishing evening, quite astonishing." He shook Edward's hand vigorously, then looked at his watch. "But look at the time, I have to give the Governor his hypodermic. No peace for the wicked. Why can't my patients confine their sickness to daylight hours?" He shook Edward's hand again. "Goodbye, sir – or should I say *Auf Wiedersehen?*" He gave a warm smile. "For I do hope we meet again."

CHAPTER THIRTY-NINE

"Completely naked please," repeated Edward to the gymnasts standing on the sun-splashed turf of the hippodrome as they looked back at him in alarm.

"But we *are* naked, Muybridge," said Louis Brandt as he fidgeted with his pickax, the muscles writhing beneath his skin like snakes struggling to escape from muslin.

Edward pointed at Brandt's loincloth. "No, you're not."

Brandt glanced at the other two similarly semi-nude athletes: William Lawton, superintendent of the Olympic Club, and Louis Gerichton, Edward's old teacher of boxing. All three shook their close-cropped heads, which contrasted so strikingly with Edward's own gray tangle now tumbling halfway down his waistcoat.

"There are no ladies present," Edward persisted, "there's nothing improper." He'd been careful to dispatch Sarah Louisa and Elsie – along with young Leland – on a shopping expedition, and Mrs. Stanford was also away as it happened, off to New York with the Governor and Frank Shay to attend a series of society parties. So there was no danger of offending any members of the fair sex – Edward hadn't forgotten the rumor that during one of Thomas Eakins' classes at the Pennsylvania Academy two female students had fainted when their teacher had stripped to the buff for the purposes of art instruction.

"No, Muybridge," said Brandt firmly, "we've already boxed and wrestled and fenced and vaulted and tumbled and performed as manual laborers – " he brandished his pickax " – for your cameras, but this we will not do. Even Adam covered his shame."

It was true, they had been very cooperative. After that unforgettable evening with the Zoöpraxiscope projection a few weeks ago, Edward had had some time on his hands; since the Governor had been up and about, he'd been spending more and more time with Stillman, although he couldn't imagine what they did together. In fact, Stanford had been acting rather strangely in other ways too: he'd allowed Edward to continue his own experiments at the ranch, but he hadn't commissioned a single new photograph from him since Edward had taken that picture of the eclipse of the sun last January. Perhaps the Governor still had not yet fully recovered from his illness. At all events, Edward had decided to use his extra hours to extend his "animated zoology" as Marey put it, to man himself.

Frank Shay had rounded up the gymnasts and brought them down to Palo Alto. He'd also hired an electrician to hook up an electric clock to fire the shutters and time the exposures of the cameras that Edward had set up at five different angles to the athletes. He had then taken hundreds of photographs of their every summersault, all performed with good will and enthusiasm – until now.

"Look, Brandt – all of you – this is strictly for scientific purposes as you know perfectly well. I now want to capture the play of *every* muscle, of *every* sinew, just like the horses."

"We're not horses," said Brandt.

All three heads shook as one.

"Thomas Eakins often poses nude for his students – the 'absolute male – '"

"*No!*" they chorused.

"Oh, for God's sake. I'll do it myself." Edward tore off his own clothes, stripping down to nothing as the muscle men looked away. For an old man of forty-nine he was still in good condition, he had to give himself that.

As Brandt handed him the pickax, Edward automatically flexed a muscle. Still not quite Brandt's dimensions, but...

He turned to his assistants to prepare the cameras, catching a smirking Arthur muttering to Matthew, "He just wants to show us his willy – " The young man stopped short, realizing he'd been spotted.

Arthur of all people, and him a married man now. But how delicious the warm California sun felt on his skin… so delicious… too delicious. He looked down at himself, oh dear, the swelling. Think of Christmas, all that freezing snow. That always did it, and it was doing it now, thank Goodness, even on this hot August day.

But here we go again: the doubts again, the shame, even when everything he'd dreamed of was coming true, he couldn't escape after all, it seemed. It is the most beautiful of Nature's works, the naked figure, is it not? Never the shame of Paul and Augustine. We are not all smutty Larkyns underneath. We can't be.

"Mr. Muybridge," said Joseph.

Oh, God, had Joseph noticed the state he'd been in? But no, he was merely alerting him they were ready to start.

Edward swung the pickax with all his might, again and again, taking out his frustration on the unsuspecting turf of the hippodrome: the world's first totally naked human being to be the subject of a motion study. Eakins would have been proud.

CHAPTER FORTY

"'Mr. Muybridge has laid the foundation of a new method of entertaining the people, and we predict that his instantaneous photographic, magic-lantern zoetrope will make the round of the civilized world... ' Sarah Louisa read from the *Alta California* the following spring. Having just returned from the latest in a series of public exhibitions of the *Zoöpraxiscope*, they were sitting in the Palo Alto studio shed preparing to take some additional pictures of moving animals. "'Most entertaining,'" she repeated.

"Yes, but that's not the point at all, I keep telling you," said Edward. But she was much too excited to listen, her eyes on the paper again.

"'Nothing was wanting but the clatter of hooves upon the turf and an occasional breath of steam to make the spectator believe he had before him the flesh and blood steed."

Talking of clatter, the sound of hammering drew Edward to the workroom at the far end of the studio shed. Through the door... was a *skeleton*. Was it California's version of the Day of the Dead? No, it was a horse skeleton, spread out on a large trestle table, its cannon, hock and fetlock bones all detached as if its legs had been smashed to pieces. Next to it, a group of carpenters were working on a series of metal joints, some of which were being screwed into corresponding pairs of bones, ready to be re-attached to the main body. Supervising all this was Dr. Stillman.

"Ah, Muybridge," said the doctor, noticing Edward. He pointed at the skeleton. "Don't worry, it's not one of Stanford's. I wouldn't dare do that. I acquired it from the Chicago stockyards."

"Why? What do you want with it?"

"As you know, we have no basis, no anatomical knowledge, relating to horses, so this is the only way to obtain it. Once the skeleton is fully articulated, we will arrange the legs in each of the successive positions of its stride and then we will have you photograph each of these phases so that we can see them with complete clarity."

"'We?'"

"The Governor and I." Stillman turned back to his carpenters.

The 'Governor and I'… really? What was going on?

Edward returned to Sarah Louisa to report what he'd seen.

Sarah Louisa placed her hand on his shoulder. "Nobody can touch you now Edward," she grinned, then flushed, "except me of course," she quickly withdrew her hand, "but what I mean is, it doesn't matter what Dr. Stillman is up to."

"But Stanford – "

"Oh, Stanford will never desert you. You've done too much outstanding work for him. And anyway your reputation is now assured. You know what your trouble is? You've too much imagination for your own good. Come back to the ranch house and let me make you a nice cup of tea."

Once again, Sarah Louisa quelled Edward's fears by stressing that the one thing he had with Stanford was security. It was true, the Governor – via Frank Shay – had always taken care of the financial end of things at Palo Alto. Good thing too, since he had no financial ability whatever. As he often told Sarah Louisa, he'd be perfectly content to mortgage himself to Stanford for a hundred dollars a month for the rest of his life. All he wanted was a living out of his business. If he could get that he'd be happy.

Sarah Louisa poured their tea along with yet more reassurance. "Relax yourself, stop worrying your head about Dr. Stillman. He's just a physician trying to help out his old friend."

She was right of course, as she so often was, thought Edward. What a comfort she had been over these – how long was it now since Flora passed away? Nearly five years, longer than his marriage. He watched Sarah Louisa as she took up her knitting in the corner of the room. She'd been looking much more drawn and tired recently than her thirty-eight years should warrant. It was almost as if the more the old pair of slippers shaped themselves to him, the more they lost their own form and brightness. But what was he thinking? He was not exactly bright as a new pin himself, was he? Fifty now, how time flies.

In the course of the next few weeks, he duly photographed Stillman's articulated horse skeleton in all the requested positions.

In the twelve-month that followed, Edward became so busy with further demonstrations of his Zoöpraxiscope and with completing his *Attitudes of Animals in Motion,* the album he'd put together of his Palo Alto pictures, he had no time to think any more about Dr. Stillman.

Even if he had been tempted to think more about him, the doctor was completely erased from his mind when a letter arrived from Professor Marey.

An invitation to come to Paris! And what did Professor Marey want him to do there? Nothing less than present his analytical photographs and motion studies to the scientific and artistic elite of that glorious city.

What an opportunity! And it couldn't have come at a better moment, for his project with Stanford was now finally concluded. Edward had presented him with a copy of his album with the Governor's name on the cover in gilt letters, and Stanford in turn had presented Edward with a settlement of $2,000, an agreement to let him keep all the equipment he'd been using – including some three thousand negatives, and – once Edward had showed him Marey's letter – a very generous offer to pay all the expenses for his second trip to France. Yet again, Edward could see that his fears regarding this extraordinary man were quite unwarranted.

He made his plans quickly: leave Sarah Louisa in charge of the South Park house – in fact place the lease in her name, one never knew with all these travels, and it might make up for her distress at his going off for what could be several months; have her look after any necessary payments to the orphanage for Florado; and leave his name and Paris address – he'd be staying at Marey's – with the Scoville Manufacturing Company in New York, who would store all his cameras and act as his agents while he was away.

CHAPTER FORTY-ONE

Even though he had tuned his Zoöpraxiscope demonstrations to a pitch of perfection after so many performances, beginning with his great triumph at Mayfield Grange, Edward was a bundle of nerves tonight. In just a few moments he was going to stand up in front of some of the greatest scientists, thinkers and artists in the whole of France. How would they receive him?

This and other such anxious thoughts raced through Edward's mind as he sat beside his host, Professor Marey, in the latter's sprawling salon overlooking the Jardins du Trocadéro awaiting their first guests.

It was at that moment that the doors of the salon sprang open to reveal the very personification of formidable talent, the man known simply by a single name.

Edward had never thought this day would come. *Nadar was entering the room!* Well, it wasn't just Nadar of course; Nadar never entered a room alone, but wrapped in the audience's collective memory of the Pantheon of poets and artists and musicians and actors he'd immortalized in his studio portraits: Berlioz, Bernhardt, Corot, Daumier, Delacroix, de Nerval, Gautier, Lizst, Millet, Rossini; a photographic roll call of European luminaries. Not that Nadar was merely a photographer; he was also a novelist, a journalist, a caricaturist, an art critic, a theater critic, a balloonist and goodness knows what else.

Edward's eyes were riveted on him. Six-foot tall, but "slightly bent like one of those Caryatides who carry a balcony on their back," as his friend Jules Verne had put it. With his tawny lion's mane, whiskery moustache and permanent smile, he looked to Edward more like the Cheshire cat. Nadar was ten years his senior, but somehow he managed to make it appear it was the other way round. His floppy velvet tie, pea-jacket and cuff-less shirt – all in a shocking red to proclaim his Republican sympathies – cried out Bohemia. He had fame beyond fame. All Victor Hugo, another good friend, had to write on an envelope to reach him from anywhere in Europe was his single-word name. As if even that didn't elevate him to a high enough pinnacle, Nadar had scrawled his signature in ten-foot high gas-lit glass letters across the façade of his very own crystal palace: the three storeys of floor-to-ceiling windows of his studio on Boulevard des Capucines.

Most of the other distinguished guests now taking their seats were from the world of science, and included Emile Duhousset, the explorer; Hermann von Helmholtz, the inventor of the ophthalmoscope; Gaston Tissandier, the editor of *La Nature;* and Jules Vilbort, the director of *Le Globe*. All of these great figures were gathered here to see *him*.

Edward made a few halting introductory remarks in his schoolboy French before he turned over the rest of his presentation to Marey, who was going to read from a translation of his lecture notes. And it had developed into a lecture now, rather than a simple "entertainment" of motion pictures.

Edward always started with a series of lantern slides of artists' renderings of the horse in motion throughout history, from the Neolithic age through the Assyrians, the Egyptians, the Greeks, the Romans, the Renaissance Italians, all the way up to modern times, demonstrating how in every instance the artist had got the positions of the legs quite wrong. He then contrasted these errors with his motion pictures of how horses actually moved, aided by the projectionist Marey had provided, a man who was himself a household word in France: the great optical technician, François-Marie Alfred Molteni.

Edward concluded his lecture with the same barnyard of animals that had cavorted across the room in Palo Alto, only now Leland Junior was replaced by a new *finale* – the climax of the entire evening – the boxing, wrestling, fencing, jumping and tumbling of three almost completely naked men (modesty having forbidden him from including his own nude work with the pickax).

Tonight, there wasn't even a second's pause before the salon erupted in almost feverish applause. Mayfield Grange was quite outdone.

* * *

The following day, Edward couldn't wait to report all this to Sarah Louisa. Thank goodness the transatlantic telegraph cable was now in place so he could communicate with her at eight words per minute instead of one missive per fortnight. And since he'd had to give up his free-lance work while he'd been on the Menlo Park project and still had Sarah Louisa herself and Florado to support, eight words was about all he could afford at $2.50 per. So he was limited to: LECTURE SUCCESSFUL COMPANY BRILLIANT NEWSPAPERS ECSTATIC EDWARD STOP

He would of course forward the French newspaper clippings by mail. Sarah Louisa was absolutely determined to keep the scrapbook up to date. And what clippings they were! Sitting in his room at Marey's a few days later, he went through some of them. Two in particular seemed to reflect the otherworldly aspects of the evening of his first motion picture projection at Stanford's ranch, with one reporter describing his moving pictures as *une chasse infernale* and *un défilé diabolique*, while *Le Figaro* predicted that much as the telephone had conserved human words like peas in a can, Edward's *"invention prestigieuse"* would make it possible to retrieve, years after his passing, a man's appearance, his gait, the very tilt of his head; *"le spectre marchera,"* the ghost will walk, Death will be defied.

CHAPTER FORTY-TWO

Edward's second *soirée* in Paris, which had also been arranged by Marey, shone even more brightly than the first. It took place in the vast studio of the artist who was without doubt the most famous painter in the world, Jean-Louis-Ernest Meissonier, the grand old man of Academic oils and glorifier of Napoleon and his armies, most recently in *The Battle of Friedland*, which because of his obsession with the exact color and contour of every tunic button and épaulette had taken him ten years to finish. Just like Marey's, Meissonier's residence overlooked a beautiful stretch of greenery: Parc Monceau.

Even though Meissonier was their host this evening, the great man had delayed his entrance and was preceded by a positive Milky Way of stars, each of them, like Nadar, enveloped in a shimmering aura of achievement. Alexandre Dumas *fils* swept into the room with *The Lady of the Camellias* at his side – how poor Flora would have loved this – and the ghost of his father at his coattails, arm in arm with *The Count of Monte Cristo* and *The Three Musketeers*. Jean-Léon Gérôme sauntered in with a bevy of alabaster-skinned oriental nudes. Then came most of the other great names of the *Académie des beaux arts*: Bonnat, Detaille, Guillaume, Cabanel. These were followed by the leading critics and dealers of the Parisian art establishment, everyone from Claretie to Wolff.

Only then did Meissonier make his appearance, not so much walking as bounding into the room. He was not at all as Edward had imagined: mid-sixties, short, ugly, with a forked beard flowing down to his waist. But he was built like a gymnast. Edward wondered if he would be as fit at that age.

After Edward's presentation was over and the standing ovation had subsided, Meissonier made a gracious speech of thanks, which ended with a deep theatrical sigh. "So much work to do, *mes amis*. Now I 'ave to adjust all ze galloping legs of my 'orses at Friedland to their true positions as revealed by *Monsieur Muybridge d'Amérique.*" He stood on tiptoe to put his arm around Edward. "Who 'as opened a new era in art."

Edward surveyed the audience that had now risen to its feet for a second time to give him another round of applause. How different the celebrated in Europe were from those in America where fame depended largely on the size of your bank account: the world of the Stanfords, the Carnegies, the Rockefellers. In Europe, far from being adulated, such men were looked down upon as mere shopkeepers, and it was the giants of the canvas and the page, the theater and the laboratory, who were placed on pedestals; they were not important because their pockets were full, they were important because their *minds* were.

Edward's public had expanded beyond anything he could have dreamed of in California. It was a good thing he had strong nerves, or he would have blushed at all the praise, not to mention all the kisses on both cheeks from gentlemen and ladies alike. Oh, the French.

And what ladies! He had never seen such a quantity of attractive women gathered together in one place. He didn't know whether the Meissonier women were wives or mistresses or actresses or models or even artists themselves. At all events, he certainly hadn't expected any members of the fair sex to be here at all – there were none at Marey's – otherwise he would never have left the almost bare athletes in the program. And yet far from fainting away or even looking away, the ladies had gazed at the exposed bodies of the young men with the same frankness with which some of them exposed their own in the Parisian art studios.

Was this the real origin of our Anglo-Saxon fascination with everything "French?" Edward mused. Not because it was naughty or saucy or hidden away like a contraceptive or a nude postcard or a harlot's boudoir, but because it was precisely the opposite, open and unashamed? But *why* did the Frenchman feel so much less guilty than the Englishman or the American about the human body? Why, when the subject was taboo almost everywhere else in the civilized world, did French artists from Boucher and Fragonard to Corot and Manet, Delacroix and Degas, feel no compunction about painting or sculpting naked women? Why did the cabarets of Montmartre frolic with such open *joie de vivre* while the Barbary Coast slunk down back alleys with its collar turned up? The French were as Christian as the English, were they not? Why didn't the dire warnings of St. Paul and St. Augustine have the same effect on them? Was it because they were Catholics? Was Catholicism less guilt-ridden than Protestantism? Three Hail Mary's and you're forgiven? If so, why weren't the Irish also more comfortable with physical love? You couldn't get more Catholic than the Irish. Or did it come down to some mysterious Gallic-Popish formula only an alchemist could fathom?

Whatever its cause, this openness about the body seemed to be one of the ingredients in the charm of the Parisian women, not only at Meissonier's, but almost everywhere Edward looked on the boulevards. It wasn't that French women were more beautiful than their English or American counterparts; they certainly dressed well, but so did many Anglo-Saxon women, and yet fashion on Regent Street or Fifth Avenue was never quite as fashionable as on the Champs Elysées. Perhaps it was something in the eyes. Perhaps because there was less shame and guilt attached to relations between the sexes in France, the ladies could look at a man more directly, more honestly? Perhaps that was what made them so attractive? Edward didn't know. All he did know was that quite apart from the amazing success he was having, spending this time in France had awakened something in him he had thought was dead. He could imagine love again – in fact, he was already in a sort of love, not with a person, but with a people. Or, so he thought. But he spoke too soon, and it was all because of Nadar.

CHAPTER FORTY-THREE

After Edward's triumphs chez Marey and Meissonier – which he still couldn't quite believe – Nadar and he had become firm friends. Who would have imagined it? But here he was, Edward Muybridge, on the morning of Christmas Day, eighteen hundred and eighty-one, sitting at the right hand of the most fabled French name of the century with the whole of Paris at his feet. Quite literally, for they were currently almost a mile above the city, far, far higher than he had ever ascended with Stanford. How absolutely he had overcome his Yosemite fears! And to make the experience even more sublime, on Nadar's left hand side, sat the most perfect Christmas present his new friend could have given him.

Nadar had taken them up in his balloon to celebrate the season – well, it used to be his balloon, he'd explained, but when he'd fallen on hard times a few years before (what true Bohemian hadn't?), he'd sold it and had now merely rented it back for the day. They were sitting in the "living room" of a wickerwork basket the size of a country cottage. At one end, was the captain's cabin, at the other, the passengers' cabin, the blood rushed to Edward's cheeks at the thought of it. The huge *nacelle* – the great aeronaut hadn't exaggerated when he'd called his flying machine *Le géant* – also contained a provision store, a lavatory, a dark-room – so that was how he managed to take his wet plate views; a well kept secret! – and a printing room, where he would lithograph accounts of his aerial adventures and scatter them about the surrounding countryside like manna from an artist's Heaven.

As they floated higher and higher, Edward had to agree with his host when he cried, "How easily indifference, contempt, forgetfulness drop away from on high, where no human force, no power of evil can reach us, *n'est-ce pas, mon ami?*"

Their friendship had begun just over a month ago when Nadar had invited him to his studio – well, it used to be his studio, but the failing business had been taken over some time ago by his son while Nadar lived in semi-retirement writing his memoirs. It was an invitation that was to change Edward's life in more ways than one. He would never forget the date: December 13th, Saint Lucia Day, the patron saint of light. Thirteen was supposed to be unlucky, but not for him.

They'd started their tour in one of the *salons d'attente* on the second floor, which were as sumptuously decorated as any of Stanford's mansions – save that here, everything from the oriental carpets and tiger skins to the suits of medieval armor was on sale.

Edward had then followed Nadar up to the third floor, an immense art gallery devoted to what his host claimed would one day be recognized as the finest collection of *plein air* art in Paris – also now on sale – and it certainly looked as if half the pictures painted by Monet, Renoir, Degas, Cézanne and Pisarro had been left behind after their much reviled "Impressionist" exhibition at the studio back in seventy-four. And the nudes! So many nudes – those by Renoir and Manet were particularly erotic – a far cry from the cold classicism of Gérôme.

Edward hadn't been able to resist posing the question that kept nagging at him more and more: why do we English and Americans get so upset about nudity and the sexual passions when the French take it all in their stride?

Nadar had given a Gallic shrug. "Everyone everywhere and at almost all times in history has taken such things in their stride. It is only you Anglo-Saxons who are out of step. Look at all the great civilizations that have had no problem with depictions of making love: the Chinese, the Indians, the Greeks, the Romans – ah – you should look at this." He had gone over to a bookcase to pull out a large leather volume, opening it before Edward.

Edward hadn't known which way to look. It was an eighteen seventy-one work by the French antiquarian César Famin on the subject of the *"cabinet secret"* in the Royal Museum at Naples. Even on the most explicit of French postcards, Edward had never seen such images. Engraving after engraving showing in exquisite detail every conceivable forbidden act, from fellatio, cunnilingus and bestiality to women with women, men with boys, dwarves with their members reaching to the ground, and all amidst a towering forest of phalluses.

"Where on earth do these come from?" asked Edward.

Nadar laughed. "Classical Rome. Are you familiar with Pompeii and the eruption of Vesuvius in seventy-nine A.D.?"

"Of course." Edward thought for an instant of Stanford's suffocating neo-Pompeian interiors. "But these frescoes – surely they – "

" – come from Pompeii. These and hundreds of paintings and sculptures like them, depicting every variety of love-making known to man and woman, were found on the walls of the houses that had been sealed in time by the volcanic ashes."

"But I've never seen these before – "

"Hardly anyone has. After their discovery, they were immediately removed from the ruins and hidden away in a secret cabinet of the Naples Royal Museum, labeled 'pornography' – the 'writing of prostitutes' – and forbidden to women and children and the lower classes. Admission only granted to men of mature age and the highest respectability... Like us." Nadar winked at him. "But my point is that the Romans attached no taboos to love-making of any description, they gloried in it, displayed it proudly on the walls of their houses for all to see." He tapped Edward on the shoulder. "That is normal, *mon ami*, not the prudery of so many of your breed. Why you Anglo-Saxons are the odd men out, I do not know, but odd you certainly are."

At that moment, as if to celebrate Nadar's panegyric upon the glories of aphroditic activity, a manservant had appeared to serve them oysters and wine; somehow there was always money for that. Edward had tried to say no, but just one small glass...

They sat down on an ottoman amidst all the buzzing beauty that so few people seemed to understand, including most members of the Academy and the majority of the art critics, who had been fit to commit murder on the upstart Impressionists. Not because of the frank nudity in many of the paintings, but because of the artists' infernal nerve in rebelling against Academy formalism.

As they swallowed and sipped, Nadar read Edward some of the reviews, translating into his fluent English.

La Presse:

> *This school does away with two things: line, without which it is impossible to reproduce any form, animate or inanimate, and colour, which gives the form the appearance of reality. Dirty three-quarters of a canvas with black and white, rub the rest with yellow, dot it with red and blue blobs at random, and you will have an impression of spring before which the initiates will swoon in ecstasy. Smear a panel with grey, plonk some black and yellow lines across it, and the enlightened few, the visionaries, exclaim: Isn't that a perfect impression of the Bois de Meudon? The scribblings of a child have a naivety, a sincerity which make one smile, but the excesses of this school sicken or disgust.*

Le Charivari had had some fun with Monet's "Impression, Sunrise:"

> *Impression - I was certain of it. I was just telling myself that, since I was impressed, there had to be some impression in it... and what freedom, what ease of workmanship! Wallpaper in its embryonic state is more finished than that seascape.*

Almost the only exception to the scathing reviews had been in *Paris-Journal*, which had been genuinely impressed with the painting Nadar then pointed out to Edward on the gallery wall, executed by Monet from the roof garden of this very studio:

> *Never has the seething life of the street, the teeming of the crowd on the asphalt and of vehicles on the roadway, the waving of the trees on the boulevard in dust and light, the elusiveness, the transience, the immediacy of movement been captured and fixed in all its prodigious fluidity as it is in the extraordinary and marvelous sketch which Monsieur Monet has catalogued under the title "Boulevard des Capucines."*

"The immediacy of movement," Nadar said, "that's what you capture with your instantaneous photographs, Monsieur Muybridge. In a sense, you and the impressionists are aiming for the same thing, although with your fast shutter you're actually ahead of them."

"Ahead of them? How so?"

Nadar pointed at the boulevard painting. "Do you see how Monet smudges the pedestrians as they walk along? He's imitating the way slow shutter speeds blur moving figures." He laughed. "'Black tongue lickings,' as another critic described them."

Edward looked at him in surprise. He was not only talented and charming and "an astounding example of vitality," as yet another of his friends, Charles Baudelaire, had said of him, he was a high-speed camera himself, not missing a single instant of life.

"Monet did something extraordinary, but – " Nadar shrugged again, " – your photographs do even better, catching life so perfectly on the fly and then preserving it – like a fly – " he laughed at his pun, "in amber. All photography defies death, but your instantaneous photography even more so. Although, you are also a murderer of course."

Edward has almost fallen off the ottoman. Could Nadar have known? Could the news have traveled as far as France?

Nadar noticed his discomfort. "Artistically speaking, that is."

"How do you mean? What I have murdered?"

"Well, if you wounded Impressionism, Monsieur Muybridge, you killed the realistic school stone dead."

"But Meissonier is most grateful to have my instantaneous photographs to correct his horse's stride. He said that I'd 'opened a new era in art.'"

Nadar looked at him over the rim of his glass. "No, you've closed an old one, *mon ami*. All Meissonier sees in your high-speed photographs is a way to remain stuck even more firmly in the past. He doesn't see that they make him redundant. Once you can photograph what's too swift for the human eye, who has need of Academy paintings struggling to represent the twinkle of a Hussar's breast button galloping at full speed? Like Gérôme and

Guillaume and Bonnat and all the rest of them, the man is nothing but a suburban photographer who's never had the shadow of an idea. And all those guns and swords in their military daubs – *épouvantable*. The taste for hardware is the surest sign of an empty head. *En tout cas*, Meissonier's days are numbered."

At that point Nadar had grasped both Edward's hands. "But your days are only just beginning to be counted, don't you see? Your photographs of multiple animals and multiple people are *merveilleux* – little frozen cubes of time," he made tiny staccato movements with the edge of his hand, slicing up the air, "the way your magic machine with the name no one can pronounce plays games with time, plays it forwards, backwards, speeds it up, slows it down, shortens it, lengthens it, breaks it up and re-assembles it, shows us all these facets of things we've never seen before, all of those in-between moments we're oblivious of, making material the impalpable specter that vanishes as soon as it is seen, leaving not even a shadow on the mirror…"

The tall gangling figure had been unstoppable, a force of nature about to take off from the ground at any moment like one of his balloons. Nothing could tether him.

"All of this," Nadar continued, "will inspire a new school of art – I, Félix Nadar, predict it!" He waved a finger as if conducting an orchestra. "Just as I predicted the school of *plein air*. But your genius will give birth to a new school, a school that tries to capture the very essence of movement itself, a school that will make the impressionists look as antiquated as Meissonier."

Edward had had only had one glass of wine, but he might have finished the bottle the way his head was whirling. Such flattery… Although at the same time, he couldn't help wondering about Nadar's judgment, the paintings of "Meissonier and Gérôme and Guillaume and Bonnat and all the rest of them" that Nadar so despised fetched three hundred thousand francs apiece while the works of his darling unknown "impressionists" were lucky to be measured in a few hundred francs – if they sold at all.

But Nadar had been so irresistibly charming that Edward had kept these thoughts to himself as they made their way up to the top floor of the studio, which was divided into a series of artists' ateliers and photographic studios Nadar's son was currently renting out for his father.

It was in one of these ateliers that he saw her, posing for a visiting painter like a statue in white marble, her back half turned, her mass of golden hair spilling down to her waist. This was no mescalin-induced hallucination – and certainly not the result of a few ounces of burgundy – this was real. Edward was perfectly sober and there was no question about it. It was Flora.

He staggered, clutching at Nadar's scarlet sleeve, as the latter breathed, "*Mon Dieu*, look at those breasts, 'a branch overloaded with ripe fruit,' as Baudelaire said of his mistress." He crossed himself. "God rest his soul."

Then the naked young woman looked round, her eyes catching Edward's.

It wasn't Flora's face, but it was her body, and it was also too late for him to avoid falling in love.

He heard a sob. Tears were running down Nadar's face. "Blanche Epler, *elle est exquise*, every time I see her, I am ravished. *Seize ans, imaginez-vous, seize ans.*" He started to recite: *"'Je suis belle, ô mortels! comme un rêve de pierre, et mon sein, où chacun s'est meurtri tour à tour, est fait pour inspirer au poète un amour éternel et muet ainsi que la matière.'"* This time he didn't translate Baudelaire.

Gazing down now at the tiny rooftops of Paris and thinking back to that moment when he'd first met his wife, all Edward could do was shake his head in wonderment. Only here in this city of light could a fifty-one year old man take as his lover a sixteen-year old girl as if it were the most natural thing in the world. Blanche Epler... Flora reincarnated, the miracle of love at first sight occurring for the second time in his life. The French for it was so apt: *un coup de foudre*, a stroke of lightning – it really could strike twice. And Edward knew his love was requited, he just knew it was. He had known it from the first moment: that spark in her eyes as they met his. This time, he vowed not to let his work destroy their happiness. He would always put her first, always, come what may. But in the next moment, he also vowed not to let what had happened hurt Sarah Louisa. If this entailed keeping his new love secret from her, so be it.

As Nadar got up to adjust the rigging of the balloon, Edward leaned over the artist's empty seat to squeeze Blanche's hand. She squeezed back, so hard it almost hurt and whispered, "My Dudu."

Only twelve days – his twelve days of Christmas and every one of them spent with her. She already had a nickname for him, the French diminutive for Edouard. It was so odd, although Blanche didn't share Flora's fear of flying, she shared the same name for him, or almost; a mere changing of the guard – of the vowels – from Dodo to Dudu.

She was his Snow White... his *Blanche Neige*... or better still, his *blanche colombe* as they said in the lovely French song, *"Apaisez, blanche colombe, votre faim du grain de froment qui tombe de ma main."* Blanche Epler... even her family name was ravishing: the "p" soft as her lips, the "l" sweet as the touch of her tongue. They'd already consummated their love in the passenger cabin – on Christmas Day of all days! (almost a mile high, but not as high as he was flying) – to which they'd been directed by a beaming Nadar: *"Allez faire l'amour!"*

What a wondrous expression, how much more civilized and honest and direct that its coy English equivalent, "to make love," meaning to play at love, to court, to flirt, to do anything rather than the physical act, for only coarse words existed for that, precisely to seal it off from love. No, the French wrapped their loving and courting and flirting and bonding physically with a woman into one simple, beautiful phrase: *faire l'amour*. Even their use of the "French letter" that Blanche insisted on could not mar their happiness.

CHAPTER FORTY-FOUR

Edward's whole life galloped faster and faster. Meissonier consulted him about making his paintings of horses more realistic; Marey was developing a "photographic gun" that would "shoot" twelve pictures in rapid succession to stop any moving creature in its tracks as surely as Jesse James; and he and Marey were building an "Electro-Photo Studio" in the Bois de Boulogne where they could advance together from Edward's "*Chronographie*" to his own "*Chrono*photo*graphie*;" Meissonier and Marey had both agreed to partner with him on a volume about the *Attitudes of Animals in Motion* as illustrated by the Assyrians, Egyptians, Romans, Greeks, the great masters of modern times (revisiting his lantern slides), and then finally – and at last correctly – by Marey and himself. So much excitement, so much promise.

And on the personal level: Blanche… Since the *coup de foudre* in Nadar's studio, they'd been together every day – in fact, every day and night, for Blanche had moved in with him at Marey's, who of course thought this perfectly normal. Edward had never realized before – even with Flora – just how many hours could be spent in a bedchamber. For one so young, Blanche had acquired some extraordinary skills, not the least of which was her ability to teach him French. Where else to master such an intimacy as language but between the sheets? She even had him reading her favorite book: *Les Liaisons dangereuses* by Choderlos de Laclos, an exchange of elegantly written letters about true and false love, whose style he emulated in the almost daily *billet doux* he left under her pillow.

And the photographs he was taking of her! Finally, an adult human being as unashamed of her body as a Beatrice. He was capturing every nuance of her perfect form from every conceivable angle. He couldn't wait to take her back to the States – he'd have to find a way to avoid the scandal of course, but where there's a will there must be a way – so that he could capture every unadorned *movement* within his walls of cameras.

Edward had shown the athletes at Palo Alto in quite a number of different motion sequences, but he knew that he'd hardly scratched the surface of the range of human movement. Now that the gelatin dry plate had been improved even further since those early examples he'd obtained from the Lumière brothers, he could take his locomotive investigations to a new level.

An encyclopedia of movement, that was what he must create next, he realized. A compendium of all the visible muscular action, of animals, men, women, children, old and young, all in their natural state; all the marble statues of the nude human form that had ever been carved, from Bernini and Michael Angelo to Auguste Rodin, all made to come alive.

Would Stanford be interested? If not, what did it matter? With Edward's success in France, there would be no end of backers. And with his new love, no end of happiness.

But still he couldn't keep the nagging doubts at bay. Did Blanche really love him as much as she declared? He who was old enough to be her grandfather? He'd thought Flora was young for him at twenty, but sixteen…

As usual Nadar had the answer when Edward broached the subject one afternoon over a carafe of burgundy; the artist always liked his *petit coup derrière la cravate* around four o'clock. They were in one of their favorite haunts, Café Procope at No. 13, rue de l'Ancienne Comédie, the oldest café in Paris, dating back to Molière. It was quiet this afternoon, no sign of Verlaine crying into his absinthe or Balzac sizing someone up for a character in his latest book. The aging owner was also absent, so they were spared his usual stream of complaints about the wild young Bohemians who had made his life such a misery back in the fifties. When they weren't bringing in their own coffee to save five sous, they were painting nude models of both sexes right under the noses of the respectable patrons. Nadar found these complaints somewhat hypocritical since the entire reputation of the café had been built on such behavior. But now all that remained of Bohemia were the framed prints of "Panthéon-Nadar" hung on the café's walls. *Was that why it was his favorite café?* As for Edward's question about Blanche, the artist replied, "She loves you because you're famous,

Edouard, the ultimate aphrodisiac, even better than oysters!"

"Yes, but she's so *young*," objected Edward. "And I know nothing about her I know she's half-Jewish 'Epler' from Hungary originally I understand related to the Hungarian word *eper* for strawberry that's why she's so delicious you can see it in her height she's taller than the average French girl but she doesn't even know where her parents are although she's not without education she's very intelligent it's quite extraordinary she never stops reading I've never known such a reader I could watch her read for hours on end just sit there watching she likes the eighteenth century best."

Edward paused for breath after this stream of words.

Nadar laughed. "For someone who knows nothing about her, you certainly have a lot to say. But as for her age and her race, well, Sarah Bernhardt is also half-Jewish, you know. How old do you think she was?"

"When you took her picture?"

"Yes, and much else." Nadar was all but twirling his moustache. "Hallucinating young woman, such a skinny creature and not very intelligent, but *une grande tragédienne* in spite of her overacting, and what a voice, pure crystal. She was already a courtesan, after all, and not much older than Blanche."

Edward tried not to look shocked. Was Blanche also a courtesan? Or did it matter? After all, the "Divine Sarah" was accepted everywhere, wasn't she? There she was, hanging on the wall nearby. Nadar had somehow managed to make her appear naked without being naked, draping her in an immense white burnoose that threatened to slip off her slim shoulders at any moment. Would he ever really understand the French?

"Sarah could help you, you know," said Nadar.

"How's that?"

"Well, you've conquered France, I know you'd love to conquer your native land as well, you've often said so."

Edward nodded. "Meissonier has already sent letters of recommendation for me to Sir Lawrence Alma-Tadema and Henry Stacy Marks of the Royal Academy of Arts in London. So I already have an entrée – "

"Meissonier, Alma-Tadema, Marks!" Nadar looked as if he'd eaten something disagreeable for lunch. "I'm talking about reaching much higher than that."

"How high?"

"I told you: Sarah Bernhardt. Now there's an entrée," a wink, "or a dessert, depending upon your taste."

"I don't follow."

"I set quite a fashion with our Sarah – between the sheets, that is." Another *clin d'oeil.* "What man of renown hasn't followed in my slippers, particularly in England, the very highest renown… "

"The Prince of Wales!?"

"*Voilà.*"

"Sarah's latest conquest. They don't call him 'Edward the Caresser' for nothing. She's in Paris now, as it happens, rehearsing Sardou's 'Fédora' at the *Théâtre du Vaudeville*, I'll send a note round so she can recommend you to His Highness – no, I have a better idea, why don't we go to the theater so you can meet Sarah in person?"

CHAPTER FORTY-FIVE

Edward was going to meet Edward, just as Nadar had promised. For here he was on the stage of the theater of the Royal Institution of Great Britain, at No. 21 Albemarle-street, summoned here for a "command performance" by none other than His Royal Highness, Edward the Prince of Wales. Bernhardt truly was divine. Between her rehearsals at that theater in Paris, they had had a most interesting talk. Apart from promising to write to the Prince about Edward, she'd told Edward all about her triumphant tours of America, including visits to Mr. Thomas Edison. What a charming woman. She lived up to every word of Nadar's description.

Edward's usual equipment was set out, everything was in place. And so it should be, he had been rehearsing for days with his London Molteni, a young man by the name of Ernest Webster. He was most grateful for Ernest, who was not only a surprisingly skilled mechanic for his age – he couldn't have been much older than Arthur – but had also given Edward some sound advice: to show only the horses and other animal pictures, the Royal Family might not be ready for semi-nude men, they were not in France now.

The Royal Institution… What heroes from his schooldays had stood upon this stage? Their presentations were a clever combination of education and entertainment by all accounts: Sir Humphrey Davy on the uses of laughing gas, Michael Faraday on the chemical history of a candle, and just last year John Tyndall on why the sky was blue. And this year, it was he, Edward James Muybridge, who was standing here!

The Institution had even lodged him in a suite on the top floor of the Langham, the most modern hotel in London, opened by the Prince himself and patronized by everyone from Napoleon III to Mark Twain and Dvorák. Edward was getting as bad as Nadar with his names. But it was impressive: a hundred water closets, thirty-six bathrooms, the first hydraulic lifts in England; they'd even installed electric light in the courtyard. Astonishing. Now it was

Blanche he couldn't wait to tell - although of course he would also cable Sarah Louisa.

It was almost five o'clock, just a few more minutes to go. Edward peered through the heavy brocade curtains. On each chair was a printed copy of his introduction to this meeting on "The Attitudes of Animals in Motion, illustrated with the Zoöpraxiscope." Just in time too, for the doors had now opened.

The aristocracy led the way, the Dukes and Duchesses, Lords and Earls and Marquises. And then came the Prime Minister, Mr. Gladstone, followed by Alma Tadema and Marks, who was sitting down next to the Darwinian, Professor Thomas Huxley, and Professor William Spottiswoode, President of the Royal Society, and Professor John Tyndall himself. Oh, the sky was blue tonight all right! And here was the poet laureate, Alfred Lord Tennyson, with – who was that? Oh, it was Dodgson! After all these years. He'd hardly changed at all. Eternal youth. That's what comes from living in Wonderland, Edward supposed. He must catch him afterwards to thank him again for getting him started on the magical path that led to his place. And now came the journalists. Edward had never seen so many in one place, and from across the world too, judging by all the different languages they were speaking.

Thump-thump-thump. What was that? His whole body was vibrating, his heart beating so hard he thought he was going to explode. The only person left to appear was His Royal Highness.

Edward wondered what he was really like? Everyone knew a story about the "play-boy Prince": a slow learner, reading little and writing less as a boy, and a gourmand and womanizer as a man, only living for pleasure, for hunting and shooting and gambling. And yet kind and charming and generous with not an ounce of prejudice towards other classes or races or religions – even Catholics. He'd once scandalized the other guests at a dinner party, they said, by sitting not only a Rothschild, but a *Cardinal* at his table. Everybody loved "our Bertie." And Edward was about to meet him, the man who – astonishingly – was cured by the same doctor as himself. Just four years after saving Edward from his stagecoach injuries, Dr. Gull had snatched the Prince from his grave.

His Royal Highness had been on the verge of expiring from typhoid fever when Gull had dealt him, as Mark Twain who was present had put it, "blow after blow between the shoulders, breathed into his nostrils, and literally cheated Death." A heroic act, for which the doctor had been awarded an instant baronetcy.

There was a sudden hush as the Royal Footman marched up to face the audience. He might have stepped out of the court of Queen Elizabeth in his long scarlet wrap doubled up over his shoulders and his gold-lined top hat. Two assistant footmen unrolled a red carpet from a side door to the center of the front row. The Royal Footman raised his long silver-headed cane.

Thump, thump, thump! It wasn't Edward's heart now, but the cane striking the floor. "My lords, ladies and gentlemen: His Royal Highness, Prince Albert Edward, Prince of Wales, Lord of the Isles and Prince and Great Steward of Scotland, Prince of Saxe-Coburg-Gotha, Duke of Saxony, Duke of Cornwall, Duke of Rothesay, Earl of Chester, Earl of Dublin, Earl of Carrick, Baron Renfrew, Knight of the Garter and Fellow of the Royal Society." What a lot of people in one man, thought Edward.

The whole edifice shook with a rumble as everyone stood.

Edward had expected him to be fat, but not this fat. Five ten-course meals a day and untold bottles of brandy and champagne had taken their toll. He was almost bursting out of the blue uniform with its scarlet facings that matched his complexion and the squadrons of gleaming campaign ribbons and gold and silver medals on his chest that looked as if they were about to take off like a flock of iridescent pigeons.

Now came the Princess of Wales, the Princesses Victoria, Louise and Maud, and the Duke of Edinburgh. If only Edward could have brought Blanche with him, but even His Highness had left his mistress behind on this occasion – or perhaps she just hadn't been able to get away from the theater? At all events, Sarah had done her job.

The royal party took their seats, followed by everyone else.

Then – almost immediately – the Prince eased his bulk upright once again like a red and blue balloon breaking free of its moorings. The entire auditorium started to do likewise until His Highness lowered a chubby hand to signal them to sit down again.

Where was he going? What was this? The Prince was climbing a small flight of steps leading up to the stage – and Edward! He gripped the curtains, feeling every corrugation of the silk and satin. He had expected someone like John Tyndall to be the host for the evening, but His Highness?

Edward narrowed the gap between the curtains to a hair's breadth: a thin slice of Prince moved to the center of the stage, and filled the gap. He was so close Edward could have poked him with his finger.

The Prince cleared his throat. "As Vice-Patron and Honorary Member of the Royal Institution of Great Britain – and in the Chair for the purposes of this evening – we are pleased to introduce the presenter of tonight's lecture – discourse – exhibition – entertainment – we don't know quite how to describe it, but we sincerely hope it is above all, the latter – entertainment, that is. Haha. At all events, we are reliably informed that it is quite extraordinary – eh – so without further ado, we present… " He left a dramatic pause. Edward held his breath. "…Mr. Edward Muybridge."

With a rustle of silk and satin and clanking and wheezing of pulleys and ropes, the wine-dark curtains slowly rose.

A sunbeam burned Edward's face: now all the limelight flooding all the actors in all the plays he'd ever seen was on *him*. He was so blinded by the light, he couldn't make out anyone in the audience, just row upon row of shadows.

The royal face looked up at him – surprisingly the Prince must have been a good six inches shorter – but so close now, the cognac fumes were almost overpowering, yet the voice was suddenly very soft, for Edward alone. "Sarah told me all about you." For an instant, he was confused. Sarah Louisa? Oh, no, of course, Sarah Bernhardt.

Edward smiled at Edward. "I know you will be wonderful."

And with that, the Prince left the stage.

Edward signaled to Ernest.

When the great waves of applause had died down, leaving only swirls of astonishment lapping around the hooves and strides, suspended feet and supporting feet, galloping and trotting, the Prince of Wales rose from his seat again and walked to the edge of the stage.

All eyes focused on His Highness. What would he, who loved racing thoroughbreds and hunting foxes almost as much as he loved chasing women – they said he'd even had all the clocks at Sandringham put forward half an hour to create more time for the hunt – what would he say about the attitudes of the horse revealed as never before by this strange gruff man with the long white beard? Would the royal thumb point up or down?

The Prince of Wales opened his mouth: "I should like to see your boxing pictures."

Edward didn't know whether to bow, kiss the Prince's hand or fall on his knees, but he just managed to get out: "I shall be very happy to show them, your Royal Highness. I don't know if these pictures teach us anything very useful, but they're generally found amusing."

He signaled to his assistant to slot the requisite disk – which Edward had stubbornly brought along just in case – into the apparatus. The two barely clad forms filled the screen, pounding away at each other over and over again to cries of delight throughout the house, with the Prince of Wales crying loudest of all.

Some of the most famous people in the land were forming a circle round him, Gladstone, Huxley, Tennyson, Dodgson – at least, he thought that's who they were, it was hard to tell, their faces were a blur as the Prince bombarded him with question after question not only about his motion pictures, but about himself.

"Muybridge… " the Prince stared at the program, "strange spelling – although I never could spell – always had trouble with spelling, they call it *alexia* or some damn thing now, you know, 'word-blindness,' but when I was growing up they thought I was the village idiot."

No wonder the people loved him. "The 'Muy' part is because of some Spanish blood in the family, your Highness," said Edward.

"Really? From Kingston-On-Thames? I didn't know it was Spanish, I always thought it was Saxon." The Prince winked. "Haha."

Edward was laughing too. *He was laughing with the Prince of Wales. When was he going to wake up?* "Yes, it was the seat of the Anglo-Saxon kings, seven of them were crowned there. Their coronation stone is still in the Market Place."

"I always wanted to change my name to E-a-d-w-e-a-r-d like Eadweard the Unready," said the Prince, "it certainly applies to me, I'm never been ready for anything, but Mama wouldn't hear of it – could never have got the spelling right twice in a row anyway. Haha." The Prince frowned. "Or was it *Aethelred* the Unready? I can never remember. I must have missed that history lesson. How do you spell yours?"

Edward blurted it out without thinking. "The same way, your Royal Highness. They got it wrong in the program."

"Eadweard…" it sounded the same, but when he wrote it at the end of his letter to Blanche, it really did look royal. He had so much to tell his darling, not only about the Prince but about yet more successes. That evening at the Royal Institution had been followed by an exhibition at the Royal Academy of Arts at Burlington House, where "Eadweard" had been unanimously elected to honorary membership. It had also been at the Royal Academy – everything was "Royal" in England, you know, my darling, he explained in his letter, even the jam – that the London correspondent of the *San Francisco Call* had said that if Eadweard were to hire a hall and give exhibitions of his motion pictures twice a day at a shilling entrance fee, he would clear enough money to greatly assist him in his researches. Imagine how rich we'll be, my dearest! Perhaps such "entertainments" as everyone insisted on calling them might one day replace those frightful charades he'd had to join in as a child. Now who was the showman?

Another highly successful exhibition took place at the Savage Club, where Edweard was also made an honorary member, joining W.S.Gilbert, Wilkie Collins, Dante Rossetti, Mark Twain, and the only – and everyone said, unrepeatable – female member, Sarah Bernhardt. Now he was up to his waist in dropped names.

Edward included with his letter his favorite newspaper clipping from the great pile that Ernest had assembled for him. It was by George Sala of the *Illustrated London News*, in which he wrote that had Eadweard exhibited his Zoöpraxiscope three hundred years ago, he would have been "burnt for a wizard." How odd; that was what they called Edison: "The wizard of Menlo Park." And what a strange coincidence that he and Edison should both have done some of their best work in a place of the same name, Edison in Menlo Park, New Jersey and Eadweard in Menlo Park, California.

The next few weeks went by so fast he could hardly breathe: the Society of Arts, the South Kensington Science and Art Department, the Royal Artillery Institute and Eton College. Who would have guessed that he would get there after all? And not as a mere student, but as a guest of honor, a person of the highest celebrity, who could pronounce his "nime" any way he liked, thank you very much.

Then, while resting on April the sixth, the day before Good Friday, a letter was slipped under the door of his hotel suite that was to change his life.

CHAPTER FORTY-SIX

Eadweard jumped up to fetch the letter: it must be Blanche, the dear, she wrote almost every day from Paris. As soon as he got back there he would take her to Laferrière, Sarah Bernhardt's favorite designer, and damn the cost.

He reached for the silver letter-opener provided by the Langham, then stopped. Embossed on the envelope was a royal crest with the words, "The Royal Society of London for the Improvement of Natural Knowledge." The Royal Society... he'd read about it of course – what scientist hadn't? Its history was that of science itself, its fellows ranging from Francis Bacon to Newton and Darwin and Pasteur and Maxwell, and recently none other than Sir William Gull.

He slit open the envelope. It was from William Spottiswoode. He was inviting him to submit a monograph on the "Attitudes of Animals in Motion" that Eadweard would read to the Council of the Society. He would subsequently be requested to present the paper formally in person so that it could be placed on the record of the "Proceedings."

Eadweard looked at his image in the cheval glass beside his dressing table. He couldn't stop grinning. How had the correspondent of the *Philadelphia Times* described him? "Like all people who amount to something, the California artist is *artistique au possible*; the loosely tied neck ribbon" – he'd learned that from Nadar – "the velvet coat, the grey felt sombrero... the true artistic style of the London and Paris ateliers." It was true, as surely as a Bernhardt in the world of the theater, he had become a star in the firmament of art, and he was now about to become one in the realm of science.

The letter said his deadline for submission was Thursday, the 20th of April. He had exactly two weeks to prepare the best description of his work he had ever written.

He completed his manuscript on time and a few days later received a proof sheet from the Royal Society. Goodness, they were efficient, but he supposed they had to be with ground-breaking monographs coming in from the greatest minds all over the world. The RS informed him that the "Attitudes of Animals in Motion" was to be read to the Council by Professor Spottiswoode on the 27th of April followed by a "Preliminary Account of the Structure of the Cells of the Liver, and the Changes which take place in them under Various Conditions" by J.N.Langley, M.A., Fellow of Trinity College, Cambridge. Eadweard was poised on the very edge of scientific research.

The RS also informed him that his own presentation to the Fellows was scheduled to take place in just over a month from now: on Thursday, the 26th of May.

On Tuesday, the 23rd of May – only three days to go! – yet another letter from the RS arrived. It was a brief note requesting his presence at the Rooms of the Society at nine o'clock A.M. on the twenty-*fourth* – why, that was *tomorrow!* They'd brought his presentation forward! Oh, my Lord. But this was excellent, excellent: the ultimate recognition of everything he'd done was coming even sooner than he'd thought.

It was only a seven or eight-minute hackney ride from the Langham to Burlington House: straight down Regent-street, turn right at the Circus and then onto Piccadilly, three quarters of a mile at the most, they said at the reception desk. But what with the traffic, especially at eight-thirty in the morning, it seemed endless, Eadweard could have got to the moon quicker than this. In a sense, he was on the moon – he was *over* the moon. He'd had many "big moments" in his career, but this was surely the biggest of all.

What a glorious spring day, the sun blazing down, unusually warm for England.

Eadweard flipped through the copy of *Twice Round the Clock* he hadn't been able to resist picking up at the hotel since it was by George Sala, the same droll reporter who had written that Eadweard would have been "burnt for a wizard" had he exhibited his Zoöpraxiscope three hundred years ago. Then he gave a start. What was this he'd happened upon? Sala was describing this very Regent-street at this very hour: "…the clattering solemnity of wooden panels, and iron bars, and stanchions as the shop-shutters were taken down to reveal the museums of fashion in plate-glass cases where young gentlemen in their shirt sleeves accomplish the difficult and mysterious feat known as 'dressing' the shop window with 'superfluities.'" This was precisely what Eadweard was seeing and hearing above the click-clack of the hackney horse's hooves on the cobblestones. This was surely no mere coincidence, this was surely a portent of the great things to come this morning! Sala went on to make gentle fun of the "rich piled velvet mantles, the *moiré* and *glacé* silks arranged in artful folds, the laces and gauzes, the innumerable whim-whams and fribble-frabble of fashion that line this great trunk road in Vanity Fair." Yes, yes, Sala had it absolutely right: the ghost of Becky Sharp could wave at Eadweard from one of these shop windows at any moment.

But do get a move on! Surely the driver could get more speed out of this old nag? Eadweard could run faster than this. What was the world record for the mile? William Cummings last year, wasn't it? Four minutes and sixteen seconds? So this would be seventy-five percent of that: three minutes and thirty seconds. He wouldn't even have to run, he could *walk* faster than this, but then he'd arrive all hot and flustered, and we didn't want that, did we? Not on this day of all days.

At last, they were turning onto Piccadilly, and there were the beadles in their top hats and tailcoats patrolling the entrance to the covered Arcade of shops that led to Burlington House.

Eadweard jumped out of the carriage and hurried past the shops. There it was: some "house," the great Palladian pile almost put Hampton Court Palace to shame. He'd already been here once before of course for his exhibition at the Royal Academy. But that had been the west wing. Now he was going to the east wing, the home of the Royal Society. How symbolic: the twin pinnacles of his success, art on the left and science on the right.

Had he remembered to put his monograph in his breast

pocket? He patted his chest. Yes, the comforting rustle of paper. Now up to the great doors, and the even greater iron knocker, you could do serious harm with that. He reached out for it – but the huge doors were already swinging open as if he were expected – which of course he was. Silly Eadweard. Oh, my Lord.

The footman bowed, then looking questioningly at him. "Good morning, sir. How may I be of service?"

Eadweard held out his carte-de-visite.

"My name is Muybridge and – P-Professor Spottiswoode – the President – I am expected."

"Ah, yes sir, please step this way."

The footman led him through a series of tall echoing corridors until they reached a massive door marked "Council Chamber." The footman knocked.

"Come," said a deep voice.

The footman opened the door and led Eadweard into a large paneled room. "Gentlemen. Mr. Eadweard Muybridge."

A dozen of so men in morning dress were seated in a row behind a long oak table. Gull wasn't among them, although several of the men looked familiar from photographs or engravings. But Eadweard was suddenly so nervous he could only attach a name to two of them: Spottiswoode himself of course, and the great student of heredity and cousin of Charles Darwin, Francis Galton, the man who had coined the term "eugenics." Galton inclined his head slightly as if he recognized him. Perhaps he'd seen some of the engravings of Eadweard in the papers. This was most reassuring. Galton's broad forehead bespoke his intelligence and wisdom and was only made more impressive by the fact that he was almost completely bald. A kindly uncle, if ever Eadweard saw one.

Spottiswoode gestured to him to be seated in a straight-backed chair set in front of the Council.

It was all very serious, but then of course this was a serious, not to say epoch-making, occasion. So it was perfectly normal for these men to appear solemn. So why was he so nervous?

Eadweard started to reach into his breast pocket for his monograph, then paused. Spottiswoode was pushing a large book on the table towards him.

"Do you know anything about this book, Mr. Muybridge?"

He read the title: *"The Horse in Motion" by JDB Stillman MD. Published under the auspices of Leland Stanford. Boston. James R. Osgood and Company.*

What was this? Where was his name? There was no mention of his name! And what was this book, anyway? Was this what Stillman and Stanford had been doing together?

He looked up at the faces.

"I've never seen this book before! I know nothing about this."

"Look inside, please," said Spottiswoode.

Eadweard opened the book. He couldn't believe his eyes. Although only a handful of his actual photographs had been tipped into the volume, there was page after page of photolithographs of drawings made from his pictures, even from some of his shots of the horse skeleton.

"Does this book contain the results of the photographic investigation of which you have *professed* to be the author?"

"Yes, indeed, it does." He could feel his anger rising.

"In that case," Spottiswoode smirked like a Stoney, "would you kindly explain to the Council how it is that your name does not appear on the title page?"

Of course he couldn't – any more than he could imagine how it could ever have come to this. He got to his feet, staring into the eyes of each of the members of the jury – for that's what it was, and no mistake, he was being judged, and this time he *was* innocent.

He tried to keep his voice steady. "I can categorically declare to you gentlemen that I took every one of the photographs depicted in this book, with my cameras and my high-speed shutters and my triggering mechanisms. In short, I invented all the means employed."

He resumed his seat.

"That's as may be, but do you *own* these photographs?" said Spottiswoode.

"What?"

"Do you have sure legal claim to these photographs?" said Galton. There was nothing avuncular about him now.

"I most certainly do."

"You must understand, Mr. Muybridge," continued Galton, "that there is a dispute as to the scientific proprietorship of these pictures."

"A dispute? What dispute?"

"The Council asked me to write a report on your paper, and as part of my researches, I cabled Mr. Leland Stanford in California and asked who owned the photographs you have been exhibiting all over London. He replied that since they were taken while you were in his employment, they belonged to him, and you therefore had no legal right to them."

"This is preposterous!"

"Furthermore," it was as if Eadweard hadn't spoken, "Mr. Stanford had his London agent send me the elaborate volume you have before you, which includes I may add a description of the conclusions to be drawn from the photographs therein written by Dr. Stillman."

"But my paper?" Eadweard brandished his monograph.

"Precisely, having read the Stillman book, I do not find that the conclusions you draw in your memoir differ in any notable manner from those of the doctor – "

"But – "

"*Furthermore*, your conclusions are certainly much less perspicacious and well expressed that those of Dr. Stillman, and they are scarcely, if at all, intelligible without reference to the photographs."

"You didn't ask me to include photographs in my paper."

"No, but for your paper to be published, it would have to be illustrated by lithographs of the photography to which you claim title, and after this – "

"To which I *have* title!"

Galton was like a steamroller. " – and *even after this* was done, the result would be a memoir much inferior in importance to an already published book, without perpetrating any novel feature of its own that I can see to recommend it."

There was a long silence. Eadweard didn't know what to say.

Galton cleared his throat. He had that look on his face, that combination of arrogance and condescension that only a well-born Englishman could summon, his voice as polished as his scalp.

"Under these circumstances, Mr. Muybridge, I am unable to advise the Council of the Royal Society to order your paper to be presented either in their Transactions or in their Proceedings."

CHAPTER FORTY-SEVEN

Eadweard could have killed Stillman, and God knows he knew how to do it. The bastard, getting round the Governor, especially when he wasn't well, to betray Eadweard and everything he'd worked for. Everything.

These and other thoughts blacker than pitch coursed through his brain as he trudged back to the hotel through a series of side alleys. He couldn't even look a cabby in the eye now, let alone Regent-street; the very name was a mockery, what would the Prince think of him now?

Back at the Langham once again, he sneaked through the lobby like a thief, keeping his head down and praying they hadn't already heard the news.

He didn't have long to wait. The repercussions of Galton's decision didn't so much ripple through the surprisingly small, closed London society as surge through it like a *tsunami*. Over the next few days, there was the same ominous hiss as missive after missive slithered under the door of his suite to slam every other door in the city in his face. All of his upcoming London engagements had immediately been canceled; the Savage Club had banned him from its portals; even the hotel wanted him out by the end of the week, the Royal Institution having refused to pay any further bills. He hadn't a friend left in the city and the only mention of him now in the papers consisted of whispered innuendo about the imposter, the charlatan, the purloiner of other people's ideas and work.

The streets of gold had turned back into mud, and he was face down in it, his reputation shredded beyond repair. How long had he been the lion of London, how long have he been "royal?" Just over two months. That was the sum total of his glory days in the land of his birth.

It was all so unfair, so grossly unfair. Eadweard had never stolen anything from anyone in his life. It was all *his* work, they were all *his* ideas; he had invented all the apparatus for his motion studies, he had performed all the experiments. Oh, Stanford had made numerous suggestions of course and had paid the bills, but the work was Eadweard's alone. And his reward, because of that damnable book, had been scandal and dishonor and disgrace. As if he hadn't already had enough of that in his life.

Suddenly, Eadweard couldn't wait to get out of the city he had been so excited to re-enter. He had to get back to America as soon as possible; he never wanted to see England again. In fact, he didn't want to see France again either, he couldn't face Marey or Meissonior or Nadar for the moment – he couldn't even face Blanche. Strangely enough, the only person whose shoulder he wanted to cry on now was Sarah Louisa. He dispatched a quick telegraph to tell her what had happened.

But how to pay for the voyage to the States? There would be no more help from the Royal Institution, that was obvious, and no more free railroad passes from Stanford, that was equally clear. And he'd received only occasional lecture fees while he'd been here, merely asking for his expenses. In short, he had hardly a penny to his name. He racked his brain: what did he have of value that he could sell? He'd had all his equipment stored in New York, but that was his whole life, he could hardly get rid of that. What else? Well, he did have with him four remaining copies of his *Attitudes of Animals in Motion*. He would just have to sell those. He spread them out on a table and scowled at them.

For the three days following the nightmare at Burlington House, Eadweard didn't step out of the suite, insisting that his food be left outside the door and the daily cleaning by the maids be put off until he quitted the hotel.

And all the while the sun that he'd always loved so much had become an inferno beating down relentlessly outside, turning his rooms so stuffy that he sat out on the balcony. He measured the distance: five floors. It was certainly high enough, especially if he fell head first, or better still impaled himself on the spikes of the railings that barricaded the ground floor of the hotel. As the minutes and hours and days went by, he leaned further and further out.

Then in the early evening of the Friday, his last day – he'd promised the management he'd be out first thing tomorrow – there was a knock on the door. Had they changed their minds and wanted him out tonight?

Eadweard drew back the bolt.

His visitor was dressed entirely in red.

"I hope they all fall into a bowl of English soup. I can't think of a worse fate."

Nadar had read all about it of course, and needed no further details. All he did need was to impress on Eadweard one simple French phrase: "*Impossible n'est pas français.*"

Eadweard smiled – for the first time in three days: the very phrase that had started it all.

"It's true," said Nadar misreading his expression.

But now Eadweard was frowning. "I'm fifty-two years old, Félix. I don't even have the money to get back to America. I don't think I have the energy to start again – yet again… It's all my fault, I brought it on myself, hubris… I flew too near the sun."

Nadar shook him by the shoulders. "*Ecoutez, mon ami. Ecoutez-moi.* I have been rich, I have been poor, in fashion, out of fashion, up and down more times than a lady's hemline. Why, as you know, I'm having to sell the entire contents of my studio to avoid bankruptcy – I've always been troubled by 'a certain looseness of the purse,' as your Mr. Dickens said of his improvident father. But like the phoenix I will rise again." His waved his finger in the air like a conductor. "I always have and I always will. And so will you, Edouard, so will you. I, Nadar, predict it!" He gesturing at the albums spread out on a table. "Why don't you sell those?"

Eadweard shrugged. "I thought of that, but to whom? Who would buy anything from me now?"

"I still have friends in London. How much do you want for them?"

"£100 each."

"I'll have them sold by Monday morning. Nadar knows everyone in London." He stroked his moustache. "And I do mean *know* in the very best biblical sense."

"But I have to leave the hotel tomorrow."

"Then you shall stay at mine." Nadar looked round Eadweard's luxurious but now extremely messy sitting room. "Not quite as grand as the Langham, but still better than the street."

"But – "

He raised his hand. "But now you must dress."

"I am dressed."

"For dinner."

"Oh no, I'm not going into a restaurant."

"You don't have to. I ordered it to be brought up. Please go and get yourself ready!"

Nadar grimaced at Eadweard's shabby work coat and trousers. "You look like – well, just dress. It will cheer you up, trust me." He made a face at the room. "In the meantime, I will try and salvage this shipwreck."

Forty minutes later, in his tails, hair washed and combed, beard trimmed, Eadweard felt, if not exactly a new man, at least a slightly more cheerful one. Nadar had been right as usual.

And when he stepped out of his dressing room his suite was not only now neat and tidy, but a slap-up dinner had been laid out for two with the finest china, steaming silver tureens, Irish linen, champagne and wine – even a crystal vase of red roses.

"When you say 'dinner,' you don't mince your words, do you Félix?"

Then he realized that Nadar himself was not dressed. "Aren't you going to change – since we're being so formal?"

"I'm not coming to dinner."

"What?"

"No, you have a guest."

A tap on the door.

Nadar opened it on Blanche, in the lowest cut and most beautiful purple velvet evening gown in the world.

The next morning, Eadweard was beyond cheerful – if fame was an aphrodisiac, then notoriety was a whole cartload of oysters. He and Blanche had been so busy making love in the French sense they hadn't slept a wink all night, a fact that Nadar registered the moment he entered the suite and saw their drowsy faces.

"So that's why they call it *'une nuit blanche?'*"

They all laughed. A sleepless night, thought Eadweard. With Blanche. How true. That was a good one.

The only thing that marred Eadweard's happiness was knowing he must soon tell his love that he couldn't take her back to America with him – at least for now – there was already enough slander echoing round his name.

In the meantime, after he had moved out of the Langham, Blanche and he spent more hours of bliss at Nadar's more modest hotel in Kensington, while their host went on a selling spree.

Nadar returned in the early evening, Eadweard's photographic albums replaced by a brown paper bag whose contents he spilled in front of the sofa where the two lovers were holding hands as if they were both sixteen.

"£400. Sold every last one of them." Nadar chuckled as he glanced at the banknotes. "You English, I always think these look like something you blow your nose on."

It was true, the flimsy white sheets of paper did look more like handkerchiefs than £5 of legal tender. Eadweard shook Nadar's hand. "I'm not going to blow my nose on these, I promise you. You're a miracle worker. How can I thank you?"

Nadar sat down in front of them. "Keep making love, that's all that really matters. Now, for your travel plans."

Blanche stared at Eadweard. "What travel plans?"

Nadar stared at him too. "You haven't told her?"

"Well… " Eadweard squeezed her hand, "I have to return to America, my darling. I have to get my career started again."

"I'll come with you," said Blanche, "I'll help, you'll see."

"You don't understand… the scandal… I can't stand any more scandal, I just can't."

Blanche embraced him, stroking his hair, soothing a child. "Dudu, Dudu…"

"But I'll send for you, I'll send for you just as soon as I can, I'll find a way, I promise – " How many times had he said that to another woman? He needed a Bible. There was one on a little table. He placed his right hand on top of it. "I swear on the Holy Bible that I will send for you, Blanche."

CHAPTER FORTY-EIGHT

"You have to sue him, you know that, don't you, him and Stillman and Osgood the publisher, the whole lot of them," Sarah Louisa said as she hugged Eadweard on the New York dockside.

They settled into the hackney she'd brought. What an extraordinary woman! Eadweard had sent her a telegraph to tell her his day of arrival from Liverpool, but he'd never dreamed she'd come all the way from San Francisco. "Well, that's as may be," he said, echoing Spottiswoode in spite of himself, "but I'm not going back there, I never want to see that man again."

"The Governor?"

"No, Stillman, he's the one behind all this… skeletons, indeed, I might have known whose cupboard they came out of. I don't blame Stanford so much."

She shrugged. "Of course it's Stillman's doing, but I still think you should sue Stanford as well. He's the one in charge. But anyway I know you're not going back to San Francisco. Nor am I. Ever."

"Ever? What do you mean? Your mother – "

"She went back to England."

"Really?"

"She was homesick – she wants to spend her last years in Whitechapel, where she grew up, although from what I hear it's not what it used to be, it's really gone downhill, they say." She sighed. "But you know how stubborn she is. I have no one in San Francisco now."

"But, wait a moment – how did you know I didn't want to return to California? I never told you."

"How long have I known you? Fifteen years… " *He'd met Sarah Louisa when Blanche was two years old*, Eadweard realized. "That's why I broke the lease on the house in South Park."

"You did what?" Everybody was running his life except him.

"Well, I knew you always liked New York, so I leased a small brownstone in Gramercy Park for us, where the Bohemians used to go, just like Paris – "

"For *us*? You're going to move in with me?" Now she was going too far.

"Well, it'll be purely – well…" Her neck exploded into scarlet. "Someone's got to look after you, and – and you know hardly anyone in New York, so no one will talk. Really – you don't mind, do you?"

Eadweard couldn't exactly say he minded, but what was he going to do about Blanche? He nodded quickly at Sarah Louise. "No, that's fine."

He watched her as she leaned out of the window to give directions to the driver. The black was draining ever faster out of her hair, leaving it a dusty gray, and her figure had all but gone. Where did figures go? To some Elysian field of pulchritude presided over by Renoir? But dear old Sarah Louisa, it was true, she did know him better than he knew himself. At the same time, she'd placed him in a terrible position, setting up house with him. How on earth was he going to bring Blanche over now?

"I hope you're not too tired after Europe," said Sarah Louisa.

"Why?"

"Because I have a lot more lectures lined up – and all at quite substantial fees. I've been working with the Scoville people; they made all the arrangements." She got out a sheet of paper and counted off the places: "Newport, Rhode Island, the Society of Arts at the Massachusetts Institute of Technology in Boston – they say they have electric light now, you won't need limelight – the Turf Club in New York, the National Academy of Design and many more. We have you booked through December."

"But the public disgrace in London, the Royal Society?" It still hurt, that look on Galton's face.

Sarah Louisa laughed. "You've forgotten what we Americans – I've grown up here so I consider myself such – think of anything 'royal.' We fought a little war over that, remember? You're more popular than ever."

"Really? I can't believe it."

"It's true."

"And you're more wonderful than ever." Impulsively, Eadweard kissed her on the forehead. Her birthmark glowed again.

She would never change, always there when he needed her, and always that blush. God bless her. And God bless America.

"Now about that lawsuit, it's embarrassing for both of us, not giving you any of the credit. You can't let them get away with it. I won't let you."

She was right of course, thought Eadweard. Not only had they plagiarized his work and violated his copyright, they had surely frightened away any potential financial backers for his encyclopedia of motion. Perhaps a successful lawsuit would yield just the funds he required.

Sarah Louisa fished out another sheet of paper and pointed at a list of names. "Your agents have recommended several excellent attorneys, you can take your pick."

CHAPTER FORTY-NINE

Over the next eight months, Eadweard led a double life, both personally and professionally. On the personal front, he lived with one woman like an old married man grown beyond physical desire while making passionate love to another in twice-weekly letters that he had to sneak out of the very house he was telling his young beauty would soon be hers. Blanche's replies were of course directed *poste restante*, no need to upset Sarah Louisa: his own variation on French letters. He'd also been careful never to mention Sarah Louisa in his correspondence with Paris. It would have been hard enough to explain his strange platonic relationship with Sarah Louisa to Blanche in English, let alone in French. So he hid Blanche from Sarah Louisa and Sarah Louisa from Blanche.

And while all this was going on, on the professional front, Eadweard was giving twice-weekly demonstrations of his motion pictures all across the northeastern United States to such praise and acclaim, he ought to have been delighted. But he was not. He was growing bored again, his ears numb with applause, his hands chapped by commendation.

The problem was, Eadweard's lectures were becoming as repetitive as his endlessly revolving motion-picture disks, when all he really wanted to do was to move on to his "encyclopedia," which he now described in optimistic terms in his *Prospectus* as *A New and Elaborate Work Upon the Attitudes of Man, the Horse, and Other Animals in Motion, by Muybridge.* As he wrote in the frontispiece, his admittedly wildly ambitious proposal was to illustrate:

> *Men… nude or draped… while walking, running, leaping, wrestling, boxing, fencing, military exercising, rowing, and while playing polo, base-ball and racquets… Ladies playing at Lawn Tennis, dancing, and other exercises of muscular action and movement… documenting the human body in its most basic acts… Birds on the wing… seals and other marine mammals. Attention will be given to photographing Actors, while performing*

*their respective parts and accurately recording the successive
attitudes, oscillations and movements of the human body in health
and disease including the successive phases of the Heart and
Lungs while in action in an apparatus I have invented for the
purpose. The results to be published in a standard work of
reference in an edition de luxe, with one hundred plates of
illustrations constituting a copy of the work. For each $100 copy
subscribed for, the subscriber will be entitled to send a horse, or
other animal or subject to my studio for a special photographic
analysis of its movements, which will be illustrated without extra
charge.*

Of course Eadweard had no men, either nude or draped, nor
ladies nor horses nor birds nor seals nor Actors, not even a studio,
so it was hardly surprising he had no subscribers.

In desperate need of funds for his project – and egged on by
Sarah Louisa – Eadweard had finally given in and sought counsel
from a Boston law firm, who'd brought suit against Leland
Stanford on his behalf for damages of $50,000. *$50,000* for a
name? Had he taken all leave of his senses? For that's all it was
about, after all: a few drops of printer's ink, a handful of raised
metal type. Put *Eadweard James Muybridge* on the cover and we can
forgive and forget. Leave it off and deposition after deposition will
pile up like the dust-heap in *Bleak House*. But he did need the
money.

Meanwhile, some funds did come in. In January, the
indefatigable Sarah Louisa made arrangements with a literary
bureau to organize yet more lectures, now to be entitled *The
Romance and Realities of Animal Locomotion*, a more "commercial"
name apparently, designed to warrant the substantial fee that was
henceforth to be charged.

After several engagements in New York, Eadweard found
himself at the Academy of Fine Arts in Philadelphia, at the
invitation of Fairman Rogers of four-in-hand in the park fame,
where the applause was led not only by Rogers but by Thomas
Eakins himself.

What an extraordinary man he was in person. If Nadar was a cat, Eakins was half monkey, half wolf. One moment he was an emaciated shuffling ape, slight willowy body, stubby hair and impish expression as if he knew some delicious secret about everyone present; the next, a wolfish creature with a haunted, shifty light in his eyes, which never seemed to engage you directly, like the poor wretches of Bedlam. Consistent with his anthropoid aspect, he had a sense of humor that defied all convention. At one point in Eadweard's post-lecture conversation with him and other members of the Academy, Eakins even broke wind to raise a laugh. Then the wolf returned as Eakins pulled Eadward aside to discuss what appeared to be his favorite subject, the bodies of Eadweard's near naked athletes.

When Eadweard expressed surprise at this, Eakins giggled, "Welcome to the City of Brotherly Love. Where else could I live with my admiration of the male form? As I always say, Muybridge, a naked woman is the most beautiful thing in the world – except for a naked man."

It was hard to tell whether he was joking or not. And yet at the same time, apart from being a fine artist – he'd studied under Gérôme in Paris for several years, no wonder he was so interested in the nude – he was a first-class linguist, with a fluency in French, Spanish, German and Italian that would have been the envy of Larkyns. Best of all, he asked Eadweard for a copy of his *Prospectus*.

As far as Eadweard's suit against Stanford was concerned, things were by no means so rosy. His legal team seemed helpless against the array of witnesses produced by the Governor's attorneys. Just about everybody who had ever worked for Stanford, from Frank Shay on down to the Palo Alto engineers, mechanics and laborers, swore on the Holy Book that Eadweard had merely been another employee just like themselves. Everything had been Stanford's idea from the start. He owned everything and everybody, "all the cameras, plates, paper, chemicals, machinery, apparatus, appliances, models, subjects, skill and labor"; they all belonged to him.

Indeed, as Eadweard stood in front of yet another enthusiastic audience for yet another lecture, this time a return engagement at the Academy of Fine Arts, the situation both at work and at home still appeared bleak. He really had no chance of prevailing over Stanford and he still had no idea how he was going to resolve the Blanche dilemma. The poor girl seemed patient enough in her letters, but how much longer could this go on? She was young, she wanted to live. What was he going to do? Was he destined to end his days with no one but Sarah Louisa for company as he endlessly turned the handle of his Zoöpraxiscope like some Italian organ grinder?

As if this were a cue for the dancing monkey, Thomas Eakins emerged from the crowd at the end of Eadweard's presentation and headed towards him, his ape-man shuffle-steps short and rapid, almost woman-like. He was closely followed by Fairman Rogers and a small army of gentlemen, whom Rogers introduced to Eadweard one by one: Edward Coates, the Academy president, J.B.Lippincott, the publisher, Thomas Anshutz, the artist representing the Zoological Society of Philadelphia, Dr. William Pepper, Provost of the University of Pennsylvania, Harrison Allen, professor of physiology, and Rush Huidekoper, professor of veterinary anatomy. This was a good omen – at least Eadweard hoped it was; after the Royal Society, he was wary of getting his hopes too high.

Pepper shook his hand: "It's a great honor, Mr. Muybridge." His arm took in the rest of the group. "I'm getting together a committee."

A committee? Eadweard didn't know what to make of this.

The Provost smiled. "Mr. Eakins showed us your Prospectus. Most impressive."

"Just what we've been looking for in our new School of Veterinary Medicine," said Huidekoper.

"And at the Zoological Gardens," said Anshutz.

"Not to mention, the Academy of Fine Arts," said Coates.

"To 'document the human body in its most basic acts,'" whispered Eakins, wolf-man again now, "how delightful."

"Of course we're still at the discussion stage," said Pepper, "but these and other gentlemen have assured me they're prepared to advance the necessary funds, secured by the subscription list of your proposed 'work of reference' – "

" – which I'll be happy to publish," interrupted Lippincott.

" – provided," continued Pepper quickly, "that you bring your subscriptions up to the point where they'll cover the amount advanced."

"A state of affairs," said Eakins, back to a monkey grin, "you'll now have no difficulty in achieving."

Eadweard could almost have hugged him. In one fell swoop, he had solved two problems: he could now create his "encyclopedia" exactly as he'd dreamed, and – as he also realized in a sudden flash of inspiration – he now had the perfect pretext for bringing Blanche over to America: as his first female nude model. *Voilà* as Nadar would say.

"Philadelphia!" Eadweard cried out to Sarah Louisa as he entered the parlor of their Gramercy Park home.

She stared up at him for a moment, then jumped to her feet, throwing her arms round his neck. "Oh, Eadweard, congratulations!"

It had taken six months, but finally the letter from the University of Pennsylvania had arrived reporting that the trustees had resolved "to arrange with Mr. Muybridge for the prosecution of his work on the investigation of animal motion, within the precincts of the Veterinary Department, starting with an advance from Mr. Lippincott of $5,000."

Although Eakins had been assuring Eadweard since February that it was a *fait accompli*, there was nothing like seeing it on paper.

"They're to provide us with rooms in a house on the campus of the university," Eadweard said excitedly. "I want you to be closely involved, Sarah Louisa, we'll be working almost daily with a committee of faculty members to guarantee the scientific accuracy of our project, so we'll have to be very careful to, um… " How should he put this?

She frowned. "Be very careful to do what?"

"Well, to say that you're... my cousin – so as to avoid any misunderstandings."

She shrugged, muttering to herself. "I suppose there are worse fates."

Eadweard did in fact have a cousin, Kate Smith, who had run off with some man to Canada and had never been heard from again. It had always seemed such a strange coincidence, Sarah Louisa having the same family name. But then Smith was hardly the most uncommon name in the world. But now it was to come in uncommonly useful.

As planned, in September Eadweard moved to Philadelphia with Sarah Louisa, each of them taking a room on the second floor of a house on 33rd Street, only a few hundred yards from Eadweard's photographic installation at Pine and 36th. Thank goodness they'd changed her identity, for the first floor of the house was taken up by two members of the faculty. It would have been impossible to avoid talk. But, instead, a cousin in such close proximity hadn't raised an eyebrow.

As for darling Blanche, he had of course told her the good news about the confirmation of his project at the university, as well as the somewhat less good news that he couldn't bring her to America until his full-scale motion photography got started, which wouldn't be until next spring. He tore open each letter from Paris with trembling fingers convinced that she would say her patience was exhausted. But never a word of complaint, never a falter in her love. Whatever the reason, he was blessed.

Meanwhile, in spite of all the setbacks, Eadweard had to say he'd accomplished a great deal. He'd established a suite of laboratories in the basement of Biological Hall; designed and set up a range of photographic equipment, most notably forty of the very latest Dallmeyer lenses from England; made operative the electromagnetic devices that would synchronize three batteries of lenses; constructed an outdoor studio around a rubber track some 120 feet long; and drafted a new university version of his *Prospectus*, which had already brought in nearly two hundred subscriptions at

$100 each from libraries, institutions, well-known artists, scientists, and dilettantes – even though he still hadn't taken a single successful picture for the project.

On top of this, the university committee overseeing his work had now become a nine-member "commission," and he had professors of anatomy, physics, veterinary anatomy and pathology, civil and dynamic engineering, and art instruction supervising every stage of his work. Everyone agreed that this was the most broadly based scientific investigation ever undertaken.

CHAPTER FIFTY

On the morning of October 16th, 1885, Blanche Epler rose from her bed, knelt down and prayed, poured water from a jar, walked and ran and skipped, and ascended a flight of stairs with a lamp, living a day in her life for Eadweard, again and again and again, making up for all the moments he'd missed over the last three years.

His wooden baton quivered in sympathy with each movement of her naked body as trio upon trio of the three dozen glass eyes that surrounded her sang *schlick schlick schlick* so fast it was a concerted triple-layered *schlieeuck* that was triggered by each touch of his thumb on the little brass screw embedded in the wood. Move move move touch touch touch *schlieeuck schlieeuck schlieeuck*. He didn't know whether it was his nerves that were galvanizing hers, or hers his, or the baton the glass eyes, or the glass eyes the baton. They were all working in synchrony, all the pieces of his life at last falling into place, the final synthesis of love and work.

Reaching this point had taken two years of constant labor and countless trial motion sequences – pictures either too fogged or incomplete or light struck. In fact, his struggles during this period had been so intense that when the inevitable final dismissal of his suit against Stanford and Stillman had come back in February, he'd hardly noticed. But at last, by July, every instrument of his 36-camera orchestra was playing in perfect harmony and he had finally been able to bring Blanche to America. She had been so patient, the poor darling.

Eadweard watched her now, beating time like a metronome with his baton, his "common stick" as he called it: Blanche simultaneously moving past his cameras, towards his cameras and away from his cameras, his glass eyes caressing her flanks and her breasts and the thick golden tresses tumbling down her back. Was that the hint of a smile on her face, a subtle Mona Liza smile, just for him? The chorus of *schlieeucks* as her movements grew faster and faster was like the metallic flurry of bone-dry autumn leaves when the wind picks up armfuls of gold and bronze and copper flakes and hurls them back on the ground: a burst of Nature's applause for her beauty.

After Eadweard had completed the last of the eleven motion studies that he'd planned for today, Blanche strode back to her dressing room as seemingly unaware of her nakedness as the clear blue sky looking down into the open studio.

The five student assistants the university had provided him busied themselves with their various tasks. Two of these young men – they were all in their early twenties – maintained the electrical apparatus, two helped in the field, and one worked in the dark-room helping the photographic expert, Mr. H.L. Bell, whom Eadweard had engaged to develop the endless stream of plates. In addition, three of these students had consented to pose for his very first full-scale motion studies here back in June: William Bigler, clothed, as he walked while lifting his hat; Robert Glendinning, nude, as he did a handspring; and Morris Hacker – the one aiding Mr. Bell – a handsome young athlete with a lean muscular body and an infectious smile, from one of the wealthiest families in the city, who'd also agreed to pose naked as he batted and threw a baseball.

Since Eadweard had known he'd end up photographing scores of different subjects, to keep track of them all, he'd given them numbers (rather like his clouds): Bigler was No. 46, Glendinning No. 98, and Hacker No. 25, while for Blanche he hadn't been able to resist reserving No. 7. He might be growing silly in his old age, but it was a magic number and she did transport him to his seventh heaven.

As for Eadweard's other nude or semi-nude models, he had encountered the greatest difficulty in finding subjects, either male or female. Most of the artisans and mechanics and farmers he'd asked to hammer anvils, drill rock, lay bricks and scatter seeds in the altogether, had refused even to strip to the waist. And the females: it had been well nigh impossible to find respectable women willing to pose unclothed. So Eadweard had had to resort exclusively to artist's models, who – with the striking exception of his darling – were as a rule ignorant and ill-bred (many of them also doubled as prostitutes), and lacked the graceful bearing essential for motion studies.

However, Eadweard had eventually found three passable candidates: Mamie, Nellie and Lily, whose lodgings Blanche was now sharing in North Philadelphia well away from where Eadweard was staying with his "cousin," but still convenient enough for visiting his love whenever he could get away; a nice long after supper walk in the park to clear his head was one of his range of pretexts. Indeed, he had been so diligent in keeping their two lives apart, he was certain Sarah Louisa suspected nothing. Not that it was a question of wife versus mistress of course, but nevertheless Sarah Louisa was so dear to him the last thing in the world Eadweard wanted was to cause her pain.

But on the subject of nudity, it was astounding that although most "respectable" people at the university understood that it was justified for the sake of science and art, some were still made nervous by what Eadweard's cameras revealed. He remembered one incident in particular. He was giving a lecture to some art students illustrated by several of his sequences of nude males. As one of the gentlemen who had posed *au naturel* for him was escorting his lady across the hall at the end of Eadweard's presentation, a student cried out: "Oh, there goes our Willie!" Roars of nervous laughter.

Another Arthur. Oh, dear, oh dear. Would this hypocrisy never end, wondered Eadweard, saying one thing and doing the other? For everyone knew perfectly well that most adult males, regardless of how "respectable" they were, were ardent collectors of what since the Pompeii discoveries was called "pornography": the sort of pictures that did such a roaring trade on the Barbary Coast.

Everyone also knew that the great bulk of the content of each new form of communication was "pornographic." This was true of the first printed books and engravings, and was now true of photography. Gutenberg's editions of the *Decameron* outsold the Bible many times over and "French postcards" had outsold reputable photographs ever since Daguerre. Only a few years back in the eighteen-seventies, the British police had seized more than 130,000 pornographic images from one London photography studio alone. And it wasn't just the new means of communication that spurred this demand, the Church itself whipped it on even further. By hiding sexuality beneath its robes and spicing it with guilt, Christianity multiplied the appeal of the forbidden fruit a thousand fold, as surely as our Lord multiplied the loaves and fishes.

Was Eadweard himself crossing the line between legitimate and illegitimate photography? Was he an in-between man like Coppinger, producing not "visions of grace and beauty" as he liked to think, but dirty French postcards? The line was as thin as the paper the pictures were printed on.

Only the other day, Blanche had arrived for some nude motion studies – Descending an Incline, Dancing the Waltz and Miscellaneous Phases of the Toilet – with her pudenda shaved. When Eadweard had asked her why, she'd told him it was an opportunity for her to earn a little extra money: "a private collector with an admiration of the female form" had approached her with a generous offer for a copy of the studies Eadweard was about to photograph. She'd added that she had often prepared herself in this way for artists in Paris, it was standard practice; many gentlemen preferred it.

In spite of his better judgment, Eadweard had been unable to refuse her, and anyway, as she'd also pointed out, this even more complete nudity would only add to the scientific and artistic value of his work, would it not? And what did it matter anyway? Why did pictures of people in their natural state always have to be justified as being done for art or science, why couldn't they be created simply to celebrate beauty? If Flora's pictures gave a little pleasure to some lonely man lacking female companionship, where was the harm in that?

So once the motion studies in question had been completed, Eadweard had personally prepared a set of handmade cyanotype album plates of Blanche, *sans* "Cupid's arbor" or "grove of Eglantine" (there was no end to the euphemisms), ascending and descending inclines, dancing a waltz, and putting on and taking off her clothes. All printed on the finest gelatin-silver paper.

After supper that night, Eadweard announced that he would like to take some air and Sarah Louisa was not to wait up. It had become such a habit, she scarcely glanced at him over her knitting.

A short time later, he was bounding up the stairs to the set of rooms occupied by Blanche and her fellow-models. He tapped on her door. "*C'est moi, chérie.*" They always spoke French to each other; especially over here in America, where it had become their own secret language. But now there was no answer in any tongue. Eadweard raised his voice: "*C'est ton Dudu.*" Still no answer. He turned the doorknob. The door was locked. There was the sound of laughter from the end of the corridor; both female and male laughter. He rushed to the corresponding door and opened it.

Four faces stared up at him: Nellie sitting in the lap of William Bigler and Lily in the lap of Robert Glendinning, each with beer bottles in their hands. Suddenly, he saw these two young men watching these same women when he'd shot their nude sequences. First, a naked Nellie spanking a naked baby across her knee, then the sequences Nellie had done with Lily: Flirting a Fan, Arm in Arm; Disrobing Each Other; Shaking Hands and Kissing Each Other; and Pouring Bucket of Water over Each Other. He recalled that one vividly. The students had melted a lump of ice in the water beforehand to cause a surprised Nellie to leap out of the tub in the altogether crying, "Oh, I cannot stand it!" Eadweard had been particularly pleased with the effect. What in God's name had he been doing? Who was playing the pimp now?

"Have you seen Blanche?" Eadweard asked.

Lily stifled a giggle as Bigler and Glendinning counted the threads in their "mobers," the legendary red and blue scarves of the university: "She had to go out with Mamie to get the money for the album from the gentleman."

"You are a one, Mr. Muybridge," said Nellie.

* * *

Did he really belong to the ranks of the *pornographoi*, the "whorepainters?" Eadweard asked himself again and again in the cab back to his lodgings, the laughter that had made it impossible to wait for Blanche tonight still ringing in his ears. What exactly was he doing with his revealing photographs? By attempting to see more and more of animal and human movement and thereby uncovering what was normally hidden was he also catering to the libidinous and the salacious? And what if he was? Eakins had been painting and photographing more and more nudes over the last three years since Eadweard had come to Philadelphia. Who was inspiring whom? But then again Eakins had never had any scruples about nudity, his entire curriculum at the Philadelphia Academy of Arts focused exclusively on the nude human figure, both male and female; no still life, no landscape, no composition. Witness all those photographs Eakins had taken of his male students in the nude. By no means did everyone approve. His latest painting, *Swimming*, had aroused even more controversy, even Eadweard had to admit to misgivings. Was Eakins perhaps an invert, a "mollie," a practitioner of Greek love? No one had ever included so many naked male figures in a single painting before. And there was something strangely feminine about their bodies. They were almost androgynous, lounging on the rocks by the lake like the odalisques of Gérôme. As with so much to do with sexuality, it was all very puzzling. He couldn't wait to talk with Blanche about all this; for all her youth, she was so much wiser than him in these matters.

"I need to talk to you, Eadweard," said Sarah Louisa as he entered their parlor.

He stared at her. "You're still up?" Could she have found out about Blanche? Even followed him to her lodgings?

"I keep house for you, I darn your socks, I do your washing, I cook."

"It's better than maggots and raisins." Their old joke, but she wasn't smiling.

"I'm glad to make a home for you, of course I am, but I always used to share in your work, but ever since we've come to Philadelphia, you've cut me out of more and more, now you don't even let me come to your studio…"

Eadweard bent down to touch her arm. "We've been over and over this, Sarah Louisa, because of the delicate nature of many of the pictures I'm obliged to take – "

"I'm not a child, Eadweard, I'm a grown woman – a forty-four year old grown women, I do know what the human body looks like."

There was a long pause. What could he say? What could he say?

"Look Eadweard, I have an idea," she was pleading now, "you said that once Mr. Bell and his young assistant – Hacker, isn't it? – finish all the positive plates next spring there'll be thousands and thousands of them, perhaps a hundred thousand in all, isn't that so?"

"Well, yes, but only the ones I've designated as 'zoöpraxiscopic' in my laboratory book will be published – "

"How many of those are there?"

"About eight hundred – "

"And how many pictures in each sequence?"

"It varies. Sometimes the full thirty-six, sometimes twenty or twenty-four, it depends how they come out. In spite of all our efforts some are still not up to the scratch. There are quite a number I'm going to have to re-do."

"All right, but let's assume you'll still end up with an average of thirty pictures per sequence, times eight hundred. How many does that make?"

"Twenty-four thousand."

"And all of Mr. Bell's twenty-four thousand positive zoöpraxiscopic plates will need arranging and classifying, will they not?"

"Yes…"

"Which I could do back here, could I not?" Sarah Louisa gestured round the quite large parlor. "Why am I with you if you don't let me help?"

How could he avoid hurting her? Not only with his love affair with Blanche, which Sarah Louisa would surely suspect as soon as she saw that little smile on Blanche's face in so many of her pictures, but also at the sight of such a quantity of other female nudes, which now included not only Mamie and Nellie and Lily, but a dozen other women. Sarah Louisa would never understand this. By no means all the pictures were nudes, of course, many were semi-nude or draped, some even fully dressed, and there were also studies of animals and children and the poor contorted souls from the hospital. But even so, it would be impossible to limit what Sarah Louisa saw.

"No, really I don't think – "

"You haven't taken me to that studio for at least six months." She was on the edge of tears.

"I took you to the Gentlemen's Driving Park when I made my motion sequences of – "

"Horses, yes." Sarah Louisa sighed. "I seem to spend my life looking at horses."

"Well, there was also the Zoölogical Garden. I don't know how many different animals you saw me photograph there."

An even deeper sigh.

If only Eadweard could have shared more of his work with Sarah Louisa as he used to do. He took her hand. "You remember? A Bengal tiger, a pine snake, a kangaroo, camels, elephants, lions, buffaloes – even a baboon."

"I am neither a child nor a baboon, Eadweard. How many times over the years have I sorted out your pictures for you? Please. Let me do something."

Eadweard didn't know whether it was the imploring look of need on her face or the deep sense of guilt in his heart, but he decided to give in. He would just have to risk it.

"Very well, you shall sort and classify the pictures."

"I missed you last night," whispered Eadweard as he and Blanche passed each other next morning at the studio.

"I'll make it up to you tonight," she whispered back.

And she did. Oh, how she did. Eadweard had never known her so passionate. Or inventive. The things she did with pink ribbons... They should both have been ashamed. Or should they?

As they lay together afterwards, her head on his shoulder, he felt a dampness. She was crying.

"What's the matter, *ma chérie?*"

She wiped her eyes on the bed sheet. "Oh, nothing, nothing."

"No, what is it? Tell me."

"Well, now that you've almost finished taking all the pictures of me you'd planned, soon there'll no longer be any reason for me to come into the studio and I shall hardly see you at all."

"I'll still come and see you after supper every night that I can."

Blanche pouted. "That's not enough."

"Well, I don't know what else we can – "

"I've been thinking: is there some other way I could help you in your work at the studio?"

Oh, no. Eadweard had never anticipated this.

"I don't want to be just a model for the rest of my life," continued Blanche, "and anyway, I'll lose my looks one day."

He kissed her. "I find that hard to imagine."

"It happens to everybody. I have to think of my future."

"I will always look after you, you know that."

She kissed him. "You're so sweet. You know I've been at almost all your photographic sessions. I'm very familiar with everything you're doing. I'd like to help, Dudu. Please let me help."

It was almost as if the two women in Eadweard's life were reading from the same play-book. But Blanche was so delightful, this was even more unbearable than it was with Sarah Louisa. He embraced her again. "What would you like to do, *ma chérie?*"

"Well, I was talking to Mr. Bell the other day and he said you're soon going to have a huge number of prints to sort out. Couldn't I help with that? I know those pictures better than anybody."

Two lives crashing together! Blanche knew Eadweard was sharing his lodgings with his "cousin," but he'd been very careful to keep Sarah Louisa in the background since they'd been in Philadelphia. How could he explain to Blanche that it was this cousin who was now going to do his sorting work?

"Um – well, I don't know…"

"Don't you want to see me every day?"

"Yes, of course I do, *mon amour*, it's just that, well, I'll think it over, it's an interesting idea."

"*Merci, mon Dudu.*" She dived down beneath the bed covers like a little squirrel.

Eadweard closed his eyes. He would think about her proposal, he would – he would love to see her every day at the studio – but he would also pray that by the time all the pictures were ready to be arranged and classified, she would have forgotten about her idea. He couldn't do this to Sarah Louisa, he just couldn't.

He shuddered with pleasure. Oh God, what was Blanche doing to him now?

CHAPTER FIFTY-ONE

The following March, Sarah Louisa held up the university's student newspaper. "There's another article about your magnum opus, this one in *The Pennsylvanian.*"

"I hope they don't deal as harshly with me as they did with poor Eakins." Eadweard thought back to the previous month and the uproar that had broken out when Eakins had finally taken his obsession with nudity one step too far by removing a loincloth from a male model in a women's life drawing class at the Pennsylvania Academy, resulting in disgrace and dismissal.

Sarah Louisa smiled. "Oh, I don't think so, but I wanted to wait until you came home so we could read it together.

She began to read, "'...the work on the subject of *Animal Locomotion,* on which he is still busily engaged, will be published within a year... Several hundred of the foremost scientists and educational institutions, both at home and abroad, are already subscribers.' That's an understatement. Who hasn't subscribed? Even at $600 for the complete set of pictures. Just look at this list: "Harvard, Johns Hopkins, Princeton, Yale,Cornell, Oxford, Cambridge, the Imperial Library of Berlin, they're all down for several copies, and then you have the Khedive of Egypt, the Emperor of China, President Hayes, Thomas Huxley, Thomas Edison, John Ruskin, Louis Tiffany, Cornelius Vanderbilt...'"

Eadweard got up to poke the fire, wishing she wouldn't be *quite* so laudatory all the time, it was embarrassing.

Sarah Louisa went on reading from the newspaper: "'The working laboratories are in Biological Hall. In one, several assistants are constantly preparing the delicate photographic plates; in another, the developing etc., of the negatives is in process...'"

Oh, God. In a flash, Eadweard knew where this was leading. Somehow – Heaven knows how, it had taken many, many cups of tea – he'd persuaded Sarah Louisa to forget about the idea of helping with the sorting of the plates and had fondly imagined the danger of her finding out about Blanche was over. But now... he'd had no idea that the student reporter who'd visited him the other day was going to write all this. He reached for the paper. "Let me see that."

But perhaps sensing there was something wrong, Sarah Louisa was already stepping away from him and continuing to read. "'… and in another laboratory, presided over by a pretty young woman with a wealth of golden hair…" Her reading became slower and slower and more and more muted as the tears started in her eyes. "…the multitudinous plates are arranged and classified…"

She looked at Eadweard over the paper. "Who is this person?" Her face started to sag and fissure, the beginning of a landslide. "It's her, isn't it? The woman you've been seeing? Oh, Eadweard. How could you?"

For someone who left such a faint impression on other people's lives, Sarah Louisa had left a very deep hole in Eadweard's, for the next morning she was gone. First stomping out of the room after the revelation in the paper, then departing from his life for good during the night as she made clear in the sad little note he had just found on her bed.

Nineteen years together. How stupid of him to think he could hide anything from her after all this time, such a long, long time…

Her note trembled in his hand. It said nothing of where she'd moved to. Back to San Francisco perhaps? Or New York? Or even Whitechapel? But even if he could track her down, what was the point? He'd broken her heart beyond repair, shattered her love for him into a million pieces; that selfless, unrequited, unrewarded love, that had never flagged all these years, with the exception of her go-between role during the Larkyns' affair, but even that had ultimately been driven by her love for him. That timid voice: "It's only me." There was the understatement of the century.

The tears ran down his face. "Only me" was gone.

CHAPTER FIFTY-TWO

"It could be the Atlantic Ocean, it's so big. How big is it, Dudu? Is it really a lake?"

Eadweard squeezed the slim waist of Blanche's overcoat even tighter; she was leaning so far out over the side of the basket. "Be careful, *ma chèrie*, be careful. And yes, it is really a lake."

"But look at it, it's huge, Dudu, so huge. What's it called?"

"Lake Michigan, and this is only the southern tip. It stretches north for hundreds of miles and then connects with Lake Huron, which then links with Lake Superior, which is even bigger, the largest lake in the whole world."

It really did take one's breath away up here, thought Eadweard, the vastness and magnificence of this country. How Sarah Louisa would have loved this, her beloved Great Lakes. But no. He stopped himself. Sarah Louisa was gone from his life now. He mustn't –

"It looks as if it goes on forever," whispered Blanche.

God, she was so beautiful: the little fur hat, the robin cheeks. How much colder it was today than that first balloon ride they'd taken on their first Christmas Day together. Five years ago today.

She turned to him. So much trust in her eyes. "Do you believe some things in life can go on for ever, Dudu?"

Oh, Lord, how would she receive what he had to say?

This ascension was his anniversary present to her. He'd been planning it for months; the culmination of their love, the culmination of his work coinciding in one sky-high celebration. He'd even brought some champagne, if only for her. Champagne: the happiest drink in the world, and the saddest. For Eadweard couldn't put off what he'd been dreading any longer, the thing he had to say to her that might bring her down to earth with a very hard bump indeed. He was about to risk everything.

How had they reached this point? He supposed it began on that terrible day on the sixteenth of March last year when Sarah Louisa walked out on him, the day he was finally free to make whatever arrangement he wished with Blanche. But that terrible day… he'd been so grief-stricken he thought he'd never recover. He'd no idea how painful it could be to lose such a friend. If it hadn't been for Blanche's unstinting love day after day as they worked side-by-side sorting the mountain of *Animal Locomotion* plates, he didn't know how he could have pulled through. He'd been careful to hide his grief from her of course, telling her simply that his cousin had been called back to England because of a death in the family, an untruth Blanche had accepted without a blink, completely unaware of how close his relationship had been with Sarah Louisa. Not that there'd ever been any intimacies, but women can be so strange.

By January of this year, he and Blanche, aided by Morris Hacker and advised by Mr. Bell, had arranged a total of twenty-four thousand instantaneous photographs (exactly as Sarah Louisa had predicted, oddly enough) on seven hundred and eighty-one plates, each containing twelve, twenty-four or thirty-six pictures in a series. Ninety-five of these plates were devoted to the horse, one hundred and twenty-four to other animals and birds, and five hundred and sixty-two to men, women and children, nude (forty-one of No. 7), semi-nude (three of No.7), and draped (twenty-one of No. 7). He had all her sequences by heart. A total of sixty-five plates commemorating the beauty of Mademoiselle Blanche Epler.

Their next task had been to oversee the preparation of twenty-four thousand highly sensitive collotype plates (as opposed to the cyanotypes he'd prepared for Blanche's private collector) which were essential for making prints of the highest possible quality. This entailed coating every single one of the metal plates with sensitized gelatin, then placing the original negative glass plates over these in a light box and exposing both to actinic or "ultra-violet" light in order to etch the metal plates with an exact reproduction of the light and action first produced by his cameras. What a long way from woodcuts! But this process was so time-consuming it wasn't until the autumn of this year that he'd been able to deliver the final batch of collotypes for printing by the New York Photogravure Company of Brooklyn.

But at last had come the great day in November, when the mighty work had finally been published: *Animal Locomotion: An Electro-photographic Investigation of Consecutive Phases of Animal Movement*, eleven huge volumes of motion studies:

Volumes I & II: Males (Nude)
Volume III & IV: Females (Nude)
Volume V: Males (Pelvis Cloth)
Volume VI: Females (Semi-Nude & Transparent Drapery) & Children
Volume VII: Males & Females (Draped) & Miscellaneous Subjects
Volume VIII: Abnormal Movements, Males & Females (Nude & Semi-Nude)
Volume IX: Horses
Volume X: Domestic Animals
Volume XI: Wild Animals & Birds

It was the greatest compendium of animal attitudes ever created, the folio-sized plates printed on the finest linen steel-plate paper weighing one hundred pounds to the ream and bound in Russia leather. Eadweard's dream come true.

The publication had been greeted worldwide with almost unanimous praise and had generated a stream of invitations to lecture on the subject and show a whole new series of motion studies. As it happened, one of these invitations had come from the Art Museum in Chicago, a city Eadweard had always wanted to visit. He'd taken advantage of his new circumstances to bring Blanche along with him for this particular exhibition, which had taken place three days before Christmas.

On the evening following the lecture, he had been free of his responsibilities and ready to enjoy the city with Blanche. What pride there'd been on her face as Eadweard had signed *Mr. and Mrs. Epler* in the guest register for the stern-faced receptionist at the small hotel he'd searched out in a remote part of the city, as far as possible from the Art Museum. At the time, he had thought her look was because of their little private joke, their little trick for getting past the morality police, who always seemed their most unforgiving when behind a hotel desk. But once they'd settled into our room, it had become clear that Blanche had been thinking of something else.

"Edouard," she'd begun – not a good sign; she always called him that when she had something serious to say, "it's been nineteen months since your 'Cousin' Sarah Louisa has gone… "

He pretended to look puzzled.

"Oh, Edouard, do come on, I may be young, but I am not completely naïve. Everyone knew about Sarah Louisa, the university world is a very small one you know."

He was the one who'd been naïve, of course, Eadweard now realized. Of course, everyone knew everything; Sarah Louisa about Blanche and Blanche about Sarah Louisa.

"But my relationship with her was not what you think, she really was like a cousin to me, or even a sister."

She pulled down her lower eyelid in the French way of saying, "Do you really expect me to believe that?"

"Anyway," she continued, "now that you're free of her – whatever she was to you – you're also free to – well, do you want me to put the words in your mouth?"

He'd hemmed and hawed, and changed the subject, although he'd have given anything, anything to let her have what she desired so much. But he just couldn't face it: another Flora… what if there were another Larkyns? A cuckolded husband for the second time over? He couldn't go through that again. It would kill him.

On that occasion, bed had resolved the situation as it often did after an occasional little tiff. She was still so young, after all. Perhaps she'd forget all about it.

But of course she hadn't, as he saw in her face so clearly now as they continued to soar higher and higher above the lake.

Her voice was so insistent. "Well, do you?"

He pretended not to understand. "Do I what?"

"Believe that some things in life can go on for ever? You know exactly what I mean."

Now for it.

"Listen, Blanche, listen to me. I love you so much, more than anything in the world. You know that. I will always be with you, always by your side, that will go on for ever, but... "

His darling stared at him, the redness in her cheeks going beyond the cold of the Chicago wind. "I thought this time together here, I thought... you wanted to... to ask me something. How stupid of me."

Eadweard turned his head away from her. He couldn't face her eyes.

"Is it because I'm an artist's model?"

"No, well..." Better to say that than to admit what he was really terrified of. "...well, yes, partly, I suppose."

"Oh, you English."

"Well, much as I love the French, I'm not French, I am English." Yes, this was the tack to take, keep going in this direction. "How can I deny the very core of my being?"

"But I thought, you and Nadar, '*la vie Bohème à Paris*,' all your nude photography..."

"As you always say, we Anglo-Saxons are a sorry lot in many ways. Always split, split about sexual matters, split about convention, split about everything, one foot in the future, one in the past. Nadar leaps into the future with both feet, but I can't, I just can't. How can I jettison everything that has taken me a lifetime to achieve as surely as if I'd tossed it over the side of this balloon?"

There was truth in this too... He looked down at the landscape. They were so high... he was so high.

He turned back to her. "I – I've now climbed a peak, Blanche, don't you see? – a peak that you've helped me climb over the last nineteen months – we've climbed it together, and we'll go on doing everything together, always, always, I promise you Blanche, but please understand, my darling."

She was redder than ever.

Was this the end?

She stepped closer to him, unbuttoning his greatcoat, slipping her arms around his waist, pulling the coat around them, nestling like a baby chick, her voice muffled against his chest.

"*Je m'excuse*, Dudu, *je m'excuse*. I know how hard it is for you with the position you've now attained, the marvelous position. It was silly of me. Please forgive me, *mon chéri*, I'm so happy with what we have together. I really am. I'm so happy."

Could this be true? He looked down at her loving face. It could be true. It could. As Eadweard felt her body against his, if he knew anything, he knew this. Oh, the joy... If she wasn't the most wonderful girl in the world, he would very much like someone to tell him who was. Oh, my *blanche colombe*...

Something was wrong. Eadweard's hand hesitated on the doorknob of his sitting-room. But what could be wrong? It was three days later and he had just picked up at the university a stack of yet more invitations for exhibitions all over the country mixed with yet more enthusiastic notices of *Animal Locomotion* that he couldn't wait to read through together with Blanche back at her lodgings. And now this strange premonition...

He laughed at himself. This was absurd. What dreadful apparition could possibly be awaiting him inside the room? Just when everything was going so well? Or precisely because everything *was* going so well? Surely not. Surely his entire life wasn't destined to be an endless sequence of triumphs and disasters, up and down, up and down, like that switchback "roller-coaster" railway they'd opened at Coney Island Blanche was always begging him to take her on? Of course not. Don't be ridiculous.

He opened the door – and breached a sigh of relief. There was Volume Three of his great work, open at plate 96, one of the last motion sequences he'd taken of her: "Ascending stairs, looking round and waving a handkerchief," waving it at him with that little smile he loved so much. Yes, there was his darling, his No. 7, in all the glory of her naked beauty, just as he'd left her before he'd gone to pick up her real-life self for their trip to Chicago.

All was well with the world.

But wait a minute, what was that slip of paper tucked into the center of the double-page spread?

It was Blanche's handwriting, but in perfect English – the first time she'd ever addressed him in his native language – but there it was in black and white with not a single mistake. Of course. It had been dictated by someone else.

> *I have eloped with Morris Hacker. He is going to marry*
> *me. I am so sorry.*

So that was what she was doing in plate 96, she was waving goodbye. The perfect integration of his public and private life… resulting in its perfect collapse.

Had he become Sisyphus now like the poor horses of Nob Hill, doomed to repeat the same mistakes over and over again, fight the same hopeless battles? Work and love, work and love, work winning, love losing. Leaving him supremely successful and supremely alone. Of course she had left him. That question she'd posed to him in the balloon had been his last chance to keep her. But if he had married her, she would have cuckolded him. If it hadn't been Hacker it would have been someone else. Of course. So many "of courses." So many events so blindingly obvious in retrospect, but at the time the man who wanted to see everything saw nothing.

Cannon to the left of him, cannon to the right of him, cannon in front of him, the *Charge of the Light Brigade* again, seeing not a one until he blundered into the jaws of death. For that was where he was heading now, wasn't it? Approaching sixty. Not many years left.

Eadweard reached for Volume Three to throw into the fire that only now did he notice had been freshly stoked.

A hand fell on his arm.

"So No. 7 left with No. 25? What a surprise."

Sarah Louisa.

CHAPTER FIFTY-THREE

So this was the man who turned night into day? thought Eadweard. There he was, sitting in the audience. Just like any other ordinary, common-or-garden human being.

It was Sarah Louisa who'd urged him to undertake this new round of lectures. For of course she hadn't left Philadelphia at all, but had stayed close by, waiting for what she knew would be his inevitable break with Blanche. Having lived through Eadweard's saga with Flora, Sarah Louisa knew a doomed relationship when she saw one. She'd also understood that the only cure for his grief would be the flurry of activity required if he was to make an adequate response to all the publicity generated by *Animal Locomotion*, the glowing reviews of which had appeared in hundreds of newspapers and periodicals. *The Nation* had declared that "the work should belong to every scientific and artistic institution in the country and across the world."

This latest exhibition had come at the invitation of the New England Society in Orange, New Jersey. Eadweard had hoped that the legend now sitting not twenty feet from him might attend since the venue was so close to the gigantic new laboratory he had recently built in West Orange after growing out of Menlo Park. He had therefore sent the Great Man an invitation, but had received no reply. Yet here he was large as life: Thomas Edison himself.

What an honor! The most prolific inventor who'd ever lived, beginning with all the telegraphic devices that grew out of his early experience as a Morse code operator and ending Heaven only knows where. By the tender age of forty-one, the man had already been issued more than five hundred patents.

Sarah Bernhardt's voice came back to Eadweard as she recounted her night-into-day anecdote after visiting Edison in the late seventies. How she'd driven from Menlo Park station in the dead of night, everything pitch dark, and then the countryside lighting up, under the trees, above the trees, in the bushes, along the paths, lights flashing into life; electric light so dazzling it created the impression of full daylight, it was godlike.

And this god had come to listen to *him*!

At the end of Eadweard's presentation, Thomas Edison applauded as loudly as anyone, then limped rapidly towards the back of the hall.

Sarah Louisa nudged him, "Now's the moment to tell him about your scheme." She was referring to the idea Eadweard had got from the article in *The Nation* that noted at one point that Eadweard was a "photographic necromancer" whose battery of cameras could make an imperishable record of any eminent man's carriage and gait and call up these particulars even after his death. The writer then going on to say that Mr. Edison's phonograph "might repeat audibly to the same audience a passage read aloud by the personage in question on occasion of sitting (or walking) for his portrait…"

He dashed down the aisle. "Mr. Edison, Mr. Edison."

But Edison's stride didn't falter as he pushed through the exit door, not even turning his head even though Eadweard was only a few steps behind him. Oh, the arrogance of fame.

Sarah Louisa caught up with him. "Never mind, Eadweard, send round a note. This is too important."

She was right. Arrogant or not, Eadweard had to speak to him. He scribbled a note to be sent to Edison's residence requesting twenty minutes of his time.

Within the hour, there was a reply suggesting seven a.m. tomorrow at Edison's laboratory. Perhaps he had also read *The Nation?*

Eadweard arrived half an hour early and was met by a whiskery young man who introduced himself as Fred Ott, Mr. Edison's "personal experimental machinist." Ott started off Eadweard's visit by giving him a whirlwind tour of the fourteen-acre idea factory, continually interrupting his running commentary about its wonders to pull his walrus mustache aside to take a pinch of snuff, followed by an explosive sneeze. The man was as full of energy as one of Edison's galvanometers as he showed Eadweard the machine shops, the library (where he glimpsed the "Old Man" already hard at work), the chemical laboratory, the patternmaking shop, the metallurgical shop. When Eadweard marveled at all this, Ott's face lit up. "With these facilities, Mr. Edison likes to say he can build anything from a lady's watch to a Locomotive."

At last they joined the shirt-sleeved inventor at his desk surrounded by a library that not only put Stanford's to shame, but looked as if it could give the Library of Congress a run for its money: three floors of book lined galleries towering over them on every side.

Before he could get in a word, Edison called out: "What is this scheme of yours, Professor Muybridge?" He was obviously not one to waste time on social niceties as he motioned Eadweard to sit across the desk from him, Ott taking his place at his elbow.

"Well, sir, you may have seen the article – "

Edison cocked his head to the left in a strange way.

Ott leaned across the desk to Eadweard, whispering through his mustache, "He's completely deaf in his left ear and has only twenty percent hearing in his right." He touched each of his own ears in turn. "You'll have to speak up."

Again, Eadweard had misjudged a man.

Edison smiled, his bright blue eyes twinkling. "I have not heard a bird sing since I was twelve – a railroad accident – but it gives me silence for my work – although I must say it made working on my phonograph a little tricky at times." He pointed at what must have been the prototype for the object in question, the perimeter of whose wooden box was etched with a series of indentations. "I had to listen to the sound vibrations through my teeth."

"CAN YOU HEAR ME NOW, MR. EDISON?" shouted Eadweard.

Edison nodded quickly. "Tell me about your idea. I'm very anxious to hear it."

He sounded a little impatient, thought Eadweard, but who wouldn't be, juggling so many different inventions at once in his mind? But there was something reassuring about his accent. Like Eadweard's own, it was definitely not the "speech of the cultivated."

Eadweard launched into his proposition, which sounded odd delivered at the top of his voice. "What I would like to discuss with you, sir, is the practicability of using my Zoöpraxiscope in association with your phonograph, so as to combine, and reproduce simultaneously, in the presence of an audience, visible actions and audible words. This scheme would afford an almost endless field of instruction and amusement. Imagine Mr. Blaine making a stump speech or Edwin Booth as Hamlet or Lillian Russell in some of her songs, with you, Mr. Edison, producing the tones of the voice while I furnish the gestures and facial expression."

Edison sat up straighter. "To do for the eye what the phonograph does for the ear. Just as Sarah Bernhardt's voice will live on long after her death, so could her person..."

Eadweard heard Bernhardt again, telling him how Edison had made the first extended sound recording of the human voice in history when he'd had her read an extract from *Phèdre*.

"Yes, that's it, yes, precisely."

"Well..." Edison's mind was obviously racing, "another London gentleman, William Frieze Greene, did suggest something similar to me in seventy-eight, 'talking portraits,' I think he called it, but he had no idea how to reproduce a moving picture, no apparatus... but now – "

"Now that my work at the university is finished," Eadweard couldn't help interrupting, "I've moved back to New York – East 14th Street – I could easily take the ferry across the Hudson to work on this – "

"East 14th Street? That's near Gramercy Park, isn't it?" Edison seemed even more excited now. "I lived there for a year at No. 25 Gramercy, right on the park – when was it?" He looked at Ott. "Late eighty-three to eighty-four?" Ott nodded.

"I used to live next to the park as well – " said Eadweard, very excited himself now, " – just before that, before I left to go to Philadelphia, that is. Right round the corner, we just missed each other, we could have been neighbors."

"You should be even nearer now though…" Edison glanced at Ott again, who seemed to be sharing their enthusiasm, for he was now grasping the inventor's bare arm just above the wrist, his fingers tapping up and down rapidly. "We could build another structure, couldn't we, Fred? Got room for it. A photographic building."

Edison rose from his chair. Then sat down again. "It's a most interesting idea, Professor Muybridge, and I shall have to think about it at my leisure, although you must understand it may not be feasible for us to start work on it immediately as we have more work to do on my phonograph. I haven't yet adapted it, you know, to reach the ears of a large audience. But I will be in touch." Rising again, grasping Edweard's hand. "Yes, I will certainly be in touch."

Oh, what would Sarah Louisa say to this! Eadweard was going to invent moving pictures that talked with *Thomas Edison*!

CHAPTER FIFTY-FOUR

"It's been nine months," said Sarah Louisa over dinner in New York the following November, "long enough to bring forth a baby – sorry – but apparently not long enough for Mr. Edison to make a decision about starting work with you."

She was right, of course, thought Eadweard. Shortly after their February meeting, Edison had ordered a large number of Eadweard's *Animal Locomotion* plates – apparently for mounting on boards in his library for him to study – but there was still no definitive word about when the inventor was going to build the promised photographic building in West Orange. As far as Eadweard knew, they hadn't even laid the foundations. But then he knew very little. He and Edison had exchanged notes – or rather he and Ott had exchanged notes, Ott was always the intermediary – but on Edison's end, the communication was always short and cryptic since he had now apparently shifted most of his attention to some ore-milling scheme.

Now Eadweard tried to hide his disappointment behind a careless shrug. "Oh, well, these geniuses are so eccentric, what can one do?"

"What exactly did he promise you? Go over that interview again to see if there's anything we've missed."

He started to go through the meeting point by point. When he got to the part where Fred Ott grasped Edison's bare arm, his fingers tapping up and down in excitement, Sarah Louisa interrupted him.

"You never mentioned that before."

"I suppose it slipped my mind."

"Do you recall exactly what sort of a 'tapping' it was?"

"Why yes, it was quite rhythmic. Ott laid his finger on Edison's arm with great emphasis for a moment, then followed this with two short taps, repeating this again and again. Taap-tap-tap, taap-tap-tap, taap-tap-tap – "

Her eyes widened. "Morse code!"

Eadweard snapped his fingers. "Of course, I'd never thought: dash-dot-dot."

"Do you know what it means?" asked Sarah Louisa.

"No."

"It's the letter 'D,' the telegraph operator's signal for danger. Ott was probably warning Edison not to promise you too much."

"That's possible," said Eadweard, "there was a sudden change in his demeanor."

"Arthur once told me that Edison instructed all his assistants to communicate with him in this way during meetings when they had something urgent to tell him," said Sarah Louisa. "Do you know what I think? I think that Edison and Ott were already planning to pursue your scheme without you."

The next day, Eadweard took the first train he could catch to Washington to file a caveat at the Patent Office declaring his intention of creating "an apparatus, combining the principles of the Zoöpraxiscope and the phonograph." He hadn't the faintest idea how he was going to do this without Edison, but there was no time to worry about details.

He was too late, the Patent Office informed him. Edison had already filed his own caveat the month before declaring his intention of creating a device that did "for the eye what the phonograph does for the ear." He called the invention a "Kinetoscope."

Betrayed again.

After Eadweard had recounted to Sarah Louisa what Edison had done, she put a hand on his shoulder. "As you said yourself, Eadweard, Edison is an eccentric genius. Geniuses don't always know what they're doing. They play by different rules. But you're a genius too, Eadweard, don't forget that. Look at all the requests you're getting from Europe to do another tour. The whole of Europe. Even the Royal Society is coming to you cap in hand."

It was all very flattering, but Eadweard couldn't get Edison out of his head. How could the man have done such a thing?

"The agent we secured for you in England, says you've got enough bookings to fill the next two years." Sarah Louisa was relentless.

"I've known other geniuses," Eadweard muttered as he picked up a newspaper to hide his frustration, "they were nearly all eccentric, Dobson, Nadar, Eakins, and then there was that extraordinary doctor who finally cured me of my stage-coach injuries. Dr. Gull – " He broke off. "Oh, my God."

"What is it?"

"He's in the paper."

"Well, that's not so surprising, you said he was very well known and – "

"Raisins," Eadweard cried out, slapping his side.

"*Raisins*? What are you talking about?"

"The Whitechapel murders!"

"What?" Sarah Louisa groaned. "Oh, no, all those unfortunates murdered in cold blood, Mother told me. That's why I never read the papers – except then they're about you of course – too many horrible things. Ugh." She shuddered. "'Jack the Ripper.' that's what they're calling the monster, isn' it?"

Eadweard looked down at the paper again. "They're still saying nobody knows who 'Jack' was, lots of names put forward... the Prince of Wales..."

"You don't mean to say the Prince you met in London? They think *he* was involved in the murders?"

"No, his son, 'Eddy'– the Duke of Clarence. He's as wild as his father used to be, apparently, always going into low places." He read further. "It says here he got one poor girl in the family way, Annie Crook, an artist's model, then the baby mysteriously disappeared... rumors of a palace plot to cover up Eddy's 'trail of dissipation.'"

"But what's Dr. Gull got to do with this?"

Eadweard continued reading. "Dr. Gull was called in to look after Annie and he put her in a lunatic asylum to keep her quiet and then – " He looked up from the paper. "Of course, and then he killed the other five prostitutes..."

"Does the paper say that?"

"No, I'm saying that."

"All those poor girls were murdered by Dr. Gull? I've never heard anything so ridiculous in all my life. The most respected man in England, you said it yourself, Eadweard, knighted by the Queen!"

"Of course, it all fits," continued Eadweard to himself, "Gull's a very clever man… he covered his traces by pretending to be a semi-literate 'Jack the Ripper.'" He read further. "And now they're saying he was a Master Mason. It all falls into place. Give me your hand."

"Now you really have gone crazy." Sarah Louisa shrugged and held out her hand.

Eadweard took it, pressing his thumb down hard between her knuckles as his little finger curled into her palm.

"What are you doing?"

"That's the handshake of a Master Mason." Eadweard released her. "That's what Gull tried on me, testing me to see if I was a Mason and he stopped when I didn't respond in kind. They always do that. I read about it afterwards."

"But I ask you again, Eadweard," said Sarah Louisa, "what does all this have to do with the Whitechapel murders?"

"All five women were mutilated in the same gruesome way that's only practiced by Masons on someone who's betrayed their secrets… and those poor prostitutes were about to betray a very important secret indeed."

"But Gull must be in his seventies," said Sarah Louisa, "how would he even have the strength to do those terrible things?"

Eadweard shrugged. "He's a surgeon. Strong hands. I know, I've felt them, believe me."

"And raisins? Why did you shout out raisins?"

"That's my whole point: raisins – dehydrated grapes."

He held up the newspaper. "They say that they now know the murderer rendered the women unconscious before he mutilated them by feeding them grapes injected with poison. They found grapes clasped in the hand of one of the victims."

"And so?"

"Gull always carried raisins with him." Eadweard shook his head. "This cannot simply be a series of coincidences. It just cannot."

"Oh, God… raisins, just like you," breathed Sarah Louisa.

All Eadweard could hear was another voice: "Remember, Muygridge, the sugar of the grape, there's nothing like it."

The room began to spin. *Inside every man there lurks a monster…* Dr. Gull? *I do not like thee, Dr. Fell/The reason why I cannot tell.* That feeling Eadweard had had. But a murderer? Eadweard couldn't really believe it himself. It was impossible, and yet it must be true, underneath that urbane exterior, a lunatic? And if it was true for Gull… *Not one of us is far from madness, Muygridge, on the edge of madness.*

Eadweard had just finished the little book that Pendegast's friend, Robert Louis Stevenson, had told him he was planning: *The Strange Case of Dr. Jekyll and Mr. Hyde.* Was that *him*? Did he, Eadweard Muybridge, have another side too, a fiend lurking inside him? Was he really insane after all? Had he been insane all along?

CHAPTER FIFTY-FIVE

Would he be able to finish it in time? Eadweard kept asking himself the same question as he dug and dug. The pains in his stomach were getting much worse now, coming more and more frequently, like a dagger some Hoodlum was stabbing into his bowels. He'd thought the arthritis was bad enough, but that was nothing compared to this damn prostate. At least that was Dr. Goodwin's diagnosis, but he was no Dr. Gull, so who knew? But whatever it was, it was agony. It had started to act up just after Christmas – *ouch!* There it goes again. But he had to keep going, he had to finish it. For her.

At least the soil was nice soft English soil, not baked hard as concrete by the endless California sun. Eadweard trod the spade down again into the ground.

Would he complete it in time? Time, always time. That was his real enemy, wasn't it? More real than ever now. Always the race against time: to escape from the stage-coach before it crashed, to make his shutter go faster and faster before the world went by, to get to Larkyns before the others to avenge his honor, to get to the patent office before Edison. Now this was his last race. Who would win?

He looked down at the squelchy earth. Ten years he'd been stuck in the mud here. They'd sailed in September of ninety-four, back to where Eadweard had started, Kingston-on-Thames. Money had been tight so they'd ended up living with Eadweard's cousin George Lawrence, the son of the uncle of the same name who'd got Eadweard his original position with the publishing company in America.

Just as in Philadelphia, to avoid any misunderstandings, Eadweard had passed Sarah Louisa off as his other cousin, Kate Smith. Since George hadn't seen the woman for some fifty years and was now bedridden, there wasn't much danger of his suspecting the truth, and even if he had, who would care? That was one thing about growing old, you gradually became more and more invisible. Even people who had once been somebodies all became nobodies with time. He should know. Total obscurity now; he and Sarah Louisa were just an old couple measuring out what remained of their lives in cups of tea and digestive biscuits. It was as if he had never accomplished anything.

What had happened? He still didn't understand it. What had happened between those heady days in eighteen eighty-eight when he'd had such high hopes of inventing talking picture shows with Thomas Edison and his decision to give it all up and move back to England? Where had those six years gone?

Everywhere and nowhere. When Eadweard consulted the sides of his battered steamer trunk, the hotel labels told him that between eighty-nine and ninety-two he must have been to more places than almost any man alive, giving hundreds of lectures on *The Science of Animal Locomotion in Relation to Design in Art* in just about every major town and city in the British Isles and across the continent. And yet all the while, there had been a faint shadow of unease looming over him. He'd had no objective evidence for any of his fears of course. Quite the reverse. He couldn't have received a warmer welcome, everywhere he went. And yet, and yet…

Now of course he knew that his intuition had been right. All those triumphs in the lecture hall were indeed leading inexorably downhill; Eadweard's pioneering Locomotive was being overtaken by faster and more powerful engines.

The first warning sign had come from Germany in ninety-three, with Ottomar Anschutz's spinning-disc peep-show machine, *Der Electrische Schnellseher,* displaying moving images of the same duration as Eadweard's screen projections, only with real photographs. Then in France, without a word to Eadweard, Marey had developed his "roll-film," which was then perfected by George Eastman. Edison had jumped on it of course combining it with his own experience with telegraphers' punched tape to create 35 millimeter perforated film for his "Kinetograph/Kinetoscope" combination; the former a moving picture camera and the latter another peepshow device. The great inventor had even opened a Kinetoscope Parlor on Broadway with banks of machines, which true to form were instantly paralleled by a shadow peepshow industry in the backstreet penny gaffs, where connoisseurs of the female form could see "What the Butler Saw" through Edison's keyhole.

Is that where some of Eadweard's motion sequences of Blanche had ended up? He'd been afraid to look.

The following year, the Lumière brothers had introduced their *Cinématographe* projector to the public at the Salon Indien du Grand Café in Paris featuring a fifty-second film of male and female workers hurrying out of the Lumière factory in Lyon. On hearing of this, Eadweard was instantly back in that darkened basement as the young Louis passed his hand to and fro over his playing cards under the ruby light, murmuring *"Encore et encore et encore et encore… le mouvement… "*

By the end of eighteen ninety-six, films were being projected all across Europe and America by the Biograph, the Theatrograph, the Bioscope, the Eidoloscope, the Phantoscope, the Mutoscope, and Edison's own first motion picture projector, the Vitascope. Scope that, graph this. They were all doing it.

One of the first of Edison's projected films had been three seconds of "Fred Ott's Sneeze," induced by yet another of that young man's inhalation of snuff. All Eadweard's decades of struggle and effort to record motion had come down to the nasal consequences of sniffing powdered tobacco?

Then had come Edison's "The Black Diamond Express," which showed the famous flyer approaching head on at seventy miles an hour so realistically it caused ladies in the audience to scream and pass out. It was such a success that it launched a host of copycat "train" films, which were soon followed by a flood of waterfalls, raging storms, burning stables, bare-knuckle boxing matches and bloody cockfights; celluloid roller-coasters and Ferris Wheels blurring the line between illusion and reality, danger and safety. All they were missing was a runaway stage-coach, which was surely not far behind.

The "movies" as the Americans now called them, eating up subject-matter like steam engines eating up miles. What was that latest one from Edison that Sarah Louisa kept begging him to take her to? *The Great Train Robbery*? The longest film ever made: twelve minutes. That seemed to be going a bit far. Who would sit still for twelve whole minutes in the dark with strangers, staring at a screen? But then everything had been going a bit far recently, hadn't it? The Wright brothers flying like birds, automobiles racing from London to Brighton. The whole world was spinning faster and faster, the human *race*, in every sense of the word.

What had happened? Eadweard continued to wonder as he dug and dug. Just at the very moment in history when everything was going faster than ever, why had he stopped dead in his tracks? At what point had he ceased to move forward and start to mark time? Had there been one moment when he was finally spent, when he'd shot his last bolt – his last picture? Who knows? All he knew was that he'd started something that had outgrown him, left him behind before he could finish it. He looked down at what he was digging: that's why he had to finish this. Why he had to finish this for her.

Would he succeed? The pain was almost constant now. But he was so close to the end. Just a few more spadefuls…

Whew. There. Done. It was done.

He stood back to see how the whole thing looked. Quite a sight. It took up almost the entire back garden.

He took the hose pipe and began to fill up what he had made. At least this was one thing he'd accomplished, one thing he'd taken to its final fruition, if nothing else.

"Eadweard!"

Sarah Louisa! He hadn't heard her coming. But then he never did, did he?"

"What is it?"

"Did you hear that coach just now?

"No. I don't hear very much of anything any more."

"You'll never guess. It was the Mayor's coach."

"The Mayor? What does he want?"

"He wants to see you – they all want to see you, all the

councilmen.”

“Why?”

“You remember that scrapbook of all your accomplishments we donated to the Kingston Library?”

“*That's* why he wants to see me? To thank me for that old scrapbook?”

She took a sealed roll of parchment out of her apron pocket.

“Where'd you get that? What's that?”

“The coachman, I made him a cup of tea, we had such a nice chat, and he didn't want to disturb you. They're going to put up a plaque, in the Market Place next to the Coronation Stone. Apparently, the Mayor's so proud. He said you were ‘Not only an Englishman, but a Kingstonian, and a descendant of an old Saxon family,’” She tapped the parchment. “He said it's all written down here, what they're going to put. But only you can open it.”

She handed him the scroll. He broke the seal and unfurled it. It was very small print. “I haven't got my glasses.”

“I'll read it for you.” She put on her own spectacles, took back the scroll and started to read: “With his camera and machine the zoöpraxiscope, Eadweard James Muybridge produced moving pictures in America in the year 1880: at Paris in 1881: and before the Royal Institution in 1882. From these inventions the modern cinematograph has been evolved.’”

“They're going to put that?”

“That's what they wrote here. The coachman said the Mayor said you were the ‘Father of the Motion Picture.’”

Agh! He clutched his side. The pain was almost unbearable now.

She took his my arm. “Come in, dear, it's time for your tea. I'll make a fresh pot.” She looked down at the series of little pools he'd just completed. “And you have finished it now, haven't you?” She shrugged. “Whatever it is, you never would tell me.”

“Now I can. It's the Great Lakes.”

Her neck flushed crimson. “Oh, I see…”

“It's my last gift.”

“For her… of course. ” Sarah Louisa's whole face and body

sagged.

"It's for *you*. You always said you'd love to see a photograph of all the Great Lakes taken from the sky. Well, this is the next best thing. Besides, I've nothing else to give you."

She began to cry. "You've given me everything, Eadweard, don't you know that? Don't you know *anything*?"

"*Aaagh!*" He cried out again, doubling up in agony.

She dropped the parchment and put her arms round him, holding him up.

She looked down at what he had done. "It's wonderful, Eadweard, it's magnificent, it's perfect. It's the most perfect gift I've ever had."

The scream of seagulls.

"Look up, Eadweard," said Sarah Louisa, "look up my darling."

He followed her gaze.

The seagulls were wheeling and dancing in the air.

"Now look down."

Together they looked down at Lake Michigan, Lake Erie, Lake Ontario, Lake Huron, Lake Superior, their faces reflected in the water.

Gently, she lifted his arms, slowly raising and lowering them in tune with the birds.

David Stansfield

Eadweard Muybridge died of a heart attack on
May 8th, 1904, while digging his scale model of the
Great Lakes in his back garden in Kingston-Upon-
Thames. Twenty-seven years later, a plaque was
unveiled at the Kingston public library, not far from
the Saxon kings' coronation stone in the market
place. Under an embossed bust of Muybridge, the
plaque reads:

EADWEARD JAMES MUYBRIDGE
A NATIVE OF KINGSTON-UPON-THAMES
BENEFACTOR OF THIS PUBLIC LIBRARY
A SCIENTIFIC INVESTIGATOR OF
ANIMAL LOCOMOTION
WITH HIS CAMERA AND MACHINE THE
ZOOPRAXISCOPE
HE PRODUCED MOVING PICTURES
IN AMERICA IN THE YEAR 1880:
AT PARIS IN 1881: AND BEFORE THE
ROYAL INSTITUTION IN 1882. FROM
THESE INVENTIONS THE MODERN
CINEMATOGRAPH
HAS BEEN EVOLVED

David Stansfield

AUTHOR'S NOTE

This is a work of fiction. We cannot know for sure whether Muybridge met the Reverend Charles Dodgson alias Lewis Carroll, though we do know he was apprenticed to a leading British photographer. The Lumière brothers Muybridge was likely, but not certain, to have met on one of his trips to France. Muybridge's doctor, Sir William Withey Gull, 1st Baronet of Brook Street and physician-in-ordinary to Queen Victoria, ranks high on many Jack the Ripper suspect lists.

But for the rest, every name, character, place and incident in Muybridge's professional work is fact, as is almost every encounter and conversation with historical figures, lesser known characters and family members. The trial chapter also follows the facts closely and is based on the court transcripts from the Napa City Courthouse.

ACKNOWLEDGMENTS

Above all, my deepest and most loving thanks to Denise Boiteau, my partner in everything, upon whose screenplay (which we wrote together over twenty years ago) this book is based thanks to the urging of Ray Bradbury, who told us from his own bitter experience with "Fahrenheit 451" that "movies disappear, books don't."

Next, my immense gratitude to the legendary Canadian director and great friend Paul Almond, the creator of more "moving picture" dramas than perhaps any other of Muybridge's "descendants," who spent endless hours taking his well-honed pruning shears to my words to give them their final shape and thrust.

More thanks to the many kind people who have commented on, informed and inspired countless drafts of first Denise's and my screenplay and then the book. These include: Arthur Penn, Richard Walter, Patrick McGoohan, Steven Nalevanski, Gary Markowitz, Charis Conn, Cécile Moulard, Chuck Nanry, Jennie Muller, Neel Muller, Jimmy Hall, Bill Musselman, Anthony Barton, Gert Basson, Steve Zimmerman, Avra Petrides and Olivia Smith.

Many thanks also for enlightening conversations, communications and contributions with and from the following: Norman Tutorow, author of the magisterial two-volume *The Governor: The Life and Legacy of Leland Stanford;* Paul Israel, author of *Edison: A Life of Invention;* Marta Braun, author of *Picturing Time: The Work of Etienne-Jules Marey* and *Eadweard Muybridge;* Mark Osterman and France Skully Osterman on the length of exposures for wet collodion out of doors and other 19th century photographic arcana; large-format vintage camera expert Luther Gerlach from the Getty Museum on minute details of the photographic apparatus used in Muybridge's day; the archivist at the Napa City Library for information about the hangman's noose that was prepared for Muybridge; Kyle K. Wyatt,Curator of History & Technology at the California State Railroad Museum, and the CPRR Discussion Group for information about trains in Napa County in the 1870s; Frank Whately, Head of School Performance and Screen Studies at Kingston University for information about Blanche Epler; Jill Lamb, Archivist at The Eadweard Muybridge Bequest at the Kingston upon Thames Museum, for providing me with a copy of Muybridge's voluminous scrapbook; David Kessler at The Bancroft Library at UC Berkeley for filming a boxful of yet more Muybridge material.

I also owe a huge debt to the scores of non-fiction books and articles about Muybridge, which have been indispensable in writing the novel, notably Robert Bartless Haas, *Muybridge: Man in Motion;* Gordon Hendricks, *Eadweard Muybridge, the Father of the Motion Picture*; Anita Ventura Mozley, *Eadweard Muybridge, The Stanford Years 1872-1882;* Hollis Frampton's seminal piece, *Eadweard Muybridge: Fragments of a Tesseract,* and the monumental three volumes from Dover Books: *Muybridge's Complete Human and Animal Locomotion* containing all 781 multi-picture plates of the stop-motion photographs Muybridge took in Philadelphia.

Lastly, I am forever grateful to the two good friends and colleagues who started Denise and myself thinking about Muybridge in the first place: Maury Whyte, who reanimated Muybridge's horse in order to contrast our 1/24th of a second perception limit with the computer's 1 millionth of a second for "Bits and Bytes," the world's first television series about the personal computer Denise and I created back in 1980; and David George who six years later planted the seed that was to lead to a quarter-century of gestation for this book when he asked us if we knew that in addition to inventing the movies Muybridge was a murderer.

ABOUT THE AUTHOR

With his wife, Denise Boiteau, David has written and produced some four hundred PBS television scripts that have been translated into more than a dozen languages and have won over fifty international film and television awards, including the selection of their "The Middle East" series in the Academy Awards Best Educational Documentary category.

David's most recent published books are *One Last Great Wickedness*, *The Seventh Coming*, *Take Nothing For Granted*, *Blood*, *Got a Couple of Minutes?* and *Attack at Noon*.

www.ingramcontent.com/pod-product-compliance
Lightning Source LLC
Chambersburg PA
CBHW021501240626
47154CB00002B/461